SEVERED SQUADRON

EARTHQUAKE WAR

SEVERED SQUADRON

PC NOTTINGHAM

4 Horsemen
Publications, Inc.

4 Horsemen Publications, Inc.
1497 Main St. Suite 169
Dunedin, FL 34698
4horsemenpublications.com
info@4horsemenpublications.com

Cover by J. Kotick
Typeset by Autumn Skye
Editor Jen Paquette

Library of Congress Control Number: 2023937020

Print ISBN: 979-8-8232-0168-1
Hardcover ISBN: 979-8-8232-0170-4
Ebook ISBN: 979-8-8232-0169-8
Audio ISBN: 979-8-8232-0167-4

To my three greatest loves: C-E-Z

TABLE OF CONTENTS

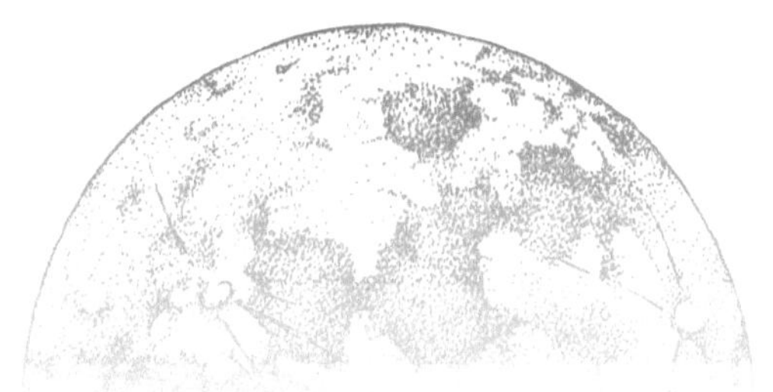

ACKNOWLEDGMENTS

THERE ARE SO many people to thank. You, dear reader, for picking up this book in the first place. The amazing team at 4HP for taking a chance on me and guiding me through this process. The phenomenal narrator who brought these characters to life. I was also blessed with some amazing critique partners: N.C. Scrimgeour, Kalen Capp, Jaci M. Lunera, D. Everett Thomas, Kaela C. Woodruff, Michael Clark, Cole Layne, Sam Barclay, Cyra King, Jon Gerung, Loren Huxley, Billie Grey, Ali Breshears, Morgan Nyx, Maia James, Lance Andrews, Tiffany O'Haro, and the whole "Cru" at the Radio Freewrite podcast: WebEater, Krispy, Murph, and The Lotus. All of you in some way helped make this manuscript better.

They're all amazing creators and worth checking out.

ONE

(JOKΛ)

**Aboard the space station "Calamity,"
floating on the fringes of Collective space**

FEW THINGS SATISFIED Joka quite like humiliating jerks, especially when they used words like "scrawny runt."

Amid the greasy locker room's clanks and conversations, Joka's new flight suit sealed onto her body with a hiss. A smirk twisted up to her eyes. She stretched her gloves and tested the suit with some lunges, considering how to spend the money her supervisor would owe her. Common knowledge dictated nobody could invent a Human flight suit to work in the more important species' spaceships, but Joka had succeeded. They'd *have* to let her join a mission.

Perhaps they would want her to puke her guts out in the spacecraft from the gravity change. Flying a sleek fighter in her suit would prove her right and win that bet. She'd show them what this scrawny runt could really do.

Joka slammed her locker shut because that somehow proved her point.

She'd need to survive this mission to spend said money, but future Joka would deal with that problem. Present Joka had exactly one more minute to bask in her glory. She hadn't been this proud of herself since joining the gang—past Joka was a drag. Not that kidnapped orphans sold into slavery had much to party about.

Joka clipped her sidearm to her belt. A dinky Human-sized pistol, meant for last ditch self-defense. But if she needed to fire it, she was toast anyway. Whoever could take down the gang's strike force wouldn't be stopped by a mechanic with a glorified tickle gun. Even if she had to hang back with the battledarts and tend to their plasma scores and nicks incurred in the descent to the target, she'd still be among the boots on the ground, making a difference in real time instead of tightening screws and checking fluid levels in the safety and stink of the station.

Lockers clanged behind her among hisses and growls while the few other Humans in the mechanic corps muttered amongst themselves. An overhead light in the corner blinked absently over the grease stain, which was somebody else's job to clean. The floor thudded as Joka's supervisor, a burly Arkouda named Tur approached, fuzzy white paws at her hips. She towered over Joka, and a smug expression crept over her bottle-shaped muzzle.

"Didn't think you had it in you," Tur said. "Symphora will be impressed."

Joka gulped. The few Humans dispersed among the other species clutched their wrenches and spanners. "So I can join? I'm allowed?"

Tur's circular ears twitched. "Symphora would kick my hairy ass into a star if I went back on my word. My three rules still apply, whether here on the Calamity or on a mission."

One Lo-sat indignantly flared her scaly neck frills at Tur's mention of "ass."

Probably Doh-riss, Joka thought. *That chick sucks.*

Fighting the urge to roll her eyes, Joka parroted the maxim. "Rule one: don't embarrass Tur. Rule two: don't get blown up. Rule three: don't be the reason someone else gets blown up."

Tur whipped her head around, eyeing the other mechanics in the locker room, all of whom nodded or waved claws in agreement. Since Tur was in charge, each refugee, orphan, or recruit who joined the mechanics had to learn her rules before they could so much as organize the screws and bolts.

Tur's appraising stare returned to Joka. "Are your pre-mission duties done?"

The other mechanics' stares of disbelief or pride made Joka stand straighter. "Yes, ma'am. The engines are humming like *fithars*."

"And?"

"I double-checked your onboard toolbox. We'll make any repairs while the alpha team kicks ass."

A Lo-sat crewwoman hissed as the last word escaped. Joka peeked out of her periphery. Yep, it was

Doh-riss. Same as before. Joka understood enough of the Lo-sat language to hear her mutter, "Such foul speech."

Somebody really needed to tell her to lighten up.

No politeness police would dampen Joka's day. The other Human women in the gang needed her to make a splash for their own sakes as much as hers. All the future girls they'd save on upcoming missions needed strong Human role models, too. Out on the fringe of Collective society, maybe the right people would hear about how awesome Humans were doing, and they'd get to climb the social ladder—become full citizens and whatnot. All because Joka was a badass inventor. While savior of the Human race would be too lofty a title, if people called her that later, she wouldn't be rude and correct them.

Tur cleared her throat, and Joka snapped to attention. "Don't get any dreams of seeking glory on your first mission. We're support staff." Tur gestured to the rest of the mechanic corps. "What are we, ladies?"

With mixed levels of enthusiasm, a chorus of Human, Arkouda, and Lo-sat voices responded, Joka taking the opportunity to shake her fists while screaming, "Symphora's engine!"

Tur placed a heavy white paw on Joka's shoulder. "Engines don't ask for thanks and don't get any either. Let's head out."

———

At takeoff, Joka glanced behind her at the shrinking Calamity station—a spinning slipshod fortress rotating through space. A heap of scraps, sure, but the only real home known to Symphora's gang.

Joka fidgeted in her too-big cockpit as bright streaks against bleak space whizzed overhead. The cockpit was designed with Arkoudae in mind, not puny Humans, so she found the area cavernous. She had to stretch and strain to reach every panel and switch. These were meant for protracted conflicts, so the fighter's rear compartment offered space for eating and sleeping—a nice perk for any situation except this one where she needed to be a small target.

Like a small swarm of plasmasippers, their battle-dart ships left formation and prepared for descent into atmospheric flight. The oblong fighters' armor panels pushed out and pulled back until the ships formed into their iconic arrow design.

Hand trembling, Joka squeezed the comm unit on her shoulder, signaling her gang's leader. "Ready, Symphora."

Tur responded instead. "You better be. Respect the chain, Joka. Report to me first."

Joka's guts tangled. Five minutes after leaving the Calamity and she already mucked it up. "Sorry, ma'am."

Tur's low growl buzzed through the comm. "I'm already regretting taking you. Don't make me look bad." Two dull chimes followed. The first came from the cockpit, signaling the increasing gravity of the approaching planet; the second denoted Tur switching to the public channel. "What's the sitrep, ma'am?"

The snarling voice of the most feared outlaw in the untamed systems responded, "You didn't read the briefing, you piece of *skata*?"

An accented hiss came over the comm. "Language," Doh-riss said. "This is a shared channel."

Joka bristled. Of course Miss Priss Doh-riss had to come. Fixing ships with her was the worst.

"Sniff my tail, all of you," Symphora said. "When you save my hairy ass, you can censor me. Until then, it's all 'yes, ma'am' to you."

Joka pushed against the controller stick, and the cockpit's pressurization adjusted to the altering gravity. "Yeah, Doh-riss," Joka said. "Boss never woulda saved you if she knew you'd censor everyone."

"Hey!" Symphora barked. "We don't joke about that. Everyone gets saved."

Doh-riss' voice followed: "And it's would have, not woulda."

"Tur, get your mechanics in line."

"Sorry, ma'am. I'll dock their pay after we return to base." Tur tutted. "Descending into atmosphere. Really, Joka... don't be such a cub. We'd all be dead or worse without Symph."

"Nobody likes a brown-snouting kisstail," Symphora said. "And don't call me Symph. Reminds me of my ex."

Joka shuddered. Nobody was allowed to talk about her. Tur's sister was the last one to make that mistake, and she was stuck on sanitation duty.

The foggy haze of the atmosphere resisted the battledarts' attempt at puncturing. The noxious environment's azure mist created the perfect place to hide a brothel where the Collective military wouldn't find it. Out here on the frontier of colonized space, the government couldn't keep up.

Ideal for outlaws.

Even better for Symphora's gang because they had tails to kick. Their methods weren't *exactly* illegal as long as nobody caught them. The only person who had it out for Symphora and lived to tell the tale had been silent for years, according to the mess hall gossip. Not that Joka ever participated in that gossip—so petty. Listening to and occasionally commenting on gossip was acceptable. It did also need to be shared with others, for the sake of corroboration and correctness, of course.

The rest of the gang's ships descended, a tiny fleet of seventeen. Each bore various painted-on clawmarks to designate their kills. Blue for a sweatshop owner, red for a brothel owner, green for a drug dealer, and yellow for a patron. A quick fantasy flashed of heroically adding some red and yellow clawmarks to Joka's crusty old ship in the service of saving some people today.

Those clawmarks were fun to brag about, but Joka knew Symphora was more interested in the painted-on hearts adorning the opposite side. White for a saved Arkouda, green for a saved Lo-sat, and pink for a saved Human. Yellow for any other species.

But each time Joka was tasked with painting a new mark on a battledart, she was reminded of the most important count: skulls painted over the "not a step" sign, representing each time someone was too late. Those hurt more than the scars anyone earned the old-fashioned way. Her little brother was memorialized as a little skull that way.

Shoom!

From below, a plasma cannonball erupted from a thick poisonous cloud and whizzed past Joka's cockpit as heat indicators beeped in automated desperation.

Symphora barked over the public comm, open to whoever was listening on the surface. "Are you gonna pretend that was a warning shot? Aim to the left, you little bitch."

"Or not?" Joka squeaked. Tur never warned her about this level of hazing.

A male Lo-sat hissed from the other end of the public channel. "Symphora, you better turn around. The bounty on you is enough to buy my own moon."

Another plasma cannon fired, and Joka banked left, still speeding toward the outpost while everyone else in the newer battledart ships sped a bit faster. From her periphery, Joka caught Doh-riss wobbling. Seemed like her flying wasn't as good as her first-aid abilities whenever someone got grease in their eye. The bunker, little more than a hunk of metal rising from moss-choked stone, came into view as the atmosphere's purple fog thinned. Plasma cannons on either side dwarfed the bunker itself.

Symphora snarled back to the man on the ground. "We can do this the easy way, Sah-slen. Let the kids out, and I'll kill you painlessly."

"So badass..." Joka's screen flashed, stealing her attention. They were close, and the next round of flak wouldn't be so easy to dodge.

One of the women in the strike team buzzed over the public channel. "Focus, ladies. Time for some fancy flying."

Seriousness seeped through Tur's voice. "No return fire, ma'am?"

Symphora tsked. "Negative. Remember what happened on Reeyaki? Not having another bloodbath on my paws."

Sah-slen's voice slithered from the comm. "Wanna storm my bunker? Good luck. I knew you'd come, and I'm more than prepared."

Symphora grunted, and her battledart lurched forward ahead of the pack. "If you really knew I'd come, you would've run." She switched back to the private comm. "Tur. Take your squad to the docks. Shoot any transport craft that's empty before you tend to our ships. Make sure you—"

"—save at least one for the survivors we can free," Tur finished. "I know, boss." Three battledarts banked left and looped around to the compound's rear.

Joka dared to open a private channel to Tur. "I'm doing repairs? I'm not storming with you?" Some part of her was relieved. This *skata* was getting real.

"Yeah." Tur dodged another plasma cannonball. "Symphora calls the shots, and I'm not arguing with her." A *doop* from the comm signaled Tur opened to the public channel. "Doh-riss, are you sure you're alright joining us? There might be a few of your kinfolk in there."

"That's where you're wrong," Doh-riss hissed. "Jerks like Sah-slen aren't real Lo-sats. Besides, ever since Symphora accepted me, you've been my kinfolk."

Joka winced, remembering the little note about Doh-riss she'd scrawled on the bathroom wall last week.

Another plasma shot hurtled toward Symphora. She dodged at the last second. "Don't get all mushy on me—I made that mistake already. Alright ladies, we're too low for anti-aircraft, but stay frosty."

A gaggle of mercenaries poured out of the moss-covered compound, brandishing rifles. The plasma bullets were too small and close together for the battledarts to dodge, so the only option left was to land, damage be damned.

Joka shook her head, mentally prepping the work she'd need to do on the ships once they landed. There'd be some scorch marks, but those could be cleaned back on the station. All the blaster fire would happen away from her.

The last words Joka heard before touching ground was Sah-slen's buttery accent. "Symphora, I'll mount your head on my office door and turn your squad into workers. They'll fetch a good price." Then he snarled, "Except the Human you brought. I'll just kill her unless some pervert wants her."

The battledarts screamed to the surface with one last blast halting their deadly momentum. Near misses from the plasma fire decorated the ships with new char and scorch marks. Supply crates big enough to move sentient cargo littered the landing zone, but there were no other ships in sight.

Joka reached for the comm, expletives at the ready, but as the cockpit hissed, she knew reaching for her sidearm was more important. Symphora certainly didn't waste the breath to tell him off, so she ought to follow suit. She watched Symphora fire up her armor as plasma bullets ripped into the grounded ships—nothing Joka and Doh-riss couldn't handle once the shooting stopped.

Smirking, Joka aligned her targeting systems, then let loose a low-impact round of bullets from her battledart, causing a few mercenaries to scatter. The bullets ripped into the bunker's outer wall, leaving finger-sized scorch marks. Tur and Doh-riss did the same, but Symphora and the other strike team members took shots with their own rifles from the relative cover of their cockpits.

Once the surviving mercenaries scrambled for cover among supply crates, Symphora jumped from her cockpit, ready for action. Landing, she let loose a roar and picked off a too-brave mercenary. The sono-fabitch plummeted with a yelp.

Symphora stood to her full three meters: big for an Arkouda, and her red-dyed mohawk made her seem even larger. She was one of the few people in the galaxy who had decommissioned Collective military armor that still functioned, making her nearly invincible compared to whatever lowlife mercenaries could throw at her. With lightning in her eyes, she fired a round, offing another mercenary.

Joka's jaw dropped. Symphora in the thick of battle was beyond anything she'd expected.

Tur's voice growled over the mechanics' channel. "Doh-riss, Joka. There's enough suppressive fire for us to get to work. I'll pick off the transports. You two get to work on repairing the ships."

Before Joka could groan, Doh-riss grumbled instead. "I'm stuck egg-laying?"

"It's called babysitting," Joka snapped. As if that somehow made it better. "Tur, don't you need more people to storm the base with you?"

"Like Nightmare you will. We can't fly home if these ships aren't repaired. Get to work."

Symphora and her alpha team picked off another four mercenaries.

In relative safety, Joka decompressed her unique flight suit, opened the cockpit, and hopped out, toolbox in hand. Her flight suit's automatic gravity harness allowed her to float down, ignoring the moon's cruel gravity.

Approaching Symphora's ship, she caught Doh-riss emerging from her battledart. Her neck frills were raised enough to show disgust, but she could still feign politeness. Before Joka could stick her tongue out at Doh-riss or do something else a mature well-adjusted adult would do, a grating creak ahead stole her attention.

The rusted bunker doors opposite the landing pad opened. Symphora's target, the crime boss Sah-slen, emerged, claws and tail raised. It had to be him—Joka recognized his image from the briefing: long brown streaks in otherwise green scales, irises a vertical line instead of the more common marble pattern. He marched out, revealing a pistol-wielding Arkouda woman behind him.

The Arkouda woman bore the government-issued armor for the detective division of the military police. She also bore a scar on the side of her snout, a brand from her former owner.

A brand that matched the one on Symphora's snout.

Tur gasped. "Symph! Isn't that your—"

A mercenary's plasma bullet ripped through Tur's throat, and she slumped to the ground, rifle clattering against the mossy stone pavement. A white-green hole smoldered where her trachea used to be.

Joka's heart forgot how to beat as her mentor's purple blood pooled on the ground.

Sah-slen chuckled. "Symphora, Goulima told me you two had a hist—"

BAM!

Sah-slen fell, green-tinted plasma steam rising from a hole in the back of his head. There was no mistaking the woman behind him: Symphora's ex, sporting the armor of the Collective military.

The one who literally got away. The reason half the gang's rules existed.

"Joined the feds, huh?" Symphora asked. "Call off the mercs, and we can talk."

Goulima shook her head. "Symphora Ianna, you're under arrest."

Symphora growled. "We'll see about that."

Plasma rifles whirred, and Joka broke into a sweat. She shouldn't be here. This wasn't the glory she imagined. She made the mistake of glancing at Tur's body again, and a tear blurred her vision.

Thud-thud-thud.

Joka whirled around. Doh-riss was charging her. "Get down!" she hissed.

Caught in a scaly tackle, Joka fell behind her battledart as plasma bolts zoomed around them.

Rubbing her head and propping herself up on her elbow, Joka moaned. "Are you fucking insane?"

"Watch your mouth." Doh-riss unholstered her sidearm and aimed over Joka. A blaster bolt whizzed overhead, the heat nearly singeing her hairs. Within the same fraction of a second the bolt left the muzzle, a mercenary "oof'd" and thudded to the ground. Doh-riss fixed her gaze back on Joka. "That scum had you in his sights. You're welcome."

Joka mouthed a thank-you. She was in over her head, and the most annoying person in the gang was the one to save her; she'd never live this down. Surviving a ground assault wasn't comparable to inventing a flight suit that could let a Human fly another species' ship. She was such an idiot. She'd be a plasma splatter on mossy pavement, a nameless casualty in Symphora's crusade.

Doh-riss pulled Joka close. "Don't have a panic attack. You want to live?"

Joka gazed up into her marbled yellow eyes. The concern in them was probably fake. "Yeah."

"Then let's stay out of Symphora's way."

More bright bursts from plasma rifles streaked through the air, along with yelps, growls, and hisses as the rounds hit their targets.

The mechanics often traded stories about how many mercenaries and lowlifes Symphora and her strike team could gun down. The guesses ranged from the reasonable half-a-platoon to the grandiose, but Joka knew everything depended on context. These weren't mercenaries. If Symphora's ex had joined the Collective military, then they were outgunned and outnumbered, and probably out-other-stuffed that Joka didn't have the combat sense to consider.

"Doh-riss, we can't finish Tur's objective. Sah-slen might not even be a real crime lord."

Doh-riss rose, fired two shots, then crouched. "Hm. Maybe he was a small-time crook who got offered a deal." Her yellow marbled eyes widened, and she gasped. "We need to repair the ships to prep for evac."

Joka gripped her sidearm tight. "Will my pistol do anything against Collective military armor?"

"It's Human-sized. Better to throw your wrench at them."

"*Skata.*"

"Language! Come on." Doh-riss, still crouched, peeked out from the cover and fired another two shots.

Joka fought the urge to remind Doh-riss she didn't need to be so uptight, but this wasn't the appropriate time. The firing around them abated. Joka dared to peek out, useless pistol at the ready. Maybe whoever was firing at them was naked. Ideally, they would be unarmed, too.

But that wasn't what she beheld.

Corpses joined Tur on the ground.

Casualties.

Friend and foe alike. Green vapors from plasma wounds wafted up from the dead bodies, mixing with the moon's natural azure haze to make a sickly smoke.

A bloodied Symphora lumbered toward them, a limp member of her strike team hoisted over her shoulder.

Through clenched teeth, Symphora grumbled. "Get me a beer and a medic..." In front of them, she let the wheezing strike team member slide off. "In that order."

Joka stood and reached for the comm unit. "Did you get her?"

"Yeah." She spit out some blood and a tooth. "And I killed Collective military to do it."

Joka's heart sank. Symphora's gang had never been on the technically correct side of the law. Granted, they disposed of criminals too small or distant for the government to bother with. But all these dead soldiers' armor recorded continuously. The whole battle, including Symphora and the strike team gunning down soldiers, was in the Collective's paws. Didn't matter that it was self-defense and a setup. What mattered was the Collective wouldn't classify them as outlaw vigilantes anymore but as a terrorist organization.

"We're fucked, aren't we?" Joka asked.

Doh-riss shot Joka the stink-eye instead of opening her snout. That was one positive from today, at least.

TWO

(RICK)

A fuel depot on the asteroid Jadwiga, Human Demilitarized Zone, Collective space

FOOTSTEPS CLATTERED THROUGH the fuel depot's wide metal corridors. Twenty Humans huddled together, bound at the wrists and knees, forced into kneeling positions. This was the typical depot that cut costs by letting dirt and grime accumulate in corners. Lots of Human businesses had no other choice out here. Cleaner bots were too expensive, and Humans were too overworked.

Commander Rick Crith loomed over his hostages, plasma pistol clenched in his only hand.

The captives gazed at him, their expressions mixed. Two obnoxious punks ogled the stump where his left arm used to be. A woman wearing her body weight in piercings nodded upon seeing Rick's lopsided haircut and tattoos which displayed allegiance to Earthquake. An older man who chose exercise over alcohol to deal with his problems smirked. Those few must be sympathizers for his cause. Potential recruits after this job was finished.

The other captives, scrawny parents by the looks of them, frowned or fought tears.

Rick sounded gruff despite his placating intent. "I'm not here to hurt you. These ships will be put to good use for Earthquake." He gestured with a nod behind him where his team checked the fuel levels and storage of the docked cargo ships.

"Sorry I can't compensate you for your losses, but you're doing Humanity a service."

One captive spat on the steel floor in front of Rick's armored boots. "You're terrorists."

With a snarl, Rick booted the jackass in the stomach. "The Collective government is what you should fear. We're fighting the good fight." Rick let out a harsh sigh. He'd gone too far and proved the damn loyalist's point. "I'll put in a distress call once we clear the area. Someone will come."

The captives observed the man Rick had kicked, some sympathetically, others with a "told you so" expression.

Another captive piped up, voice steady despite streaks of tears on her cheeks. "You're taking our livelihoods. How do you expect us to feed our families?"

"You could join us instead." Rick's flat tone verged on discouragement. None of these pilots and traders seemed like they knew which end of a rifle to hold, but that could be fixed. And once he rebuilt Earthquake according to his vision, he'd need more help outside of combat roles. Rick's purified Earthquake would help people with services they needed instead of robbing them.

One captive struggled to stand but toppled over instead. "I'll join. You're a legend, Mr. Crith."

Phantom pains tickled Rick's missing left arm. He was too old for some damn fanatic to rehash his exploits. "You can come if you shut up. Any other takers?"

A few heads nodded, so Rick motioned for a squad member to come over. "Untie the ones who want to join and submit them for processing."

"Is it true you fought an alien demon?" one of them asked.

"Ask again, and he'll toss you out an airlock," his crew member responded. Rick's team learned the hard way to avoid questions about his past. They knew enough.

The jackass who spit huffed. "Ask him about enlisting in the Collective military just to turn around and defect."

Rick glared at him. "Yeah, first Human to enlist. I defected when I saw how rotten they were. I joined Earthquake to make a real difference and help people."

"Some help."

The asshole had a point. Humans would be free again, even if that meant snapping some bones first.

Rick turned to Jake Rawltz, his lieutenant in charge of inventory. "How many did we score?" The kid did his job well enough. Rick reminded himself to stop calling people in their thirties "kids," even if their presence made him feel like a dinosaur.

"Eleven," Rawltz mumbled.

Damn. These metal scrapper ships and cargos were supposed to be one-man crews. Rick clenched his teeth. This teetered on not being worth their time. "Good. Send them back to base after we drain the depot of its fuel."

The captive in the center, the one Rick knew was the station manager, grunted. "You're going to make me homeless. I owe people money."

"We know." Rick glared at him. "Now your debt with Earthquake is settled. If you had other creditors, tell them to take it up with us. Otherwise, there's a homeless shelter a few systems down from here."

Asshole Number One dared to speak again. "What'll you even do with these ships?"

"Classified." Rick signaled another squad member. "The three who protested..." Rick let the silence hang in the air while his recruit approached. A faint temptation rose to order their execution. None of his recruits would question it. Other commanders in Earthquake certainly did similar things. He shook the thought from his mind when he remembered his list of names. He couldn't extend that list today by killing anyone. "... take their credits. We'll redistribute that wealth, too. Then we'll head out."

Robbing Humans left a sick knot in Rick's gut, but the galaxy needed to learn the three options of dealing with Earthquake: comply, get out of the way, or get hurt. Whether for individuals or the whole

damn Collective government, it didn't matter. At least he didn't have to kill anyone.
    Today.

THREE

(INSPECTOR)

Great Mystery Monastery, New Lodestone, Polemistes System (known locally as Boudica), Human Demilitarized Zone

INSPECTOR BIKKOLOS WONDERED if his current migraine was more from the planet's magnetic field or the conversation. His mouth was sore from speaking the Human language. It had been years since he said more than a word or two of pleasantries. The Human across from him bore a content expression, as if he enjoyed the verbal gymnastics.

Bikkolos resisted the urge to sneeze from the braziers burning incense around them, hanging off the red pillars supporting too-low archways. Geometric shapes he couldn't begin to understand decorated the walls.

"Brother Maynard." Inspector Bikkolos scratched at the fur on his neck with his paw. "I could've brought you to the government offices above. More cooperation would be appreciated." The floor of this monastery was uncomfortable. They didn't have any places to sit intended for an Arkouda. It was annoying, but he understood. These monks were more of a sit-on-cushions than sit-in-chairs type. He supposed the floor was a better seating arrangement for him than pushing two chairs together.

"I'm acting as cooperatively as possible, officer. I ask that you respect my monastic vows." The monk seemed middle-aged by the fading of his scars and complexion, but Bikkolos never was the best at discerning Human ages. A series of precise scars on his face suggested a traumatic childhood. The sensitive part of Bikkolos was pleased this guy found some solace in religion. Too many abused Humans traversed darker paths.

"Aren't you supposed to attempt to end suffering? For all creatures? Do you know how overwhelming this planet's field is for me?"

"I can't imagine, officer." The monk's pheromones smelled honest, but Bikkolos always suspected that Humans enjoyed seeing Arkoudae uncomfortable. "I could ask our botanist to craft you some medicine."

Inspector Bikkolos waved a paw. "That won't be necessary." He withdrew a vial from between his trench coat and the low-grade body armor meant for emergencies, not combat. "I have my own stash." He downed it, wincing at the chalky taste. It stank like an armpit barbecue. "But I'm running out, and you haven't given me any answers."

The monk pulled back his dark hood as if to show he had nothing to hide. "I've answered all of your questions, officer."

Bikkolos furrowed his thick brow. "Not satisfactorily. I suspected you'd be more cooperative since the person I'm trying to find is your brother."

A slight twitch from the monk. Finally. "My brothers are the other monks here. We're a community and have disavowed all other attachments."

"Don't you care at all?" Bikkolos removed his cap, hoping it would show the monk his own sincerity. "He's missing."

"I don't want anyone to go missing, but I haven't visited him in years."

A salty pheromone rush attacked Bikkolos' nostrils. Something wasn't true.

"Have you had other contact?"

The monk paused, eyeing the inspector. This guy had something. "He has attempted to reach out to me."

Another pheromone whiff. Only a partial truth.

"And you responded, didn't you?" Inspector Bikkolos leaned forward. "Is someone threatening you? Or him? Blackmailing, perhaps?"

The monk shifted on his meditation cushion, blinking a little faster than before.

A surge of the planet's magnetic field hit the inspector. It was like when the explosive detonated near his ear during his last tour of duty. Wincing, Bikkolos continued. "He could be alive. Surely, there's something you know."

"He's a scientist," the monk said. "So is his wife."

Wife. That revealed a bit about this guy's politics. He acknowledged their marriage if he used that word.

Breathing through the pain of the magnetic flash, desperate for the medicine to kick in, Bikkolos nodded. "Did you know she's missing, too?"

"You'll have to forgive me, officer, but the Collective has a checkered past with Humans. I appreciate that you're speaking Human, but understand that I do not wish anything I tell you to create more suffering for someone else."

Progress? "I don't blame you." His mouth dried, and he asked the question he'd been dreading. "Are you with Earthquake?" This planet was adequate for a base, Bikkolos surmised, because of the oppressive magnetosphere. Their presence on this ferrous rock was one of those open secrets that the Collective couldn't quite legally prove, and few people on the force had the patience to deal with the paperwork to get there.

Earthquake wasn't why Bikkolos was here, though. He wanted to stay as far away from them as possible. He'd heard the rumors about their bounties on Arkoudae heads.

The monk's eyes widened at the mention of the Earthquake organization. His pheromone scent shifted to the stink of fear.

"Is Earthquake threatening you?"

The monk exhaled. "No. They don't know about my brother."

More progress. "I imagine they wouldn't be too happy if they knew about his wife."

He chuckled. "No, they wouldn't."

"I'm not here chasing Earthquake." Bikkolos wished Human olfactories developed enough for the monk to know Bikkolos was honest. "You're right to be suspicious. There aren't many detectives who go after crimes against Humans." He pointed to the "Crimes against Provincials" unit logo emblazoned on his badge.

"I don't know what kind of research you're able to do from your monastery, but you can search my badge ID. I was a military medic and became fed up with how the government treated Humans." A knot formed in his stomach, remembering his friend, the first Human in the military and the only one in his unit. The guy he had to patch up constantly. The reason Bikkolos learned to speak Human in the first place—until that friend received the untreatable injury, and they never spoke again. He shook his head. "I really do want to find your brother."

The monk moved his jaw to the side. Bikkolos had seen a few Humans do that before. It was a "mulling it over" expression.

"Inspector, do you understand that my cooperation comes from a place of compassion for all creatures, not any familial attachment?" A single bead of sweat formed somewhere on the monk's head.

"Of course."

With a speed known only to Arko ice snails, the monk rose from his cushion. "I have some recordings to show you."

FOUR

(JOKΛ)

Aboard the space station "Calamity," floating on the fringes of Collective space

SYMPHORA PROMISED A memorial for Tur and the fallen strike team members after they could relocate the station. The odds of discovery by the military or government-funded hunters were too high to remain here.

In Joka's years with Symphora, the gang had warped the station, but this was the first time they needed to. Joka massaged the migraine from her temples—this wasn't fun mayhem. She was crammed in the engine room with the other mechanics and engineers, everybody straining to get each rusted gizmo and lever in the proper positions.

If real badasses instead of me and Doh-riss joined the mission, would we be this deep in the skata?

The warp drive's hum bristled, radiating a gentle heat despite harnessing half the power of a condensed sun. Yet all that energy only facilitated fleeing from Tur's death instead of making it meaningful. Joka wiped sweat from her brow and stepped away from the drive core. She was still on the wrong side of the safety divider, but that precaution was meant for the Arkoudae who didn't handle the heat as well.

From the safety of the guard rail, her bunkmate Devy called to her. "Jokes… is it true Tur died protecting you?"

Joka tsked to mask her shriveling heart. "Who told you that?"

"Is it true?" Devy leaned over the rail and frowned.

"No. Didn't the mission debrief make it to the mechanics' dungeon? Symphora got duped. Sah-slen didn't have a pedophilic brothel or sweatshop like we thought. The operation was a sting. Tur died because she was in the line of fire. Following Symphora's orders, I might add."

Devy whistled. "Yeah, that's what came down, but some of the others said the official debrief was worded without mentioning you because—" she winced and averted her eyes, "you screwed everything up."

Joka ducked under the rail to join Devy, as if there weren't bile threatening the back of her throat. "Unbelievable."

Except it wasn't. She and the other handful of Humans were the social pariahs in Symphora's gang, just like Humans were in the greater galactic society. None of them were on the strike team, and Joka was only the first allowed to directly participate in a mission.

Tur lost a bet.

The whole mission was a joke.

Symphora saved Humans when they liberated some scumball's lair like other species, but very few were afforded the opportunity to join the gang. Joka puffed out a breath as she focused on the drive levels. Everything was stable. She hoisted her green flag and noticed other green flags held aloft. It would've been more appropriate for her to hold a white flag.

Joka's knuckles turned white once she realized how much fuel this would burn. If they picked the wrong spot to warp to, this would be the worst relocation attempt ever. Right in the center of a black hole or amid a swarm of Drowned Star pirates.

Devy nudged her again. "Uh, who is everyone flagging?"

"*Skata*, you're right. Tur's gone."

Other mechanics made eye contact with each other and shrugged or waved their tails, everyone making the same realization around the same time. Even Doh-riss, thankfully too far to hear Joka's profanity over the engine's hum, seemed confused.

Doh-riss strutted to the engine room's center, the only area unoccupied by a clunky hot machine. Over buzzing converters and beeping monitors, she hollered, "I'll inform Symphora we're ready."

Tail kisser. Joka rolled her eyes. "Should you bother her? Maybe go to the engineering chief instead?"

An Arkouda growled. "Is that what Tur said we should do, Joka?" Sounded like Marka, who was certifiably the worst. Well, Doh-riss was the worst, but Marka was runner-up.

Murmurs followed from around the room.

Doh-riss slapped her tail on the metal floor, snapping attention back to her. "Tur was nowhere near Joka when she died. I'll tell the engineering chief we're ready. We don't have enough time to point claws at each other."

Joka clasped her flag as sweat beaded on her forehead. Doh-riss was the only one sticking up for her. Earth, she was the only other mechanic who knew the truth. Her lunch threatened to resurface, realizing Doh-riss deserved some gratitude.

Devy tsked. "Sucks that Doh-riss is on your side. At least she's loud."

"I'll fart on your pillow tonight."

"Doh-riss wouldn't do that," Devy taunted.

"A Lo-sat wouldn't fit in our bunks, and I don't think Doh-riss has farted once in her life."

Devy cocked an eyebrow. "That would explain so much."

Each mechanic either returned to her workstation or putzed around in tense anticipation in the five minutes before Doh-riss arrived with the engineering chief, a haggard Arkouda who'd been with Symphora since the early days.

"Alright ladies," she barked. "We know Tur wouldn't want us moping around. I'll do double duty until we get stuff sorted. We're ready on my end. Can I see some flags?"

Maybe Doh-riss would raise a red flag over some minor issue and slow everyone down like last time.

The engineering chief grumbled a "thank-you" to everyone and thanked Doh-riss individually. Instead of joining the crew's muffled groans and eye rolls, Joka relaxed, thankful the attention had shuffled elsewhere.

Minutes later, the space station alarm blared, and everyone strapped in. Joka and Devy squeezed together in a chair meant for an Arkouda, as did the few pairs of Humans. The Lo-sat mechanics coiled their tails around pillars.

With a squeal, space warped outside the station, and everyone lurched forward. Riva puked at the gravity change, which garnered guffaws and groans from everyone else.

After an hour of adjustment to hyperspace acceleration, the mechanics were free to move about the room again and twiddle their thumbs, lose to Kahrenn and Marka in cards, clean their spilled vomit in shame, or get drunk. Joka preferred option four since that was the easiest way to blend in. Devy also had the good hooch hookup.

As Joka approached the stairwell to the mess hall above them, heavy thuds sounded from above. Footsteps.

Everyone stood at razor-sharp attention as Symphora descended the staircase with a measured cadence.

Symphora waved a paw. "What'd I tell you *skata* stains about acting like we're military? Saluting me is a one-way ticket to the ass-whooping station."

Everyone slackened, but Joka caught Doh-riss in her periphery scowling and mumbling. Joka considered the ethics of making a fake ping address for the purpose of sending Doh-riss pictures of Arkoudae feces.

"Good." Symphora crossed her muscled arms. "Before we do memorials of the sisters we lost, I need to go through Tur's stuff. Since her cousin died last year, she didn't really have a next-in-line picked." Symphora uncrossed her arms and checked a nearby clipboard. "Where's Marma?"

Marka stepped forward, ready to defend the unofficial title of the literal second worst. "Marka? That's me."

"Sorry." Symphora's tone wasn't apologetic as she squinted at her clipboard again. "You have the best commendations from Tur's last review."

A Lo-sat called from across the room, "That was over a year ago!"

A collective gasp rang out as everyone stared at the idiot.

Symphora snarled. "The next person who interrupts me gets a week-long booze ban." As the women quieted, Symphora continued, "Marka, you and the other two mechanics on the last mission come with me. We'll sort Tur's belongings and see if she left any other recommendations. She was in the process of finalizing reviews last week."

Eyes drifted from Symphora toward Joka and Doh-riss.

Joka let out a long exhale and eyed Devy. "Wish me luck?"

Smiling, she mouthed, "Eat *skata*."

Joka shook her head and chuckled. "I love you."

"You'll wake up with pink eye tomorrow."

Joka followed Marka, with Doh-riss' slapping foot-steps not too far behind. The trio followed Symphora up the staircase in silence. Goosebumps erupted on Joka's skin at the prospect of hearing Tur's last recording. Even though Tur never showed it, in some corner of Joka's mind, she knew Tur was proud Joka invented a Human flight suit. In some dorky way, Tur was like Joka's big sister, maybe even mom.

Sure, the first mission was a tragic bust, but more of the Humans in the gang could pick up the slack. Prove their worth. All because of Joka.

The starships designed for and by Humans could never fly fast enough or survive enough fire to be useful on the missions they went on, but plopping a Human in a ship made for an Arkouda? Surely, that was worth some merit. And if Symphora fired her, at least she could go into the inner core of the Collective worlds and sell off her design. Someone had to want it. Someone had to want her. See her worth.

When they passed the mess hall, Symphora led them down the private hallway meant for the strike team. These were the station's nicer quarters. Kah-renn and Doh-riss both swore the members of the strike team had private rooms, but nobody believed them. Unable to see past Symphora or Marka's bulk in front of her, Joka eyed the wide doors on either side of the hallway.

Shooting range.

Private bar.

Neither of those were surprises.

A hot tub?

"What the hell?" Joka whispered.

A derisive snort came from behind her. "So unsanitary," Doh-riss whispered back.

Marka cast a glance over her shoulder, lingering by the hot tub room's door before shaking her head.

Under different circumstances, Joka would've attempted commiserating with her about the strike team's privilege, but after seeing what they had to endure, she thought better of it. Having to take life to save another's... it was noble, but damn if it wasn't dirty.

Joka's heart froze. She had fired at people on that mission—even if none of the people she shot from the safety of her cockpit died, she was in just as much *skata* as everyone else.

She thought they were nameless mercenaries defending a scumbag slaver or pimp, but they were soldiers. Defenders of the Collective. Not bad guys. Joka's eyes widened. She had never been religious and didn't know much about the main Human religions, but she might need to talk to a cleric or a damn good therapist about what she'd done.

The quartet turned a corner, arriving at the war room. A metallic oval table with a projector in the center spread before them.

Symphora dragged a slow paw across her muzzle. "Take a seat, girls."

Occupying one of the chairs was the heavily bandaged strike team member Symphora carried earlier.

Too many empty chairs in a room where the walls were lined with trophies from missions: skulls from drug lords, branding irons from slavers, and framed thank-you notes and drawings sent in by rescued kids.

Marka snagged the unoccupied seat closest to the door and waved Joka and Doh-riss over. Joka could've lain down and still fit for how large the chair was, and Doh-riss sat, legs and tail akimbo across from her. She stared at Joka as if unaware of her own status as the galaxy's biggest pain in the ass. How anyone could be so oblivious was beyond Joka.

Symphora slumped into the seat at the head of the table. "I haven't seen this yet, so I don't know what we're in for." She checked her clipboard before glancing back at Joka and Doh-riss. "Yoka?"

"Joka," she squeaked.

"Mm. Sorry. Long day. And Hor-iss?"

"Close, ma'am," Doh-riss said through a wide smile, serrated teeth on display. "Doh-riss."

"Right. Do either of you have anything to add about today's mission? *Skata* happened in a blink. I didn't see Tur go down."

Joka's legs dangled off the edge like she were a child in an adult's seat. "No, it happened so fast. Maybe a sniper?"

Doh-riss shrugged. "I helped Joka take cover." Her eyeridges raised, and a smile crept up her snout. "I even made some covering fire, which connected to one of—" her expression fell, and her shoulders slumped, "one of the... the soldiers."

Damn, Joka thought. They both had fired at good people. They really were criminals. Together.

Tears budded behind her eyelids.

Symphora drummed her paws on the table. "Don't beat yourself up. We had bad intel. Any soldiers with my ex were either super green or had it coming. You didn't take out anyone who would actually serve the Collective."

Joka smelled how freshly that line was pulled from her ass. It was some kind of defense mechanism to protect her from the realization of what she'd done. Of what they'd all done.

Doh-riss nodded. "Thank you."

The other strike team survivor grunted, straining to speak. "Symphora's a legend. Anyone worth their scars in the Collective knows she's doing the Goddess' work. Nobody good would take on the job to hit us. Especially to fight so dishonorably."

"Quit tail-sniffing," Symphora grumbled. "I'd be careful about banking on that anymore. There's full reason to rain Nightmare on us now. There's gotta be recordings of us killing Collective soldiers. Popular opinion might not care or believe it was a setup." She ran a paw through her red-tipped mohawk. "Either way, I need a new mechanic chief. We'll see what Tur had to say."

Joka fidgeted again. Tur had started their reviews, but she'd told Joka she'd get to the Humans in the mechanics' corps after today's mission.

Symphora tapped a button and a projection of Tur sprang up. She was in her standard mechanic chief gear, not the combat armor from the botched mission. Seeing her boss and mentor in her element, looking like herself, hurt in a way Joka hadn't expected.

Joka blinked hard. Symphora had found her years ago as an orphan, shucking kernelfruit husks with her tiny fingers, working as a slave for a farmer too cheap to buy a bot. Over the years, Tur took advantage of

Joka's tiny fingers, showing Joka how to manipulate the smallest gears and wires. Tur had other mentees, other "children," although she'd never label them as such. Yet Joka always felt a special connection to her. Now she was stuck with Marka, whose nurturing skills were on par with anal fissures.

The recording of Tur cataloged the members of the mechanic corps, starting with the Arkoudae women. Marka received top marks, of course. Polla, Mael, and Graia scored average ratings. The Lo-sat women received mixed reviews. Joka cast a glance at Doh-riss, who clutched her tail, scales turning white at the knuckles. Tur's recording gave middling marks to Kah-renn and Senh-dan, high commendation for Whas-trom, but groaned at the mention of Doh-riss.

Tur sighed and pinched the bridge of her snout. "Symphora, I know on the last review you told me I couldn't demerit a member for being a pain in the ass, but you have to believe me, Doh-riss is unbearable. She's an absolute tail-sniffer. The worst kind, too. When I bring up an assignment, she raises her claws and volunteers before I can finish my sentence. Her hearts are in the right place, I think, but Nightmare—"

Doh-riss had chosen to stare at the floor instead of grumble at the profanity at this point.

"—we need to find an excuse to ditch her. She wants to get promoted, but I tell you, I'll lose half the team if she does. People will quit. Your strike team is too reckless for me to be down any mechanics. I'm bringing her on the upcoming mission so you can see what I mean." The recording of Tur chuckled at the last remark.

Joka's eyes widened, watching Doh-riss' eyebrow ridges and snout contort, fighting a battle against unraveling in front of everyone. Maybe Doh-riss saw Tur as a mentor, too.

Joka tensed. The recording had gone through all the Arkouda and Lo-sat candidates. Tur should be wrapping up soon.

"Finally," the recording continued, "we have the Humans. Some of them actually hold some promise. Riva Lavanta and Agatha Park do well with lighter tasks, and the new cub we got, good ol' whats-her-face, she can get in the tiny spots. With the right direction. She's better than the last runt." A sigh followed, and sweat beaded on Joka's neck.

Tur told Joka she would review the Humans later. Tur either lied to her and skipped Joka or she skipped the evaluation process altogether.

"Last up, Devy Rajpatel and Joka Bunear..." Another sigh. "Devy does well enough. But hanging around Joka is slowing her down. Bunear is a distraction. Honestly, Symph, she's not much different than Doh-riss. Some part of Joka wants to help but finds the pain-in-the-assiest way to do it. She'll be bragging about her flight suit in the next few days, I bet. I'll let her test it out; I'm thinking we could take one of the more skilled Human mechanics with us for field repair on future missions. They could do the stuff too dangerous for a repair bot. A Human on your strike team could potentially sneak in somewhere to plant a bomb. If this invention works, it could help us out. We could even sell the design for a quick buck. If it blows up and kills her or cripples her, we're not missing much.

Good heart, but she'll never be leadership material. Now that I got a new runt, Joka doesn't even have the smallest fingers on the team."

Symphora hit a button, pausing the recording. "Well, *skata*. You need a minute?"

Joka assumed she was talking about Doh-riss, but when she absently touched her own face, she picked up moisture on her cheek. After clearing her throat, Joka shook her head tightly. "No, ma'am. Allergies. I'm alright."

"Bitch did you dirty," the strike team member said with a huff.

Symphora waved a fuzzy finger in her face. "Tur was a good woman." Her expression soured. "I trust her opinions." After casting a sympathetic glance at Joka and Doh-riss, she added, "Sorry. I hope you can take her evaluations to heart and improve your performance. Marka, stay. Everyone else is dismissed."

FIVE

(RICK)

**Tecton Homeless Shelter, New Lodestone,
Boudica System, Human Demilitarized Zone**

RICK'S FOOTSTEPS ECHOED through the tile
mess hall of the homeless shelter named after one of
the few Human representatives in the Collective government. Any connection Monsieur Jacques Tecton
had to Earthquake and Rick couldn't be proven. Not
legally at least.

After the misadventure on that damn moon, the
recruitment videos featuring Rick were pulled, and
Tecton wanted an extra layer of protection and plausible deniability. Yet on New Lodestone, few people
were interested in tattling to the government.

In his periphery, Rick caught one of his squad members jumping behind the counter to assist the serving.

It was about damn time. He'd had enough issues with old recruits joining Earthquake for the wrong reasons. Punk kids who wanted to make an illegal homemade gun or unload their daddy issues on Arkoudae. He needed people who wanted to advance Humanity, not just xenophobes.

Rick snaked through the tables of people, greeting and mingling with the patrons as appropriate. One veteran waved to Rick as he passed, and phantom pains in his missing arm tingled since he couldn't return the gesture with the same hand.

More new faces this week, along with the same ones from before—that made four consecutive weeks of additional mouths to feed. As Rick left another patron to his meal, his nostrils flared.

He wished he could blame the surge on New Lodestone's breathable atmosphere drawing Humans, but he knew that wasn't the reason.

Was it another mining operation closing this time? A government agency pulling some funding again? Each possibility churned hate and hope in equal measure. Places like this were where people would truly see why Humans needed Earthquake. Suffering under the Collective as provincials without full rights or representation served nobody except the damn Arkoudae. Human labor was cheaper than building and maintaining bots to do it.

En route to his office, the brightest star in his unit greeted him.

Amanda Martinez.

The platonic nature of her radiant smile twisted his insides.

"Why so grim, Mr. Sunshine?" Her curly dark hair bounced like a forest of happy springs. He had approved her request to forego the mandatory lopsided Earthquake haircut as well as cover the required tattoos. Tecton would never know, and if he did, Rick had a good cover. She was officially the shelter manager, after all, and they needed plausible deniability. Rick's name wasn't on the officially registered forms, and this was far enough on the frontier that Collective agents didn't bother examining too closely. People on this side of Human colonies wouldn't dare turn in Rick. They didn't see him as a traitor the way the damn loyalists and appeasers did.

Rick huffed a chuckle. "New faces. Wonder what shitty thing the Collective did this time."

"More people we can help." That was why Amanda was perfect. "Got my money for new coolers and freezers?" She bade him follow through the kitchen to the back offices.

"As promised." Rick sidestepped around a busser carrying tin cups. "Any new recruits?"

"Two. One of them is pretty good. Former physicist. Came out here in the colony's early days to study the planet's magnetism—see if there were any spots for Arkoudae to settle."

The guy washing dishes behind them slowed his pace and leaned closer.

Rick's eyes widened. "There aren't any, right?"

"Calm down. No. He was the guy who told the Arkoudae the planet was uninhabitable for them."

"And they thanked him by cutting his funding?" His tone would've been harsher if he'd been speaking to anyone else.

A cook silently lifted a ladle from a pot, motioning for Rick to taste. The scent of tomato and salt ignited memories. Rick politely shook his hand to refuse. Some part of him was leery about how fast imported Earth vegetables grew in New Lodestone's stronger magnetic field, but the smell was at least right.

Amanda glared. "Jimmy, no cross-contamination. Use a bowl." She turned to Rick as they looped around the prep area. "Yeah. After that, he worked as a schoolteacher, but..."

A waft of rising bread hit Rick, a tempting distraction from the physicist. "They cut the school's funding?"

Amanda waved a playful finger. "Thus the legend of Rick Crith continues. Super soldier and super detective."

"Please never say any of that about me."

"You know my rule. Take my aunt out to dinner if you want me to stop."

She was a flower in bloom with a digging thorn.

He needed to let this go. "I'll have time to date when Humans are independent from the Collective."

Amanda rolled her eyes. "Whatever. I've got some more good news."

Outside the view of anyone in the public area of the shelter or kitchen, they reached the "Employee Hygiene" poster. She tapped the piece of mismatched tape on the corner, and a panel on the metallic wall rolled to the side, revealing the door to Rick's office.

Amanda switched her clipboard to her other hand and gestured like she'd open the door for Rick. He cut in front of her with more sharpness than he would've liked and opened it himself. He wasn't the damn charity case in this shelter.

"Is your news that my conference call with Monsieur Tecton was postponed?"

"Funny. Two minutes to get your swears out. Maybe don't flare your nostrils this time when he says something you don't like?"

Releasing the door handle, Rick pinched his nostrils shut.

Amanda sighed. "I'll establish the connection. You're still on his good side, remember?"

Rick entered his office and wished he could forget why he was on the leader's good side in the first place.

That damn tomb they shouldn't have opened three years ago.

The thief he shouldn't have hired.

The archaeologist he almost murdered.

All for functioning Collective armor, finally his to study and exploit for Earthquake's benefit.

Dozens of dead Humans, some loyal to Rick, others damn mutineers. Malodorous death surfaced in his nightmares, defying years of therapy.

Whether the prize of the invincible Collective armor was worth the cost remained to be seen. His engineers' prototype hadn't been tested yet.

Rick's office in the shelter was almost as bare as his previous one on his old mobile base. One wall had the solitary decoration of a printout of the newsletter from his home station, bragging about the first

Human accepted into the Collective military. Beside it hung his dishonorable discharge papers from the Collective military. A generic watercolor of a beach graced the opposite wall. Staring at it whenever the dark thoughts threatened helped a little, remembering the last vacation before Mom died. No pristine shores or cawing wavegulls could allay the pessimism of a discussion with Monsieur Tecton, though.

Rick huffed, initiating the connection on his desktop tablet. He had a brief glimpse of himself before the screen clicked on. He'd need a shave soon to get his haircut back in the ridiculous regulation. Lopsided hair. Neither tactical nor practical in combat.

The screen buzzed to life, revealing the grinning visage of Monsieur Jacques Tecton, Human Affairs Representative in the Collective. Whether or not he was also the leader of Earthquake was mere speculation on all official channels. He left being the face of the operation to his field commanders like Rick. It never stopped him from taking credit in conversations with them, though.

"Morning, Monsieur." Rick steeled his voice into formality.

"There's my boy," Monsieur Tecton said, running his left hand through his normal hair, jackass that he was.

Sonofabitch had to rub that in Rick's face. Amanda suggested once that Tecton did it subconsciously, but the grin on his face was too smug for the benefit of the doubt.

"How was your most recent haul?"

"Not what I'd hoped," Rick said. "We'll need more targets to hit. The cost of the homeless shelter is rising."

"So shut it down. It's a cover. Do something cheaper." On the other side of the screen, Tecton fiddled with a pen as if he hadn't suggested allowing the homeless to starve. "Or you could be like my less problematic commanders and choose something that generates income. Ever thought about that?"

Rick's eyes narrowed. "I get better recruits than they do."

"But fewer. Sometimes you just need a warm body and a gun arm. Now..." Tecton steepled his fingers. "I heard you have a slimeball on your crew. Tell me what that's about."

"The Lo-sat? He's not on our crew. Not officially. I don't trust him, but he has no love for the Collective. He's stolen enough supplies and funds to prove his worth." Rick sighed. "I hoped having another species nearby would alleviate some prejudice associated with our organization."

"Sounds like you're insulting half the members in *my* organization."

Rick clenched his teeth. "If we rid ourselves of them, our ranks would swell with more level-headed individuals. That's what we need. The thief has almost paid off his debt; we've made a profit off him." Rick didn't explain how the thief danced on the border of more trouble than he was worth, but that wouldn't do Rick any favors.

Tecton furrowed his brow and leaned in closer to the camera. "When he's outlived his usefulness..."

Rick understood it as an order and closed his eyes slowly after a pause.

"Ensure your men see it. Now, you will give me some good news next week. Otherwise, our discussion will be about whether you have outlived *your* usefulness." The transmission ended.

Rick huffed and tapped the button on his tablet, letting the world outside his office know that he was no longer occupied. Of course a knock came at the door.

"Enter," he croaked.

In walked a member of Rick's field team, a stocky colonist who everyone except Rick called Fat Don. The sonofabitch who was dating Amanda. A dark part of Rick considered sending him on the most dangerous missions, but the dumbass was so incompetent that he'd end up getting more people than himself killed. Rick motioned for him to take the seat opposite his desk.

"What do you have to report?"

He situated himself opposite Rick and avoided eye contact. "The monks weren't interested."

Through a growl, Rick asked, "And why the hell not? Did you give them the pitch?"

Fat Don shrugged. "They heard what the Collective says about us. The racist stuff."

"Shit. What was your counter?"

"That we're not racist."

Rick fought the urge to strangle the bastard. "That's what every racist says about themselves."

"That doesn't sound right." What Amanda saw in this loser was a puzzle for the contemplatives hanging out in the monastery.

An image flashed in Rick's mind of taking a hammer to this moron's face. He exhaled and released the rogue idea. "You didn't tell them we have a Lo-sat on our crew?"

"That slimeball? He's an embarrassment. Total asshole. No reason in keeping him around or mentioning him."

Rick clenched his fist under the table. If the monks would lend some support, it would go a long way to bringing more sympathy to their cause and garnering more recruits. "Did you at least tell them about our work for the homeless and downtrodden?"

Waste of Flesh nodded. "They said that was commendable and the only reason they didn't forcefully remove me with their martial arts."

"And I'm assuming they also weren't willing to provide a teacher so we could learn their techniques?"

The loser shrugged. "They weren't interested in anything I had to say. They got it in their bald heads that we're the bad guys here."

With nincompoops like him, it was a small wonder anyone thought differently of Earthquake.

"Thanks," Rick said. "We'll figure something else out."

If he couldn't garner their support, he at least needed to glean their unarmed fighting style from them. Collective soldiers were trained to fight against conventional warfare and combat strategies. Prehistoric Human fighting styles weren't anything even the most learned Arkouda warrior could counter against without resorting to brute force. They didn't know most prehistoric Human martial arts were meant to subdue a stronger and bigger foe: literally and symbolically true of the Arkoudae.

"Dismissed."

After the dumbass saluted and left, Rick pinged Amanda.

[Rick: We need to get one of our own in the monastery. Someone who can learn their techniques without drawing too much attention to himself. Someone who also knows how to learn and teach effectively. Having a candidate who only meets some of the criteria will be insufficient. Understood?]

[Amanda: 👍]

For now, he'd have to settle for an agent infiltrating the monastic order. Their symbolic blessing was too valuable to surrender. Get them on his side, and the skeptics would follow. Maybe even some loyalists, too.

[Rick: I'm going to the monastery myself.]

SIX

(NED)

**On a research station in
{LOCATION CLASSIFIED}**

THEY WERE HAPPY once. A real family.

On tiptoes, Ned Porandi rubbed his wife's back as she sobbed. Even through her lab coat, her rough, ridged scales slowed his hand. It wasn't as soothing as releasing pheromones, but it was the best he could do. He imagined Human dads never gave their sons a "how to release positive pheromones" talk, but Ned knew his birth parents probably wouldn't have approved of their son marrying another species. His wife's parents sure didn't.

Ned winced as the hovering bots shoved their son away from them.

La-hok placed her hand over his, her claws pressing against his skin, but not to the point of pain or puncture—they'd made that mistake enough times when they were dating. Yet today, their touch couldn't flood adrenaline into Ned's system with their young son screaming on the other side of the dura-glass.

The boy pounded against the partition with his malformed fists.

"It's harder every day," La-hok hissed.

Ned winced back a tear. "We'll figure something out and escape. We'll give Mui-xe the future we imagined. Together. As a family."

Her tail curled around his wrist and drew his hand away from her back. Her dry scales scratched and tugged at the hairs on his arm. "You say that every day. It hurts more each time we fail."

Mui-xe was thudding his shoulder against the glass. His hairless skin, mottled with flesh and scales, cracked in different places as the gasses in the chamber swirled.

Ned averted his bleary eyes. "Dr. Diastrevlo can't keep us forever. Once he figures out how we made our son, he'll turn us loose."

"He'll kill us, Ned."

Maybe if he'd received a proper education, gotten a real degree, he would've been smart enough to save them or stop this from happening all those years ago. A worm-riddled pit tore in Ned's stomach. "I won't allow it."

La-hok slapped her tail against the floor, staring in horror and disgust at their child's torture.

We're lucky our son's shrieks will muffle what we say. Diastrevlo is always recording. Ned dropped to a whisper. "La, I know how to save us."

She wouldn't meet his gaze. "I love your hope, but … you can't."

Ned reached for her wrist, interlacing his fingers with her claws. "I already did."

She whirled on him, neck frills slightly extended. "Your hologram machine is ready?"

"I prefer to call it an image inducer, but no, that's plan B."

Over her shoulder, he caught sight of Mui-xe vomiting through pained heaves. His tail, not quite as long or thin as La-hok's, wriggled helplessly.

Ned wished to trade places with the boy—Mui-xe never deserved this. "Do you remember the lab assistant who was fired?"

"The Arkouda girl? Koray?" Her eyeridges slanted. "She quit."

"But not before she did me a favor. I saw her growing compassion for Mui-xe. I knew she'd quit or say something to Diastrevlo and get fired." A cautious smile spread on Ned's face. "She agreed to help us."

La-hok pulled her lab coat tighter and crossed her arms over her chest. "She did that for a Human?"

"There's an outlaw who lives on the fringe of the galaxy." Ned hated the bluntness in his voice. In other circumstances, he would've cracked a joke or flirted with La-hok. But no more. "The one who made headlines by killing those slavers. I asked Koray to contact her for us."

"Symphora Ianna? The Arkouda vigilante? Why not ask for a superhero or a wizard?" She pulled her claw away from his hand and turned her attention back on Mui-xe.

"She saved me."

"But you were so young." Her tone was soft. "You could've been mistaken."

"I remember the factory." Ned massaged his forehead in a tight circle. "The stench. The beatings. And I remember the Arkouda with a mohawk who splattered my manager's brains over the floor. Those things stick with someone, my love."

"But why would Koray of all Arkoudae have the contact information for a folk hero?"

Ned reached between the buttons on his lab coat to the undershirt pocket where he kept his wedding ring and withdrew a small card. "She doesn't, but I do. There are some orphanages under Symphora's protection. *I should know.* I know who can reach her. Doing it myself—"

"Diastrevlo would notice. Right." A pained smile stretched across her snout. "You really are a genius, my love."

Mui-xe's screaming reached a new intensity. This wasn't the shrill cry of a child throwing a tantrum or plain agony, but something more primal. Visceral. Ned's thrumming eardrums melded with his tightening chest.

Through the far side of the dura-glass, behind their writhing son, lurked Dr. Diastrevlo. Some part of Ned wished a diabolical smile would creep up the Arkouda scientist's snout, but the doctor remained cold as ever. He scribbled notes on their tormented son as if this were a lunar mineral survey.

La-hok clamped on Ned's shoulder. "Ned," she whispered, "his hands."

Amid the whirling maelstrom of poisonous gasses in the container, two lights flickered, right where Mui-xe's hands ought to be. The gasses ignited, and the container snapped into a pillar of bottled flame, redder than a dying star.

In the instant of combustion, La-hok's neck frills flared to their fullest extent while husband and wife screamed "NO" in their own native languages.

Before logic could kick in and remind them that fire needed oxygen to burn, the flames dissipated, and their son lay in a crumpled heap, struggling to breathe. If Dr. Diastrevlo would have granted their request to allow Mui-xe some clothes to protect his dignity, they would've been burnt to ash on his body. Some small part of Ned appreciated that instance of Diastrevlo's cruelty today.

Ned slammed his fist against their side of the partition. "Let him out, you goddamn monster!"

A drone descended from the ceiling and shot a taser at Ned, sending his convulsing body to the floor. La-hok crouched over him, claws on his shoulders. His stiffening body rattled against the floor. Fury bubbled knowing how much more pain his son was in.

Dr. Diastrevlo's monotone boomed over the PA system. "How can you call anyone a monster when you created one? Today's trials were successful."

From the floor, Ned heard the blessed *whoosh* of Mui-xe's container lifting. Today's nightmare was over. Tomorrow's was only a few hours away. But somewhere, he knew, Symphora would hear his plea. Dr. Diastrevlo wasn't an enslaver or pimp, but he was the kind of scum Symphora would rip apart.

He imagined her kicking down a door, entering triumphantly like a vengeful spirit, champion of good, red-tipped mohawk following her movements like a graceful horse mane as she slaughtered Diastrevlo and blew up his security drones with all manner of grenades. Ned cursed himself for not thinking of his guardian angel sooner. He also cursed his slow progress on the image inducer. If he could manage some more time away from Diastrevlo's prying eyes, he could finish and escape.

The partition raised, and an emerald light over their son's observation chamber flashed, indicating the last toxic vapors had dissipated. La-hok released Ned and ran over to their heaving child. Feeling returned to Ned's appendages, and he propped himself up. Where he expected burn marks on Mui-xe were instead rippling scales and flesh squelching and reforming, burnt scabs unceremoniously plinking to the metal floor.

When Dr. Diastrevlo had begun experimenting on Mui-xe's macrophages and healing, it had started with cuts. The abrasion experiments gave way to forcefully broken bones. Those graduated to poisons and microbes. Each time, Mui-xe regenerated, while Ned and La-hok were left to soothe him at night and panic over what new horror Diastrevlo would concoct next. But this was the first trial where his body attempted self-defense. The ignition had come from him.

Realizing their son was developing some defense mechanisms gave Ned the adrenaline needed to scramble to his feet. When he joined the two people who meant the whole galaxy to him, his wife and child conversed in gently whispered Lo-sat. Through her hisses and his croaks, Ned caught the soothing nursery rhymes of his wife's kin. The words were too lyrical for him to understand, but the melody of mother and son made sense.

Ned wrapped them in an embrace. "We're proud of you, Mui-xe. You just keep fighting back." *We're working on a way to rescue you.*

Mui-xe's red spherical eyes rolled up to him. With mouth and teeth that almost matched his father's, he spoke in his scratchy prepubescent voice. "I know, Dad."

"Are you hungry today?" Ned asked.

La-hok scoffed. "He ate this week already, Ned."

Mui-xe gave a defeated shrug. "I'm sorry, Mom. I think I need to eat today."

The light show must've drained tons of energy, Ned surmised. "Whatever you want, son."

Praying for Symphora to swoop in and save the day wouldn't suffice. They needed to escape immediately. He needed to finish his image inducer. Their son had endured enough.

SEVEN

(JOKᴧ)

**Aboard the space station "Calamity,"
floating on the fringes of Collective space**

JOKA DRUMMED HER fingers against the communications relay dashboard, the dull echo permeating the cramped room's silence.

A hiss came from beside her. "Do you mind? That's distracting." Doh-riss, of course.

Joka yawned and wheeled on her new coworker, spinning in the squeakiest Human-sized chair on the station. "What're you being distracted from, exactly? Messages aren't pouring in."

Another woman's voice cut through, the head comms officer, an Arkouda whose paunch may have sported its own gravitational pull. "Hey, you never know what we'll get when we stabilize." Officer Iasona leaned between them, balancing her paws on the communication table. "Not like those brick-headed engineers ever tell me when they're stopping. So you always kinda need to be at the ready. But Symphora doesn't care if we play Block Bash on our omni-tablets in between messages." She wiggled her round white ears. "Which is some pretty cool *skata*."

The sad part for Joka was how she spoke unironically.

Doh-riss bristled at the curse, making Joka wonder how to coax their new boss into swearing more often and colorfully.

With an "oomph," the comms officer pushed off from the dashboard. "And now there's three of us, so we can take naps and cover each other during the shift. Won't be so lonely, which is awesome."

Joka frowned. Demoted to the most useless job in the gang. Stuck with the most annoying coworker. The only way this would be worse is if they had to clean toilets after cheese block night.

Ignoring Joka's visible disgust at the situation, the rotund officer continued. "And besides, you never know when a new message will come through. The hard part is deciding the legitimate messages. After that last one I sent up..." She sank her head. "I bet that's why she gave me two employees. I don't think she trusts me anymore. Maybe I played too much Block Bash." A sober clarity darkened her voice. "Their blood is on my paws."

Symphora earned fame for her marksmanship, skullbashery, and that one time she ripped out a pedophile's throat and stuffed his manhood down the new hole, but this was a social slap in the face the likes of which Joka never imagined before.

She'd insulted Iasona by sending her helpers who also were pariahs, then humiliating Joka and Doh-riss by sending them to the shamefully easy job.

Officer Iasona smacked her forehead. "Stupid, stupid, stupid!"

Doh-riss' tail snagged Iasona's wrist. "Symphora approved the mission herself, so it wasn't really your fault."

"Lots of people screwed up that day," Joka said. Images of Tur's corpse flashed in her mind. "It's my fault Tur's dead. I took a strike team member's spot on that mission."

"Our fault," Doh-riss whispered. "Don't put it on yourself—we both took spots meant for fighters. Besides, not everyone thinks that you're the reason she's dead."

"Correction," Iasona intoned. "You should see what people wrote on the bathroom walls about you."

The cramped office lacked the engine room's hums and the bustle of the other mechanics. The laundry suite next door was probably more interesting than this, but unfortunately, Symphora didn't have an ax to grind with whoever ran that.

Joka had nowhere to escape this ridiculous and embarrassing new station. But at least she was alive.

Symphora reassigned her bunk and gave her the crap shift with the crap meal break times. Everyone in the gang was valuable, sure, but Joka's greatest value according to her superiors was staying out of everyone else's way.

A blinking light on the dashboard caught Joka's attention. "Hey boss, is there a way to see messages while we're in hyperspace? The old ones, that is?"

"Yes, we learned that during orientation." Doh-riss grinned wide. "Officer Iasona did an excellent job explaining it."

Iasona waved a dismissive paw. "Come on, ladies. You can just call me Iasona."

Without knowing the dirtiest anatomical expletives in Lo-sat, Joka settled for mumbling, "Right, I forgot."

Reaching in front of Joka with her long verdant-toned arm, Doh-riss tapped the blinking light.

"Huh," Iasona said. "Musta come in right as we were entering warp space."

"Let's see what it says." Joka sat straighter and squared her shoulders.

"Don't be so hasty," Doh-riss said. "Officer Iasona—excuse me, Iasona. Do we have your permission—"

"Yeah, hit play. Let's see what we got!"

A female Arkouda appeared on the projection, draped in a lab coat. Her round ears were flattened against her head. The projection of the woman leaned toward whatever camera she had and whispered. Joka slammed the volume button like it owed her money.

"I was given this contact information by someone Symphora saved many years ago. A Human man. He's being held prisoner with his wife and child. I…" The woman winced. "I've watched them get tortured for science experiments. What's happening to them…" She paused to wipe away a budding tear. "Monstrous. Truly monstrous. The scientist keeping them captive is—" She lowered her voice again, and the listeners leaned forward.

Of course Doh-riss was a mouth breather.

The woman's voice shook. "Dr. Diastrevlo."

She said the name as if it were supposed to mean something to whoever was listening. It just sounded like every other Arkouda name Joka had ever heard.

Officer Iasona and Doh-riss made eye contact with each other and shrugged.

"We're on an asteroid," the recording continued. "I'll upload current coordinates and angular projection. I didn't have time to calculate the telemetry of where we'll be in the coming days. I managed to secure transport for myself. But if the other scientists leave, Dr. Diastrevlo will kill their son. You just—" She let out a shaky exhale. "Symphora, you're a legend. You saved this Human once. I had some friends at university who were saved by you when they were cubs. Please… Dr. Diastrevlo has to be brought to justice."

Joka tapped pause. "This is pretty suspect. She didn't tell us her name or the name of these scientists who need to be saved—"

"Shh!" Doh-riss, of course.

Iasona slumped in her chair, running a paw over her face.

The recording continued, "The scientist who gave me your information is a Provincial, but I know that's never stopped you before. His name is Dr. Ned Porandi. His wife is—"

The screen shook and tilted. Whatever camera she'd used to make her message must've clattered to the floor. When it settled, it displayed a skewed angle pointing up her lab coat that only a sicko would've found useful.

The woman stepped back, and her voice was muffled. "D-d-d-dr. Dias-s-strevlo," she stuttered.

A stony-voiced male Arkouda responded, "Submitting your resignation?"

Joka leaned in so close the projection was practically beaming up her nose.

"Uhm, yes." The scientist cleared her throat. "I was booking the next transport."

With a sun-chilling tone, the response came. "Liar."

Shoom.

The telltale burst of a plasma pistol. Joka shuddered, the sound conjuring too-fresh memories.

The woman slumped to the floor in a smoldering heap. A new pair of feet appeared on the projection. They cast a shadow over the body, stepping over the corpse to reveal himself at a nosebleed angle. He resembled any other Arkouda man Joka had seen, only with less emotion: ears and muzzle stiff. He aimed the still-smoking plasma pistol at the recording device, and the transmission cut.

Joka whipped around to Officer Iasona. "How do we replay that? Is there any way to know if there's more?"

The communications officer shook her head. "If there were, it would've started earlier. Looks like she broadcast this live in case this happened. Or whoever shot her, that statuey science guy, must not have realized she was transmitting."

Doh-riss rose from her chair. "We need to take this to Symphora. These scientists are in danger."

Joka was glad nobody else was around to witness what left her mouth. "Doh-riss is right. There's no way this is some kind of setup."

"Not gonna happen," Iasona sing-songed, as if injecting mirth into her voice might dissuade them.

Joka snapped up beside Doh-riss, wrists on her hips and scowling. "Excuse me? We have innocent people, including a child, in clear danger. If the main scientist is funded by the Collective, the government won't do anything to help them. This is a classic Symphora mission. Save the neglected and vulnerable."

Their new boss who bragged about being super chill grunted. "This could be a setup. Even if it's not, there's too much heat on us. We can't go somewhere, battledarts blazing. This is begging to get everyone arrested or killed."

"Then what the *nguc* are we even doing?" Doh-riss immediately covered her snout with her claws. "Excuse me." In a softer tone, she added, "Officer Iasona, I mean, Iasona, we should at least give Symphora the message so she can make the decision for herself."

Inhaling deeply, Joka straightened. "I'll say it again, Doh-riss is right. If this turns out to be legitimate, public favor might return to Symphora."

Iasona rose and leaned over Joka, letting her feel the height difference between them. "I forbid it. This could be a trap."

Joka whipped out her omni-tablet and hip-checked Iasona. She may as well have done that to a wall for how much the comms officer moved out of her way. Joka began the file transfer, but a heavy fuzzy paw clamped on her wrist.

"I said no, ladies."

Doh-riss cleared her throat and displayed her own omni-tablet. "Now I have a picture of you being aggressive with a subordinate. A weaker species, no less. I think Symphora's chief of staff might be interested in seeing this image. We know how Symphora tells us to treat people who prey on the weak."

Madam Communications Officer who probably had fun nicknames ready to go for their mandatory bonding session released Joka's wrist with a huff. "I'll arrange a meeting with Symphora. Happy?"

"No," Joka said. "All three of us need to be there. And none of us are touching the recording in the meantime, so we can tell her it wasn't edited or doctored in any way."

Doh-riss beamed her rows of serrated teeth. Joka hadn't expected her greatest accomplishment after inventing the flight suit would be outsmarting a middle manager with Miss Priss, but after the demotion and bloodbath and her subsequent pariah status, she would accept any win.

———

Hours later, Joka, Doh-riss, and Officer Iasona situated themselves in Symphora's war room. Joka exchanged uneasy glances with Doh-riss, remembering the last time they'd occupied these seats.

The recording looped, and Joka strained for new details. Doh-riss leaned forward as it played, as if she were doing the same.

Same message, interruption, and murder. A flicker arose in Joka's heart realizing this Arkouda woman died for some Humans. Ned Porandi and whoever his wife and kid were... Joka imagined a pair of college professors studying some Human-specific subject, living an idyllic life with their perfect baby, kidnapped by a Human-hating Arkouda scientist who did Earth-knows-what to them. Joka chewed the inside of her cheek as she faced the reality of what she was projecting onto this stranger's life.

When the recording ended, Joka, Doh-riss, and Officer Iasona cast nervous glances at Symphora.

Symphora leaned back in her chair and unfolded her arms to scratch the base of her mohawk. "*Skata*," she sighed loud enough to cover Doh-riss' tiny sneer. "Iass, didja run the telemetry? Where are they now?"

Iasona pulled her paws behind her back and recited the coordinates, all while Doh-riss muttered, "*Did you.*"

Symphora flattened her ears before rising from her chair. "We can't go."

"Excuse me?" Joka asked.

Symphora's fur stood on end, making her seem even larger as she loomed over Joka. "Watch your tone. It's only three people. It's too far away. It's right where Collective patrols are tight. Too much risk." She let the pregnant pause hang in the air before baring her teeth. "Need another reason?"

It was Doh-riss' turn to risk a punch to the snout. "But Symphora, isn't that the whole point of your mission? Risk ourselves to protect the weak?"

The grizzled legend pulled away from Joka's face to glare at Doh-riss. "If my hairy ass gets arrested or killed saving three people today, I can't save a factory's worth of enslaved people tomorrow. We need to lay low, and that means saying no to some requests. I'm saying no."

Somebody had to do this. Leaving this family was not an option. Joka winced and gulped. "What if *you* didn't go?"

Eyes trained on her.

"I'll go. I don't have a recognizable face." She considered adding "or hairstyle," but decided against it. "Everyone's hunting you. Not me."

Symphora appraised her. "No."

Doh-riss sidled beside Joka. "What if I went with her? We could find a believable cover. We could pay for our own transport."

Joka fought the inclination to ask Doh-riss to stop volunteering.

Officer Iasona piped up. "I could go back to running the comms relay by myself."

Symphora rubbed her chin. "A lone Human can't walk around Collective interior without a good pass..." After a sigh, Symphora waved a paw. "No. You'll get caught. That'll land you in prison or a morgue. We're passing. Comms isn't working out, so I'll find a spot for you two in sanitation. Dismissed."

Joka deflated further as she left the war room. Symphora didn't think they'd succeed. Tur's last testament was the mechanics' corps would be better without them, and Communications Officer, First Class Iasona didn't want them, either. The whole station blamed them for selfishly taking up spots on the mission and therefore botching it.

And innocent people would die.

Doh-riss draped her tail across Joka's shoulders. "Isn't this great? No more Iasona."

Pinching as gently as possible, Joka lifted the tail off her. "She's throwing us away. Symphora thinks we'd die or get arrested. What's the point?"

The clink-clink of their footsteps and gentle buzz of the cheap overhead lights filled the silence. "Symphora found me in a brothel when I was a hatchling," Doh-riss eventually said. "I was used but never loved. I was a tool. But… I found a new mother in Symphora, and a big sister in Tur. I thought they were my kin." She met Joka's eyes. "I … want to get something right." She stiffened and returned her gaze forward. "I can clean a toilet right. Maybe that's all I'm good for."

Decency dictated she should thank people for sharing and opening up like that. Instead, Joka could only clench her fists and match her pace. "No. Let's sneak out of here and save that family. Symphora can go fuck herself."

"Language!"

"Come on," Joka pleaded. "Did you really want to walk away from that meeting with a refusal and demotion to toilet duty?"

"I … do wish Symphora had acted otherwise."

Joka loathed the words at the tip of her tongue. "I can't do it alone. Are you in … sister?"

Doh-riss tail-embraced Joka. For how prim she was, she should've smelled less like forgotten eggs.

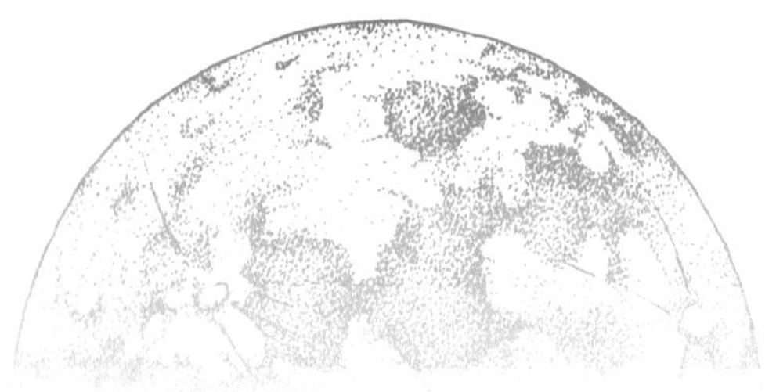

EIGHT

(RICK)

Great Mystery Monastery, New Lodestone, Boudica System, Human Demilitarized Zone

UNDER A MAROON sky, Rick glared at the robed monk in front of him. "I can pay."

Some younger monks, probably five- or six-year-olds, lobbed rocks against the monastery's outer wall, seeing which would magnetize and stick.

Humiliation probably fell outside monastic vows, yet refusing Rick's entrance cast doubt on the assumption. They stood under the stone entryway to the monastery, built so the shadow profile resembled hands in prayer.

The scrawny guy's age and the importance of his position didn't match. Either these monks were desperate or this guy was well-connected.

Brother Maynard, the abbott, smiled and shook his head. "We have a vow of poverty. Your money is better spent on the homeless, Mr. Crith. You do such good work there that one could think you've laid down your weapons."

For being just over Amanda's age, the monk sure talked like Rick's grandfather. "You want something."

The monk winked. "One of the joys of giving myself to the Great Mystery is forsaking desires."

An avian hammering at a brickbark tree behind Rick broke his concentration. He felt like one of those birds, robbed of a beak.

A younger Rick would've threatened to punch Maynard in the mouth so he would desire a dentist. "You say you want to end suffering, but every day you let the Collective off the hook." Rick turned around and pointed at the Collective's space elevator in the distance, piercing the atmosphere like prehistoric skyscrapers on Earth. "You're allowing more innocent Humans to suffer. All our wealth on this planet is sucked up to the government offices and shipped around the Collective." He faced Brother Maynard again. "Get on the right side of history. I know what other people in Earthquake do. Help me purify it. Make it better."

Brother Maynard bowed with his hands together. "I wish you well, Mr. Crith. Let me know when you have moved beyond violence."

Rick glared at him, hoping his eyes telegraphed the message of "Let me know when you pull your head out of your ass." Instead, he said, "Yeah. I'll do that." He turned and sauntered down the dirt road where his autocab waited.

Leaning against the hovering autocab was the second biggest liability in Rick's organization: the lanky Lo-sat thief under his employ, Binh Ten-trom. The green of his modified Earthquake armor would've matched his skin if he were an ordinary, healthy Lo-sat, but his scales adopted a gray pallor from a genetic condition. With his long, thin tail, he absently picked at something in his teeth while his arms sat crossed over his chest.

"Hey, Lefty's back." Ten-trom pushed off the autocab. If what the damn thief said was true, his flawless command of Human language came from growing up on Earth. He blamed his sarcastic nature and general assholery on that, too. "And here I thought you'd left your one diverse friend behind. How'd it go with the hood crew?"

"Don't call them that." Rick motioned for the thief to enter the autocab.

"Did you tell them about the mole who joined them a week ago?"

"Watch your mouth."

"Snout," Ten-trom corrected. "This place is too secluded for those holy rollers to hear my silky voice."

Slamming the door and entering the coordinates to the driver bot, Rick shook his head. "They didn't seem to be onto the mole."

"Gotta say, Ricky Rickster, you're smart for a Human. If anybody had suspected your ploy, coming up here yourself would've redirected any suspicion."

Rick knew better than to respond. The autocab bobbed, rising half a meter over the ground, and plodded toward New Lodestone's city, a smattering of two- and three-story buildings huddling around the planet's lone space elevator like toddlers clinging to a parent's leg. Yellow-barked trees thinned on their approach.

"Did you get the new medicine for yourself?" Rick asked.

Ten-trom pulled out a vial from the diagonal chestpiece he wore, functioning as a portable heat source for his circulation. "Yep." He jiggled the container between his claws. "My Planet Magnet Torture migraines will be reduced to headaches again, which lets me focus on my other constant sources of pain."

Lacking the magnetic sense of Lo-sats and Arkoudae, Rick couldn't fathom the overload from living on a heavily magnetized planet like New Lodestone. "Doesn't seem like much," Rick said. "How long will that last?"

"Two weeks."

Rick cocked an eyebrow. "You've gotten bigger supplies before. Was more not available? Did that pharmacist have an issue with her supply?"

The Lo-sat's neck frills extended halfway. Never a good sign among his kind. Rick adjusted in his seat so he'd be ready to pull out his pistol if it came to it.

"I debated not picking you up from here after I got this." He jiggled the medicine bottle aggressively. "I only have two weeks left with your stinky ass. My debt is almost paid off."

"You've kept a ledger?"

Ten-trom's neck frills flared fully, and his eyeridges sank low. "You haven't?"

Rick held up his hand in a placating gesture. "I have. I'll show it to you. I know what you've been skimming off the top, and I've been deducting."

Ten-trom exhaled and relaxed back into his seat. "Sorry I need to eat once a month." He lazily drew circles with the dull side of his claw against the window. The darkening maroon sky made his blotched scales appear even more drab and dry.

"Don't forget I'm paying for that medicine you shook all over the place. It's expensive."

"Sorry I need to live."

Rick sneered. "Can the act. You're not that close to paying off your debt, but I'm a man of my word. When we're settled, you can join us fully or be off on your happy way."

"Is that why you dragged me along, Lefty? So you could taunt me?"

"Taunt?" Rick shook his head and stared out the window, counting the rain-thick clouds, the space elevator coming more into view. "Our new weapon prototype goes into trials today."

"Don't want me swiping it to sell?"

"I don't want them testing it on you."

Ten-trom waved a claw. "You made that thing to puncture Collective armor. I have this lovely outfit designed by your fashionistas. Their ability to design rivals your ability to clap, so I'm not worth testing on."

"*That's* why they would—you're annoying. You're not much shorter than an Arkouda, either. We were able to procure more intact armor for testing. With me gone, there's a chance they'd put you in it for a shot."

The thief snorted. "Still worried about mutiny after our time on the moon—"

"Don't finish that sentence."

"It's just us." Ten-trom gestured to the empty passenger seat. "We were both there."

"Doesn't mean I want to discuss it."

Ten-trom sighed. "Fine. We'll ride in comfortable silence."

———

Rick inspected the under-construction medical office before he strode a labyrinthine path through the tables of the homeless shelter's cafeteria. He exchanged quick hellos as warranted and entered the kitchen. One of his squad had joined the serving line, and another stirred soup over a stove. Amanda basked in an open refrigerator's glow, inventorying on her omni-tablet. She rested her stylus above her ear, using her fingertips to type instead.

"Rick," Amanda called, "they have some messages for you in the downstairs office."

Thanking her, he approached the decommissioned walk-in freezer, safely tucked out of sight of any potential patrons. Before he opened the door, the clip-clip of Amanda's footsteps trailed behind.

"Something else?" He broke his gait to face her.

"Two things before you go see your new toy." Her expression soured. "You're getting the bad news first."

"Go on."

"Leaked rumors of a refugee camp. Human population, guarded by Collective soldiers. Some patrons whispered about it. I wrote it off as garbage, but I heard it enough times that I did some digging. I have no clue where it is, but I've found a few mentions in different sources about a refugee camp that went missing. Families who went there never reunited. Want me to investigate more?"

"If it gets you off my ass about new refrigerators, sure." Smile fading, he asked, "You had good news?"

"The first scrapper ships returned. They sold some trashed satellites and a tiny asteroid. The space elevator docking tax snagged a big cut, but we got a good influx of money and material. If we can keep this up, it'll boost the settlement economy."

"And our coffers. Thanks."

"Enjoy the show down there…"

Letting the heavy metallic door close behind him, he flicked the light switch four times, and the tile floor unhinged, revealing an elevator. Rick entered and descended to the sub-basement.

The underground hangar made use of a natural cavern, smoothed out as much as possible by their engineers when they began construction on the complex last year. The cave network extended far enough to allow deploying ships outside the space elevator's shadow, letting them deploy and land ships on their own terms.

Monsieur Tecton gave them a tidy cash infusion to fast-track the building, back when Rick was riding a wave of popularity in Earthquake, when he got his hand on the first functioning set of Collective armor off an Arkouda. Since then, Earthquake had risen in the galaxy. Some skirmishes against Collective soldiers happened and weren't total bloodbaths. This armor was their ticket to perfect defense.

If his engineers delivered on what they promised, he would have the required countermeasure as well. Since more of Rick's rival commanders in Earthquake gained favor with Tecton using more brutal methods, Rick's wave of popularity had crested.

Until now.

Derrickson and Zhou met him at the elevator. "Come to see the cannon?" Zhou asked with a grin, her eyes ablaze with pride.

"Of course."

Their stolen cargo and scrapper ships, in various stages of rebranding, decommissioning, and modification, lined the wall of the yawning space. In the center, three engineers coordinated to push one of their greatest prizes on a gurney. A preserved Arkouda corpse, outfitted with one of their cherished suits of Collective armor. The corpse in question was not the previous owner of the armor, so the fit wasn't precise, but it was close enough.

"You waited?" Rick asked.

Derrickson winked. "Using a harpoon design was your idea. Nobody else would've thought to try that."

Three responses seemed plausible. Rick could chide her and the rest of the crew for ignoring sources about prehistoric Earth. Alternately, he could explain that brute force over plasma fire had been on his mind since his first debacle with Ten-trom, but he chose the third response.

"Thank you. I'll take the blame if it doesn't work."

A senior engineer joined them. "Would you like the honor of firing?"

Rick clicked his tongue. "That looks like a two-handed weapon." In reality, it would need a fire team of at least three. For the harpoon and accompanying cannon to be large enough to do the requisite damage, a single Human lifting it in standard gravity was asking for a hernia or a snapped bone. Rick flagged the lead engineers. "Ayen, Byrd. You two can get the honor of firing the first shot. Reeve and Kathreft, get the cadaver ready. Everyone else, clear the floor. This could get messy."

After everyone took appropriate precautions, Rick signaled the countdown. The cannon, shaped like prehistoric Earth bazookas, but wider and heavier to accommodate the payload, aimed at the dummy target. It fired with a *thunk* toward the hapless corpse and connected with a ripping squelch. In the space of a blink, it clanged against the floor, covered in rotted entrails.

Rick circled to the back of the body and examined the gaping hole, which the engineers on either side used to wave to each other. After giving them the appropriate death stare, he barked, "Celebrate some other way. Respect the dead. Respect the enemy."

The crewmen stiffened.

"Reload the chain and see how much cleaning needs to happen before it can fire again safely. Analyze the harpoon tip and see how many shots this can take before it would need to be sharpened or replaced. Once you've figured that out," Rick paused to make eye contact with each person assembled, "start production and training for strike teams. I know where we'll hit first."

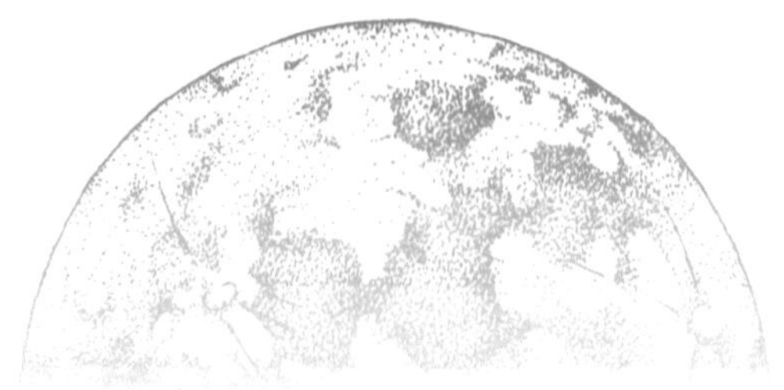

NINE

(INSPECTOR)

**A shaman's hut on the
Lo-sat homeworld of Vee**

INSPECTOR BIKKOLOS PULLED his collar away from his neck and tapped the cooling unit on his armor. He was stuck between being uncomfortable or rude by lolling out his tongue to cool off the old-fashioned way.

The aging Lo-sat woman before him probably wouldn't have approved. Her hut was claustrophobic by anyone's standards, and the cloying swamp's humidity didn't lend itself to greater comfort. She dried a single tear from her eye, a conical bone talisman shaking gently as she lowered her arm. "You don't have any news, inspector?"

"I have something better, ma'am, if you cooperate." He wished he could commune with her in Lo-sat to let his tongue out of his mouth more, but he'd likely wind up insulting her by accident.

"I've always cooperated."

Eh. "Which I appreciate. I'm one step closer to finding your daughter and her husband."

Her neck frills jiggled at the word. "They were not married on Vee. The gods did not preside. There was no marriage."

Bikkolos knew the other half of the story: she didn't approve of her daughter's choice in partner, thus there wasn't anything official. Flattening his ears, the inspector continued. "I have reason to believe they were kidnapped together."

"I could have told you that." Her scales chafed against each other as she adjusted in her wicker seat.

"But I have a clue where now."

Her neck frills extended. She bore a glaring hole into his eyes.

Since joining law enforcement, Bikkolos saw that expression often. This shaman didn't seem to care much for official Collective law. Her devotion to the Lo-sat gods superseded any other devotion to law and order. His cynical side understood why the monk's brother and shaman's daughter eloped.

After she calmed, she intoned, "If you know where she is, you should be there, not here torturing an old woman."

"Benedict reached out to his brother. I have the message."

She snarled at the mention of her son-in-law's name. Maynard had called him that, too. Bikkolos had assumed using the formal version of the name would soften her irate stubbornness. Perhaps the multisyllabic name reinforced his Humanness.

"Ned, sorry."

Some tension released from her shoulders. Her neck frills regressed to the side of her face. "I tried to pronounce his name in Human. Too many syllables. I could only say 'Neh-dah.'"

"Understood. Anyway, I have an idea of where he is, but I need another message to calculate where he will be."

The shaman touched the tip of her talisman with her claw. It let out a faint cyan glow, a cute party trick. On Bikkolos' next inhale, he realized he couldn't smell anything. Noticing his disorientation, the shaman smiled.

"I killed our scents for the time," she said. "This is true trust here. You won't know if I'm lying."

The old cover-the-scent trick. It was standard psychological warfare. One of the first things to be incapacitated by the enemy before dogfights and skirmishes on hyper-sanitized spaceships became the norm.

"So what do you want to ambiguously tell me, then?" Bikkolos leaned back in the thatch chair, then pulled forward after hearing a few snaps. At least this planet didn't have the oppressive magnetic tug.

The shaman furrowed her eyeridges. "If any harm comes to my daughter, when I die, I will force myself to become a ghost and haunt you."

If Bikkolos were a few years younger, he would've waved her off with an "expect a boring afterlife," but the Lo-sat religion was one that became deeper the more he learned about it. If there were one person he didn't want to test in this situation, it was her.

All he could find to respectfully respond was a simple "yes."

"Ned arranged for La-hok to send me messages. There's something she hasn't told me. I don't know if Ned is abusing her or if she's worried their captor will come after me, but I'm scared. I also grow tired waiting for results."

Bikkolos appraised her, pondering how to explain if her daughter had gone missing by herself, this would've received much higher priority. Her son-in-law's standing as a Human meant they earned the slow as needlebark molasses treatment, having to go through the understaffed Crimes Against Provincials Unit.

"Let me analyze those messages," he said. "If I can triangulate, I'll be able to figure out where they'll be by the time I can catch them."

She fiddled with her talisman using her thumb claw; Bikkolos wondered if it were for some kind of spell or incantation. "Tell me, inspector," she said, eyeing his badge, "what do you gain if my daughter and Ned are found?"

His response was supposed to be that he was just doing his job, but she wasn't the kind of woman to feed *skata* like that to. "I had a friend once. A Human." That garnered a raised eyeridge. "He left the Collective because he believed they didn't care about Humans. In my own way, I'm trying to prove him wrong."

"You haven't spoken to this friend in years." It was worded like a question, although said flatly. "You're a man of faith."

He hadn't been to Temple in a decade and had forgotten a good chunk of the prayers to the Sleeping Goddess, but he nodded. "I'm glad you don't think it's childish."

"Inspector, some people wish to force themselves from our lives. I hope that my daughter hasn't done that to me and that this former friend of yours hasn't done that to you. I'll show you those messages."

TEN

(JOKΛ)

Aboard the space station "Calamity," floating on the fringes of Collective space

IN THEIR CRAMPED bunk space, Joka pulled her mechanic jacket over her personalized flight suit.

Doh-riss clutched her tail in her claws, wringing it. "Symphora's going to kill us."

Joka displayed a sheet of paper. "Look, it's the schematics for my flight suit. This will be worth the ship we're taking." After clearing her throat, Joka muttered, "Probably."

"If you say so."

"I found the oldest battledart in the hangar. It's been decommissioned and doesn't even have a full tank of fuel. Practically trash."

"I suppose dying in a ship we stole isn't the worst way to go."

"I've messed around with it enough times to know it's reliable."

Eyeridges and tone lowered, Doh-riss asked, "That's what you want to use to travel halfway across the galaxy? It doesn't sound safe."

Joka didn't have time for this. "Please trust me."

"Fine. Can the older model fit us?"

"With an Arkouda-sized cot! We can take turns sleeping." Joka didn't care to add she hoped they would alternate sleeping so they wouldn't have to interact. "My question is, did you do your homework?"

Doh-riss unclenched her tail. "Of course I did." Her obnoxiously familiar confidence returned. "I found a space elevator with a refueling station not too far from here. Since we're taking an older ship, the traffic controllers won't bother to trace our location."

"Never been around those parts. Is it Human space?"

"The whole galaxy is Collective space, Joka."

She waved a hand. "Tell that to the Blekk and rebel Makawe running around."

"The star is called Polemistes, but the Human name for it is Tu-dik-ha, and the planet with the space elevator is called New Lodestone."

Joka cocked an eyebrow. "That doesn't sound like a Human name for a star. We usually do famous people from Earth's prehistory." Joka hoisted her duffle bag over her shoulder. Barely bigger than a toolbox, it held all her life's possessions. "Got all your *skata*? Ready to go?"

"I leave that in the toilet," Doh-riss huffed. "With your language. But yes, I'm ready."

Joka clenched her teeth. This would be a long trip.

Navigating the Calamity's maze of corridors and open areas, they passed various gang members, none of whom wore their uniforms—apparently getting properly dressed was only for when times were good. Support staff ignored Joka and Doh-riss, the backups in training to be the new strike team offered pitied smiles, and worst of all, the other mechanics, their closest sisters in arms, sneered. They probably passed everyone in the entire gang before they arrived at the hangar for decommissioned ships. Joka's old bunk-mate stopped them.

"Jokes... been a while." Devy avoided direct eye contact.

"Barely a month," Joka said. "I left some of my stuff down here."

"Oh," Devy said, more embarrassed than surprised. "Nobody turned anything in. I-I would've forwarded anything to you if someone did."

Joka resisted an eye roll. "I know. Barely anybody comes down to this hangar. I was expecting it to be deserted."

"It was when I arrived." Devy gestured absently to the wide room and rusting ships, half of them obscured by the decommissioned hangar's flickering lights. "I got the joyful duty of deciding which ships get scrapped for parts. We're cash-poor, and it's time to liquidate. Marka's orders."

Joka studied Devy's almost-clean jumpsuit. One extra stripe over her monogrammed name. She'd been promoted quickly with Joka gone.

"Liquidate?" Doh-riss asked, claws over her heart. "She can't do that."

Devy shrugged. "Not my call." She tapped something into her omni-tablet. "I pinged Marka and let her know you're down here. She'll kick your ass out."

"I thought we were friends," Joka said.

Through pursed lips, Devy replied, "We were until you got Tur killed. That's why I gave you the heads-up. Find your *skata* and leave."

Once Devy's back was turned, Joka signaled to Doh-riss. Nonchalantly as possible, Joka bobbed in between the ships opposite Devy, absently checking her omni-tablet.

The *plash-plash* of Doh-riss' footsteps echoed above the steps; Joka glanced up as the exit bubble initiated. It wouldn't be long before the hangar doors parted, and they'd be protected against the vacuum of space.

That was, of course, assuming Devy didn't turn around or check to her left.

Sweat beading on her forehead, Joka approached the ship she'd designated for them. She'd worked on repairing it months ago, daydreaming that this would be her personal ship one day, taking it along with Symphora on missions. It was only slightly crappier than the one she actually piloted on the debacle from a few weeks ago. Doh-riss caught up as Joka stepped onto the ladder. At the metallic echo of Joka's first step, Devy wheeled around.

"For the love of Earth, what are you doing, Bunear?"

Last name. Not the nickname. All pretense of their friendship disappeared, replaced by incredulity.

For a flash, Joka wondered if Devy had ever considered her a friend, or if every other Human mechanic had glomped on to someone else already and Joka was just who remained.

Doh-riss passed Joka the ignition card. As Joka accepted it and jumped into the open cockpit, she called to Devy, "Taking a bit of a vacation."

"Are you insane?" Devy shouted, running over. "You're stealing a ship?"

Doh-riss plopped in behind Joka as she thrust the ignition card into the feeder. Only a few more seconds.

"No." Joka tsked. "I left Symphora some payment. You said this was garbage."

The thrusters and antigrav groaned to life, and a series of too-dim lights flashed across the dashboard. As the ship taxied toward the widening hangar exit, Joka called out again, "Tell everyone we went to kick some ass."

Before Doh-riss could speak, the cockpit whistled shut. Open space outside the hangar was on full display, colors skewed and obscured by the protective bubble trapping the oxygen.

Devy stamped like she was screaming something, but Joka couldn't hear.

Couldn't care, either. Joka may have hit social rock bottom, but she was finally fulfilling the reason why she joined Symphora in the first place—she didn't just want to escape that factory farm but help other kids like her.

Like that poor child in some distant research lab. Tortured.

Maybe this called for a two-woman operation, not a full-blown Symphora shoot-fest. This required stealth.

The gang would understand when she and Doh-riss returned. They'd have to. They'd save an innocent family from a horrific jerkwad, unnoticed by the Collective military, thanks to Symphora's radar disruption tech.

Joka's omni-tablet vibrated. She'd just gotten a ping.

[Devy: I'll get demoted because of your ass.]

A few colorful retorts came to mind, but finding fuel took priority. Not responding was also fun in its own way.

Over her shoulder, Joka said, "Doh-riss, can you punch in the coordinates for that New Lodestone planet? Use the Arkouda name for the star, since I know you didn't give me the right Human name."

"Excuse me. Human sounds are harsh. Don't get me started on the syllables."

"You speak Arkouda just fine."

"It's a refined language. Human is as crass as the people who speak it."

"Yeah, alright."

The navigation unit chirped, signifying acceptance of the coordinates. Joka confirmed the destination, and the ship lurched forward at warp speed. The dazzling spectrum of cosmic color distorted and whirled around them like a grenade had been detonated in a paint store. It was dizzying and breathtaking in equal measure.

"Wow," Doh-riss said. "Seeing this from a space station is one thing, but this? Indescribable."

"Yeah." Joka stole a glance at the array of purples and whites. "It's pretty special. So, uh, what can you tell me about this New Lodestone place?"

"Nothing. Small Human settlement. It seems like all the Collective government presence is located in the space elevator, not on the surface."

Joka's heart froze. "We have to deal directly with government officials?" She never had the opportunity to sneak into the hangar to paint over Symphora's insignia. "Shit. Shitty shit shitty shit."

"Joka," Doh-riss moaned.

"Sorry." She huffed out a breath and inhaled a plan. "If they notice Symphora's symbols and ask, our story is pretty close to the truth. We were scared of arrestation—"

"—arrest."

"Whatever. Point is, we quit. We were mechanics who spent most of our time tightening screws. We stole this and have no idea where Symphora is since we left in a hurry."

"That's mostly true."

"Damn straight."

"Joka..." Doh-riss tutted. "This will be a long few days if you insist on constant profanity."

"Fine." A smirk rose. "Darn straight. How's that?"

"Better. Thank you."

"Penis."

ELEVEN

(RICK)

Tecton Homeless Shelter, New Lodestone, Boudica System, Human Demilitarized Zone

IN THE DAYS since the new weapon's first successful test, operations proceeded smoothly—until the night before the plan's next phase.

Engineer Zhou approached Rick in his office. "Sir?"

"What's wrong?" Rick stiffened. "Did something happen to the new weapons?"

She waved her hands in front of her. "No, not at all. We have five fire teams trained on them, and we solved that 'dragging the guts' issue, too." Her expression lay on the spectrum between proud and disgusted. "We, uh… we never got an official name for the weapon and wanted your input."

This wasn't a huge deal, but bonding exercises were important for any team. Having a fancy name might attract more attention, too. Possibly fear in the Collective military or hope in Humans. "What did you have in mind?"

"Some of us like the name 'Gungnir.' It's from prehistoric mythology."

"Spear of Odin." Rick's expression hardened. "I'm familiar. Absolutely not."

"Oh. Alright, well, the other name some of the Abrahamist folks suggested was 'Spear of Destiny.' I think that's from—"

"Prehistoric Earth before the different Abrahamist sects syncretized. No. Nothing religious or mythological. When people think of Earthquake, I want them to see us as they see themselves. Average, regular people who are sick of Collective bullying. If we drape ourselves in these larger-than-life symbols, the wrong image is implanted."

Zhou stepped back. "Sorry to bother you, then."

Rick shook his head. "Equalizer. We'll call it the Equalizer. That's what it does. It allows us to fight armored Arkouda on their level. We'll finally be a match for them and can engage them in standard combat. No more killing civilians or paying through the nose to get our hands on any of their armor or weapons. Real fighting like a real military against another. Equalizer."

Zhou muttered, "Gungnir still sounds cooler."

Rick followed her from the office to assemble for the briefing. They would only have one shot to display the Equalizer guns and show they were a force to be reckoned with, all while accomplishing their mission before the Collective Fleet could arrive to counterattack.

Today, they would conquer New Lodestone. All they had to do was commandeer the space elevator and disrupt traffic. Thus, they'd prevent the bigger Collective machines of war from approaching too quickly, giving them time to fortify. But if Rick's plans worked, it wouldn't be long before he could take on a warhive, the backbone of the Collective Fleet. If a warhive could be added to Earthquake's growing armada of refitted civilian ships, Humans would have a defense force. There'd be no reason or incentive to stay within the Collective fold. Rick descended the elevator to the hangar.

Inspecting his crew, he paced the row of them. Some wore plain clothes, concealing illegal homemade pistols. Others were adorned in the green and blue plate armor of Earthquake, brandishing homemade assault rifles.

"We go in silent. Shock troops, you don't budge until we get the precise signal. We're not letting anyone get caught. We have one chance to liberate this planet from the Collective, and that's in our use of native resources. Once we can turn the space elevator's defenses outward, we can repel Collective threats."

Seeing the smiles and nods among his troops, Rick cast a glance at Ten-trom, leaning against the back wall and shaking his head. Remembering the nightmares Rick had endured, both with Earthquake and before, he proceeded to balance their enthusiasm with sober reality.

"There will be armed Collective soldiers. Some of your comrades will fall today, and we'll remember them as heroes. Equalizer gun squads, line up your shot and take it. You have targeting software. Don't eyeball it. You only get one shot before they start moving. Everyone else, your job is to provide covering and suppressive fire for the Equalizer squads. You might get lucky and find an exposed joint to hit but don't bank on it."

This had the intended effect of balancing their expectations, if their faces were any indicator.

"Remember, we're going into a space elevator," Rick said. "Expect civilians. Humans. Avoid collateral, even for Arkoudae and Lo-sats. They call us terrorists." The very word made him want to spit. "But I say if the Collective did right by Humanity, we wouldn't exist, would we?" He paused to allow for murmurs of agreement. "They call us names to justify their refusal to look in the mirror." He drew a deep breath for his parting words. "We'll win. Honorably. We're declaring independence. New Lodestone will be a new start for Humankind." He eyed his ground troops. "Who's ready to storm the elevator?"

Homemade guns held aloft, they responded with cheers and "hoo-ahhs."

Rick smirked and turned to the space team. "And who's ready to show the galaxy what Human ingenuity can do with ordinary civilian ships?"

As the second group drowned out the first, Rick nodded. This would mark a new turning point for Humans. A new era would begin today.

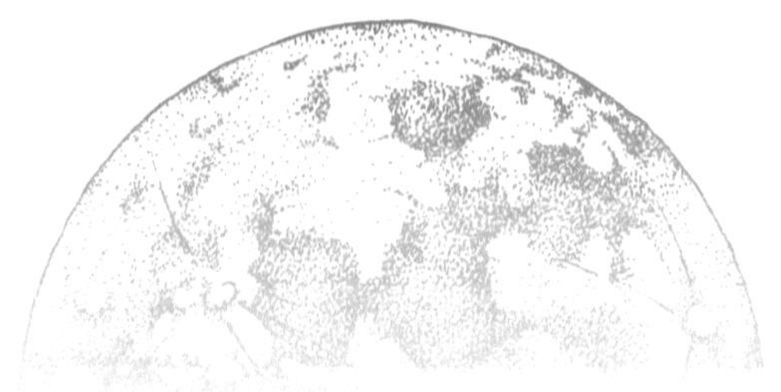

TWELVE

(NED)

A happier time

IN THE CRAMPED quiet of their makeshift home laboratory, Ned stroked the duraglass tube. It would be a matter of seconds before—

His hairs stood on end. "La…"

She cocked an eyeridge in his direction.

"The temperature is higher than the others were."

She slinked to his side, pulling his shoulders tight to hers with her tail, constricting him with her anticipation and love. "You don't think…"

"I don't have to," Ned breathed. "It worked."

"You're positive?"

"The temperature is above the expected range, but we have cellular fusion." Ned draped an arm around her waist. "Batch thirty-two took. We're finally parents."

La-hok's neck frills jiggled above him. "Can we be positive before we celebrate?"

Ned cracked a smile. "What else could I expect from the greatest scientist on this station?"

"Don't let the boss hear you say that." La-hok brought up the display, zooming in on the spinning cell. "It split. The cell split." She pulled away from the screen and gazed down at him, eyes as warm as her blood was cold. "All thanks to your fantastic engineering and machinery."

"I had a good muse."

La-hok eyed him. "Myu-suh? Is that a Human word?"

"Who cares? Our kid is right there in this tank. You were right."

She tapped the duraglass with the tip of her tail. "My theories about galactic evolution and DNA editing viruses don't feel as important now that our child is floating here."

"Humble as ever," Ned said. "Are you sure you're OK with not sitting on an egg?"

"Not the way my mom complained about it. Every time I did something wrong as a kid, she'd remind me of how many hours she spent laying on my egg."

"She didn't use an incubator?"

La-hok scoffed. "It's my mom. She had to be traditional and plop her own butt on my shell."

Ned knew having a child would alter their intimate lives, but he hadn't expected it to already. "Great image, sweethearts. Have you thought of a name?"

"I tried not to." She sank into her chair in their cramped apartment, between her heating lamp and food terrarium where unsuspecting rodents clambered around. "All those failures. Thinking of names only made the process harder."

"Well," Ned said. "No more failures. At least in the lab with the creation. I'm sure we'll have some other parenting failures down the line."

"Like when you say something offensive?" She offered him a weak smile.

"I meant when we forget to help him with his homework or something. But sure."

"Homework, school…" La-hok gripped her tail in her claws. "His life will be a challenge. Fitting in either with my people or yours." She bit back a tear.

"Sweethearts, we figured out interspecies procreation. What in the galaxy can't we solve? We'll be his people. He'll fit in with us. I hope other kids accept him… but maybe they won't, and that's fine. Kids don't always like other kids. We can't protect him from all the meanies out there. And once we publish your findings on cell regeneration and natural heat induction in Lo-sats, we'll buy our own asteroid and live an easy life. The three of us."

La-hok nodded. "We can protect him. As much as we can. That would be the real parenting failure, being unable to stop the evil of the galaxy from descending on him."

"What's that supposed to mean?" Ned asked, eyebrow cocked.

"It means stop hinting at us having a secret project at home around your coworkers. Could you imagine if Diastrevlo knew—?"

"Hey, we don't mention that name here. This is a happy place."

La-hok stared into the glowing green tube where their perfect multicellular child floated. "Yes, it is. Now come here."

THIRTEEN

(JOKA)

Orbit of New Lodestone, Polemistes System, Human Demilitarized Zone

NINETY HOURS OF warp travel ended with a jolt. Doh-riss had complained about how Joka chewed with her mouth open so many times she considered opening the cockpit to the whirling kaleidoscope of space above. She would've been compressed into a thread of pulp and pain; however, it would have relieved her from Doh-riss.

Focusing on that scientist's kid kept her sane.

Their ship neared the azure planet, so Joka's flight suit constricted, adjusting to the gravity. The dashboard display flashed some basic information about the planet—probably expired, given the ship's age.

Naturally, Doh-riss wanted to know everything. "Come on," she chided. "What's it say?"

Joka considered grabbing a snack so she could list these off while chewing with an open mouth. "Small population, one landmass, main export is oceanic methane. Only one space elevator?" Joka tsked. "Talk about backwater. Oh, and how's this? Says here the planet was deemed unfit for colonization: intense magnetosphere." She closed her eyes for a moment, trying to remember what she knew about other species' biology. "That won't, like, kill you, will it?"

"No," Doh-riss said. "Depending on how powerful the magnetism is, I would feel sensory overload, like staring into a nearby star."

"Or going into the bathroom after an Arkouda?"

"Joka!"

"Don't act like you never held back a puke after someone forgot to flush. It's gotta be worse for you with your strong nose."

Her neck frills jiggled in what Joka assumed was a Lo-sat's approximation of blushing. "*Got to*, not gotta. I think Marka never flushed on purpose as a dominance thing."

"Ha!" Joka beamed. "Where has this Doh-riss been hiding?"

Their communicator buzzed, and a female Arkouda voice followed. "Unidentified civilian ship, you do not have authorization or clearance to approach the space elevator with weapons. Identify yourselves."

Joka winced. Doh-riss had warned her to take a different ship, but in the back of her head, Joka worried they might need to fight or escape some goons, and she didn't want to fly unarmed. Plus, this rust bucket was faster than the unarmed civilian stuff.

Biting her lip, she turned to Doh-riss. "You talk to her. If I do, they might blow us out of space, thinking I'm some nutjob from Earthquake."

"I don't know what a nutjob is, but it sounds filthy." They switched seats, and Doh-riss accepted the comm. "We're defectors from Symphora's gang. We're here to refuel and nothing else." She spoke as if she would never correct someone's grammar.

A pregnant pause followed, and two growing dots emerged from the space elevator station. Joka clenched her fists, knuckles turning white as she realized those dots were twin battledarts, the newest model used by the military.

The Arkouda woman's voice returned, more rushed. "Do you have information that could lead to her capture?"

After reading Joka's body language, Doh-riss continued, "No. We left after she committed the crime, and they went into warp space to relocate her base as we were leaving. We'll cooperate with any search."

Doh-riss switched off the communicator. "How was that?"

Joka shrugged. "Good enough, but I'm not too excited about these battledarts coming at us. They could shoot us before we'd have a chance to run."

Doh-riss flashed a toothy smile. "Good thing we don't have enough fuel to go anywhere else."

"We have to work on your joke delivery."

The battledarts flanked them, and a new voice broke over the communicator. "We will escort you inside, and you will answer our questions about Symphora. You won't deviate from the flight path and will maintain constant speed. Deviation will allow us to legally open fire. Understand?"

After Doh-riss hissed a "yes," one battledart whooshed over their cockpit, cascading right in front of the ship's nose. A warning beeped on the dashboard, signifying the other one had taken position directly behind them.

Desperate for distraction, Joka peered through the side of the cockpit, examining the space elevator shaft. A wide cargo car hurtled toward the top, where ships would take off to their intergalactic destinations. Unlikely that it held people with how low the reported population was. As the elevator car raised, she imagined the childhood she wished she had, where she and her hypothetical friends would lie on rocks, staring up at the endless sky.

Their decrepit ship ambled along behind the newer Collective one. Some part of Joka wished she could see one of those new models in action, but the rest of her hoped she never would. Unless she could snag one and someone in Symphora's organization could reverse-engineer it. Otherwise, she dreaded the possibility of seeing a fleet of these sleek fighters come up against Symphora's gang. After what happened in the firefight, it would be another bloodbath, and she might not survive. She'd tackle that grander issue later but kept plugging away, keeping the ship as steady as possible between the escorts.

They approached a hangar yawning open to greet them. They passed the protective bubble and lowered, thrusters and antigravity slowing as they descended.

Joka turned to Doh-riss. "How bad is the magnetic field?"

Doh-riss shrugged. "Probably better up here than on the surface. It's not horrible." She stretched her head as she undid her safety harnesses. "This might give me a headache after a few hours, but I'm fine. I can definitely feel it, though."

"How bad do you think it is for the Arkoudae?"

"I don't know, but I imagine it's noticeable. You really can't feel it?"

"No, and it's weird to me that you can."

"Don't you get lost all the time, though?" She sounded authentically curious.

"Is there an unsarcastic way to tell you about maps?"

After the dashboard lit to signal the safe landing, the first voice from before buzzed over the intercom. "Exit the vehicle with all hands, paws, claws, tails, or tentacles raised high."

Not how Joka wanted this to begin, but here they were.

They left, and a trio of armored Collective soldiers followed them with their rifles.

A lightly decorated Arkouda officer approached them. "Two members of Symphora's squadron." Paws clasped behind her back, she ambled to the ship's side, looking for Symphora's famous symbol. After a pleased grunt, she added, "I didn't know Symphora kept Humans in her gang. I assumed she'd turn your kind loose."

Doh-riss narrowed her eyeridges. "Symphora takes the strong."

Joka flashed a meek "thank you" with her eyes.

The officer nodded, her neat white fuzz poking out from under her officer's cap.

A soldier bristled. "Ma'am, can we commence searching?"

"In a moment." She eyed Doh-riss. "What are you transporting?"

Joka's lips burned to respond, but she didn't have the rights and liberties a Lo-sat did. Instead, Joka raised her eyebrows, hoping Doh-riss could read her body language.

"Just ourselves. Food for her." She pointed at Joka. "We fled Symphora's gang. We didn't want to be arrested or implicated. There's not much room in there for more than us."

The officer turned to her detachment and waved a paw. Two soldiers lumbered into their battledart, and Joka tensed. All she had was her duffle bag and the message from that dead lab assistant. Doh-riss probably didn't have much except a rodent for her meal next week and spare heat cells.

"You two," the officer said, indicating them. "Follow me." The remaining Collective soldiers fell in line, forming a barrier around Joka and Doh-riss. Arkoudae towered over Humans, but seeing these soldiers— clad in their armor, muscles like professional athletes, assault rifles that would make Symphora drool—Joka felt smaller than she had in years. Not since her days in the factory farm.

Joka guessed at the odds of these Collective soldiers being relatives or friends of those Symphora killed in the setup or any of the ones she or Doh-riss shot. Sharp ice filled her veins. Would they believe her story, even if Doh-riss corroborated?

A white-haired muscle wall around them prevented Joka from absorbing the scenery inside the station's hangar. But high silvery ceilings overhead left plenty of room for civilian ships of most sizes to maneuver without bumping into each other, unlike the Calamity's cramped hangar. Organizing ships in and out of that was like level ten on "Line Align," which nobody could beat except Kah-renn.

The design boasted a grand sense of planning the Calamity lacked. Part of their old station's charm was how sections were added on piecemeal as Symphora stole money from crooks and received donations, slowly building her reputation over the decades. The Calamity was slapdashery and function-over-form at its finest. The organization and consistent architecture tugged at unsavory memories.

With little warning, the detachment of marching Arkoudae turned sharply, and the officer stepped aside, opening a door to a moderate office. Movies had conditioned Joka to assume she would be forcefully nudged in by the butt of a rifle, but the officer bade them enter. Doh-riss and Joka complied with neither complaint nor kerfuffle.

Resisting would be pointless, anyway. They were outnumbered, outgunned, outmuscled, outeverythinged. Joka's only course of action would be to act like a good little obedient Provincial while the scaly Citizen beside her exercised her rights.

Habit pushed her to mutter something colorful, but she stopped herself, unwilling to let Miss Priss ruin their shot of departure.

Inside the office, an amber light flashed near the metal door. The officer stared at it for a moment, then flipped a switch. She pressed a button and spoke into an obscured intercom. "This better be important."

A shaky Arkouda voice responded. "Ma'am, we've got a dozen unregistered ships floating our way."

"Are they armed?"

"N-no. They're scrappers."

The officer groaned. "They're probably just wildcat asteroid miners who got lost and need fuel. Tell traffic control to make them show identification or find somewhere else."

Joka and Doh-riss sent strained glances each other's way.

The nervous guy on the other side of the comm responded after a few stutters. "They refused and said they're coming anyway. How do you want us to proceed?"

"What the actual shit?" Joka asked.

Doh-riss glared at her.

"Oh, right, a Provincial shouldn't speak that way. What the actual *skata?*"

The security officer's reaction made them stop cold. "Intercept and destroy them."

FOURTEEN

(RICK)

**New Lodestone Orbit, Boudica System,
Human Demilitarized Zone**

SCRAPPER SHIPS WERE never designed for combat, which was a damn shame in Rick's eyes. They sported armor meant to repel and withstand asteroid impact and heat shields strong enough to defy a star. Cargo hulls were expansive enough to transport minerals from entire asteroids or satellites—or a detachment of soldiers.

Not only were scrappers slower than a slimeshell, they also lacked combat capabilities.

Until now. Rick and his team had infused Human creativity into their mineral magnets. New Lodestone's powerful magnetosphere had more uses than repelling Arkoudae and Lo-sats from the surface. It would increase the scrapper's powers of attraction and repulsion, a natural amplifier for their already formidable magnets.

Rick's comm unit buzzed. His civilian cargo ship's viewscreen displayed enough of the space before him to suffice as a mobile command post for the coming conflict.

"Give me good news, Rawltz," Rick said.

From behind, Ten-trom snorted. "You put Flakey-Jake in charge? Watch this turn to shit."

"I'll toss you out an airlock," Rick said.

"Don't tempt me with a good time. Maybe when your mole with the monks comes back, he can show you some fun moves."

Rick didn't have time to ponder how his agent was faring with the Great Mystery monks. That was a long con, and he couldn't worry about it now, although the thought did nag him. For whatever military successes he'd have today, they would only go so far without the monks' blessing.

Jake Rawltz's chirping colonial accent whistled through the comm, breaking Rick's distraction. "They told us to present identification or leave."

Rick grinned. "Tell them they have the option of leaving New Lodestone. A full withdrawal of the Collective government from the planet. Allow the people there to live independently."

"…You think they'll go for that?"

"No," Rick said. "But they need to know our terms before we embarrass them."

"Understood."

The thief slinked beside Rick. "You grow up so fast, Lefty. When we first met, you were threatening that sweet little archaeologist. Say, did I tell you about the first time I met Jakey?"

"Don't call Rawltz 'Jakey.'"

Zhou snickered behind them.

Rick whispered so only the Lo-sat could hear. "Mention the archaeologist again, and I'll increase your debt."

"You can't do that." The Lo-sat lowered his voice and added some gravel to it, imitating Rick's clipped Earther accent. The sonofabitch even pulled his left arm behind his back. "I'm a damn man of my damn word, dammit. And I'll be damned if damny damny damn damn."

From the space elevator, a slew of dots billowed out. Rick's shoulders stiffened. "Someone get an exact count. This is the first wave."

"On it," came Zhou's voice.

"Sixteen," Harvat added.

Rick switched his comm to the public channel to get his miniature fleet of scrappers' attention. "Alright, troops. Follow plan theta-two. Precise movements. We drilled for this."

The viewscreen displayed the dots approaching Earthquake's scrappers in a honeycomb shape.

"Rawltz," Rick said. "Give them one more chance to surrender."

"Roger." After a few seconds, Rawltz added, "They laughed at me. They said they'd blow us out of space."

Hope they enjoyed it. "Corner ships, engage. Remember, we want at least one as a trophy, but your lives are more important."

At Rick's command, the four scrapper ships on the corner of his square formation activated their asteroid magnets. They targeted the four approaching battledarts on the formation's edges by casting a translucent violet ray in their direction. Once in the beam, the scrappers yanked them toward the center of their honeycomb, smacking four other fighters with them. The collisions triggered two explosions and three clipped wings. In one swoop, half the offending ships were obliterated or incapacitated.

Cheers erupted from behind Rick with a semi-impressed "hmpf" from Ten-trom, but Rick didn't join them. "Center ships, engage."

The approaching battledarts, close enough for Rick to see their black sheen, opened fire against the scrappers. For all the damage they did, the battledarts may as well have been miners' children on New Lodestone, tossing magnetized pebbles at buildings to see which ones would stick.

The two center ships activated their magnetic beams, trapping the top two remaining battledarts. They flung them toward New Lodestone, letting the planet's gravitational field catch them. They'd burn up in the atmosphere over the ocean while their sensory overload from the planet's magnetism would make it impossible to activate any emergency ejection.

"Shtagg, Rawltz," Rick barked over the comm. "Let's take these two home with us if we can. Once you trap them, spin their ships to disorient the pilot. Are your Equalizer teams ready?"

"Yes."

"Locked and loaded."

"Good," Rick said. "Remember, offer a chance to surrender. They lay down their weapons, deactivate their armor, and hand it to you. If they refuse, that's when you hit them."

"Easier to kill them," the Lo-sat muttered.

"Faster, too," Rick sighed. He cast an eye at Ten-trom. "But we're not who they say we are."

"You're exactly who they say you are," Ten-trom muttered.

If he'd said it loud enough for anyone else to hear, Rick would've reprimanded him. But he couldn't afford to get riled up or distracted.

The scrappers pulled the final battledarts toward them. The spinning wasn't as graceful as Rick had imagined, but it appeared jarring enough to rumble his own gut.

Watching them from afar tugged at a memory of flying a specially-made Human skirmisher from his time with the Collective military. They had put about as much effort into safety as Ten-trom did minding his manners. Each ride in that threatened vomit and vertigo.

Guilt pinched him for ordering the scrappers to spin the encroaching pilots, but he couldn't risk any wild shots from the battledarts or them attempting to open fire inside the scrappers' cargo.

As the battledarts hurtled toward the scrappers, Rick gripped the comm. "Don't decelerate the ships, do a hard brake. If we're lucky, that'll concuss the pilots and make life easier."

A nebulous mass of dots emerged from the space elevator, approaching fast on radar. "All units, prepare for the next wave. We need an immediate count."

Harvat's voice came from behind. "Forty-one."

Rick couldn't unclench. "Someone double-check."

"Forty-one, sir," Zhou said.

After a tight sigh, Rick steeled himself again. "This is their whole force. Execute plan epsilon six. They'll fan out in two complete honeycomb formations with the remaining five forming a smaller one in between."

Some murmurs rustled behind him. Ten-trom peered over his shoulder at the rest of Rick's crew. "Lefty learned how the fuzzy stinkies fly and fight during his time with them."

"When their first attempt doesn't work, they come in with triple their original number. Since we're not seeing that here, they're throwing everything at us."

The murmurs melted into a mix of "ahhs" and grumbles.

An update came from the two center scrappers that captured the last battledarts from the first wave. Both captured pilots refused to surrender and were summarily executed. Rick would need to learn if any celebration came from an execution so he could nip that in the bud.

"Brasileo," Rick called into the comm, "release your payload on five."

The flank scrapper pilot's voice buzzed through. "Consider it done."

"Kenyatta and McGare," Rick continued, "get your repulsion fields prepped."

The leftmost of Rick's scrappers plodded toward the oncoming battledarts and rotated. Ferrous asteroids that Rick's team had meticulously carved into spiked balls spilled from its cargo hold, bobbing along in zero gravity.

As it did, the two other scrappers on the outermost flanks circled around.

The battledarts kept formation. Rick smirked. Of course they didn't deviate. They were trained to fight pirates and crime bosses with mercenaries. They didn't have a plan for this.

As the battledarts neared the released asteroids, the two scrappers on the flanks activated their repulsion fields. The asteroids and the bulk of the battledarts halted with a jerk and proceeded to bounce off each other, ricocheting and colliding with small explosions.

From the field, only five battledarts escaped, which all opened fire.

"Good work, everyone," Rick called. "Montgomery, Grayfort, L'onesea, Ayoob, Dragunov, try to grab the battledart nearest to you and pull it into your cargo. If you don't have an Equalizer team ready to welcome the pilot, repulse it down to New Lodestone and let it burn up in the atmosphere or sink in the ocean."

Rick refused to bask because this was only phase one. He switched channels and radioed the troops on the elevator. "Herrod, what's your status?"

Weaker than the other responses from pilots, Herrod responded, "The elevator was stopped because of the attack. We were stuck, but the scrapper you left behind has us in a mag field and is pushing us up to the station."

Rick flipped the comm to the public channel. "Begin phase two of the operation. Let's get boots inside the hangar."

Ten-trom grumbled. "You're keeping me aboard right, so I don't cause any mischief?"

"No. I might need you to break into an office."

"How many do I need to break into to pay off my debt?"

Rick couldn't divulge the truth. If Tecton discovered the thief had filled his debt, Rick would be ordered to put a bullet between his eyes. His options were to extend the debt or let the damn blabbermouth die, but Ten-trom knew too much to let him loose.

"A good number."

The Lo-sat huffed. "Is it more than a handful? I don't know if you could handle more than one."

"Earthquake," Rick called, ignoring the thief. "Let's move!"

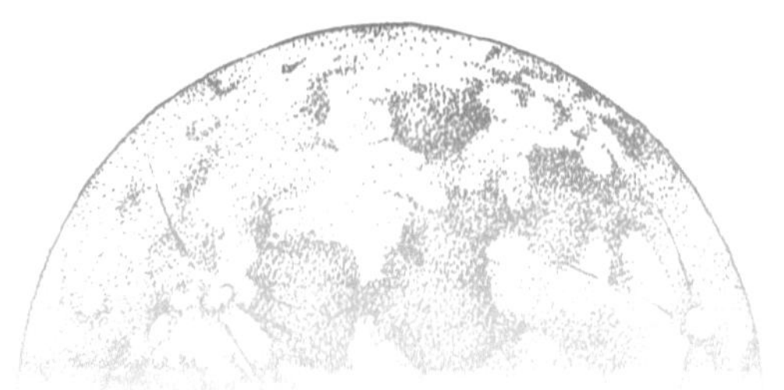

FIFTEEN

(INSPECTOR)

**A Collective space station government office,
near the frontier outpost**

HAVING ENDED THE recordings, the magistrate peered down his mono goggle at Inspector Bikkolos with the scowl of someone begging to retire. His office bore the cramped shelving of a midlevel government worker: someone who boasted enough experience and skill to handle tough cases and was too useful and complacent for a promotion in a long career. Two plaques for years of service adorned the wall behind his desk.

Bikkolos dealt with these types before. Patience and gratitude were the only options when at the mercy of someone like Magistrate Aletos.

After a harrumph, the magistrate pawed the omni-tablet back to the detective. "These are some serious allegations, officer."

Bad sign number one. "They are. I've investigated this case for the better part of a year."

"If this mushrooms, you could implicate higher officials who approved this scientist's funding."

Bad sign number two. "You're right. I hope that won't happen, but it's a possibility. These Human uprisings keep happening because they're treated like second-class citizens."

"Legally, they are."

Skata. "Magistrate Aletos, do you believe organizations like Earthquake would exist if Humans were treated justly in the Collective?" Telling an old magistrate the system was unjust was likely the spark of the funeral pyre. Bikkolos wondered if he should quit now and try some other route to secure this warrant.

With a deep sigh, the magistrate removed his goggle and pinched the bridge of his snout. "My son was killed by Earthquake."

Touched a nerve. Bikkolos should just thank him for his time and leave.

Possibly noticing Bikkolos' defeated expression, the magistrate held up a paw. "He was an archaeologist. You know that Human who was allowed to join the military but defected?"

Bikkolos' hearts forgot how to beat. Did this old timer know Bikkolos was the medic who patched up "the defector" Rick Crith? The memory surfaced of telling Rick, his one-time friend, that the Collective wouldn't pay for a prosthetic arm.

All the inspector could do was nod.

"Well, he killed my son. He asked my son to admit that Humans were abused and mistreated by the Collective, that we allegedly stole their culture."

That sounded like an unhinged Rick, alright. "What did your son do?"

The magistrate glared without anger. "My son refused … and insulted him. Told him Humans were filth, more or less. I had to watch the defector shoot a plasma bullet through my son's eye. Crith and his Earthquake minions recorded the whole Goddess-forsaken thing. Went viral before the censors got to it." He winced and sighed. "It was … a massacre."

Nodding slow, Bikkolos removed his detective's cap. "May he find rest in Her Divine Dream."

"Thanks. Wherever this Crith guy is now, he must be somewhere the Collective stopped caring about. You know, I wasted so much time screaming about how Humans were an evolutionary mistake from a backwater planet." After an old man cough, he continued, "But all that hating didn't bring my son back. Nothing will. I've thought about what I did wrong as a parent. If I had raised him to be more loving and compassionate, he would have admitted the truth to the defector. He would still be alive today." Moisture beaded around his sunken eyes.

"I wish more people thought like you did, Magistrate Aletos." He needed to get back on track. "Maybe if I can find these missing people, they will."

"I'll sign off on this search warrant. You may legally search Dr. Diastrevlo's laboratory. Keep your armor camera on at all times, understand? I can't give you a whole squad."

Skata. That wasn't what Bikkolos wanted to hear, but he knew he shouldn't push it. As the magistrate scrawled his approval on the search warrant, his words lingered in the inspector's mind. Maybe if he had been a better friend to Rick all those years ago, that magistrate's son would be alive today, too. Not to mention the other sons and daughters Rick had probably killed since joining Earthquake. He wondered if his old friend was still inside that killer somewhere, buried under the feelings of hate and betrayal.

And if his old friend weren't inside the killer, he shuddered to think who or what lurked there instead.

SIXTEEN

(JOKΛ)

Space Elevator Station, Orbit of New Lodestone, Polemistes System, Human Demilitarized Zone

THE OFFICER DOMINATED the table, separating herself from Doh-riss and Joka, who only came up high enough to rest her chin on the surface. Ironic how these government offices above a Human world never considered Humans in their design.

There wasn't much in this room beyond a locked cabinet beside the door. What passed for decoration was a single painting of a hunting scene, a pod of ancient Arkoudae on all fours barreling down on a hapless Arko mammoth rabbit. Not that Joka could see much from her vantage point, dwarfed and cramped at the same time.

Joka's omni-tablet chimed with notifications, likely because the device wished for Joka to crap herself.

Whoever the hell was pinging her needed a kick in the teeth.

"So what you're telling me," the officer said, expression stony, "is that you both saw Symphora in action?"

After eyeing each other, Joka and Doh-riss nodded tentatively.

The officer checked over both of her shoulders, even though the three of them were alone. "How awesome was it?"

Joka blinked. "Excuse me?"

"Sympora Ianna. Legendary badass outlaw. Are the stories true?"

"Yes!" Doh-riss perked up. "She's as wonderful and strong as everyone says. She's the best shot in the galaxy and her crack team…" Her voice lowered.

The officer grinned. "I heard one time she caught a bunch of slavers, sold them to a dumb pimp, stole the money, and blew them all up together. Is that true?"

Joka peeked over the edge of the table, repositioning her spine as much as possible to eke out an extra millimeter or two. "I never heard that one, but maybe. We got to live on her station. The Calamity—"

"Her station!" the officer interrupted. "So you saw her in the fur?"

"We were in the thick of it," Joka said, desperate to relax and slouch.

The officer's eyes widened. "Were those pings on your omni-tablet … from her?"

Cringing, Joka checked the notifications: all pings from Iasona the comms officer, asking if they took her stash of protein butter.

"These pings…" Joka cracked a grin. "They're about how Symphora was set up by the military—"

"Setup?" The officer's ears flattened. "Are you saying the Collective military actually tried to frame her? That she didn't turn on her own kind?"

Doh-riss nudged Joka under the table. "What the Provincial is trying to say is that Symphora had false intel." She shot Joka a glance as if to apologize for calling her that. "She thought we faced a criminal's mercenaries. Instead, it was a rogue military officer who had a grudge against her."

The officer leaned backward, arms crossed over a once-muscled chest. "Everyone says stop listening to conspiracy theories, but Symphora? A murderer? I knew something was up. She's the guardian of the fringe! Worse than the Goddess' Nightmare to any wrongdoers on the frontier. She wouldn't do anything like what people are saying."

This officer never met Symphora and only had an idealized version in her head, but Joka decided now wasn't the time to remind her. "So we hoped spreading the word might save us from getting arrested as well as let people know that Symphora was set up and innocent. She's in hiding, and we don't know how to reach her."

"And after the last mission," Doh-riss said, "Symphora lost most of her strike team. We could certainly put in a good word for you."

Joka eyed Doh-riss. Maybe she'd underestimated her. That was certainly worth a beer or two. Not that Miss Priss drank, but she'd at least offer.

The officer rubbed the bottom of her snout. "Just imagine … fighting alongside the legendary Symphora. That's every cub's dream." After a chuckle, she added, "Adults, too." She clicked her tongue and rose. "I can see to it that you get the fuel you need to spread the word. Take my contact information so you can let Symphora know where to find me when you—"

An alarm blared.

Joka cringed. Perfect timing.

The room's comm buzzed. The officer muttered something about how she shouldn't have put it on mute to get some stories about Symphora. Once she did, the message boomed. "Unauthorized entry. Hangar breached. Traffic control, respond. Reception, respond. Security, respond."

The officer's eyes widened. She darted to the closet in the corner of the room. With a *ch-thunk*, it unlocked. The officer pulled out a suit of Collective military armor that hadn't seen use in years. Swearing and fumbling over it, she allowed the armor to graft itself onto her. The frame made her look jacked, along with pleated armored skirt folds draping to her knees. The helmet boasted an enlisted officer's badass spike. Once it formed to her body, she slammed a plate near the side, and a compartment opened. She dug a small cube out of it, which unfolded in her paw into a handgun.

"You two stay here."

Her eyes expressed more of a "Oh *skata* on a platter. What the Nightmare just happened" type of message, though.

The immature part of Joka wished the officer had expressed that out loud so Doh-riss could react, but her repressed adult assessed the situation. When the officer closed the door, Joka turned to Doh-riss. "So we definitely can't stay here, right? Whatever that alarm was, it ain't good."

"*Wasn't* good." Doh-riss gasped, claw over her chest. "You wish to defy an officer of the Collective?"

"We're working for Symphora, so we're criminals already."

"I don't want to break the law."

"Sister, you can't be serious. Whatever just came through here and spooked her is trouble. We need to get back in our ship and float to another station, even if it takes months going at sublight." She dropped her voice and smirked. "Or maybe we could borrow a fueled-up ship."

"Steal?"

"Again, criminals." Joka jostled the door handle— she had to reach with both hands and it barely budged.

"Joka, you're—"

"Shut up. I'm saving that kid, which is impossible sitting in here."

"Joka—"

"You can help or get out of my way," Joka grunted— the doors on the Calamity station never gave her this much trouble.

"You're pulling on the door, and it's a push. How's that for help?" Doh-riss harrumphed. "Also, I thought I might mention you're not leaving that way. She locked us in here."

Joka sighed. "How do we get out?"

"What sarcastic response would you have if I asked that question?"

Slumping her shoulders, Joka replied, "Sorry." After a deep inhale, she straightened her posture. "But we're in a locked room with Earth-knows-what happening on the other side. No way we're safe."

Doh-riss furrowed her eyeridges. "An officer wouldn't suit up over nothing."

Vibrations rumbled through the floor, knocking Joka off balance. A chorus of pained Arkoudae howls followed. Doh-riss rose from her chair after the shouts and rumbles stopped.

Angry moments passed as Joka ripped apart the room, and Doh-riss rummaged through the closet, searching for some kind of key.

Upon hearing the door to the adjacent room thud open, both froze and stared at each other. Angry voices with mismatched accents spoke in Human.

"This the control room?" one asked.

"Gotta be, check that PA system," another said.

"Go tell Rick we found it," a third said.

"Call him Commander Crith unless you want him to rip you a new asshole," the second chided.

"Do you want to be the one who tells him if we're wrong?" the first voice said.

Doh-riss pressed an ear against the adjoining wall. "Can you understand them? That sounds like Human."

"It is," Joka said. "But I have no idea who they're talking about. They mentioned a name I think I've heard somewhere, though."

The third voice grumbled. "Just start pressing buttons, man. We'll figure it out."

A click in their room stole their attention back. Joka's eyes widened. "They just unlocked the door. Doh-riss, if you found another gun in that closet, arm yourself. On the zero percent chance you found a Human-sized one, I'll take that, too."

Doh-riss tutted. "There weren't any other weapons. Are you sure you want to leave?"

"Maybe they'll help out a Human." Joka cracked open the door.

They peeked out, watching civilian ships hover in the hangar. Simple scrappers and cargo ships.

Joka scoffed. "What the hell got her so worked up? Is she afraid of them not paying docking taxes? Come on, let's go."

"You're being impulsive. Wait—!"

Joka nudged past Doh-riss and left. As she re-entered the station's hangar, one of the scrappers activated a magnetic field. Joka hadn't seen one up close, but its cloying indigo light snapped her attention first to the source, and then to the target.

The scrapper, cargo hull opening, had targeted her battledart.

"Nononono—"

"What?" Doh-riss asked before yelping. "What're they doing?"

Joka prepared a scream and geared up to sprint over to her ship but stopped in her tracks.

The officer they'd spoken to seconds ago lay splayed on the floor, twitching.

Scattered near her were other Collective soldiers.

Most weren't twitching.

Gawking, Joka noticed each one had a rocky, reddish ball balanced on their chests. They almost resembled tiny asteroids, but whatever they were didn't change the fact that she and Doh-riss were in deep *skata*.

The silence of the corpses splayed before her sent her stomach into convulsions.

Humans clad in green and blue patchwork chest plates sported matching lopsided haircuts. They loomed over the fallen Collective soldiers, brandishing homemade weapons. Seeing something made for a Human by a Human without the hallmarks of Arkouda design made Joka take a second glance. She'd never seen anything like them—their cylinders and angles contrasted with Arkoudae's oblong honeycomb shapes. Her flight suit was the closest equivalent.

But these people were here to wreak havoc, and she didn't want to get in their way. She held out her arm to hold Doh-riss back. "Let's hide."

Doh-riss tutted. "Should we play dead?"

"No. Left stairwell," Joka whispered.

The gun-toting Humans didn't seem to notice Joka and Doh-riss, focused as they were on the fallen Arkoudae. They tiptoed forward, and Joka noticed a second wave of civilian ships engage landing gear and touch down, sending vibrations through the floor.

On reaching the first step, a male Human voice boomed over the intercom, speaking in Human with a clipped accent. Joka couldn't tell if the speaker was an Earther or from somewhere near Earth, but he spoke with a confidence she hadn't heard in a Human before.

"Attention, all Humans on this station. This is Commander Rick Crith. New Lodestone is a free planet now, liberated by Earthquake. We're giving the Collective Citizens on board the chance to surrender in peace. We'll deal with whoever resists. Stay in place and stay safe. You will see armed men and women. We all have tattoos of Earth on our bodies. That's how you know we're on your side."

Doh-riss arched her neck over her shoulder. "What did they say? Sounded like a threat."

Joka descended the steep stairs, careful not to rip her flight suit with each overextended step. "You're positive you don't have a gun or anything?"

"I didn't lie, Joka."

"Look, I don't know who these goons are, but they don't seem keen on—"

The same voice boomed over the PA system, changing to minimally-accented Arkouda. "Citizens of the Collective, your station has surrendered. You are now on the station of a free, sovereign planet. We do not wish to shed innocent blood. We will see to it that you are delivered to the Collective safely."

Doh-riss tutted. "How different was that from what he said in Human?"

"Enough that you better let me do the talking now."

They bolted down the rest of the stairs—each step a lunge for Joka—toward an Arkouda language sign labeled "Provincial Government offices." A red alarm light oscillated, but any warnings it made had long since echoed out or been cut off by those three button-mashing guys from the room beside their holding cell.

The lines of doors towered over Joka. Within seconds, Arkouda burst out of them. Some carried guns, and others had household tools and kitchen implements, all with steel in their eyes.

"Sounds like they aren't too fond of the new direction from that PA system guy," Joka muttered.

Doh-riss cocked an eyeridge. "What do you expect? An Arkouda take orders from a Provincial? They wouldn't bear the shame."

The office nearest them had government symbols Joka didn't recognize, but she knew it was something important. An older man stepped out wielding a Collective military pistol which looked like it hadn't seen action since before Joka was born. He wheeled on them and aimed the weapon at Joka.

"Are you with those Humans above?" he barked.

Doh-riss stepped in front of her. "No, honored Citizen." She hoisted her tail, shielding her eyes from the oscillating alarm light. "This is my assistant. We stopped here for fuel when this nonsense began."

"Hmpf." He holstered the handgun. "Best be on your way. You can hide in my office and let the—!"

Shoom.

A plasma bullet ripped through his throat, and he crumpled to the ground as indigo blood sprayed from the wound. The singed fur stench made Joka wince.

Behind them, Arkoudae howled and roared, collapsing to the floor.

"Shit," Joka whispered.

Gunshots continued, met with Arkoudae howling.

Doh-riss pointed at the end of the hall. "Humans!"

Joka's eyes widened. More gun-toting Humans like the ones upstairs, sporting matching lopsided haircuts.

Heavy boots thudded from the stairwell behind them, and Joka dove into the grumpy dead guy's office with Doh-riss close behind. Inside, they crouched in front of a wide window looking out into the corridor. Between the overturned chairs and Arkouda-sized desks, they had ample cover.

Collective military guards ascended from a lower level. This seemed like a small detachment to Joka since this station didn't have much to defend, but different parts of her relaxed and tensed at the sight. The last time she saw Collective military was when they were disguised as mercenaries. These soldiers wore the invincible Collective military armor.

If the soldiers noticed Joka and Doh-riss, they didn't care. Their only target was dead ahead, these Humans. Joka never saw Humans gunned down before, but there was no other option. They'd defied the Collective. Yeah, they brought some Arkoudae down with them and stole Joka's battledart, but this uprising or whatever it was couldn't last. The Arkouda soldiers passed them; Joka and Doh-riss craned their necks to see the warriors stand in formation and open fire against the Humans at the other end of the hall.

"Can you see through their legs?" Doh-riss asked.

"Looks like the Humans have some kind of hand-held shields."

"Shields?"

"Weird..." Joka squinted. "They seem like they were made from chopped up Collective armor plates. They're forming some kind of wall and advancing."

A round of flashing *shooms* erupted as the Collective soldiers unloaded against the advancing Humans. But when the lime-colored plasma dust settled, a trio of Humans emerged, holding a tube that rivaled the length of Doh-riss' tail. From the end closer to them, a shiny pointed blade stuck out. Before the Collective soldiers could react, the trio aimed at one of the soldiers, and fired.

A bright metal alloy, shining like a hateful sun, shot forth with a series of clanks, attached to a chain. The projectile connected to a soldier's abdomen, causing a bone-shattering howl Joka hadn't heard since the botched mission. The harpoon exited the soldier's other side, leaving a gaping hole as the corpse fell, phlegm-colored intestines spilling.

When the nearby soldiers gasped and stared down at their fallen comrade, another four projectiles launched from both sides of the first one, connecting and boring holes into the soldiers' stomachs.

Gore and blood splattered on the glass.

Joka shook herself from the stupor. She and Doh-riss turned around and found an abandoned desk in the office, which they heaved to reposition, providing some cover.

Joka peeped through one of the desk's cord holes; gun-toting Humans passed.

"None of them look familiar to you?" Doh-riss asked.

Joka lacked the energy to curse. "Remember that viral video from a few years ago? A one-armed Human murdered an Arkouda archaeologist. This is them."

"Urt-quake?"

"Earthquake."

The last one passed; Joka strained to listen while Doh-riss sniffed the air. "They went back down that stairwell where the soldiers came from. Maybe if we go back where they came from originally, we can find a new ship in an alternate hangar or some bay for emergency escape pods."

"Let's go. There might be someone who needs help." As the words left, she remembered the scientist's kid. That child needed her help, too. Each passing second in this space station was one step closer to the kid never getting a chance to live a real life.

They exited the office, crouching, because apparently that made them invisible. Joka gasped at the sight of the Collective soldiers who'd died fighting those Humans. The spikes that killed them were gone. But the soldiers had been stripped of their armor. Loose organs and matted chunks of fur littered the floor.

"Holy *skata*," Joka whispered.

Doh-riss hissed.

"No, look. Those shields they used really were made out of sliced Arkouda armor. They must have figured out some way to chop them up."

"Hm. They'd need to since there's no way a Human could fit into a suit of their armor."

Just like how there was no way a Human could pilot a single-person fighter meant for a bigger species or wield a weapon tailor-made for the Arkoudae. The sprawled-out soldiers, stripped to their underclothes and bereft of their power along with their dignity and legacy, wouldn't get the funeral they deserved. Symphora always gave fallen sisters proper burials or cremations according to their religion. It was probably the closest Symphora's gang came to acting like a real military.

The families would be mortified if they found out their children, brave soldiers of the Collective, couldn't achieve oneness with the sleeping goddess. These Humans had taken that away.

Joka sympathized with the desire for independence, but staring at the mangled bodies, she wondered if this was the way to go. Perhaps there was something she missed in her years in Symphora's extended family.

Thinking of family brought her back to the flashes and half-memories of her own parents. Strangers, really.

Doh-riss knelt before the bodies, muttering some kind of Lo-sat prayer, holding back tears if Joka understood her body language correctly.

"Come on, Doh-riss." Joka gently nudged her to her feet. "We can't help them. But there might be someone else we can. If nothing else, we've got to help the kid. We can't let him get orphaned."

"Right. The child. We must save the child."

They continued their trek down the corridor, ears straining for any signs of more Humans approaching.

Another announcement boomed over the PA system, and it was the same male voice who made the previous speech, speaking in Arkouda. "Any Collective citizens must report to the hangar bay on the top floor. If you choose to flee, you will need to contend with us. We have all the ships in this station commandeered and are reappropriating them for ourselves. We will arrange for your transfer once we are guaranteed sovereignty and autonomy."

Before Joka or Doh-riss could comment, the voice came on again, this time in Human. "We'll be through momentarily to take a census. We are declaring independence. If you wish to remain with the Collective, come join the Arkoudae and Lo-sats who will approach the hangar. If you wish to join the new nation we're building on the surface, remain where you are until further directions come."

Joka and Doh-riss rounded a corner and found more dead Collective soldiers and citizens with gaping holes in their stomachs. The only distinguishing factor between them was the soldiers had their armor removed, as opposed to the others with less definition to their muscle mass—they retained their clothes and some dignity.

If this had been on a planet, any number of insects would've made pilgrimage to these feasting sites. Guts and blood lay on display unceremoniously, like an animal caught and killed in a turbine engine.

One of the bodies coughed.

Doh-riss sniffed, eyes wide. "Somebody is alive."

Joka bit her cheek to keep the sarcasm inside. "Yeah, it's one of the older ones on our right."

Joka led Doh-riss to an elderly Arkouda woman whose chest rose and fell a hair's distance.

Crouching, Joka spoke in her best attempt to be loud and gentle. "Ma'am? Honored Citizen? Can you hear us?"

With her tail, Doh-riss cradled the dying woman's neck, propping it up. Voice straining like her tail muscles, Doh-riss hissed, "We're here to help."

The woman struggled to open her dark eyes. Upon seeing Joka, she blinked hard and yelped. "Don't hurt me."

Joka backed away and displayed her hands in a placating gesture. "I'm not with them."

The barrel of a pistol cooled Joka's neck. Doh-riss looked up and gasped.

A male voice spoke in Arkouda. "No sudden movements, ladies." The voice repeated the phrase in flawless Human.

Joka dared to follow the barrel of the pistol. A clawed hand covered in gray scales held it. The hand belonged to a Lo-sat man wearing the same color and style of mismatched plate armor as the invading Humans. His gray scales reminded her of some sick Lo-sat kids she'd seen in the factory in her younger days.

With a raised eyeridge, his marbled yellow eyes bore down on Joka, a sick smirk running up his snout. "So I got a pilot and a, what, mechanic?"

Doh-riss laid down the woman's head and hissed something in Lo-sat which sounded hostile. After catching a glance at Joka, she switched languages to Arkouda. "We're not with the Humans who attacked this station. Can you help us escape?"

The Lo-sat man flashed a toothy grin and eyed Joka's flight suit. "Yeah, you don't smell like them. I'll help. Just follow me."

Joka slowly rose from her crouch, trying to create some polite distance from the weapon. "Who are you?"

The gray Lo-sat responded in Human. "Binh Ten-trom, at my service. If you're wondering about my fashion choices, I did this to blend in with those Earthquake *ke-noks*."

"What's Earthquake?" Joka asked, playing dumb.

"I thought everybody knew them. Well, they're invading, and they aren't too keen on people like her and me," he said, indicating Doh-riss. "But I can take you to someone who will keep you all safe from them."

Joka kept her eye trained on his gun. "That's great, but our business isn't here. We just needed to refuel. We don't want any part in this."

Doh-riss hissed. "What are you saying?"

Binh switched languages to Arkouda. "I'll keep you safe. My guy will show you what to do. Now, will you follow me or do you want to wait until the haircut crew comes back through with their ouchie guns?"

Doh-riss cocked an eyeridge. "Ouchie guns?"

He waved a dismissive claw. "I don't care enough to learn its name. Now come on, follow me, and you won't bump into those chumps."

Joka's eyes darted between him and the heaving elderly Arkouda on the floor. "We need to save her before we do anything."

"Humans," Binh muttered. "Move fast, alright?"

As Joka and Doh-riss started the basic first aid Symphora required everybody to know, Binh took out an omni-tablet and idly tapped, casting an occasional wary glance at Joka's outfit.

"And what are you doing instead of helping us?" Doh-riss asked.

"Playing Block Bash," Binh responded as if there weren't corpses all around them. "What? I don't know first aid."

SEVENTEEN

(RICK)

**Space Elevator Station, rechristened "Shaka."
Orbit above New Lodestone, Boudica System,
Independent Human space**

THE STATION MANAGER surrendered without complaint from the local governing officials on the station. Rick's captives were mid-level clerks. No official recognition came from the Collective governors, but this sufficed. A docking bay wasn't the most glamorous stage for a victory, but it didn't diminish the significance.

Hand behind his back, Rick observed his crew and prisoners of war. He turned to Zhou. "Inform Monsieur Tecton of our success. Give him the full update."

"Right away."

Rick prepared what he'd say to the captured Arkoudae and Lo-sats before him, but a ping notification on his omni-tablet distracted him.

[Ten-trom: I have a good find for you, Lefty. Send some goons with guns to block Delta on the office level. This will pay off my debt.]

Another ping followed before Rick could respond.

[Ten-trom: There's a Humie and a member of the master race down here with me. Both unarmed. No need to send your tummy tickler guns.]

Paying off his debt—the one thing the damn thief took seriously. Rick motioned for two of his local recruits and sent them to intercept Ten-trom. As they passed, he whispered, "The thief is never too far from a double-cross. Eyes open."

Rick scrolled through his other notifications. Nothing from his agent with the monks, which was probably for the best; less is more with those operations. One update from Amanda, planet-side.

[Amanda: Good luck up there, not that you need it. I got more intel on the guy who is experimenting on Humans. Might be a good follow-up if you can get the shiny new toy you want.]

A smile broke through Rick's grim exterior, which he suppressed after he noticed some eyes trained on him. He kept scrolling. Update from Cohen on the number of captured ships, refreshing enemy casualty lists and surrendered prisoners, with an update from the team of engineers on the surface about how many commandeered ships they could modify at once.

Among the captured ships, bulky cargoes and sleek transporters lined the hangar, each boasting the polished sheen of a Collective vessel. None of these were operated by Humans. This was all part of the planet's exploitation. That changed today.

As Rick inventoried them, a lone battledart stuck out: an older model that had seen better days. It was probably still a gravitational nightmare for a Human, but having an older one to make comparisons could help the engineers deduce how to make them safe for Human use. Or at least operate them with drones.

Stowing his omni-tablet, Rick called for comms officer Johnson. "How far out is the nearest detachment of the Collective fleet?"

"Hours, sir. Either our estimates were wrong about their location, or they got the signal earlier than we anticipated."

Rick nodded. "It's also possible they're moving faster. They could be eager for some action." His voice turned grave. "Were we right about the size of the detachment, though?"

Some tension left her voice. "Yes, one warhive."

Eighty armored Collective soldiers with an escort subgroup of six battledarts. Rick held up a finger signaling Johnson to wait while he plotted. "Call every Equalizer team to come back to the hangar. Then let everyone know we're executing plan gamma two for this operation."

She smirked. "Of course. They'll never know what hit them."

Rick refrained from chiding her over the cliché. After another glance at the gathered prisoners, he bellowed out to them in Arkouda. "A delegation from the Collective government is on its way to retrieve you. We have demands and conditions for your release. Until they're accepted, you'll be moved to a secure location to ensure you are not harmed during negotiations. Your cooperation is appreciated." Rick signaled Ramakrish, who opened a cargo vessel hull, one they hadn't modified. Addressing the crowd again, he continued, "Everyone in."

Members of Rick's fire team escorted the Collective civilians inside the cargo ship, amid grumbles, hisses, and muttered threats.

Rick got a ping on his omni-tablet from Monsieur Tecton.

[Tecton: Kill the prisoners if you can't use them, or they don't have any information. See if they have any of our people rotting in some prison, too.]

The Leader wasn't military. He didn't understand that prisoners had value. Especially these prisoners—they weren't soldiers. Mere civilians doing their jobs who were more useful alive. Tecton did have a good point about their own people being locked up. There were also probably some Makawe rebels and Blekk pirates who would appreciate a release, too. Humans weren't the only ones relegated to being Provincials, after all. The thought lightened Rick's spirits.

For the first time in his life, he was a free man. He no longer had reason to call himself by the Collective's designation. It didn't matter that the Collective didn't and most likely never would respect New Lodestone as a free and independent population, but he had declared it for himself and for the small number of people on the surface.

Soon more Humans, weary of Collective oppression, would flock to his side. The fact that the Arkouda would refuse to surrender the planet, even though it was uninhabitable for them, proved all of what Rick said about the Collective. They wanted to dominate those they considered inferior more than they wanted to create a just society where all people had a communal stake and vision.

Rick had a vision, too.

Grumbles bubbled behind him. Two of his men escorted a Human and Lo-sat woman, looking sullen, betrayed, and the worst kind of pissed off. Ten-trom flanked them with a smug expression. The Human woman in particular caught Rick's interest. Not because of how she carried herself but because of what she wore. Peeking out of a mechanic's jacket was a Collective flight suit, except modified for a Human. One glance at her sensible haircut was all it took for Rick to know she wasn't a member of Earthquake. Didn't have the same kind of chip on her shoulder that most New Lodestoners did, either. Why the hell she'd be on New Lodestone's space elevator was anyone's guess.

If this unknown person had created a flight suit a Human could use to pilot a smaller Arkouda craft, that would change the direction and momentum of the conflict in Earthquake's favor.

Rick didn't have much time before the incoming warhive popped from hyperspace demanding surrender, but he needed as much of that time as possible to get the flight suit or the wearer to join him. Those massive monstrosities boasted armaments adequate to level a city in minutes.

None of that answered why there was a Lo-sat woman with her, but Rick didn't care. What mattered was that flight suit. The Lo-sat woman, dressed as a mechanic, didn't resemble any soft government agent, either. Lacking sun damage, she bore the look of someone who spent most of her life on space stations. This pair didn't make sense, but there would be time for answers later.

As Rick advanced, an unbidden memory surfaced—when he violated his principles and threatened the Human archaeologist to get her dead Arkouda friend's armor. He gritted his teeth. He'd done what he'd needed to then and would do the same now. If he hadn't crossed that line, he never would've gotten the armor to experiment on, and they wouldn't have enjoyed today's success.

Ten-trom split the difference and strode in front of the women, then turned to Rick. "Ever heard of Symphora? They say they work for her. Sounds like a crock of shit to me, but you never know."

Rick arched an eyebrow and whispered back. "The vigilante? The same one who sodomizes criminals with her rifle?"

"Know any other Arkouda famous enough to go by their first name only?"

Many Humans Symphora freed wound up with Earthquake, and the ones who didn't usually weren't too keen on the Collective. Symphora was good for Earthquake since she was proof the Collective didn't care about people on society's fringe. If these women really worked for her, he might be able to get in her graces.

The two women glared, no doubt pissed at Ten-trom for whatever boveeshit he pulled to get them here, and also carried the entitled indignance one got from association with a celebrity. But all legends about Symphora said she had her own space station and a veritable city's worth of support staff behind her.

Rick stood in front of them. "Welcome to our station, ladies. My name is Commander Crith. My associate," he indicated Ten-trom, which garnered a barely perceptible "aw" from him, "says you work for Symphora. Why are you here?"

The Human responded and her accent was that of a spacer stuck around Arkoudae her whole life—not too different from the archaeologist. "Symphora is in some legal trouble. We bounced. We stopped here to refuel."

That sounded rehearsed. She couldn't make direct eye contact, either. A raised eyeridge from Ten-trom suggested he caught onto a half-truth, too.

The Lo-sat woman flared her neck frills and used the most formal construction in Arkouda possible, still bearing the hissing accent of a Lo-sat. "We're also on a mission to save someone. You're getting in the way. Give us our ship back."

Rick shook his head. "You sound like someone who's used to bossing Humans around. I'm sorry to hear that's how it worked for Symphora's organization, but we don't operate that way."

Ten-trom hissed to the other Lo-sat in their language.

Rick could write a novel in Arkouda, struggle through a polite chat in Maak, or read a children's book in Blekker, but the Lo-sat language was beyond him. He only remembered a few words, most of which were unrepeatable curses learned from Ten-trom. In their exchange, Rick caught the word for "left" while the thief was indicating Rick.

The Human woman's nostrils flared. "We have nothing to do with you or your attempt to liberate this planet. We couldn't care less about the Collective. We've got somewhere to be and you stole our ship."

The Lo-sat woman tapped the tip of her tail on the floor. "The brown battledart, it's from the Kappa series from about twenty years ago. It has Symphora's branding on it."

"So that flight suit you're wearing..." Rick indicated the Human woman. "You developed that?"

Defiant pride beamed on the inventor's face. "Yes."

"I have a new mission for you," Rick said in a level tone. "You'll make more of those."

The Lo-sat woman flared her neck frills. "Like hecks she will!"

Rick waved to Ten-trom. "Put them in a separate room from the other prisoners." Rick only had a few more minutes until the warhive would roll up, ready for conflict. He clenched his teeth and breathed deep. He was prepared for casualties, but he knew who he needed to protect and how. Getting flight suits for Humans would be an accomplishment all on its own, as would capturing a warhive or a space elevator. Rick had accomplished one and planned to do all three before the Boudica star set on New Lodestone.

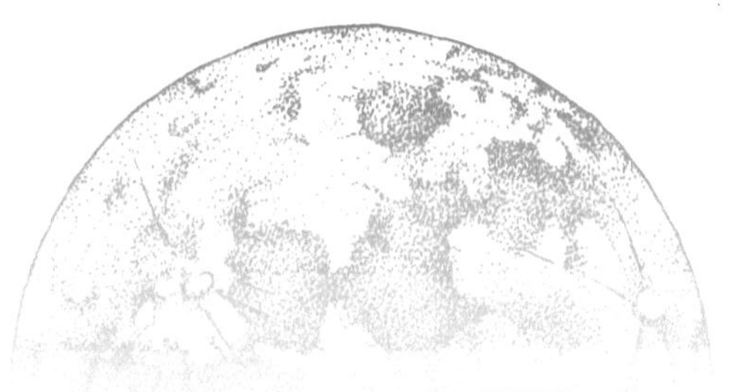

EIGHTEEN

(NED)

**On a research station in
{LOCATION CLASSIFIED}**

NED CAREFULLY SLIPPED his image inducer over his wrist and input the command. A gentle warmth tickled the hairs on his wrist.

La-hok made a quarter turn to her left, pretending to examine notes on her clipboard, comparing data on their biological readout screens just like they'd rehearsed. He stared at the tip of her tail intently. Their observation room which doubled as their home and laboratory hummed with equipment. That gentle buzzing provided the soundtrack to their misery.

Then came the signal. She crumpled the end of her tail into the shape of a Lo-sat's heart. Success so far. He let out a tight sigh. Then came the five-count wait. Four. Three. Two. She shifted, letting her tail fall flaccid.

Good.

"Can you hear me?" Ned asked.

No reaction from La-hok.

He restarted the five-count. No reaction from her. Four. Three. Two.

"Can you hear this?" Ned was louder this time.

She remained natural, loosely following standard procedure and pretending to make notes. No reaction from her.

For the third time, he restarted the five-count. No reactions. Four. Three. Two.

"Your mom gets on my nerves!" Ned shouted. "She's a buzzkill. Sometimes when I'm in a sarcastic mood, I tell myself that the only good thing in our isolation is not seeing her."

Thank Earth. Ned allowed himself a smile before the five-count finished.

Ned sent her a ping, even though she was within arm's reach.

[Ned: I love you.]

La-hok glanced down to her omni-tablet and tapped a response with her claw.

[Sweetscales: I hope you always say that as loud as possible. I love you successfully. I'd love you even if I were blind and deaf.]

Ned couldn't hide his smile. His first trial of the image inducer succeeded. The field it created allowed for a false image to project over his body as well as baffle his soundwaves enough to mute a rant about a mother-in-law.

La-hok did another quarter turn, toward his general direction. She cast eyes at where she probably thought he was, in an "I'm proud of you" expression. She was a few degrees off from where he was in reality, but that was more good news in the long run.

The next step was to increase the field so they could escape.

They knew Dr. Diastrevlo monitored the pings they sent to each other, so they couldn't continue to deliberate together or speak in more code, lest the doctor's prying eyes piece anything together. Ned initiated the encrypted call to his brother, halfway across the galaxy.

After a bout of sitting on the edge of his seat, squirming to remain within the boundaries of the hologram, the connection finally established.

The screen clarified, displaying his brother. Maynard Porandi, or Brother Maynard as most people knew him, was the Abbot of the monastery dedicated to the Great Mystery on New Lodestone. The planet was a total backwater, which Ned assumed probably made for a good place to pray.

When Symphora rescued them as kids, Ned found science, and Maynard found faith. It had taken them both far in life.

Ned could hardly believe Maynard was even willing to speak to him. Renouncing family ties was one of the first vows Maynard swore, but somehow, he found it worth it to bend the rules every few months to check in with Ned. But in the years of his confinement under Dr. Diastrevlo's thumb, those communications grew sparser and shorter, more for safety.

Maynard had an unspoken attachment that he hid from the other monks. An attachment to being an uncle. A love that drove him to break their other rules.

Ned smiled, seeing the older version of his own face. Bald, per the monks' rule, an awkward nose teetering between bulbous and beakish, and the soft eyes of someone who overcame childhood trauma. Maynard's scars and face brand hadn't healed the way Ned's had. It was jarring to see them each time since Ned's scars only lingered in memories and nightmares.

On the other side of the screen, Maynard softly clapped his hands together and bowed, beaming. "It's good to see you."

"Likewise. I don't have a ton of time."

"You rarely do. How's La-hok?"

"As good as you could expect for someone who has to watch her son get tortured."

The smile melted from their faces in tandem.

"I pray for the three of you. My heart breaks for Mui-xe every time I remember him. The authorities I called are searching for you... I wish there was something else I could do, Neddy."

"It gets harder every day. Maybe we could turn that prayer into action?"

A shadow passed over Maynard's face. "The legends of prehistoric monks on Earth who could teleport were myths. I thought you were a man of science."

"I'm not asking you to come to me."

On the other side of the screen, Maynard leaned closer and dropped his voice. "You've found a way to escape?"

"It's how I'm talking to you. I invented something that can project an image and muffle noise. We'll come to you."

Maynard's expression allowed Ned to absorb what he left unspoken. Openly admitting he kept contact with a blood relative could cost him his position as the abbot and shame the order. Yet his greatest call was to demonstrate compassion for all creatures and denying them would ignore that.

"If you can find a way here, we'll take you. Be mindful there are elements of New Lodestone that would prove difficult for La-hok and possibly Mui-xe."

"I told her about the magnetic field. She said she'd rather have a constant migraine than live like this. We haven't figured out a way to test it definitively, but we don't think Mui-xe has the Lo-sat magnetic sensitivity."

Maynard closed his eyes and shook his head again. "That's good to know, but that wasn't what I meant. Have you heard of the terrorist group called Earthquake?"

"Our knowledge of the outside is limited. I can program a little better than Diastrevlo, which lets me talk to you and La-hok to her mom, but not much else. Getting news isn't a priority."

Maynard rubbed his chin. "I can imagine. Well, suffice to say Earthquake fooled lots of Humans that they aren't terrorists, but I see through them. They are here. If they hear about Mui-xe, let alone that you married a Lo-sat…"

"Nobody's keen on our relationship, Maynard. The invasive questions people think they have a right to ask… But as for Mui-xe, my invention will protect him. He'll hide in plain sight."

"And ignore his true self? Lie about his identity?"

Ned's expression dimmed. "Until we can figure something else out, yes. I would take anything over his constant torture."

A crease formed in Maynard's brow. "Do you have any particulars about your departure?"

Ned explained his plan before saying goodbye.

When he disconnected, he moved to the spot where the image inducer projected himself and lowered the field.

La-hok didn't react: another good sign. He gently took her hand into his and kissed the scales just above her knuckles.

"There's my little space heater," she said.

A chuckle escaped. "I thought we agreed you'd stop calling me little."

"You're shorter than me, and you radiate heat like an open flame." She brought his hand up and lowered her head, allowing her to plant a dry kiss on his hand. "How did your 'prayers' go?"

"We proceed as planned."

"If we die, my love…" La-hok draped her tail around his shoulders, pulling him close. "I'll die satisfied we did it for our son. But I will fight like the gods of rage and fury before that happens."

"Normally hearing you talk like that would be sexy."

"I just come to you for warmth, you know." She released his hand and kissed the side of his neck.

"I'll find a place for you that has rocks all over the place, and you can sun yourself all you want." Ned pulled at the collar of her lab coat, but an alarm blared. The sound was one they knew too well at this point. Dr. Diastrevlo's next round of experiments would commence.

NINETEEN

(JOKA)

On the stupidest space elevator in the
galaxy. Not Collective space now?
Can they do that? Whatever.

THAT COMMANDER CRITH guy had instructed
the liar to take them to a separate room from the
other prisoners, but here they were, marching
toward a cargo ship at the end of the space elevator's hangar bay.

Now, the Lo-sat asswipe who Joka wanted to
strangle escorted them to a cargo ship. Doh-riss shot
him a few cold stares and acidic hisses, which he
shrugged off.

Joka puzzled over this guy's actions and motiva-
tions. "Where's this ship going?"

"New Lodestone, down to the surface," Binh said.

Assuming they could trust him.

"We can strike some kind of deal," Joka said. "You and your one-armed boss give us a chance to leave quietly? We could put in a good word with Symphora and all?"

"Is all you see his disability?" Binh asked, eyeridges raised. "That's so heartless and shocking. I honestly forget he's differently abled. Is my softscale all you see? For shame."

"All I see is a lying son of a Galsan worm," Doh-riss said.

Joka snarled. "Give us a straight answer."

"Look *ke-nok*..." As the word left his lipless mouth, Doh-riss gave a sharp indignant gasp. "I'm not in charge of this operation. Slick Rick over there is. Now go into this cargo ship and shut your traps."

Doh-riss addressed Joka but glared at Binh. "In Lo-sat culture, liars are condemned to the worst afterlife."

Binh leaned down and nudged Joka on her opposite side. "Imagine the irony, since religion is a huge lie already."

Doh-riss gasped.

Joka stared at him, slack-jawed. "That's awful. Just because you don't believe doesn't mean you should—" They had arrived at the door of the cargo ship.

That lanky shitsniffer distracted them with his stupid tangents. She couldn't decide if she was more annoyed or impressed, so she made a gesture considered offensive in most cultures.

Smiling like a jackass with his three-forked tongue dangling between his teeth, Binh returned the gesture with both hands and attempted a facsimile of the gesture with his tail.

Doh-riss averted her eyes.

Someone with a lopsided haircut and a tattoo of Earth on his arm pulled Joka aboard the cargo ship. Another person grabbed Doh-riss and did the same, albeit more forcefully. The other guy grimaced like he was disgusted to touch a Lo-sat yet also pleased with himself for manhandling one.

Under the cargo's dim lights and forced between crate shelving, Joka gave Doh-riss a reassuring pat as high on her lower back as she could reach. "We'll figure something out. If all else fails, we can write mean things about that guy in every bathroom in the galaxy."

Doh-riss harrumphed. "Is that how Humans relieve stress? Defacing bathrooms?"

"Yeah, it's not super mature—"

"So who wrote those things about me in the locker room?"

Joka almost responded with "everybody," but paused. "Humans have chips on our shoulders. We're pissed at the galaxy for being born into second-class status."

"I…" Doh-riss pushed Joka's arm away with her tail. "How do we get out?"

Joka assessed the cargo ship's inside hull. It was designed to hold containers of whatever could fit, but an unscrupulous smuggler would have no issue transporting living merchandise this way. They'd be stuck in this tub for the duration of the descent to New Lodestone. If they left the space elevator, their chance at saving this kid would jettison into orbit. They had to escape.

The other Human passengers inside, maybe a few dozen, huddled around the viewscreen displaying the outside environment in various states of panic and jaded detachment.

"What's there?" Joka asked.

Doh-riss rose to her full height, a half meter above everyone else's heads. "Looks like a bridge from a bigger ship extending into the hangar."

Another captive folded his arms. He eyed Doh-riss with a frown and spoke in Human. "It's a Collective warhive." Shaking his head, he added, "They're beyond screwed."

"A warhive," Joka whispered. She wished she could've seen it. If they'd stuck with Symphora, a warhive may have come after them eventually. She'd rather see it here than on the victim's side. One of Symphora's dead strike team members bragged about serving on one before hooking up with the gang. The 'hives were supposed to be the backbone of the Collective fleet.

A single warhive could protect a convoy or a base on an asteroid, and a detachment of them could defend a planet. She wondered how many the Collective fleet would've sent after Symphora, but she shook the thought from her head. She'd kicked Joka and Doh-riss to the curb. Whatever happened was out of their control and concern.

This pitiful and bloody revolution would soon come crashing down, with Joka and Doh-riss caught in the crossfire.

The extending bridge locked into the hangar with a *cha-clank* loud enough for them to hear inside the cargo, sending reverberations through their feet. Joka and the other Humans inside lost their balance. She would've tripped, but Doh-riss steadied her with her tail.

"Thanks," she muttered.

"Write that I helped you on a bathroom wall," Doh-riss snapped. "What did that other Human say?"

"A warhive docked the station," Joka said in Arkouda. Whispering, she added, "We gotta board that ship. There will be battledarts inside. We take one. Simplest thing ever."

Doh-riss groaned and stooped down to match Joka's whisper. "You want to steal from the Collective?"

"That would be one less battledart to use against Symphora. Do you really think they'll miss it? This is the Collective we're talking about here. They're not exactly strapped for resources."

"They'll definitely notice. And how do you propose we stow away? There's only one entrance, and we have to walk in front of everyone to get on there. Do you have a way to turn invisible?"

"No, and you forgot to mention that I don't know how to escape this cargo." Joka peeped around at the other people aboard, all of whom were fixated on the events unfolding on the viewscreen. "I mean, we could sneak into the cockpit and hijack it."

"What about all these people?" Doh-riss asked, gesturing to the increasingly louder crowd. "Do you want to take them with us?"

"There's got to be some way to open the cargo doors."

"They'll close them again. We should find an alternate release."

Joka's eyes widened. "This is a cargo unit; they didn't only have solid matter on here. There should be a release valve."

Doh-riss' expression brightened. "Which will let us crawl out."

Rows of metallic arches formed a ribcage for the cargo hold. In between two arches, Joka spied the depressurization valve. Getting up there would be a challenge since it was twice Doh-riss' height above them.

"The structural arches," Joka said. "That's our way up. Come on."

Joka and Doh-riss slinked away from the crowd around the viewscreen, demanding to see it and arguing with each other about what the commotion was.

The two center arches flanking the release valve were slightly farther apart than Joka had estimated.

Between two arches, Joka held out her arms and braced one foot against an arch. She motioned for Doh-riss to do the same. Doh-riss complied, grabbing Joka's wrists, using her tail to assist her brace on the arch behind her.

"We balance ourselves and climb up," Joka said, steel in her eyes. "Ready?"

Doh-riss let her tongue slip out. "I suppose the fall will be more socially painful than whatever will happen next."

"See? That's the spirit. We probably won't get seriously injured if we fall. And hey, who says we have to fall?"

"Gravity."

"Good point." Joka thumbed her grav harness, adjusting the setting to allow her to be a fraction lighter. She wondered if her next model of flight suit should have a built-in grav harness. Her insides lurched, and she got an instant headache. "Do yours now. It'll make the climb easier."

"That gives you a belly ache. Adjusting my gravity will give me an aneurysm."

Joka considered muttering "wimp" but reconsidered. Lighter on her feet, she held onto Doh-riss as hard as she could and pulled her second leg up to brace against the arch. Doh-riss did the same, her bulging eyes dilating like she ate the wrong candy at the wrong party.

"Don't look at me all nervous like that," Joka said.

"I'm not as confident as you are."

She was confident enough to insert herself into any conversation she wanted.

Inching up the arch, bracing each other, they cast occasional glances to the people watching the viewscreen. Joka noticed the Crith guy outside gesticulating as if giving orders while the haircut brigade fanned out around him, forming some kind of semi-circle around the entryway. She couldn't count how many, but there were quite a few of the harpoon cannons she'd seen in the hallways.

As they neared the curve before the ceiling, Doh-riss' tail slipped.

Joka noticed the appendage growing limp. "Hey, watch your tail," she said.

"Watch your right foot," came the retort.

They clutched each other tighter as they corrected their balance, inching ever closer to the center. As Doh-riss adjusted her grip, her claws dug into Joka's skin. She fought the urge to flinch. Symphora had hardened everyone on the crew to withstand worse, even the scrubs who weren't supposed to go on missions.

Arriving at the release valve in the ceiling's center, Joka's heart raced.

Doh-riss sniffed. "Why are you scared?"

"I'm not scared," Joka whisper-hissed back, barely audible over the commotion below them.

"I can smell your pheromones."

"Fine." Joka eyed the stupid thing. "I have no clue how to open the valve."

Doh-riss studied it. "We should go back down."

"No. Can I trust you?"

"Of course, but—"

"Good. I'm letting go to grab the valve. You can keep balance by holding on from here. Use your tail to help me spin it."

"You can't be serious."

Joka forced a smile. "Do I smell serious?"

"Your kin below are stinking up the place with their fear."

"I'll take that as a 'Yes, please be careful.'"

They inched toward the valve's wheel, and Joka released one of Doh-riss' hands to grab its rim. Doh-riss did the same, then adjusted. Teeth clenched, Joka swung to get her other hand on the valve; Doh-riss dug both claws into a tangle of pipes. Joka gripped tight while she dangled. Time to see if her pull-up competitions with Devy had paid off. With her tail, Doh-riss pulled Joka by the wrist and spun her as hard as possible, unscrewing the latch.

Accumulating sweat threatened Joka's grip, but Doh-riss steadied her.

After a few rotations, the latch dropped enough for Joka to swing up. Her shoulders would burn for the rest of her natural-born life, but damn she felt like a badass. Breathing the semi-fresh air of the hangar, she allowed herself one victory sigh, then leaned back down to extend a hand for Doh-riss.

Doh-riss hissed a "thank you" and wrapped her tail back around Joka's wrist. She clasped onto her hand, and Joka strained to pull her up.

"Damn, what'd you eat this month?"

"I don't eat every month. I'm not a glutton."

Knees buckling, Joka hoisted Doh-riss as much as she could with the Lo-sat aiding the ascent, grabbing a foothold where possible.

Once they were both atop the cargo ship, their attention snapped to the carnage below.

The Rick dude stood in front of the bridge amid a pile of Collective corpses. His tattooed haircut goons milled between the bodies, removing weapons and armor in teams.

"*Skata*," Joka whispered. "They beat them."

Doh-riss gasped. "The Collective is supposed to be invincible."

So was Symphora.

Joka peered over the edge of the cargo. "We're in some major trouble if we can't safely get down. I don't know how we'll sneak on that warhive."

"You still want to go on?"

Joka shrugged. "Got a better idea? That warhive will have a hangar with ships we can steal. I have some hair clips, and I can pin my hair to look like one of them. I could collapse my flight suit and stuff it in my pack."

Doh-riss lowered her eyeridges. "Your duffle bag that you left in our battledart?"

"Um, yes. Crap."

"And how do you propose I sneak aboard?" Doh-riss said, waving her claws around her neck frills. "I don't exactly have hair to pin."

"That was almost funny, Doh. I did think about that. They have a Lo-sat on their crew. If we can go in with a big crowd away from him, maybe nobody will notice."

"He has softscale. He looks nothing like me—we're completely different colors. Not to mention he's a him. And don't call me Doh."

Joka let out a soft sigh. "I know, but they," she gestured toward the Humans below, "aren't too keen on Collective Citizens. They probably don't notice details like that. Please don't take this personally, but it's hard for Humans to tell male from female Lo-sats. *I* know you don't look alike, but we can take advantage of their ignorance. We also don't have other options."

"Hpmf. So we need to wait until they start piling aboard?"

"Yeah. Do you have eyes on the Binh guy?"

"No, but I can smell him." Doh-riss took a sniff and pointed to Joka's left. "He's over there somewhere. Scum."

Joka smirked. "I thought you were about to say *skata*."

"Please stop swearing. They're on the move, and we don't have much time."

A worse word formed on Joka's lips, but the Earthquake leader caught her attention. They were high up enough and far away enough that she doubted Commander Crith could see her, but she rolled down to lie on her stomach nonetheless and tugged at Doh-riss until she did the same.

Whatever he was saying down below was a muffled mumble by the time it reached Joka's ears, but she was fairly confident she heard a "damn" in there somewhere. People lumbered toward the bridge, entering the warhive. Teams carrying the spear cannons led the way behind the guy Binh called Slick Rick, followed by other gun-toting thugs.

Doh-riss sniffed and pointed rigidly with a claw. "There's the scoundrel. Let's float down. We have a small window for this to work."

"I thought lowering your gravity too much would fry your brains."

"I didn't say that." She winked like they were friends or something. "You'll lower yours, and I'll hold onto you, so you can slow my fall."

Joka shrugged as she redid her hair to match the lopsided ugly of the Humans below. "I'll lower my gravity enough to make you regret that I ate this month."

"Hold in your vomit," Doh-riss warned. "The thief will be able to smell it, and he'll find us. He'll know it was yours."

"Gross," Joka said, thumbing her grav harness. "How could he identify me from the stink of my puke?"

Doh-riss scooted down the curve of the cargo ship until she was low enough to clutch Joka's ankle. "The same way you could recognize my voice on a recording. Stop wasting time."

Joka's insides rose along with a sulphuric burp, and she regretted her penchant for spicy food. If she messed with the setting anymore, her bones might not stay together with Doh-riss' weight on her ankle. She definitely needed to make the next model of her flight suit work with a grav harness to avoid this feeling. After a deep breath, she pushed off the cargo hold, letting her boot scrape the side of the ship.

Their collapsed landing was as graceful as a fart at a funeral. Groaning and tangled in each other's bodies, Joka adjusted her grav harness back to standard and swallowed her vomit, eyes watering. Breathing heavy, she helped Doh-riss to her feet. "Ever hear the joke about why Makawe shells are so flat?"

"Please don't tell a dirty joke now."

Buzzkill. "Well, I feel like I was *stepped* on by an Arkouda, how's that?" The dirty punchline was better, and significantly more appropriate for the moment. Without the lowered gravity, she would've snapped a bone or six. "Let's get out of here."

TWENTY

(RICK)

**Space Elevator Station, rechristened "Shaka."
Orbit above New Lodestone, Boudica System,
Independent Human space**

RICK MARCHED INTO the city-sized warhive at the front of his brave squadron. He was finally the damn hero. He knew they'd meet more resistance, but he had the best recruits behind him. Assuming the subadmiral commanding the warhive followed standard procedure, the welcoming committee would be their toughest marines on the ship. Rick's team would perforate any fighters like the rest since the bastards would never accept his terms.

Before he reached the bridge's midpoint, he got a ping from the surface. It was his mole in the monks.

[Mole: Big news when you get a chance.]

[Rick: Good news?]

[Mole: Not what you want but not bad news. Interesting.]

Of course the thief had to ruin the moment by looming over Rick's shoulder. "Any good updates, Ricky Rickster? Did the girly-girl with the curly-curl agree to a date?"

The ping was definitely unexpected, but having some confirmation the mole made progress was useful, especially before he did any gallivanting in space. His unit neared the bridge's end into the warhive's main hangar. They would either open fire or surrender. If Ten-trom provoked them, they would choose the former.

A faint smile flickered onto Rick's face, realizing the small pistols and knives the Collective engineers and mechanics would have for emergencies wouldn't do anything against Earthquake's refitted and modified armor. This would be the inverse of the first skirmishes against the Collective and Earthquake.

Fitting.

He noticed some splattered indigo blood from an Arkouda had stained the sleeve of his armor. It wouldn't wash off easily. It didn't bother him.

Rick motioned for the Equalizer teams to fan out beside him, prepped to fire at any second. When they reached the threshold of the warhive docking bay, a subadmiral greeted them, fully armored, brandishing an assault rifle. The bay had eight docked battledarts ready as escorts. It would have been an intimidating sight if the marines meant to pilot them hadn't been slaughtered by Rick's troops already.

"Not one more step, Provincial," the burly Arkouda veteran growled. "You can surrender now. We'll keep the killing to a minimum if you comply."

Rick puffed his cheeks for precise Arkouda pronunciation. "I was about to make the same offer to you, subadmiral. Perhaps I should make the offer to your superiors instead. I'd like to do this peacefully."

"Funny." The subadmiral waved; a team of too-thin and too-fat Arkoudae spread out from behind him, limply holding pistols. Not one sported armor. They'd never had anything beyond basic training and never appreciated the need to stay combat-ready. Why would they?

Rick lowered his pistol and addressed the warhive's support staff.

"Your leader refused the surrender offer." Rick furrowed his brow. "You lot aren't fighters. We'll kill or capture him, then give you each the chance to surrender peacefully. I don't want to harm noncombatants."

Binh wedged himself beside Rick and pointed at himself, shouting. "Look, he's got one diverse friend! You can trust him."

"Shaddup!" the subadmiral barked. "Don't listen to them. Let's kill—"

Fhoom!

An Equalizer harpoon careened across the bay like a dark lightning bolt with a dense oval head— the malice of downtrodden Humans made manifest. It sailed directly into the center of his stomach, pushing him back and stapling him into the wing of a docked battledart. He howled for a half-second before falling limp around the harpoon, tongue lolling out, eyes frozen open in the last painful throes of death. A nightmarish last second, but the spectacle had the intended effect on the crew. Rick hadn't ordered the kill, but his crew was listening to their training and instincts. He'd address the problematic high-fiving and fist-bumping later.

An engineer was the first to drop his sidearm and throw his paws up in surrender. A deckhand and engineer followed. One by one, the crew laid down their weapons and stepped forward.

One mechanic, trimmer than the others, clutched his pistol tighter and advanced. "You're dead. You think you can fight the Collective, you—"

A crack rang from Rick's pistol, shattering the tense quiet. The poor fool fell to his knees, gazing at the point between his eyes where Rick's plasma bullet punctured his skull.

Remaining support staff gasped. Some yelped his name.

It was a shame. He didn't have to die. But he didn't have to defy Earthquake, either. Rick made a mental note to learn that guy's name so he could add it to his list.

As the surrendered Arkoudae gathered to the side of the docking bay, Rick faced his brazen crew. "We'll keep them aboard and stow them in the cargo hold." He switched languages and addressed his captives. "You'll remain here as prisoners of war until we can negotiate your surrender to the Collective. When they recognize our independence, we'll hand you over to them, unharmed."

Ten-trom spoke up. "Impressive kill, Ricky Rickster. Those will be fun stains to clean up."

"What do you want, Ten-trom?"

"Just wanted to ask what level of quality control your boys are doing for the people coming aboard this warhive of yours." He sniffed a few times. "Do you know who you're letting enter your new murder metropolis?"

Rick wheeled on the Lo-sat, daggers in his eyes. He didn't have time for any garbage about how Humans stank or how Earthquake members were unintelligent. This sonofabitch had three jokes, and they'd grated on Rick long enough. "Talk straight before I toss you out an airlock."

The damn thief folded his arms over his chest. He cast a marbled eye toward the group of captured Arkoudae and tsked. "Looks like you found new non Humans to be nice to so you can make yourself look good. Don't have much need for me, do you?"

"You're one nickname away from uselessness," Rick sneered.

"Useless, huh? The Human flight suit isn't worth anything to you, then?"

Rick backed off, firmly holstering his pistol. "Not enough for you to continue mouthing off."

"One victory and it all goes to your head. Well, Rodrick Crith, that flight suit makes us even."

Rick stared at him. "Almost."

The Lo-sat sniffed. "Will anything be enough?"

A heavy silence passed.

The captives were staring, and Rick glared at the Lo-sat. "Don't try to read my scent for information. I won't tell you here. Not now."

Ten-trom's neck frills flared for a half second, as if he had something insulting or snarky to say, but whatever he had in mind stayed behind his snout. He took a deep sniff, smirked, and turned on his heel.

More people from the bridge entered, a mass of warriors and technicians ready to unshackle themselves from Collective tyranny. Rick found a spot where he could address them, on top of a staircase leading to a docked battledart. "This warhive is ours. This'll defend New Lodestone. Our first order of business will be to adjust the gravity so we don't have to walk around with our gravity harnesses dictating how we feel. We've been successful so far because surprise and underestimation by our enemy have been in our favor. We can't assume that'll happen again. The subadmiral's armor would've notified the fleet once he died. They'll know to come here. So they'll take negotiations seriously, or we'll be in for a hell of a fight. Either way, we have a planet to defend. We have prisoners to bargain with, and we have families on the surface. Let's get to work, Earthquake."

From his periphery, Rick caught sight of the warhive's docking bay widening. Someone must have rigged the hangar bay oxygen bubble to initiate. The semi-permeable barrier the color of quartz allowed oxygen to stay inside coated the bay hatch.

Sweat beaded on his neck.

It didn't make sense because there weren't any of his engineers or mechanics in the upper decks yet to make that call. Unless this ship had some other mechanism where someone could open that from this floor, he had someone aboard who hadn't surrendered.

Rick's heart raced. "Sabotage! Equalizer teams, charge the upper decks. We didn't get the whole crew. Expect armed resistance. The rest of you, stay here. Nobody else gets on the bridge."

Rick hopped off his platform and bolted toward the upper deck, Equalizer teams and shock troops behind him. Whoever had the bright idea to surprise Rick was in for some pain.

TWENTY-ONE

(INSPECTOR)

Hyperspace lane to the Collective frontier

THE WORST PART about the mindless flying through colorful hyperspace was the memories it brought on. As a cub, Inspector Bikkolos could relax and enjoy the colorful dazzle melting around him, but the end of his life loomed closer than cubhood. The display failed to amaze or distract.

Bikkolos longed to switch off the autopilot and guide his disk-ship, but he couldn't fool himself into thinking he had the reflexes for manual control during faster-than-light travel.

Despite his best intentions, the memories resurfaced. Always the same ones.

When his special forces unit learned they'd get the military's first Human, the whole squad was apprehensive. His dad was an Eleva War veteran but never saw Humans as lesser. His dad reasoned Humans had the gumption to fight the Collective; therefore, they were worthy of respect, despite losing. So for a young Bikkolos to have a Human in his squad who could be the descendant of someone on the other side of that conflict was more exciting than unnerving.

It made sense they'd put this Human in their unit, after all. They were a mixed group of Arkoudae and Lo-sats. The only thing Bikkolos wasn't excited for was learning Human anatomy to treat this guy if he ever got banged up.

Which he did.

Rick always went where the fighting was toughest. A Makawe rebel nearly snapped his spine, and a Blekk pirate came within a breath of strangling him. Bikkolos practically became an expert in those one-hearted anomalies because of him.

As the missions zoomed toward destruction, Bikkolos developed a growing suspicion they weren't the type of unit who was expected to survive. Casualties were kept at a minimum because of Rick, and despite what everyone thought, Rick rose in the ranks. He would've risen faster with fewer scrapes to show for it if he were Lo-sat or Arkouda. When their unit was sent to contain some pirates without close air support, Rick knew they were walking into a slaughter. They engaged a whole contingent of pirates. Outnumbered ten to one. Rick, Bikkolos, and two others—Zha and Kurna—made it out alive.

Bikkolos heard rumors Earthquake worked with Blekk pirates and Makawe rebels now, or at least intended to. He knew that was Rick, through and through. Rick respected his enemies the way Bikkolos' dad did.

After that mission, the four survivors got hammered; nothing left to do. Zha, a Lo-sat, cried into his bloodmead. Poor guy wanted to be a poet but couldn't find any work. He was devastated and wracked with survivor's guilt. Rick consoled him, but Kurna, the most hateful Arkouda Bikkolos had ever met, chastised Rick. The waste of fur said Rick shouldn't coddle the Lo-sat—the wannabe poet ought to feel guilty.

Rick glared at Kurna. "He deserves to express himself. The Collective tells us we're brothers-in-arms. He ought to feel something for our losses. Back off."

That was where he went wrong.

The *skata* stain challenged Rick to an arm-wrestling contest. Maybe it was because they were drunk, maybe it was because Rick was overconfident, but the poor sap agreed. Rick held his own, but Human strength couldn't match that of an Arkouda. Simple biology.

When Rick lost, he smirked as he nursed his arm. "That took you too long," he'd said. "You should have beaten me in seconds. I lasted a whole minute. That's embarrassing."

Bikkolos smiled, remembering that cocky sonofabitch. The smile faded to a grimace.

Kurna roared in Rick's face. He latched onto Rick's arm.

And pulled.

The wet snap of Rick's shoulder dislocating still haunted Bikkolos to this day. But that was nothing compared to what followed. The bully twisted and yanked until he lifted a leg and pushed off against Rick's chest.

Rick's arm detached completely.

In Bikkolos' memory, he was as stonily passive as someone watching a movie. His friend's arm was forcibly removed, and Bikkolos just stood there, frozen in place.

Each time this Goddess-forsaken memory resurfaced, Bikkolos blamed his inaction on something different. Sometimes, he was too drunk to do anything. It happened so fast in the moment, despite replaying in slow motion in his memories. Sometimes he convinced himself they were just messing around; the bully wouldn't actually incapacitate another member of their unit. In more optimistic times, Bikkolos told himself he believed the Collective would let him patch Rick up with a prosthetic, just like he had sewn stitches and iced his joints on earlier missions.

But on this replay, Inspector Bikkolos knew none of those excuses were valid. He chose cowardice. Having a Human friend was bad enough, but actually siding with one over an Arkouda was the worst kind of social heresy.

Bikkolos hadn't intervened until it was already too late. When the bully held the bloody stump that used to be Rick's arm, he actually laughed. Rick protested, then Kurna sneered and smacked Rick with the bloody end of his own arm. When bone connected to Rick's face, that was when Bikkolos intervened. All he did was stand and say, "I think he's had enough." He could have told this guy that the sleeping Goddess wouldn't approve, that this was more Nightmarish behavior. He could have reminded this guy of all of Rick's exemplary work and how his cunning and leadership got them out of more than one scrape. Honestly, Bikkolos should have threatened to do the same to him or arranged a court martial. Something. Anything.

Sure, he got Rick to an operating table to stop the bleeding. He'd treated Rick's other wounds. All the cuts earned inside a Blekk pirate ship were all the more painful and serious from the saltwater, but Bikkolos had come through and prevented infection back then. But this hadn't been like those other times.

He even filled out the paperwork to get Rick a prosthetic arm. But this hadn't been like the other medical documentation.

Bikkolos' paws clenched as he remembered holding the notice from the military high command. They wouldn't authorize Rick's prosthetic because it didn't happen in battle. It came from horseplay and roughhousing. As for the bully, nothing happened to him as far as Bikkolos knew. Not that he stuck around the military much longer after Rick left.

He had failed Rick on that day, but he refused to let himself fail any of the Human victims he had encountered since switching careers. Bikkolos couldn't make it up to Rick, but he had saved a few dozen Human lives. When he exited hyperspace, he'd try to save one more.

TWENTY-TWO

(JOKA)

Aboard the captured warhive Rick would probably rename, New Lodestone orbit, in Human independent space, apparently. Good luck with that.

ENTERING THE WARHIVE'S docking bridge remained simple. Doh-riss got side-eyed from the Earthquake chumps of course, either from racism or guessing at her personality. Keeping enough distance from that asshole Lo-sat worked since nobody outright said anything to them, and nobody was really scanning the crowd. A few people ogled Joka's flight suit under her mechanic's outfit, but most people preoccupied themselves with congratulatory whoops and hollers.

Once off the bridge and inside the warhive's loading hangar, docked battledarts greeted them. Joka wondered how they would fare in a dogfight against these goons. Within seconds of getting on the hangar with the others, she held Doh-riss back. A standoff unfolded between Rick the asshole and a subadmiral.

Fighting erupted quickly—cracks of gunshots and death screams muffled the splattering blood against the walls and floor.

"*Skata*, we gotta go," Joka said. "Cover me. I'll rig the hangar to open."

"Now?" Doh-riss asked then muttered, "*Have to* go."

"If we're lucky, they'll get distracted and look up to the engineering deck."

Joka didn't wait for a response. Using the noise and shock in the front of the docking bay for cover, she jogged toward the hangar bay oxygen bubble blast door. If the Collective model of warhive was similar to the patchwork of decommissioned Collective military tech comprising the Calamity station, there should be a panel she could cut into and force open.

Ten paces away from the crowd, seeing Doh-riss huff and approach, Joka faced the hangar bay door and increased her pace. A fizzing plasma shot came from behind her along with a series of gasps and screams.

Thud.

Another dead body today.

Joka shuddered but pressed forward. Nearing her target, she eyed the hexagonal panel about a half meter above where she expected it to be, which wasn't too bad if she said so herself.

Doh-riss caught up, then recoiled as if she sniffed a rancid egg fart. "That double-crossing scum licker is close."

Joka bit her lip. "Can you see him?"

"No. I'm hoping nobody nearby can see both of us."

"Whatever. Try to look relaxed. At least not more suspicious than that Binh asshole."

Joka unhinged the panel and set to work. The lattice of wires would never exist on the Calamity station, complicating Joka's task. She could work in chaos. But this organized business? Awful. She squinted at the matrices of circuit boards and found just the right panel to tickle with the thin wrench hiding in her mechanic jacket. After a few failed attempts and some unwelcome suggestions from Doh-riss, Joka hit the correct spot, and the hangar bay panel lit orange.

"Run," Joka whispered. They set off in different directions, taking cover behind docked battledarts. Soon after, the shut hangar bay doors groaned, slowly opening like a grand eye waking.

Commotion at the front of the hangar erupted. But many eyes and heads craned up to the third deck, where the engineering office overlooked the hangar. Lots of people were pointing up to it, and after some shouting, the one-armed asshole and a few other haircut assholes left to storm the top deck, clanking up the stairs. Hopefully there wasn't anybody up there, otherwise she had sentenced someone to death.

The battledart before her was a wider model meant for longer excursions away from a base or carrier. With any luck, it would carry enough fuel that they wouldn't need to refuel and run into another debacle like this *skata* show. She'd had enough of these Earthquake goons in one day to last a lifetime.

Joka beckoned Doh-riss over, but she shook her tail like there was a louse she wanted to scare to death. Was she really denying their ticket off this place and this Earthawful detour because it was the bigger model of batteldart? Joka huffed and ascended the ladder to the battledart anyway.

Doh-riss waved her arms and jumped on the balls of her feet, but Joka ignored her and climbed. After she reached the halfway point of the ladder, she caught Doh-riss scuttling toward her. Finally.

Joka piled into the cockpit, flipping the requisite switches and smacking the buttons needed for takeoff. "Hurry up," she spat. They had only a few seconds left before someone noticed and opened fire. She didn't want to consider what those harpoon cannons would do to the hull of a battledart based on how they performed against Collective armor.

An angry *dank-dank* of wide footsteps on the metal ladder followed, and Doh-riss piled in behind her, grumbling the whole time.

"This is a bad idea," Doh-riss said. "Will you—"

Joka closed the cockpit even though Doh-riss hadn't strapped in. They needed to leave this hangar. She would be fine. Doh-riss would be fine. No Humans in that hangar in the warhive could chase them, and those scrappers and cargo ships in the space elevator's hangar couldn't give proper chase.

"Buckle in, Riss," Joka said as she engaged the liftoff, and her flight suit read the ship's antigrav signals and contorted around her.

Finally, she'd get to put this new model through the wringer. She hadn't bumbled into any disasters in this new and updated version, which was an added bonus. All her screwups were in the older kind, which is where she intended to leave them.

Doh-riss grumbled more about how this wasn't the right thing to do, but the ship had already left the floor, floating toward the mauve oxygen bubble field.

"Ready to rock?"

"Can you wait until I'm strapped in?"

Doh-riss squirmed behind Joka, filling the cockpit space meant to accommodate an adult Arkouda, which allowed for them both to sit in the pilot's seat.

Joka initiated the hyperdrive sequence. "Fuel levels look good."

"I can't see into the back area of the fighter, Joka. I don't know what's back there." She took some nervous sniffs. "Will you please listen—"

Her whining was overpowered by the lurch of the ship into warp speed. Galactic colors danced around them like a collection of different paints swirled into each other. "I can't believe we got past those chumps," Joka said, sighing and relaxing her shoulders.

A different voice answered. "I wouldn't say that." She'd heard that voice before.

Doh-riss snarled. "You."

"Me," the buttery voice responded.

Joka whipped her head around.

Emerging from the back of the ship was the Lo-sat shitstain who worked for Earthquake. The scumbag who sold them out to other scumbags.

"Don't tell me you forgot my name, ladies," he pulled a cocky grin. "Mr. Ten-trom, at my service."

"That wasn't funny the first time, asshole. What're you doing?"

"Escaping Earthquake," he said, as if they could trust him and he was wounded they even asked.

Joka knew she couldn't actually reach to kick him in the snout but considered threatening it anyway.

Doh-riss hissed something at him in Lo-sat, then turned to Joka and switched languages. "He'll sell us out to them again."

The thief dropped his act and changed his tone. "Ladies, I get that you'd have some hesitations. You may recall I allegedly gave you over to Lefty so he could yoink that flight suit off you. See, I owe the mammals in Earthquake a fair bit of money." His eyeridges lowered, and he sighed. "I thought Lefty had some kind of honor. A noble prick. The kind of lowlife who convinced himself he wasn't a lowlife."

Joka sneered. "Give it to us straight, or I will fly us into a star."

"Threats have to be believable." Binh sighed, and the grin that made Joka want to strangle him faded. "The straight answer is Earthquake basically made me a slave. I'm not about that lifestyle. Once I sniffed you two sneak *onto* the warhive, I knew if you had the smarts to escape that cargo ship, you could sneak *out of* the warhive, too." He shrugged. "I needed a ticket out."

Joka folded her arms over her chest. "Boveeshit. How'd you know I'd pick this one?"

"I watched you eye it. This one was closer to the access panel."

Doh-riss huffed. "I *tried* to tell you not to take this one. It stank like him."

"Hold on," Joka said. "That doesn't explain why you put us on a cargo ship with the others instead of the separate room like your Commander—"

"Lefty."

Joka clenched her teeth. "I'm not calling him that."

Doh-riss snarled. "Stop trying to distract us. Answer her question."

Binh shrugged. "He was going to look for you, see you were gone, think you escaped. I'd find you again and bring you to him again in a less tense moment, so I could negotiate my release. Happy?"

"We can't trust a word you say," Joka said.

The thief shrugged. "You can't, but how's this for you? If I wanted you dead, I had my chance. If I wanted to sell you out to Tricky Ricky, I missed my chance when you flung us into hyperspace. That good enough?"

"You betrayed us already," Doh-riss hissed.

"I'll go with whoever I can to save my scales. That is reliable. Trust my self-preservation. Once you park wherever you're going, I'm gone. I ate this month so I won't touch your rations, and I won't touch the auto-pilot since you don't trust me." He gestured to the whirling colors around them. "So where are we going?"

"We're on a mission," Joka said, eyebrows lowered. "Which doesn't concern you."

"Well, no *nguc*. You two greaseballs really work for Symphora?"

Doh-riss flared her neck frills. "You don't deserve to say her name. And we aren't telling you."

"So that's a yes," Binh said, eyeridge cocked. "Hey, is it true that she once force-fed a rapist to a pedophile? She's into some sick *skata*. No wonder everyone's afraid of her."

Joka's smile snuck through. "That story gets passed around a lot. The best part is after the pedophile had to eat that creep, she tossed him into a nest of Galsan worms. It was legendary."

"Joka!" Doh-riss tutted. "Don't encourage him."

"What? I don't trust him, but there's not much we can do now."

Doh-riss whispered, "We can't take him on the mission, and we're not stopping."

Binh clutched the tip of his tail in his claws. "Ladies, I'm begging you. I was a debt slave. I was forced to do whatever Rick the Prick and his henchmen made me. Aren't you supposed to help people like me?"

Joka faced forward and called over her shoulder, "We'll do some actual work that would make Symphora proud. We didn't save you; you stowed away. If you want to earn your keep, you'll hand Doh-riss any communication devices you have."

"Ooh," Binh said in a mocking sultry voice. "Full cavity search on the charming rogue from the uptight chick. Sounds like the premise to a romantic comedy."

Doh-riss grumbled something in Lo-sat before switching languages. "Why can't you search him, Joka? He's disgusting."

As Joka opened her mouth to respond, Doh-riss waved a finger to silence her.

She craned her neck and sniffed deeply. "Joka, he has a gun."

"And I haven't threatened you with it," Binh said. "We're a happy crew of three now. You'll drop me off wherever you need to, and I'll be on my merry way. I'm assuming from your tone I won't be eligible for an autograph from Symphora."

"You assumed correctly," Joka deadpanned.

Binh leaned against the curved wall of the living quarters, tail dangling over the Arkouda-sized bunk. "So, a real mission for Symphora, but she's not going herself. Is she too old now? She's gotta be getting up there in years, based on the number of crazy legends and hearsay about the lady."

"Don't speak ill of Symphora," Doh-riss mumbled.

Binh ignored her. "No, that's not it. She'd send another badass Arkouda with an arsenal if this were her standard fare. No, this is something stealthy. Potentially a suicide mission. Been on those before. Those don't end pretty. This also has to be something only a small crew could handle." He paced the cramped living quarters in front of the refrigerator fit for an Arkouda.

Joka tsked. "You're delusional."

"So I did get something right," Binh said. "I'll figure it out. In the meantime, make one more threat so you feel better about yourself. It will also be good if you second guess everything your buddy says about our side conversations in our superior language." He switched languages from Arkouda to Human and smirked. "If it makes you feel better, we can have our own private conversation. She'll never know. It's so naughty."

Joka glared and responded in Human. "Fine. Come here, there's something I need to tell you."

A smile slithered through his snout. He leaned in close, and Joka snapped around, grabbing his neck. Over the sound of his gags, Joka switched languages. "Hey, Doh-riss. Grab his gun." She snarled at Binh, "You're going to shut up and sit down, or I'll club you with a wrench. We're heading to an asteroid field."

TWENTY-THREE

(RICK)

**Aboard the rechristened warhive *Salamis*,
docked on Shaka Space Elevator Station.
Orbit above New Lodestone, Boudica System,
Independent Human space**

A SABOTEUR PICKED the wrong day to test Rick. His first thought went to the thief. If Rick couldn't see Ten-trom, the bastard was concocting something. He'd even warned his crew about a double-cross. Teeth clenched, Rick wished he'd left Ten-trom to die on that damn moon where he found him. Keeping the Lo-sat around brought in good money but hadn't exactly slowed the racial epithets among his crew like he'd hoped.

A ping came from the surface. Rick should've ignored it to assess the situation and give his troops new orders.

[Amanda: I got more information on that lead—he's an Arkouda scientist. There's hard confirmation he's experimenting on Humans. Kick his tail and bring him to justice. I know where he is now.]

Shouldn't have looked—now he needed to know more. Without saying it, Amanda showed she was thinking a few steps ahead. If they had hard proof Collective scientists were experimenting on Humans, their recruitment would skyrocket and the average Citizen would sympathize with Humans more. They had time before the Fleet arrived to New Lodestone in force, and Amanda would handle things in his absence. Besides, New Lodestone was safe for now, and bringing a corrupt scientist to justice was the right thing to do.

As he pondered, another ping came from his mole in the monastery.

[Mole: I can't sit on this information much longer. It's been hours. Call me. I have something huge.]

Rick's breathing steadled. From the deserted engineering deck, he addressed his crew. "No use denying someone tricked us and stole a battledart. If it wasn't a rogue Arkouda prisoner, it was the Lo-sat." His words echoed across the too-big room. "No Human could pilot one of those." Except one, Rick knew. But now wasn't the time to share that information.

The crew's expressions ranged from pissed to confused.

"Bring our own engineers up here," Rick said. "Adjust the ship's antigrav to meet Human standard. It's time for the Arkoudae aboard to get a sense of what it's like to live chained to a grav harness. We don't have much time before the Collective retaliates with three more warhives barreling down on us. These next ones won't ask nice." He found the comms officer in the crowd that followed him. "Johnson, play a looping broadcast about our prisoners and our willingness to exchange. Make sure you use the formal construction when you phrase it."

Amanda's deputy hadn't joined him on the engineering deck. It was time to start assigning jobs and delegating so he could deal with these lingering issues. Rick turned to the engineering deck's main switchboard, scanning until he found their PA system.

After clearing his throat, he grabbed the comm unit and addressed the whole ship. "Earthquake, you know your skillset. Those who had the opportunity to get a basic education, raise your hands so your brothers in arms can see you. Good. Those of you who were never forced to learn to read Arkouda, find a buddy who can. Spread out through the warhive. Find what you can operate. If there's nothing you're comfortable operating, guard the prisoners. Every job is important, and remember that something designed for one Arkouda might take two of us—there's no shame in that. The Collective will strike back. Make us proud."

Rick assigned the nearest grunt to investigate the hangar while the rest scattered.

In the following minutes, the bustle was close to organized chaos as people navigated the warhive. They'd drilled schematics, blueprints, and layouts of the various 'hive designs and a few pirated orientation videos for new recruits, but actually traversing one was overwhelming for most of them. Rick hadn't set foot on one in years, and he fought on the wrong side of the conflict back then.

He met the still-mustering navigational team on the main bridge. Ramakrish and Curtin were both there, reading telemetry displays and delegating to the other recruits trickling in. Both women straightened when Rick entered. He was tempted to say "at ease" but decided against it. "How close are they?"

Ramakrish and Curtin eyed each other. Ramakrish took a sheepish step forward. "Sir, I hate to say that you're wrong, but—"

"I'll stop you right there," Rick said. "Always tell me when I'm wrong."

She regained some composure. "Commander, unless there's something wrong with the warhive's navigation or scanning systems, there aren't any other Collective ships heading our way."

Some phantom pains tingled in Rick's missing tricep. "What are the odds the ship is cut off from the Collective network?"

Curtin spoke. "That wouldn't affect navigation. In case the ship got blown too far off course or something."

Humans getting experimented on rattled in Rick's mind. He needed to save them. "So how long would we have before another warhive arrives?"

"A few days," Ramakrish said. "This sector never got hit by pirates, so this ship was all they had out on patrol."

Rick radioed to the engineering deck. "Zhou, figure out how to cut us off from the Collective network after we broadcast our demands one more time."

Those on the bridge shot Rick confused looks.

Rick turned to address them. "We'll assemble an expeditionary fleet. We have some targets we need to expose elsewhere in the galaxy."

Ramakrish raised her hand. "Would that leave New Lodestone undefended?"

"We'll take the modified scrappers. They can defeat a warhive as long as the planet's magneto-sphere amplifies their strength. The Collective isn't moving against us right now. They're ignoring us, or they're developing a new way to fight us. I can only make so many assumptions, so we'll assume they're planning a way to take us out."

Worried mumbles rose up, which Rick silenced with a gesture.

"We'll let them chase us on our next mission." A few minutes ago, he thought he'd need to choose between defending his conquest, following the mole's lead, or following Amanda's. The winds of war had finally turned in Humanity's favor because Rick now understood he could do all three at the same time. In the few days he had before any official retaliation, he needed more warhives.

Rick hailed comms officer Johnson. "Establish a connection with the Leader."

TWENTY-FOUR

(NED)

**On a research station in
{LOCATION CLASSIFIED}**

NED PULLED HIS wife to his side, supporting her between sobs. "We can leave soon. Once we get our opening—"

The *whirr-hiss* of their son's torture chamber cut Ned off. Even behind a partition, it creaked loud enough to snap their attention. Mui-xe collapsed to the floor, heaving. The boy hadn't ignited since the trial a few weeks ago when he overcame Dr. Diastrevlo's poisonous gas experiment. But the torture only worsened in the following days. The mad scientist needed to replicate his results, after all.

Rage pumped through Ned's veins as he sprinted to his son, the blinking lights of their laboratory practically an illuminated runway. He and La-hok wrapped their wonderful boy in their arms, blanketing him in their apologetic embrace.

Ned whispered, "This was the last time. We leave today."

La-hok lowered her eyeridges and whispered in her language to their son. "What Father means is we'll attempt to leave today. We hope we'll succeed, but we can't promise."

Mui-xe croak-huffed, averting eye contact. "We've tried so many times. You can't get us out of here."

Ned shook his head, eyes steely. "I can. I will. I'm saving my family." He tapped a button on his wrist and let the image inducer do its work, creating a holographic field around them. "Dr. Diastrevlo knows how long we take to console you after you're hurt, Mui-xe. We're moving now so he won't know. Let me and Mom help you to the door." Even though he was only a year or so from hitting puberty by Human standards, the boy seemed so old. So much of a childhood had been stolen from him. He never got to teach him how to play hiveball.

The trio inched toward freedom, and Ned's spirits soared. He saw the image left behind of the parents consoling a crying child. The scene had played out dozens of times in that very spot, easily replicated. All he had to do now was leave while the scientist was distracted. Freedom loomed inches away.

Maybe he would get to show his son how to toss the hiveball around.

Except the door already gaped open.

Ned blinked hard. The feet of Dr. Diastrevlo appeared before him.

After a series of sharp sniffs, the doctor spoke in his icy monotone. "Stand up now."

Ned glanced over his shoulder in abject horror. The projected image of their family didn't react. Of course it didn't. Ned wasn't a sorcerer.

Diastrevlo adjusted and sniffed the air again. "You neglected one layer of illusion, Porandi." The Arkouda lifted his foot and swung it forward.

Ned's vision darkened as the skin around his septum ripped off. He careened backward, reaching for Mui-xe as he fell. Dizzy, eyes watering, face throbbing, Ned collected himself, realizing he strayed outside the image projection.

The bastard could smell them. Ned cursed his negligence. Too short-sighted. Too desperate to rush production.

La-hok's olfactories were fried by the months of Diastrevlo's sanitizing chemicals—they never thought to test for scent in their trials. Ned winced, desperate to stand, but his bones and tendons forgot how to coordinate. In full view of Dr. Diastrevlo, Ned scrambled to his feet as the scientist kicked again, this time hitting La-hok.

Like Ned before her, La-hok took the brunt of the blow and slid against the metal floor, using her claws to slow her trajectory.

Mui-xe crawled forward, huffing.

Dr. Diastrevlo approached La-hok with the casual indifference of someone grabbing dropped paper. He raised his foot for another stomp, but she wrapped her tail around his ankle and yanked.

She lacked the strength to trip him. Rather, she jerked herself forward, sailing into his shin. He flailed his foot to get her to unravel and hit the wall.

Ned scrambled and charged the doctor. "Mui-xe, run!"

It didn't matter that the Arkouda had a meter on him. This hateful tower of fur hurt Ned's child and wife. Ned's time in the lab had softened him, but he remembered how to scrap from his days in the factory with the other kids. He could fight like he was a hungry animal.

Diastrevlo had preyed on his family for too long. Ned would rip out his eyeballs and feed them to him in a way that would make even Symphora proud.

The doctor faced Ned, readying another strike.

But Ned banked left and adjusted his image inducer. He used it as an intense light beam and directed it at Diastrevlo's eyes, making him recoil. The twisted Arkouda must have assumed he could slap Ned around like a rag doll again. No more.

Ned bolted over to La-hok, then hoisted her to sit as Diastrevlo rubbed his eyes. He made eye contact with Mui-xe, shaking on the floor. His son stared at him, slack-jawed.

"Dad!" He held out a limp arm, pointing behind Ned.

Dr. Diastrevlo had recovered and backpawed Ned with enough force to turn his face and spin his shoulders. La-hok slipped from his grip.

With a snarl, Dr. Diastrevlo extended his claws, slashing down at Ned's thigh.

Ned's vision went fuzzy again. He was about to lose a lot of blood.

La-hok pounced on the Arkouda, neck frills extended. Like a badass warrior out of Lo-sat mythology, she swiped at his face with her claws, but he grabbed her wrist and slammed her to the floor with a thud. As she gasped, Dr. Diastrevlo used his free paw to reach into his lab coat and unholster a pistol.

Ned's eyes widened and heart froze. "No!"

Grimacing, Dr. Diastrevlo shot La-hok in the stomach once.

He sprinted, yet his legs could not move fast enough. The world slowed down around him as the monster murdered his beloved.

Twice in her thighs.

Mui-xe wailed, but that didn't stop Diastrevlo. He shot her again in the base of her tail. All her flailing stopped. She would be alive for a few more minutes, but he had paralyzed her with the shot to her spine. Lime plasma smoke rose from the bullet holes.

"Damn you—" Ned hissed. Sweat and blood ran together on his face, stinging his eyes. He'd wring his neck if it took the last ounce of his life from him.

Dr. Diastrevlo raised his pistol again, this time pointing at Ned.

"Your image inducer is promising but requires work. Perhaps you could have earned a doctorate, given the chance. You must find an olfactory baffler for it to fool an Arkouda. Or an *intelligent* Lo-sat. One who isn't so blinded by her hormones."

He fired. The plasma bullet ripped into the side of Ned's neck. Searing plasma cauterized his skin as it streaked across his body. Every cell in his body tingled in revulsion from the pain, and the sulfurous odor of burnt hair snaked into Ned's nostrils.

It didn't matter that this would kill him. He just had to take Diastrevlo down with him.

Ned wailed—his vision blurred as his once aflame body numbed. He was paralyzed now, too. His nerves were dead. It was only a matter of time until he was, too, from the blood loss. He knew too much anatomy to pretend otherwise.

Through stammers, Ned let out one last shout. "We love you, s-son. We-we're s-sorry."

As the room spun around him, Ned's vision turned red. This pristine emotionless scientist had made a bloody massacre of a mess in this sterile lab and walked away. His ears rang with such intensity he could barely think.

He needed to reach for his son, his wife. Needed their touch one last time. Needed to tell his son to defend himself and apologize he couldn't show him how to play hiveball. But his finger wouldn't even twitch to life. Instead of spending his last moments with his family, some mindless bot would vacuum his blood and grind his bones into powder like a failed lab rodent.

Death felt warmer than he would have guessed.

Hot, almost. Maybe the Abrahamist religion was right, after all. Maybe he'd transgressed on some divine proclamation. Too bad he couldn't tell Maynard.

Some feeling returned to Ned's fingertips. Maybe this was the beginning of reincarnation, and Maynard's Great Mystery religion was right instead.

Enough feeling returned to form a fist. He dared to move an arm. His vision clarified, and the ringing in his ears quieted. Crouched over him was Mui-xe, tears gently falling from his mottled face. "Stay still, Dad," the boy whispered.

"Mui-xe?"

Ned's legs and spine regained sensation. Squelching slurps signaled the gash in his thigh closing. Ned sat straight, watching his son.

Mui-xe's hands were splayed out over Ned's torso. They glowed like they had when he ignited in the chamber, yet this wasn't a burning heat. It soothed, like some kind of massage therapy Ned could have never afforded.

"How are you doing this?" Ned asked.

Mui-xe stayed focused on Ned's torso. "I have to do this for myself each time." His voice didn't sound like the innocent kid who wanted to hear another story.

Ned's head snapped to the left where La-hok lay in a heaving pile of scales and mangled tail. "Please, take care of her. I'll be fine." Some part of him wished he could scream at his son for choosing him.

Diastrevlo loomed over them, head tilted. He muttered a "Hm" as if he were counting speckled avian eggs.

The glow faded from Mui-xe's hands, and he cast an innocent look at Ned. "You were dying. I'm sorry."

Ned wrapped him in a tight hug, sensation flooding his arms. "You don't have anything to be sorry about. Let's go to your mom." Standing on his new thigh made him feel like a hill-dwelling hoofbeast standing for the first time, but he did it.

He walked.

No occupational or physical therapy like after surgery. Full recovery. His eyes widened as he examined his hands. He felt strong.

As the boy moved away from Ned, he realized the experiments had never been on Mui-xe, but on Ned and La-hok. The determined fury raging through the boy suggested he understood that reality now as well.

"Ss-stay away from my p-pparentss!" Mui-xe's hands shifted to a deep crimson. The temperature raised enough for sweat to bead on Ned's neck. Mui-xe stomped toward the partition, raising his glowing hands.

From the other side of the partition, Diastrevlo jotted something on a notepad. Mui-xe raised a shaking hand toward the beast, then glanced over his shoulder. Ned watched the murder in his son's eyes melt as he gazed upon his mother.

The crimson faded from his hands, and the temperature decreased as Mui-xe trudged over and knelt over La-hok, and Ned lifted and cradled her head. She cast a tired, bleary eye at him.

"Shh," he cooed. "Our son is here."

Mui-xe's hands glowed, this time iridescent.

Ned glanced up at the partition. The mad scientist was there with his notepad, still observing. A few crimson dots lined one of his paws. Ned's blood.

This had been another experiment. At the realization, Ned swatched his son again, healing La-hok. Sensation returned to her tail as she stretched it anew.

Their son was given the choice of revenge or love, and he chose love.

Diastrevlo hadn't broken him. Ned and La-hok had succeeded.

A grim realization stirred in Ned's gut like he'd swallowed a razor. Dr. Diastrevlo knew about the image inducer. Ned hadn't tricked him at all. The doctor probably even broke the encryption on Ned's supposedly secret messaging system. Dr. Diastrevlo knew about La-hok's mom and Ned's brother. Nowhere in the galaxy was safe for them. They had no means of escape.

Where Ned and La-hok thought they were creative and sneaky, engineering their escape and saving their son, they had merely been furnishing Diastrevlo with free research. They'd offended the galactic order by creating a hybrid, and this was their cosmic punishment.

Dr. Diastrevlo would kill Ned in his next experiment. He already knew about the image inducer, which was the only thing Ned could have done that Diastrevlo couldn't. If he told Ned what he was missing in the design, he already had some grander countermeasure prepared. Until Diastrevlo cracked the secrets of Mui-xe's genetic code, he would keep La-hok alive. That was some consolation, even though Ned was doomed. If Mui-xe could resuscitate Ned, that wouldn't erase the trauma of watching his father die. Diastrevlo would keep killing Ned in different ways and would eventually prevent Mui-xe from resurrecting him for periods of time to see the extent of his powers.

Ned would die over and over again. For science. Advancing the Collective and whatever dark agenda

Diastrevlo had. He'd be the one tortured instead of his son, and he hadn't known relief like this in years.

Teeth clenched, he knew there had to be another way. He would find it.

TWENTY-FIVE

(JOKΛ)

**Aboard the battledart rechristened
Binhsux, approaching an asteroid belt
in the Collective frontier**

DOH-RISS ARCHED AN eyeridge at Joka. "Why name the ship something I can't pronounce?"

Joka groaned. "You won't even say 'sucks'? What's your problem?"

She lowered her voice and furrowed her eyeridges. "Foul language reminds me of my time before Symphora saved me. And that wasn't what I was talking about."

"Wait, you mean can't say Binh's name?" Joka asked.

"Ladies," Binh shouted. "Check out the stars outside. Pretty, right?"

Doh-riss craned to scrutinize Binh. "You didn't tell her your Lo-sat name?"

Joka glared. "Is that why you talk to us in different languages?"

Scratching behind his neck frills, Binh forced out a chuckle. "You got me there, Strangle Girl. Humans can't pronounce my Lo-sat name. You need to fold your tongue on itself. Nobody could say it the right way and most wouldn't bother trying. 'Binh' is easier for mammals. In my line of work, having aliases never hurts."

Joka wheeled on Doh-riss. "What have you been calling him?"

"Scumbag," she said.

"I like Scumbag better," Joka replied.

———

Days of warp-speed travel in a cramped battledart had confirmed a few things. Neither of Joka's companions could shut up. All of them wished the others would shut up. These were established as facts. Also established: Binh sucks.

For as much as Binh could be trusted, he filled in the gaps of their knowledge about Earthquake. Human separatist terrorists seeking independence from the Collective. Commander Rick Crith was a big deal but not the head. If Joka had lived a normal life on a Human settlement, she would've learned about this Crith guy. Whenever his name came up on news vids aboard the Calamity, the Humans would moan about how they needed to show him shirtless, and then somebody would groan and turn the news to a hiveball match.

Binh skirted around how he and Rick met, as if concealing some memory he didn't wish to revisit.

The more Binh described him, the more Joka thought this Tecton leader guy sounded like a war profiteer working with both sides. He sounded like the scum Symphora would snap in half.

Other commanders besides Rick sounded gruesome. Torturers and drug traffickers.

Binh estimated these Earthquake people, minus Rick himself and one of his staffers, were all hyper-xenophobic and would rather see Humans on top, dominating the Collective as opposed to existing as an independent neighbor or being elevated to Citizenship.

"So how did he lose his arm?" Doh-riss asked.

"Gross how Humans can't grow back appendages, right?" Binh asked. "Tail-less freaks."

Joka harrumphed. "We have tails; they're inside our body."

"Sounds useful," Binh said. "So to answer your question, Super Prude, rumors are floating about how Both-y became Left-y, but the tightass won't let anyone discuss it in front of him or confirm anything. He does keep his dishonorable discharge and the rejection letter from the medics like they're trophies."

Joka tried speaking their language. "Time. For. You. Up. Shut." Her smirk faded with the subsequent gagging from poor pronunciation.

Doh-riss tutted and corrected her vocabulary.

"Bet that hurt your tongue, Jokels. Go ahead and cough up a lung while you recover. *Jat-je* over there won't watch because she respects your dignity."

She had no clue what horrible name he called Doh-riss, but she inferred plenty from Doh-riss' flared neck frills. Joka had her rebuttal ready, but a chime interrupted them. They were leaving hyperspace soon. Joka's flight suit whistled, and it constricted around her limbs in anticipation of the incoming gravitational loop-de-loop they'd endure. The Lo-sats' cold blood and better-adapted nervous system would spare them from these issues. She envied them for a split second but brushed it off since she was still the badass inventor who made this flight suit, which was in the process of saving her life.

The menagerie of whirling colors slowed and solidified back to the smoky purples of galactic clouds and sharp whites of vibrant stars.

"We're here," Joka said.

Binh snorted. "If I knew where we were or what we were doing, I could help."

"Or betray us," Doh-riss snapped.

"Fair."

Joka pulled up the specs on this asteroid belt. This was on the fringe of Collective space, but these asteroids weren't named. She cocked an eyebrow. "Do either of you think this was cut off from the Collective fleet's network and that's why nothing is coming up for these asteroids?"

"You were sent on a wild puddlefowl chase," Binh tsked. "Symphora must be getting senile."

"No," Doh-riss said. "This is a real mission. Maybe these asteroids' names are blocked because they're supposed to be hidden?"

Joka's eyes widened. "So the battledart is still connected to the Fleet's network. They could find us. We're screwed unless either of you have electrical engineering skills you've been hiding."

"If there's anyone who wants to stay hidden on one of these rocks," Binh said, "they know you're coming by now."

One of the nearest asteroids, only a few meters smaller than the battledart, rotated toward them.

"The other asteroids are rotating the other direction," Joka muttered.

"It's not an asteroid!" Doh-riss shouted.

"Shitty fuck fuck shit piss—" Joka scrambled to remove the autopilot as the false asteroid rotated enough to reveal a glowing turret.

Binh snarled. "I know that model. Bank left."

Joka didn't have time to second guess the shit-wad's self-preservation instincts, so she snapped into manual pilot and swerved left. Her insides remained intact, and the force didn't concuss her. In her head, she gave herself a point. The flight suit saved her life again.

"Dohey, can you handle the weapons system?" Joka asked.

"Yes, if—"

"I know," Joka sighed, leaning in the swerve's direction. "I'll stop clipping my toenails on your side of the bunk."

"No you won't. If I destroy the turret, that might alert more false asteroids about our direction."

"Little late for that, Sugar Snout." Binh pointed above them in the cockpit, indicating three more false asteroids careening toward them.

"Well hot *skata*," Joka said. "This'll make for a fun ride. Dohey, just fire at everything."

The inflection of Doh-riss' grunt suggested she didn't like this new nickname.

"Scumbag, operate the telemetry. See if you can calculate the asteroids' trajectory and maybe we can figure out where they're coming from."

Joka banked left again, barreling away from their fire. One blast clipped their wing, rocking the ship. Eyeing their position closing in on her and paying attention to their fire rate before the reload, she kicked the drive forward, threading the space between them. The twin asteroid turrets fired at each other, and they both broke in crumbled debris.

Two remaining.

Joka spun the battledart toward the one on their left, and Doh-riss shot a round of plasma fire.

At the brilliant green light from the plasma, a sharp memory rose of when Joka had let loose a barrage of plasma fire from the old battledart, unknowingly killing Collective soldiers.

But she didn't deserve all the hate. Doh-riss didn't either. Joka refused to screw up again.

She pushed the thought from her mind once she realized she hadn't flown at the right angle for Doh-riss to align a good shot. Doh-riss deserved a better friend than she was.

"Let's try again," Joka said.

"Another shooty-rock inbound," Binh said. "I think I figured out the launch pad's location."

Doh-riss cheered, flaring out her neck frills to the point where they poked Joka's head. "I got one! Good flying."

"Good shootin'," Joka said.

Binh hissed. "Won't matter if another angry mineral hits us."

Joka spun the ship around, and Doh-riss took the cue. She fired another round of plasma bolts, which connected to the final asteroid turret. While disintegrating, the turret fired one last shot, which grazed the cockpit. It left a burning streak in the duraglass. One millimeter closer, and it would have opened a hole.

Joka sighed. "Let's hear that trajectory path. Time to land and see where these things are coming from. Must be the mad scientist we're hunting."

"Head left," Binh said. "But do it without hurtling us like you're playing a video game you suck at."

"We weren't supposed to play video games on the Calamity," Doh-riss muttered.

"Maybe Symphora is a heartless monster. A life without Block Bash isn't one worth living," Binh said, as if anyone cared.

Doh-riss' tone soured. "You have no idea what it's like to live a hopeless life."

Joka needed to change the conversation; she'd heard rumors about the life Symphora saved Doh-riss from and didn't want Binh getting a whiff of them. "I'm getting weird signals from the smoother asteroid up there." She pushed the battledart on course.

Two asteroids rotated into view, the smaller one on the left and a significantly larger one on the right.

"You're sure it's not the big one?" Doh-riss asked. "Look, there's an oxygen generator on it. That could support a small settlement."

"The turrets came from the small one," Binh said.

Joka shrugged. "There's got to be one last decoy. The bigger one is probably where he wants us to look."

Doh-riss fixated on the larger asteroid. "Fine, but I'm telling you, something is on that bigger rock. It can't just be a decoy."

Joka initiated the landing sequence. As the asteroid rotated more, she spied a landing pad on it. On closer inspection, she realized the two asteroids rotated at the same rate. She squinted. "Well butter my ass and call me Marka," Joka whispered.

"No thank-you." Doh-riss gasped. "They're connected."

"The thought of buttering Pokey Jokey's ass made me—"

"Shut up or say something useful," Joka said.

Binh exhaled. "Fine. That's definitely a connecting bridge. Carbon nanotubes, black so you can't see it too well from the outside."

Joka's heart rate skyrocketed. "Let's check this place out. Binh, did you see any small guns back in the living quarters when you raided it for valuables?"

"I did no such thing."

Doh-riss sniffed. "He took a credit chit." Two more sniffs. "From between the cot cushions."

"Fine," Binh said. "I did some rummaging. Not like the owner is coming back any time soon. There was also a piece of forgotten hoofbeast jerky in there, but I didn't hear you mention that."

Joka scowled. "Guns, assface. Did you find guns?"

"No," Binh said. "All I have is my sidearm. It's a stolen Collective military pistol, not the slipshod homemade stuff Earthquake makes."

Doh-riss sniffed again. "I can only smell one gun in here, and it stinks like him."

Joka clicked her tongue. "What are the odds those asteroid turrets were the only security?"

"About as high as either of you getting a date," Binh said.

Joka elbowed him in the snout, which was more satisfying than it should have been. "Sorry, just finalizing the landing gear. Dumb Human mistake."

Doh-riss chimed in. "Before you say her parents' copulation was a dumb Human mistake, you should think twice about what Symphora will do to you if you double-cross us."

Massaging his snout, Binh muttered, "I'm sure Symphora would mutilate me in ways a serial killer would find disturbing."

"Or we will," Joka said. She checked the ship's status. That clipped wing would need more than what a simple autorepair matrix could handle. They wouldn't be able to scratch lightspeed. Joka closed the notification—this wasn't the time to tell them.

TWENTY-SIX

(RICK)

**Aboard an unmarked civilian cargo ship.
Orbit of Palaios planet, Uperaygos System,
Collective space**

CONFIRMATION CAME TO Rick ahead of schedule. Blekk pirates hid a detachment of raider ships near New Lodestone, ready to flank and pounce on any surprise attacks from the Collective fleet against his base.

If successful, this mission would result in another warhive or two. If it didn't, he'd need to find another soft target for the Blekk pirates to hit since their patience only extended so far. Rival Blekker factions all liked Rick for eliminating the self-proclaimed "pirate king" during the business with the archaeologist and Ten-trom, but they didn't yearn for living in a society the way Humans did. Their goals only aligned for the moment.

Getting Makawe rebels' assistance was another matter entirely. Monsieur Tecton forbade it, of course, but Rick was gaining clout. He had these victories behind him. The only leverage the other commanders had on Rick was higher body counts on missions. Slaughter did not equal success.

Rawltz interrupted Rick's plotting. "Sir? We only have a few minutes before that patrol will notice us."

Rick observed his strike crew, polishing their Equalizer guns and fitting their patchwork armor over their chests.

The women from Symphora's gang arose in his mind. They must've been part of whatever double-cross Ten-trom prepared. If the thief knew what was good for him, he would've told the women to run back to Symphora and stay the hell out of Rick's way.

Even if Rick couldn't snag that flight suit prototype, he knew it worked and what it looked like. That would be enough for some of his more clever engineers, at least as a starting point.

For a brief second, Rick considered inviting Symphora and her gang to join in Rick's growing coalition. If the legends about her were true, she couldn't be happy with how the Collective treated its lowest members. He clenched his fist, knowing why she wouldn't help. Unsubstantiated rumors circulated that some of the other leaders in Earthquake had deals with drug dealers and manufacturers. Tecton denied it, of course, and Rick couldn't verify without diverting resources from more important projects.

But knowing the wild stories of what Symphora did to drug dealers was enough to give him pause.

If he could replace Tecton, that wouldn't be a concern.

He unclenched and huffed a tight sigh. This wasn't the time for any ambitious ladder scrambling. Enough eyes were on him now—he couldn't delay his orders any longer.

"As some of you know, I led a team that hit an archaeological dig site on Palaios in the recent past. Since then, the Collective fleet has kept a small force in orbit, just in case we would try hitting here again."

A few of the crew peered into the hull's viewscreen, observing the pink-hued rock below them. Two lone dots hovered above it. Warhives.

"They won't expect us to attack them without the warhive we captured."

Rawltz fidgeted.

"Speak," Rick commanded.

"How do you know?"

"They're haughty and conceited. They're telling themselves our success over New Lodestone was an isolated freak stroke of luck. They're assuming future attacks will be with their weapons and ships."

An Equalizer striker piped up. "Wasn't that the whole point?"

Rick shook his head. "We can win without their stuff. We know that and proved it over New Lodestone. We need to show them and the galaxy we can beat them. Our small flotilla of scrappers and cargos won't register as threats. They'll regret that."

Rawltz raised his hand. "So are we giving them the option of surrender? We don't have enough cargo space to transport two warhives' worth of prisoners anywhere."

"Today's casualties..." Rick forced steel into his expression. "Today will be a bloody day. Palaios has a network of observational satellites orbiting the planet for archaeological research. We'll use those in our attack. There are no population centers, so we don't have to worry about collateral damage like we did over New Lodestone. We'll destroy one warhive and commandeer the other. The survivors will be stripped of their armor and weapons and left with our message."

"Easier to kill them," one of the recruits said, which garnered some chuckles.

"It would be," Rick said. "We do what's strategically advantageous, not what's simple. Collective propaganda can't spin the narrative if there are dozens of naked soldiers sharing the same story. If we just killed them, they could claim it was a reactor accident or something. We won't give them that chance." Rick gave a definitive nod to signal he'd finished and motioned for Rawltz to toss over the communications device.

Rick radioed the other ships. "Everyone in position?"

The ten scrapper pilots all rang in with affirmatives and call signs.

When they were in position, near enough the planet's orbit to see the outline of continents, one warhive transmitted a public broadcast.

"Unidentified civilian vessels: this is not an authorized travel area. Return to your—"

"Now," Rick barked into the comm.

Outside, four scrappers formed a square, then shot magnetic beams at nearby satellites and flung them at the warhives' bulbous protrusions at opposite corners—communications arrays. The satellites careened toward the Collective ships.

A garbled Arkouda voice came over the comm, which melted into static.

Rick grinned. "Good. Now they can't cry for backup. Initiate phase two. Remember, we don't have the luxury of a super strong magnetosphere."

He was a predator, and the realization as he enclosed his prey made him warm.

The closer warhive on their right ignited side thrusters, engaging in a sharp turn toward them.

"Expect battledarts from the turning one," Rick said. "Thirty seconds before the other closes in and does the same. Montoya, get the empty cargo ship in position. Drone operators, get ready."

More affirmatives came as a detachment of fifteen battledarts poured out.

"That's more than expected. Scrappers, you might take some fire, but trust in your hulls. Proceed."

The empty cargo transport moved in front of Rick's ship and opened its hull, letting chunks of asteroids and jagged boulders of scrap metal float out into the zero gravity space.

"Not yet." Sweat beaded on his neck. The second warhive was close enough now to start rotating. He had another five seconds before its battledarts would scramble out.

In Earth's true prehistory, hunters banded together to take down creatures larger than their homes.

One.

The mammoth prey stood before him.

Two.

And Rick was the lead hunter.

"Now!"

At Rick's command, the asteroid chunks and heaps of scrap metal spun to life and hurtled toward the approaching battledarts. "Call out your targets."

The drone operators sounded off, announcing which fighter they'd strike. After the first two hit with precision accuracy, the battledarts shifted formation and opened fire on the scrappers.

A hushed gasp ran through the recruits in Rick's ship. This was earlier than anticipated. They would lose at least one of their pilots.

"Scrappers, don't let the drone operators do all the work. Turn on those magnetic beams and do as we drilled."

The scrappers ignited their indigo magnetic beams. Three caught battledarts whose pilots made the mistake of flying straight. Two snagged bobbing satellites and hurtled them at oncoming ships.

Ten remained.

The next wave of battledarts should have joined, but nothing came up in Rick's periphery, and the navigator was silent.

Maybe they were adapting faster than anticipated.

"They have something up their flexweave. Scrappers, work together to cast a net and toss all the 'darts at the nearer warhive. Aim for the bridge if possible."

The pilots managed to trap eight of them. This was the part where the drones would pick them off for the sake of symbolic spectacle, but he didn't have much time. Once trapped in the net, the battledarts struggled against the magnetic force, likely frying their internal systems along the way.

"Full power on the repulse! Let's take down that 'hive!"

The scrappers flung the eight trapped battledarts toward their carrier ship. As they hurtled forward, the remaining two battledarts careened toward Rick's cargo ship.

They would be in range for opening fire soon.

Panicked murmurs filled the hull.

"We planned for this. Drone operators, hit these last two."

The drones weren't fast enough. The first battledart opened fire on the cargo ship, denting the hull. The viewscreen clicked off.

"Shit," Rick muttered. He turned to his navigator seated at the helm. "Borson, can you still see what's happening?"

"Y-yes," she stammered. "I think that hit only got the viewscreen port."

"Damn." Rick wedged himself over her shoulder. On the less elegant heads-up display, he caught the blinking light of the two rogue battledarts caught by the drones. "Can you tell how much damage was done to the first 'hive?"

"We didn't destroy it," she said. "Looks like they're both prepping their main cannons for firing."

Rick barked into the comm. "Scrappers, get every last satellite in your beams and pelt the warhive as much as possible. Don't worry about the second one. We'll handle that."

"Soyen, get us to the other warhive." He flicked the comm device back on and double-checked he was on the Earthquake-only channel. "I'm going to fake surrender. Our Equalizer teams will make short work of the soldiers inside. Scrappers, all ten of you together won't have enough power to destroy the other warhive if things go south. If we fail, scatter and regroup on New Lodestone. My second in command is Amanda Martinez. She'll take care of you."

He flipped off the radio and addressed his crew. "Who's ready to kick some tail?"

The nearer warhive's main turret glowed crimson on the navigational screen. Rick parked in front of the tiny porthole, the "actual" window of the ship and a poor excuse for the viewscreen.

The opposing ship unleashed its cannonade at the scrappers. One pilot shot a magnetic beam at a nearby satellite, pulling it in front of her ship to absorb the impact. Rick smiled at the cute trick, but there were only so many satellites on the near side of the planet, and they were running out of time.

From the porthole, he watched the turret illuminate turquoise and launch streaking plasma cannon fire, hitting the scrapper with a red zigzag paint job. It was gone instantly.

At least it was painless. *Kayla Jefferson.*

Behind him, a recruit shouted "No!" as shrapnel scurried from the blast. Rick recognized the tone, not the voice. One of his recruits had not watched a sister-in-arms die, but a sister.

Rick strained for a moment to remember Jefferson's faith. *May you accept the Great Mystery's embrace into the next life.* Rick spun away from the porthole and grabbed the comm device. "Scrappers, use the empty cargo ship as a weapon if you need to. We have others. See if you can at least mess with the turret's aim with your mag fields. Drone pilots, if there are any left, dive into the bridge on that 'hive."

Rick switched the channel to the public broadcast. As he prepared his false surrender, his eyes widened. They had disabled the communications array on both of these warhives. They wouldn't get his message. The individual battledarts would, however.

"Soyen, flip the ship upside-down and continue our path toward them."

The pilot shot Rick a quizzical look but complied. The ship's antigrav kept everyone in place as he completed the maneuver.

Behind Rick, a recruit muttered about one of the other Earthquake commanders being unable to pull off this exact maneuver. That other commander had a much higher kill count than Rick and was favored by Tecton for it.

Instead of turning around to thank the recruit, Rick addressed the pilot again. "Good, now wiggle the back end left to right."

"Sir?"

"Cargo ships resemble Arkouda cubs. Upside down ass wiggling is how they surrender in wrestling matches. If nothing else, it'll confuse and distract them for a second."

They were close enough now to see into the war-hive's oxygen bubble from the porthole. They had battledarts at the ready, and since they were now too close for the turret to aim at them, Rick tried one more gamble.

Radio comm on the public channel, Rick spoke in Arkouda. "If you can hear us from your battledarts, we offer our full surrender. Our leader was in the ship you destroyed."

A youngish-sounding Arkouda responded on the other end. "Uh, I can't authorize a surrender. I think. Um, can you stop approaching and let me give my helmet to my commander?"

"We'll wait." Rick lowered the comm device and stared through the porthole. The scrappers attempted to fan out. In the time it had taken Rick's ship to get to this position, another scrapper had been blasted into oblivion. He couldn't tell who the pilot was from his vantage point, but he'd be damned if he didn't learn later so he could give them a proper memorial and inform their family their child died a hero.

Once the scrappers were staggered enough, they concentrated their magnetic beams onto the shimmering turret. The coordinated scrappers yanked their translucent indigo beams, but the turret didn't budge. Rather, it prepared another shot, aiming at the center scrapper. As the turret's tip ignited, the scrappers' beams shifted colors, repulsing the turret so it faced the warhive's command bridge, and the hulking warship fired its most powerful weapon on itself.

The flash of destruction arced like a peaceful rainbow into death and shrapnel.

He'd need to learn the ship's name and procure a copy of the manifest. He'd never had so many Arkoudae killed at once. Knowing each death inched the conflict toward its end mitigated the burden on his shoulders.

The cheers inside his cargo ship drowned out his thoughts. Rick shielded his eyes against the explosion's blinding turquoise light, but pulled his hand down and squinted, desperate to see if his brave pilots survived the explosion. Before he could tell, the comm device chirped.

"We accept your surrender. Please come aboard. Any weapons will be confiscated." It wasn't the same rookie pilot who'd answered. Good.

"Thank you," Rick responded.

Behind him, knuckles cracked.

———

In Earth's prehistory, a general won a battle at too high of a cost. Pyrrhus. As Rick surveyed the dead bodies around him, Human and Arkouda alike, he wondered if Pyrrhus had a list, too, if he delivered the news to the families of the fallen.

Rawltz passed Rick a washcloth. "Some blood on your cheek." After a second, his eyes widened and he hastily added, "Sir."

Rick accepted the dripping cloth. The cool fabric against the stubble on his cheeks failed to dry the blood on his hand. Five shivering prisoners huddled before him.

After returning the cloth to Rawltz, Rick approached the prisoners, the five survivors of this massacre. He puffed his cheeks to get the precise pronunciation. "This didn't go according to my plan. I didn't want a bloodbath."

The technocrats, all too soft to be combat-ready, stared at Rick. He knew they understood him perfectly well. "Your comrades died heroes. They fought well and will be remembered as such."

One civilian prisoner pointed at Rick's missing arm and whispered something to another.

Rick ignored it. "Your officers had a whole luxury suite on this ship, didn't they? If you cooperate and assist in piloting the warhive, you can have all the comforts associated with that station. I had provisions and accommodations ready for an entire crew. It can all be yours. Seems like a few of you recognize me. I don't know if my reputation precedes me or not, but let me be clear: I don't want to kill a prisoner. You all surrendered. I'll get you home somehow when my mission is complete."

One of the prisoners whimpered. "You'll kill us."

"I would have already. You know what I did to the other warhive. It would have been simpler to do that again."

Glances were exchanged among the five prisoners.

"How do you know we won't take you to the Collective?"

Rick unholstered his pistol. "Katochos, Kreas, Apatay, Aspida, Plerosis." He aimed at each one as he said their names. "I broadcast your names to my allies. I was honest when I said I don't want to kill a prisoner. Some of the other leaders in Earthquake, not so much. If I don't call them off, they will come after your families."

"You're bluffing," Aspida said.

Rick eyed him. "Your grandmother's name is Babush."

Katochos gulped. "Fine. We'll pilot the ship."

"*Noryang*," Rick said. "That's the ship's new name. I'll adjust the ship's gravity to Human standard, so make sure your grav harnesses are in proper working order."

He motioned for Rawltz and an Equalizer strike team to escort the prisoners to the bridge. Then Rick turned to his other surviving crew. "Johnson, secure a link to Monsieur Tecton. We'll do it from inside the cargo ship. I need to update our Leader on today's fight."

———

Rick's footsteps echoed around the empty cargo hold where an hour ago they would've been muffled by the sheer mass of people inside. He clenched his omni-tablet and got a quick glimpse of himself in the blank screen before the connection established.

He'd earned a few more grays. His widow's peak became more pronounced with the mandatory lop-sided haircut. The spot on his neck with the Earth tattoo had wrinkled some more. He was every bit as haggard and exhausted as he felt.

Then the vibrant and virile face of Monsieur Tecton greeted him. The sonofabitch didn't sport the tattoos or haircut but carried all the smugness and swagger of the punk kids who joined Earthquake for the wrong reason. From behind Tecton, the almost-clean sky of Earth stretched in the background, a potent reminder of what could have been and what could still be.

"Give me some good news, Rick."

Rick checked the time estimator on the side of his omni-tablet. "Good afternoon, Monsieur. We destroyed one warhive and commandeered another. Heavy losses, though."

A crease formed in Tecton's forehead. "You aren't calling from New Lodestone. Where are you?"

"Uperaygos system. We're orbiting Palaios. I knew they had a rookie patrol guarding this area since we hit it a few years ago."

"And who told you to go there?"

Rick forced himself to remain calm, but his nostrils disobeyed orders and flared. "I needed another warhive, and I have reinforcements coming to defend New Lodestone."

Tecton ran his left hand through his full hair. Jackass always had to taunt Rick like this. "I didn't authorize this."

"I didn't have time to wait. I have confirmation about a clandestine Collective laboratory where

Humans are being experimented on. I needed to act immediately."

An eyebrow cocked. Tecton's gaze bore into Rick. "Human experimentation? How did you hear about this?"

"I've been telling you for years we need something to prove to the whole Collective that Humans are mistreated. Something tangible that even the most nationalistic Arkouda or brainwashed loyalist couldn't ignore. I have people digging for things."

"We don't need the Popsicles on our side."

Phantom pains tingled. "If we want independence from them, I think we do."

"This," Tecton gesticulated with his left hand, "laboratory. Where is it?"

Rick huffed. "In an unnamed asteroid field on the Collective frontier. When the imperialists don't name something, they are covering something up."

Tecton's eyebrow twitched as he muttered, "The fringe." He straightened his posture and adjusted his tie. "Do you have the name of any scientists there?"

"One, yes." Rick opened the tab on his omni-tablet, pulling up the information Amanda sent. He'd read the name a few times already but didn't want to say it wrong. "Diastrevlo."

Tecton clicked his tongue and took a bit too long to respond. "Wait until you have a bigger force before assaulting him. Retreat to New Lodestone."

"It's a moving field. I will have to reset a lot of the telemetry and lose progress if I don't act now."

"Are you ignoring orders?" Tecton asked, acid in his voice.

"No, sir."

"Good. My other leaders are using those Spear of Odin guns your eggheads developed. Very effective. Do what they're doing."

"We named them Equalizers. Sir."

"No. Spear of Odin is better. Liberate a planet instead of chasing rumors."

"Understood."

The transmission cut from the other end.

Rick radioed his pilot. "We land on the asteroid in ten minutes." Nobody had the right to experiment on his people.

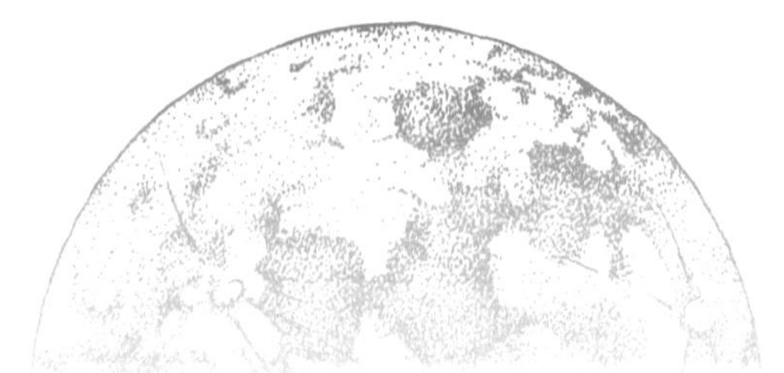

TWENTY-SEVEN

(INSPECTOR)

Asteroid field in {LOCATION CLASSIFIED}

EXITING HYPERSPACE BROUGHT Inspector Bikkolos into the promised asteroid field. Finding this unmarked location was a challenge on its own, and locating a single asteroid in a field felt daunting.

The scanner on his dashboard chirped, signaling an anomaly. Metal shrapnel inconsistent with the surrounding asteroids. Bikkolos cocked an eyebrow and zoomed in on the scanner. Forged metal floating. It looked like a scrap of a ship, maybe a mangled piston or an engine part.

Not even a buzzed pilot would get clipped by an asteroid. This wasn't close enough to any population centers to warrant a pirate skirmish. Maybe some rookie mechanic dumped trash from a passing cargo.

Scratching the end of his chin with one paw, he dialed the environmental scan with the other and the screen flashed white.

The scanner chirped to a three-beat.

Plasma fire had been exchanged within a few hours of his arrival. On closer inspection, his eyes widened. The shrapnel belonged to a gun. Small-scale cannon by the heat path's suggestion. The type meant to eliminate a single small ship.

Like what he found himself in right now.

Bikkolos adjusted the settings on the environmental scanner, widening the search for automated weapons, but nothing came up. Someone had beaten him here and cleared out the defense systems, but not with ordinance able to vaporize these turrets. Interesting.

He directed his police speeder past a smallish asteroid and spied another two similarly shaped bits of shrapnel. He adjusted the environment scanner to detect ionized trails left by smaller ships.

His pulse quickened reading the data. He got a zig-zagging line to an asteroid, similar enough to fool a casual onlooker. It was smooth and in synchronized rotation with a larger asteroid above it. He instinctively patted the pistol holstered to his chest and piloted the speeder closer, then he glimpsed the earlier ship. The ionized trail led straight to it. A battledart. Interesting.

A lone Collective pilot tracking this kidnapper? It didn't make sense. The idea of someone stealing an individual battledart for this kind of thing was more likely. But what kind of person would have the means, guile, and motivation to do all of this?

Bikkolos knew the answer before he finished asking himself the question. He knew exactly what kind of person would steal a Collective battledart for an altruistic reason instead of selling it to the highest bidder.

Rick Crith.

How Rick managed to pilot a Collective battledart was beyond Bikkolos. Perhaps Rick held the pilot at gunpoint. But even then, battledarts were too small to have ship-wide gravity adjusters, and the grav harnesses suitable for Humans couldn't cope with the anatomical demands made on their frail bodies by the shifting gravity in a small fighting ship.

Unless Rick discovered a solution. Maybe he'd invented some kind of flight apparatus or miniaturized gravity suited for a nimbler ship. Both sounded far-fetched, and Bikkolos dismissed the idea. The galaxy was too big to assume his former friend had come here. As he approached for the landing, he performed one final scan on the battledart. Whoever had been inside that ship had already exited.

Bikkolos grinned. Maybe this mysterious adventurer and savior of the downtrodden would eliminate any internal security as well.

One final theory about the pilot's identity crept into Bikkolos' mind.

Symphora.

The woman, the myth, the legend. Bikkolos had interviewed a few too many of the people she rescued as kids to deny her existence. The stories about her carried the air of wild exaggerations, though. The last one he heard at the water cooler was about how she forced a drug manufacturer to snort his own supply until blood leaked from his eyes felt fake.

But saving a kidnapped couple? That was the legendary folk hero he needed. Maybe if more Arkoudae like Symphora were running around, shooting up the bad guys until the galaxy was a better place, Rick wouldn't be known as the defector. Maybe Rick would've made more positive inroads for Human advancement years ago instead of setting them back with his defection.

Bikkolos recently heard a PhD was awarded to a Human for the first time. She was an archaeologist or a paleontologist or something. He could never remember the difference or care enough to remember. But still, that was the kind of progress Humanity needed. They didn't need this Nightmare version of Rick who went around killing people. They needed the real Rick. The version he knew, and maybe nobody else.

He shook his head and engaged his speeder's decontamination spray; he hadn't come so far to save this couple just to kill them with some microbes he contracted on the way. The spray hissed over him, and the ammonia stench made him wince.

Hearts racing, Bikkolos affixed his breather to his light armor, undid his flight suit, and prepared for his first steps into this compound, where he could hopefully find the two scientists alive and well, desperate for rescue.

No time for complications or obstacles.

TWENTY-EIGHT

(JOKΛ)

**Aboard *Binhsux*. Location:
Data Unavailable. Wait, what?**

"DATA UNAVAILABLE?" JOKA asked. "That sounds wrong." Her knuckles whitened as she fought the ship's urge to wobble.

"So does makeup for Lo-sats," Binh said. "But you should see all the beauty products in my sister's garage. Hey, would either of you be interested in an incredible business opportunity?"

"Would you be interested in keeping your snout closed?" Doh-riss asked.

Landing with a clipped wing occupied too much of Joka's attention for her to rattle off an insult. "Either the navigational system on the ship is faulty, or someone's scrambling us."

The ship landed with a *thunk*, delicate as Symphora's knuckles.

She tapped the top of her flight suit; her breather mask extended over her neck, covering her mouth. After another two taps, it extended again to cover her head.

"It got us here, so the battledart isn't the problem." Doh-riss followed Joka's example and prepped her breather for exit.

"I'll wait with the ship," Binh said.

"Waiting with the ship, my ass," Joka snapped. "You'll leave us stranded."

"Fine," Binh huffed. "The charming rogue will strap on his breather and plunge into mystery yet again."

"You're as charming as a leaky hemorrhoid," Joka said. "Double-cross us and—"

Binh waved a claw. "You'll tattle. Look, there's a list of people I don't *nguc* with. Symphora is up there with the Drowned Star pirates and the lady on Earth who sells me hot sauce."

Once their breathers all lit green, Joka disengaged the cockpit and float-jumped from the battledart onto the landing pad.

A few meters to their right, a conspicuous rock formation, redder than the rest of the asteroid, jutted out at an angle that didn't quite seem natural. Carved into it was a hatch, big enough for an adult Arkouda to walk through upright.

Gravel crunched under Joka's boots, and a few loose bits floated away in the absence of gravity. She gazed skyward at the emptiness above and felt smaller than she ever had.

"Do you feel like we're being watched?" Doh-riss asked. "Or that someone is behind us?"

Joka glanced over her shoulder. She couldn't detect anything unusual in the bobbing asteroids around them. The spinning rocks did make for good cover, though.

They approached the hatch, the *clank-clank* of boots against semi-hollow rock the only noise puncturing their silence. Joka, like any Human living among Arkoudae, had always felt small, but walking on this comparatively tiny asteroid against the void of space made her appreciate her truly insignificant role in the universe. Symphora didn't know or care where she was.

Nobody did.

Just her, Doh-riss, and the asshole. But maybe she could make a difference to this scientist guy and his kid. And maybe she'd get recognized as the hero for once. Or at least not a colossal screw-up. Not that she cared.

The hatch's angle in the jutting rock suggested it either led to a ladder or stairwell. "If nothing has come out of thin air to try and shoot us, we're probably past the point of locks. We're past this place's security."

"So you open it." Binh cocked an eyeridge.

"I mean, I *could*," Joka said, "but I haven't been bragging about my thieving skills. You should open it." These two didn't need to know how scared she was.

"Semantics." He crouched in front of the hatch's door and examined its lever. Without touching, he bobbed his head around it and took a few sniffs near its perimeter. "Needs some kind of code, I think."

"You could also just grab the handle and pull instead of being a baby."

Doh-riss hissed in agreement.

Binh switched languages to Human and glared at Joka. "Even in this void, I can smell your fear. Your pheromones are through the roof. The Prude Queen isn't saying anything because she wants to preserve your feelings or whatever, but you can't fool me."

Joka glared at him. "If you're not scared, you're delusional."

Returning to the latch, Binh slithered his tail to the handle and gave the lightest tap. To their left, a loose rock floated up off the surface. It wasn't the strangest sight on a zero-gravity asteroid, but it did snap Joka's attention.

Under the floating rock, a mechanized bot the size of Doh-riss' head whirred. Over a spinning orb, a telescoping pole sprouted two mechanized arms on either side.

"Out of the way!" Doh-riss shouted. Before Joka could look back at her, the little mech's arms extended and expanded, unfolding into the shape of two guns.

Joka fumbled for her own pistol, but as she realized she no longer had it, two more mechs rose from the ground. The first one rolled toward Joka, arm cannons glowing.

The thief unholstered his gun and fired at the mech closer to Joka.

The lime-green plasma bolt sailed past the bot. Perhaps his target was the ground four meters away. "Aw, *nguc.* Either of you good shots?"

"When did you take that gun back?" Doh-riss cried out. "There's another two over here!"

"Toss me your pistol," Joka called.

One of the bots shot at her, and she jumped away. The little bolt of plasma seared her flight suit.

Another shot rang out. "Incoming!" Binh jumped.

The thief's pistol floated toward her. Her eyes widened. He used a Collective weapon meant for an Arkouda or Lo-sat, not a puny Human. Hopefully the low-gravity environment would be a bit more forgiving. Joka pushed off and leapt toward the floating weapon.

Grabbing it with both arms mid-air, she looped her hand through the trigger guard and sloppily aimed at the little mechs encircling Doh-riss. Using her forearm, she pulled the trigger, a challenge even without gravity. She also missed wildly, but the shot dug a hole in the rock. The mechs around Doh-riss hesitated, shifting toward the new hole. Doh-riss swung her tail, forcing them into the new hole. Joka fired again, vaporizing a few of the little robo-punks. The plasma bolt disintegrated them from the center, and charred metal floated into the void.

Binh, for his part, hopped about them like someone doped on ravedust, dodging their shots with the grace of a stumbling child wearing shoes on the wrong feet.

"Stand still!" Joka shouted. "I don't want to hit you." Muttering "on purpose," she pulled the trigger, hitting one of the mechs assaulting him, and she descended to the asteroid with the panache of an inebriated bird.

Doh-riss leapt toward him, unable to jump quite as high as Joka in the lowered gravity.

The two Lo-sats swung at the remaining mechs, but one fired a shot, going right through Doh-riss' palm.

With a yelp, she clutched her wounded hand with the other, pressing it tight to her chest as green plasma smoke rose from the wound.

Joka's heart froze. Cold blooded Doh-riss' body temperature would plummet if they didn't get her inside. Joka didn't know enough Lo-sat anatomy to be sure when hypothermia would kick in or how bad it would be, but they couldn't keep messing around with these pint sized bots.

Binh snarled and kicked one into the surface, and she used the opening to shoot it. One left.

As Joka's feet connected to the asteroid, the final mech shot Binh, sending a bolt of plasma through his tail.

Binh howled.

With a running leap, awkwardly cradling the too-big pistol, Joka fired again, hitting the final mech. She floated back down, panting. The two Lo-sats collapsed on top of each other.

"Are you dead?" Joka asked.

"No, piss brain," Binh said. "I'd almost rather be dead, but Miss *Nguc* and I need to glomp onto each other for warmth."

"Don't call me that. We just need some time to heal where it's warm," Doh-riss said.

"That's not here." Joka adjusted the pistol to full power and aimed at the joint.

"Wait, *ke-nok*!" Binh hissed. "I thought shooting problems and asking questions later was an Earthquake thing. I can see now it's genetic in Humans. So sad."

Joka lowered the pistol. The asshole was right. There was bound to be some airlock and decontamination system inside. "*Skata*. We're screwed."

"Don't say that," Doh-riss mumbled.

A different voice broke through. Male. Arkouda. Unfamiliar. "I wouldn't say that. Depending on why you're here, of course."

Eyes wide, Joka looked over her shoulder. An Arkouda, graying around the muzzle and eyes, wore the garb of a police officer over the flight suit variation of military armor. He reached into his officer's uniform and withdrew a badge.

"Inspector Krisbat Bikkolos. I'm with the Crimes Against Provincials Unit. I'm investigating a missing Human scientist. Who are you?"

Joka blinked hard, then looked to Doh-riss, still cradling her hand and smushed against Binh.

Before Joka could say anything, Doh-riss piped up, "We're looking for a missing Human, too!"

Binh hissed. "Say officer, you probably saw those little mechs. Got a spare heat cell for two wounded Citizens?"

Inspector Bikkolos indicated the holstered pistol on his hip. "One of them came after me."

Joka followed his gaze. He'd zeroed in on Symphora's symbol on her suit and his eyes widened. She hastily covered the insignia because that's how mature people behave.

"Part of Symphora's gang, huh? Did she really—" His eyes drifted back to the injured Lo-sats. Bikkolos turned and walked away. "I'm getting my first aid kit. I was a field medic back in the day. I've patched up enough Lo-sat scales and Human flesh to make your head spin. Sit tight."

"What're the odds we can trust this guy?" Binh moaned, nursing his wound.

"We're still asking that question about you," Doh-riss retorted.

Joka clenched her fists. "Neither of you are in a position to deny a medic with a heat cell." Additionally, Joka had no clue how to open that hatch, and a cop might, but she kept that to herself. "It makes sense that somebody in law enforcement is looking for our guy and his son."

"It's weird that they put that much effort into a Human," Binh said. Doh-riss shot him a look, but he waved her off. "I'm serious, you prude. The Collective doesn't divert a ton of resources to Humans and Makawe. They're not Citizens like the Arkouda and the master race. If I wanted to insult her, I'd sarcastically say she looked cool holding the cartoonishly big gun."

Joka folded her arms over her chest. "Did you use the phrase 'master race' to refer to yourself in the same sentence you said you weren't racist?"

"Same paragraph."

Doh-riss moaned. "You're insufferable."

Inspector Bikkolos jogged back, medic's case in paw. He knelt before the two Lo-sats and pulled out a heat cell for each. He examined their wounds and applied the glowing disks under their bandages.

Doh-riss winced as her charred scales flaked off and new ones squelched to the surface.

"Watch it," Binh hissed. "We never agreed to a safe word."

Bikkolos ignored him. "Apply pressure on it with your claw and count to sixteen."

Joka watched Bikkolos, jaw dropping in her breather. His precision and speed in the procedure demonstrated what must've been countless repetitions. It didn't seem like he had to think about it. The whole backstory of being a medic felt credible. He would've put the medics on the Calamity to shame, but she surmised that must be the benefit of a formal education.

Joka approached him. "How could you patch up a Lo-sat so well if you were a field medic? Only Arkouda are in the Collective military."

He rose from his crouch and leaned away from her. Most Arkoudae Joka knew would lean over Humans to let them feel the height differential. He didn't. "That's not true. A few units have representatives of different species. I served in one. Like I said, I've patched up Lo-sats. Maybe you ought to re-evaluate your assumptions."

"Ha! Inspector Stitches showed you."

Bikkolos glared at Binh. "No nicknames."

"Arrest him, then," Doh-riss said.

Joka backed off her interrogation. "You said you were coming here to investigate a missing person. How'd you know to come here?"

"Confidential. I could ask you the same question. Did Symphora send you here?"

Doh-riss looked like she was about to speak. Joka couldn't let that happen, so she sidestepped in front of her. "That's also confidential." Hopefully, Doh-riss would get the hint and avoid mentioning Symphora.

"Kidnapped persons here managed to send messages. I triangulated to figure out where this asteroid would be." Bikkolos folded his arms over his chest. "If you aid in my investigation, you can keep your secret. I don't want to get on Symphora's bad side."

"And what else could we get for aiding?" Binh asked. "Hypothetical pardons?"

"He's joking!" Doh-riss hissed.

"We're stuck with this door." Joka pointed at the hatch. "Any idea how we can open it? I tried touching it, and you saw what happened."

"I tried swearing at it," Binh said, "but that didn't work, either. It's my usual go-to."

Joka glared at him. He was a professional thief. He knew how to burgle doors like this. She pondered the odds of him letting her trigger any traps on purpose.

This guy would double-cross them at some point. Joka just had to be ready.

"Speaking of this door... are there some tools you might need, officer?" Doh-riss asked.

Bikkolos shook his head and crouched in front of the oval hatch sized for an Arkouda. "I'll knock. I couldn't get enough signatures for a no-knock warrant."

"Whoever's in there," Binh tsked, "knows we're here. Or they're long gone."

"I have laws to follow," the inspector replied. The accompanying huff signaled this guy found those laws as annoying as Joka did.

After some taps on the hatch, Bikkolos barked into it. "Collective police. Open up."

Nothing.

He snarled and added, "I have a warrant."

Nothing.

Joka would've guessed that would convince everyone except the hardest and dumbest to exit their shelter. But whoever held this scientist guy must not be home or not care. Joka's heart sank. There was also the possibility they were in the wrong place entirely.

The Arkouda rose from his crouch. "I have a prybar and a lever bot that'll let me open it. Unless any of you happen to be professional lockpickers."

Joka cast a wary eye at Binh, but he kept silent.

Bikkolos returned a minute later with another bag covered in Collective police symbols. He pulled a yellow crowbar out, tapped in a number, and a bot peeped out of the crowbar's edge. He pushed the crowbar into the hatch, and the drone, arachnid in shape, scuttled to the end of it. It dug between the crowbar and the hatch, repositioning the crowbar for maximum leverage.

When Bikkolos started pushing down, the drone scurried near his paw, similarly adjusting his grip. It cast a thin loop around the crowbar's handle and jumped down to the surface, assisting the inspector's attempt to pry it open. The hatch came undone with a hiss.

Binh whistled. "Nice to know the best thieving tools are in the police's hands. I'm sure there's a Makawe protest song about that."

Bikkolos rose, placing the crowbar back in the bag. "Two that I know of, but I'm not much of a fan. Their knuckle drums give me headaches."

Joka peered into the dark hatch. "Binh, you're going first."

He glared at her. "You're starting to sound like my previous employer."

"That's never a compliment," Bikkolos said.

"You have no idea," Doh-riss hissed.

Joka shot Doh-riss a "stop giving this guy clues" expression. "I'll go in after."

"No." Bikkolos' voice hardened. "Single file. I will be in the rear."

Binh winked at Joka, which she assumed was an invitation to step on his tail the next chance she got, and he took the lead as Joka suggested. They descended the steep steps. These weren't intended for a Human by any means. Joka hated it, but it wasn't any different from wherever else she'd been her whole life. Tailored to Arkouda. Lo-sats could handle the steps and heavy door handles without much issue, their tails giving them the added balance, but Humans had no hope of actually walking their stairs. Hop down, swing a leg up.

Whoever built this, and likely whoever kidnapped this scientist guy, was an Arkouda or Lo-sat, not a Human. Some part of her felt relieved, but she remembered the footage. The lab aide murdered on the recording.

The feet. She cursed her stupidity for considering any other possibility. She might even recognize the killer from the feet alone.

Reaching the bottom of the steps, they found themselves in a metal-rimmed corridor, brightly lit. Binh sniffed and recoiled as if he'd opened an armpit scented candle. "You smelling the same thing, Officer Fuzz-fuzz?"

"No nicknames," the Arkouda grumbled. "There's some kind of sterilizing agent in here. If this is a laboratory, there must be some strong cleaners. I can't smell anything other than it."

A bot rolled out in front of them—some type of assistant mech meant for clerical work or reception. It spoke in metallic Arkouda, addressing Bikkolos. "Welcome to the laboratory, Officer." It turned to the two Lo-sats, starting with Doh-riss. "Citizens." Addressing Joka, it added, "Others."

Inspector Bikkolos advanced from the back of their line. "I have a search warrant. Where's Dr. Diastrevlo?"

The bot wheeled back, folding its lithe body for a deep bow. "Of course, Inspector. Before I take you to the back to meet with the doctor, I must ask that you deposit any firearms. Scans show there are—two—firearms on your persons."

Bikkolos waved. "You can't make that request. I'm an officer of the Collective."

The mech rolled to its left, its spinning wheel a wide orb. "Invoking Reasonable Safety, Precautions, and Jerky Prices Act of the year—"

Inspector Bikkolos advanced on the retreating bot. "That act doesn't exempt you in this situation. The more you protest, the more proof you're giving me that your operator has something to hide."

Joka glared at the little robo-fucker. It was stalling and distracting with banter. That was her trick.

"I'm finding our guy," Joka called, walking away.

"Provincial, you must not—*initiate code 6322.*"

Soft whirs sounded from behind Joka. The thing followed her. As she marched through the corridor, she couldn't find a single door or window. Not one change in scenery. After a few steps, two more bots unfolded from the walls in front of her. They locked mechanical arms and barred her passage.

A male Human voice caught her attention. Whoever he was, he spoke in Arkouda, but that didn't bother her. "Excuse me? Are you here to rescue me?" His accent didn't resemble any she'd heard before, making her process the words for an extra second.

Joka turned from the bots. A man maybe ten or so years older than her stood before her, wearing a pristine lab coat. Instead of resembling the sexy movie star like she'd maturely hoped, he had the weathered look of someone who'd lived lifetimes' worth of pain in a few decades.

He eyed her flight suit. "Are you with Symphora?"

She checked the corridor in both directions. She couldn't see the other three. Had she walked that far?

"Yes," she said. "We got your message. Symphora couldn't come herself, but you're in good hands now."

A rush of air hurtled toward her from his direction, which didn't make sense. It was as if something a meter over her head were swinging at her, yet she couldn't see anything. In the time it took her to register what was happening, a mass of hair she couldn't see hit her in the forehead, and the force knocked her backward.

Landing hard on her ass, the bots descended on her, removing her breather mask and placing another one on top of it. Despite her thrashing screams, her eyes lost the battle with her eyelids, flailing until she went limp, and she slipped into darkness.

———

Joka blinked the fog from her eyes as a scaly hand tapped her cheek. She slowly opened her eyes to see Doh-riss crouched above her. "You're back," she hissed.

Doh-riss gave her some space, and Joka rubbed her eyes, then propped herself up on an elbow. She was lying down on the floor in a cramped room with her companions.

"What got you?" Binh asked, nursing a lump on his head and leaning against a wall. "Was it the sexy scientist chick?"

"Huh?" Joka asked.

Doh-riss offered her tail to help Joka stand. "For me, it was Symphora."

"Symphora's here?" Joka asked.

Inspector Bikkolos paced the mirror-lined room, which took him about four steps in one direction. "No." He gave Joka a once-over. "Look at the light above my head, and do two long blinks."

"Excuse me?"

"I need to see if you're concussed," he said flatly.

Joka complied. Her head throbbed, but she'd survived worse.

Bikkolos rubbed his chin. "You'll survive. We were all duped by some powerful hologram technology."

Binh pushed off against the wall with his tail. "The cop won't say what tricked him."

Joka cocked an eyebrow. "If it was just a hologram, why couldn't you smell through it?"

Doh-riss draped her tail around Joka's shoulder. "This place has a strong chemical smell. I'm surprised you didn't catch it. It's so strong that we can't sense other things."

"So... scientist who kidnapped somebody has us all in prison and can fool any of us." Joka sighed. "Splendid."

"He also nabbed our omni-tablets," Binh said.

"And weapons," Bikkolos added.

"Whoever our kidnapper is," Joka said, "why not just kill us? I mean, I'm not complaining, but..."

Binh scoffed. "There's gotta be some other motive."

"Got to," Doh-riss whispered.

Binh waved her off. "Maybe he's afraid of what'll happen if Symphora hears you two got killed or if the Collective learns Detective Fuzzbutt isn't reporting in for duty."

Doh-riss nodded. "He could also want to ransom one of us."

"Joke's on him, then," Joka muttered. "Experimentation is more likely."

As she finished the sentence, a whirring made the floor near her vibrate. A panel from the floor opened, and a medical bot rose out. It was conical, maybe the size of Joka's hand, gently floating toward her. It's shining chrome made it look expensive, like everything else on this asteroid.

"Don't touch it!" Bikkolos shouted.

Binh hopped over to the floor opening and dug his claws into it.

The medbot puttered in front of Joka, and a scanning laser spilled from a sensor, running an analysis.

"Don't move," Bikkolos said as he crept toward her.

Binh grunted, straining to pry the floor panel open. "I can almost see down in there. Miss Tightass, come help me."

After flaring her neck frills and frowning, Doh-riss joined him.

The medbot blinked a blue light. Joka passed whatever random inspection this thing had for her. When the blue light blinked a second time, Binh and Doh-riss started coughing. Joka's eyes widened. Lime-tinted smoke billowed out from the missing floor panel.

"Poison!" Doh-riss shouted.

Joka scrambled to her feet. "Calm down, we're wearing breathers."

Bikkolos met her gaze, and his dark eyes watered. Even through his breather, she heard him wheezing.

A tendril of smoke infiltrated her breather. It stank like a mix of dust and salt, but it didn't make her own eyes water. The stink made her cringe, but she wasn't having difficulty breathing. She turned to the two Lo-sats on the floor, collapsed in a heap.

This poisonous gas, whatever it was, defeated the fancy breathers full Citizens could wear but was harmless to Humans. At least as far as she could tell. The medbot hovered in front of her and emitted another scanning laser. She eyed the bot carefully. Once it made the two blue blinks, she snatched it.

Frantic, Joka rotated the medbot until she found the hatch for its wiring. Nobody expects tiny Human fingers to come in handy until they're faced with a mechanical or wiring issue. She'd hotwired plenty of these things, plundered from pimps and enslavers.

Symphora kept a few medbots on hand in the Calamity's infirmary, but most of the medbots they found got donated to hospitals and homeless shelters.

Squinting, she found the little switch she needed on its bottom panel. Just like she thought, the stupid thing was set to information-gathering mode. One half-tweak and… "Gotcha." Joka placed the conical bot on the floor. It sputtered in place, rotated thrice, then zoomed toward Inspector Bikkolos.

"Triage mode." Joka's smirk soured. Doh-riss could die if she didn't act fast enough, and she couldn't override this thing's preference for Arkoudae. If she had any chance of resuscitating any of them, she'd need that bot's assistance. While the medbot did base assessments for the Arkouda, Joka attended Doh-riss.

She rolled Doh-riss onto her back and checked her breathing. Without a response, she started chest compressions. She considered messing with Doh-riss' gravity harness, possibly allowing Doh-riss to open her lungs wider, but she couldn't risk going too far. Kah-renn had passed out from some ionized fumes once, and Devy was the one to help her. Joka strained to remember what her former friend bragged about doing to save a Lo-sat's life. Apply heat from your skin if possible.

Check.

Clear obscured breathing paths. Should she take off the breather? Joka panted, sweat beading on her forehead. Those fumes must have compromised her breather, and they were in a sterile lab environment. She did another chest compression and then placed her ear on Doh-riss' chest. One heart beat, but not both.

"Come on, come on," Joka whispered. "I'm never swearing again if you wake up."

One wall panel clicked to her left. Joka snapped her neck in that direction. All she saw at first from her vantage point on the floor were feet.

Feet of an Arkouda.

Feet she'd seen before.

This was the guy she'd seen on that recording. The murderer.

Joka followed the line from his feet up a simple lab coat, leading to an Arkouda man holding an omni-tablet. A small breather covered his snout. His eyes were hidden behind a pair of mono goggles, but the eyebrows and round ears above them were still.

"Who are you?" Joka fought like Earth to keep the tremble from her voice.

The scientist tapped something on his omni-tablet, then glared down at Joka. "You may continue to resuscitate her, but leave the two men alone." His voice was like stone.

He had his chance to kill her, so she must be safe.

Probably. "Bite me," Joka sneered. "I'm saving them all."

"You won't interfere in my experiment."

"Experiment?" She ran through the list of possibilities in her head. Maybe he was the proud type who would want to monologue about his greatness. "What experiment?" No evil scientist could resist that. Symphora loved getting *skata* lickers to wax poetic about their exploits before shooting them in their manhood mid-sentence. Joka had learned from the best, and she'd get her opening. Lacking a weapon was problematic.

But the asshole stayed silent.

"Excuse me? I have a right to know if I'm being experimented on." She glanced around him. The hallway behind had a more bluish tint than she remembered. The earlier illusion, hologram, whatever it was must've been more pervasive than she realized. Those bots which blocked her may not have even been there before.

Joka stood and marched forward. This guy might be an illusion, too.

"Not one step farther," this guy or illusion of a guy warned. The lack of inflection made her squirm, but it solidified this was definitely not a sentient—

Thwack.

She'd marched into an unseen yet solid wall of furry muscle.

"Foolish," the actual guy said. It wasn't a taunt. It was stated as fact. Which was so much more annoying.

"Let me out," Joka snarled, rubbing her definitely bruised nose.

"You'll remain here until the experiment is—"

Joka punched him in his manhood. The height difference allowed her to fully uppercut him.

He thudded to the floor in a howl, his natural bulk shaking the floor, rattling Joka's spine.

Worth it.

"Experiment on that." Joka turned around to the others. Bikkolos was shuffling to his feet, as was Doh-riss. The medbot had taken care of both of them already and was working on Binh.

Bikkolos coughed. "Impressive. Never saw someone take down an Arkouda that way."

Doh-riss helped the groggy Binh stand. "I'll tell everyone. Binh won't believe us."

"Whazzawhazza?" Binh murmured.

"Let's go." Joka waved them forward. "I don't know how long before that jerk can stand again."

The scientist was already clawing at the floor.

Bikkolos crouched in front of the scientist and ripped off the breather mask. "We'll see how you like your knockout gas. I'll be back when I have handcuffs." He rose and kicked the scientist in the chin.

As the four of them hobbled out, Doh-riss hissed something to Binh. His eyeridges popped up over widening eyes. "She did what? Damn! Sell that technique to Earthquake. My sister should've done that to her ex. Boom!" He laughed and Doh-riss let him slide off her shoulders.

"It was still undignified. You're fine to walk," she said.

Once they were out, Joka stood in front of the open door. Upon finding a panel, she hit the standard sequence to close. As the door zipped shut, Joka's heart froze.

They didn't have much time at all. The medbot would attend to Diastrevlo. Shit. She hoped she'd done enough damage to his manhood that he wouldn't walk correctly.

"Punchy the Mechanic." Binh whistled. "You remind me of someone on Earth. Old broad. Sells hot sauce. Un-fuck-with-able."

"Keep talking and you're next," Joka said. "We've got a kidnapped person to find."

"Right," Bikkolos said. "A Human male, Ned Porandi. Middle-aged scientist. Also missing is a Lo-sat female, La-hok. They're married."

"Ooh," Binh cooed. "They're into some freaky *skata*."

Bikkolos glared at him.

Joka arched an eyebrow. "Our message mentioned a son."

Bikkolos rubbed his chin. "I wondered if there might be a third person. When I interviewed people, I got the feeling there was one layer to this they wouldn't say."

"He must have remarried," Doh-riss said. "So we're looking for two Human males and one Lo-sat. Simple enough."

"Not if we can't smell," Binh muttered.

"Let's open doors 'til we find them," Joka said. "Let's see if we can barricade this door or something first. I don't want that creepy doctor coming out after us."

Joka led them through the hallways, which, like the entire galaxy, were tailored to Arkouda. Everything made her feel small. She wondered how this scientist guy, Ned, must have felt as a captive here. And his poor son. Little Human kid growing up with a Lo-sat as a stepmother while captive to a hostile Arkouda. She bit her lip, realizing the symmetry to her own life. Her time as an orphan on the farm would've been paradise compared to the nightmare this kid must've endured.

In the lab's sterile monochrome, the doors all looked the same, and there weren't many of them. None of them were marked. Makes sense for a kidnapper with a staff of drones to leave it like that.

Doh-riss called for a halt. "This door ahead smells different than the others. It's hard to catch it because of the chemicals in the air, but trust me, it does."

Bikkolos and Binh sniffed.

"Miss *Nguc* is right," Binh said.

"Of course she is," Joka commanded. "Stop calling her that and open it."

Inspector Bikkolos cast a sideways glance at Binh. "If you have some opening skill, Citizen, that would be helpful. I don't know where they took my tools and gun when they tossed me in that room."

A smile curled up Binh's snout. "I do have something." He tapped the side of his diagonal chest strap, pulling out a thin piece of bone. "I thought Earthquake might do something similar to me, so I do have a lucky lockpick."

After a sniff, Doh-riss' eyes widened. "Who did that belong to?"

"Not that it's any of your business," he said, smirk fading, "but my dad."

"That's tiny," she hissed. "What did you do with the rest of his claws?"

They devolved into a few quick sentences in Lo-sat while Binh set to work on the door. Inspector

Bikkolos leaned down and whispered to Joka. "Lo-sat funeral ritual—"

"Yeah, yeah. You make something from their claws if you were the person they loved the most."

Bikkolos stiffened and cocked an eyebrow. "Excuse me." His tone was kind. "You're only the second Human I've met to know that."

"Thank Symphora for bunking me among other species."

As Binh continued to work and swear at the door, Bikkolos leaned down again.

"We hear rumors about Symphora all the time at the station. Is it true she fed a drug manufacturer his own supply until he lit himself on fire?"

Joka shrugged. "We're not supposed to confirm or deny any legends about her. Part of her mystique." *Shit, this guy is a cop.* Joka stiffened. "That's not an admission that I have any affiliation with her."

Bikkolos waved a paw. "I can smell a setup from a lightyear away. Symphora wouldn't kill soldiers. Either the story was falsified, or someone tricked her. I don't know who in the government would have a claw to sharpen against her, but you don't get to be in her position by making enemies with the Collective."

Slackening slightly, Joka eyed him. "If you believe that's true, would you be willing to get her crew a pardon? Prove her innocence?"

"Not my jurisdiction."

Joka rolled her eyes.

After a few more frustrated groans, Binh glanced over his shoulder at them. "Let's see what Dr. Dirtbag kept locked away in door number one."

Using their tails to assist their grip, Binh and Dohriss pulled open the door, letting Bikkolos and Joka see inside.

Back on the Calamity, Joka used to think the engine room was huge, yet it could have fit inside this circular room, practically an auditorium. A duraglass semicircle at the back half of the room was the clear focal point. Rivers of wires and a jungle canopy of pipes sprawled out in every direction from it. Monitors of every sort lined the walls. As a mechanic, Joka needed to know a good bit about electronics and engineering, but the display in front of her was beyond her capacity. Joka and Bikkolos entered, approaching the duraglass partition.

The untouched computers and observation desks they passed told her this facility was designed for a bigger team. How many lab assistants had Dr. Diastrevlo killed?

Thud-thud.

Swinging her head around, Joka scanned the area. That noise came from in front of them, a bit to the left, and— "There!"

Inspector Bikkolos gasped, and the two Lo-sats plodded behind them.

The noise had come from someone on the other side of the duraglass partition.

A Human man banging his fist, wearing the face of someone as afraid of holding out hope as he was of losing his last shred of it.

"That's Dr. Ned Porandi," Bikkolos said.

All this way, and they'd done it. It wouldn't bring Tur back from the dead or end anyone's legal troubles, but they'd arrived. They finally did something right. Smile plastered, Joka turned to Doh-riss. "We found him."

TWENTY-NINE

(RICK)

Aboard the warhive rechristened as *Noryang*. Hyperspace lane toward an unnamed asteroid field on the Collective frontier

RICK COULD FINALLY connect with his mole from the monastery. Apparently, Brother Maynard had a weak spot. The guy had a blood relative he kept in contact with; the mole managed to intercept a message exchanged between them. There was talk of a nephew, too. The mole even got confirmation on the brother's name. Benedict Porandi, "Ned" for short. Blackmail wasn't Rick's preferred method of eliciting cooperation, but this would certainly give him the leverage he needed to get the damn Great Mystery monks on New Lodestone to pledge their support and blessing.

He counted his blessings on New Lodestone. With the warhive defending the atmosphere and Amanda managing ground operations, the people there would flourish until he returned.

The repair bots had done an adequate job patching up the damaged communications array to Rick's specifications. The five captured survivors didn't give him any trouble, especially when Rick let on that he knew they could operate the warhive with only three of them. He had no clue what kind of propaganda they'd been subjected to about Earthquake, but they took his threat seriously.

Rick knew he'd be reprimanded by Tecton for disobeying orders. But if Earthquake ignored someone experimenting on Humans, this would be all for nothing.

The whirlwind of astral colors solidified, and the ship hummed a gravitational shift warning. Rick stepped to the command bridge's viewscreen and ordered his recently promoted navigator to scan the field. "We'll send out a scrapper to snag any minerals," he told her. Turning to the captives, he switched languages. "Set the autoturrets to vaporize only the asteroids that will damage the hull if they get too close. When the environmental scan finishes finding minerals, do another scan for any signs of suspicious activity. An unmarked settlement or even a building."

The scans came through quickly. Rick smirked. He could get used to this level of technology at his fingertips. Earthquake could progress with this level of support, and Rick had only begun to unlock the secrets of this new warhive.

"What'd you find?" Rick angled his chin to meet the Arkouda's snout line.

Katochos, the captured civilian who'd become the de facto spokesman, stared back at Rick. "We found two asteroids locked in synchronous rotation. Turns out they're connected." His voice was a defeated grumble.

"Perfect. Signs of life?"

"Both have landing areas for smaller ships, connecting to bunkers leading to sublevels."

"Anything else?"

Katochos made a flimsy paw wave. "Two ionized trails from ships recently. They've dissipated a bit. We missed them by anywhere between an hour and a day."

Rick turned to his Human crew and switched languages. "We'll keep a skeleton staff aboard here. We're taking the captives with us so they don't get any funny ideas." Noticing the exchanged scowls, he added, "Maybe they'll see firsthand how we're treated."

Rick stepped down from the commander's perch, joining the Human crew. "I don't know what kind of resistance we'll find. Expect security. Might be soldiers, might be defense drones. We do want to protect them," Rick indicated the captives behind him, "but that's not the first priority. First priority is saving as many lives as we can. We've shed enough blood. Time to save some. Earthquake, are you with me?"

Raised fists and tight nods formed the response.

He had less than half the crew available that he'd intended. Too big of a fight here, and he wouldn't return home. But if he didn't, nobody would. "Rawltz, Harada, Johnson. You're staying here. Everyone else, suit up and come with me." Rick sauntered toward the Arkouda captives. "Listen, you're joining. If there are Collective officials there with bargaining power, I will negotiate for your release. You step out of line, and I will kill you. I can only promise I'll try to make it pain-less. Are we clear?"

Slow growls followed.

Unsatisfied, Rick leaned toward them. He'd found Arkouda respected a straight spine, even if the head sat a meter below theirs. "Humans are being exper-imented on with the Collective's blessing. You'll see how your government really treats us. Why we have to do what we do."

The group shifted uncomfortably, and Katochos stepped forward. "We'll cooperate, but don't expect us to smile about it."

Over the next few minutes, they clinked through the warhive, heading toward a docked scrapper.

———

The ride to the larger asteroids consisted of the captives eyeing the Equalizer guns while the strike teams exchanged stories of their kills before joining Rick's crew. One boasted about killing a parent and child with the same grenade. He called it saving two Human lives by removing two oppressors, making Rick shudder. Any other commander in Earthquake would have promoted somebody for that story.

The whole crew Rick had to work with could fit in the hull of one scrapper. Even with the prisoners, there'd be room aplenty for rescued civilians. Rick wondered how many were in this facility dug into the asteroid, and why this mad scientist needed two asteroids for his work. If they could save even one life and share the story, this rogue mission in defiance of Tecton would be worth it. Success would be the only way to salvage his job. Barring that, success here might let people forget about his darker deeds—triggers he shouldn't have pulled. Lives he couldn't save, including the fiasco to get this second warhive.

That changed today. He'd only ever tried to do the right thing. Nothing was wrong with a hunter felling dangerous prey.

The scrapper touched down on the asteroid's surface. "We don't have time to politely ask them to open the door. Shepherd, turn on the magnet and start pulling until that hatch opens. Everybody else, make sure your breathers are ready to go and double-check the grav harnesses."

With a groan, the scrapper's magnet beam triggered and pried open the door.

"Shepherd, keep your comms unit open. That door can make a last-ditch projectile if you get some unwelcome company. Earthquake, let's move."

His recruits and captives filed out before him, approaching the wide opening where the bunker door once stood. As Rick stepped onto the asteroid's rocky surface, he wondered how many Humans were funneled into this place a year.

Rick inventoried his too-small crew. Five Arkouda prisoners in the center. One Equalizer team of three to their left, another to their right. Two gunners in front of the left team, three gunners on the right team. Rick in the center. Including him, that made twelve members of Earthquake to defend the five Arkoudae. Handling one adult Arkouda proved enough of a challenge. They could turn on them at any second; claws and teeth paired with their sheer size advantage would take out at least a third of his crew before he put them down. Rick relied on the strength of his threats and reputation to keep them in line.

They descended the stairs under dim lights, forced to shuffle. Whoever designed this meant it to be disorientating for whoever went inside—incongruous lines and zigzagging tubes created an illusion of a bashed arachnid's web. His crew seemed to be more affected than the Arkoudae due to the architecture.

A security drone rolled out in front of them, a thin tube atop a spinning orb. It spread guns from its side and beeped a "stop" command in Arkouda. One of his gunners shot it in the center before it fully unfolded.

"Good shot, Marquez," Rick whispered. There was a reason these few survived the earlier fight.

Three more bots emerged from the walls to their left, and their targeting nodes stuttered, unable to get a lock on anybody.

"Fry them," Rick said. His soldiers complied.

The prisoners murmured among themselves, and Rick's eyes widened. These security bots couldn't fire on Arkoudae. They were designed to stop Humans. Proximity to the fuzzy Citizens must scramble or at least slow down their targeting parameters.

"Stick close together," Rick said.

Lunging like idiots, they reached the bottom stair, entering a wide cavernous room. Tanks a bit wider than a large Human and shorter than a tall Lo-sat lined the walls, accenting the room as if they were pillars. These tanks held bubbling green liquid. Their purpose didn't matter. Their size alone was enough to make Rick sneer. "Search for signs of life," he said. "But stay close."

Hoses, tubes, wires, and monitors occupied the cramped spaces between the tanks. Scanning the room, Rick counted sixteen tanks on both sides. As they approached the center of the room, a PA system buzzed to life, and a male Arkouda voice echoed from the ceiling.

"You must be the rogue Earthquake agent. My instructions were to give you one chance to leave." Whoever spoke those words had a voice that carried no inflection, yet Rick caught heavy breathing.

The speaker had a recent injury. Other explanations for the wheezing surfaced, but it reminded him too much of his days with the Collective to consider them seriously.

They knew he was coming. Collective government must want him. Rick spun around and shouted back, "Sure. Give me the Humans you're experimenting on, and I'll be on my way."

"Be sure to use all manner of your weaponry and tactics here. This data will prove useful," the emotionless voice on the PA replied.

Human and Arkouda eyes alike settled on Rick. He shrugged. "Seemed to know who we are and that we're coming. Be prepared."

Behind them, the landing at the bottom of the staircase rumbled. A panel he hadn't noticed in the floor opened, and a steel wall rose, sealing them from the stairwell with a thud. "Shit," Rick whispered.

From the side, plodding thumps echoed. Something encroached, concealed by the tanks.

Rick switched languages to Arkouda and addressed his captives. "What do you smell?"

Katochos shouted, "Something I've never smelled before." The other four exchanged glances, eyes bulging.

"R-R-Rick..." Marquez, the crackshot who once stood down a snarling Arkouda commando, pointed a shaky homemade pistol at a shadow on the wall.

Whatever created the shadow wasn't anything Rick had seen before in profile—it was also dripping. This might have just left one of those tanks.

This thing approaching on the left loomed taller than Rick for sure, but definitely not as tall as the shuddering Arkoudae behind him. The bulbous object Rick's subconscious hoped was a head had an elongated feature suggesting a snout, but too chunky to be from any species Rick knew. He checked to the left, and a similar shadow appeared on the wall.

Rick turned between both sides and shouted in Arkouda. "Surrender. You're outnumbered. If you're victims, we'll help you get home." No response. The shadows advanced. In Human, Rick whispered, "Get those Equalizers ready." He tried shouting his message in simplified Human, "We came to save you."

Between the thudding footsteps closing in on them, two low groans emanated. Great.

The PA chimed. "Don't bother. They're here to kill you."

"Back to back, everyone," Rick said. "Something tells me this isn't a standard—"

The approaching interloper on the left came into the light from behind the row of tanks.

Rick's heart dropped. There weren't any Humans here to save. Whatever these dripping aberrations were, they weren't Human, maybe not even alive.

He'd seen real monsters before. That damn tomb he should never have entered with that archaeologist and Ten-trom two years ago. The whole experience made him question his sanity, faith, and place in the greater cosmos. But through it all, the unspeakable abomination he saw in that tomb could logically fit into an ancient culture's mythology, deified avenger or demonized reaper.

Not like this.

What approached was a hulking mutant made by some twisted deviant, released from a stasis tank, suggesting dozens more waited at the ready.

This aberration mixed Human with Lo-sat features. Or Lo-sat with Human features. Both were wrong. It shambled toward them, naked. Mangled genitals resembling a female Lo-sat's cloaca grabbed his attention first.

Whatever covered this creature's body was an unholy mesh of scales and flesh, a pockmarked mix of not-green-enough and not-flesh-toned enough. A sickly gray brown from sagging scales that hadn't quite molted, causing a too-dry squelch with each footstep. It had Human-shaped feet with the proportions of a Lo-sat. Four toes on the left foot, five on the right.

Different toes on the feet had claws. A tail protruded from its backside, misshaping the shadow—more of a malformed nub than anything prehensile or serviceable for balance. Not a hair to be found on the whole body. Its ridges and spikes bore the curves of a Lo-sat female.

Aimey and Wystone gagged. He didn't blame them. But they'd need to compose themselves soon in order to fire.

"Identify yourself!" Rick shouted. Nausea and bile threatened when he caught this thing's eye. It had the marbled pattern of a Lo-sat but with a red iris, like a sick Human. Hairless eyebrows where there should have been Lo-sat eyeridges quivered: a sign of agony in their species.

Teeth clenched, Rick commanded, "Put this damn moaner out of its misery. Equalizers, line up your shot."

From the right, another limping abomination approached. It wasn't a precise copy of the other, yet it bore the same hallmarks that made his hair stand on end. It had different proportions, but the pattern of bastardized Human and Lo-sat remained. It flared out stubby neck frills, the Lo-sat attack stance. Opening its mouth, it groaned, exposing mismatched Human teeth and Lo-sat fangs. A molar fell out and plinked against the floor.

"Shit! Right flank, prepare to fire on the other one."

His left side shakily took aim with the Equalizer, readying the harpoon.

Rick barked in Arkouda. "If you all think that will discriminate between us and you, you've got another thing coming. The only way we're leaving alive is if we work together. Those get close, you slash and bite, understood?"

Aspida tsked. "We don't take orders from—"

Rick shoved his pistol into the offender's chest. "Don't finish that damn sentence." Switching languages back to Human, he called, "Equalizers, fire once it's in range. Gunners, start shooting. These things aren't wearing armor."

Marquez shuddered and fired the first round. The blast sailed past the shambling attacker and shattered a nearby glass storage tank, raining molten shards across the room.

Aimey wiped the puke off her chin and fired at the left beast. The plasma bullet connected to a partially-clawed hand. A sizzling stench spread, yet the mutant had no reaction except to continue trudging forward, groan-croaking all the more as lime-green plasma smoke rose from its wound. Wystone was still a shivering mess, more likely to drop his gun from the vomit coating his hands. Rick wheeled to his right and fired. He missed by a half-meter, shattering a light.

The raining shattered glass didn't slow or startle the mutant. It marched closer.

"Damn it, Earthquake—light them up!"

All six gunners opened fire, Rick trading glances and shots on each side. Most of their bullets missed, and those which connected didn't seem to do much. They only hit extremities.

"Aim for the heads and torsos. There's gotta be some organs in there."

Vibrations underfoot told him the Arkouda civilians were huddling closer.

"We're their prisoners," Katochos shouted. "Don't hurt us!"

The mutants continued their groaning march.

Rick wheeled on his captives. "You couldn't listen? These aren't sentient. An Arkouda made them this way, so I'd stick with us if I were you."

Ca-thunk.

The left Equalizer team fired its harpoon, sailing toward the advancing monstrosity. Like with the practice cadavers, the harpoon sailed through the center, taking the mutant along with it. The harpoon stapled it to the wall.

Cheers.

"Right team, take your shot."

They did as instructed with similar results. Rick read its expression as the harpoon connected with its abdomen. No change. Exact same amount of anguish with an Equalizer harpoon in its gut as when it shrugged off their bullets. These creatures had their pain thresholds already maxed out or were bred to not have any in the first place.

More cheers as the right beast thunked to the laboratory floor.

To his left, a series of wet squelches and snaps made him glance over. The creature, still with the harpoon in its gut, rolled over. Crawling on mangled mutated hands and knees, useless tail bobbing midair, it pulled itself off the harpoon, blood and entrails cascading out as it did.

"Sh-sho-shoot it!"

Everyone had frozen solid. Once this aberration pulled its body off the harpoon, it stumbled to a standing position. It advanced again, close enough to display a mix of mismatched fangs and molars.

"Retract the chain. Aim for the head!" Switching languages, he snarled at the prisoners. "Kreas, Apatay: when we pin it down, charge and slash until you find the brain stem. Aspida and Plerosis: get ready to do the same. Katochos, stay here."

Both harpoon chains retracted, tripping the beasts. The left team fired again, this time aiming at the head. It connected between the eyes.

Rick fired another round, grazing the side of its neck as it careened backward. The right team fired, aiming too high. It chopped into the monstrosity's crown and chunks of skull went with it. Puffing his cheeks, Rick shouted in Arkouda. "Attack them!"

Nothing.

The cowards stood there. Rick wheeled on them, teeth clenched. "You want to get out alive?"

Katochos nodded. "Come on!"

Apatay and Kreas started at a slow jog. They weren't soldiers. Shit.

"Get the Goddess-damned lead out!" Rick's voice was getting hoarse.

They glanced over their shoulders at him. Scared shitless. They thought they were getting sent to a slaughter.

And they were.

The beast flailed mismatched limbs like muscled whips at the approaching Arkoudae.

But the right side needed more help. "Plerosis and Aspida, get the other one. I'll cover you."

Equalizer teams respooled their harpoons while Rick led the right gunners and flanked the creature. They lit it up with gunfire. "Concentrate on the—" A coughing fit seized him from all his shouting. *Shit shit shit shit*. He hoped they got the "head" message. By the time he collected himself, the monstrosity splayed on the floor, face first. The two Arkoudae hunched over it.

Rick nudged the gunner beside him and pantomimed slashing, still clutching his pistol and coughing.

In an accent so thick it was practically useless, the gunner called out in Arkouda. "Slashy slashy now!"

The Arkouda roared. It wasn't the powerful, guttural stomach-turning battle cry he'd heard before, rather a civilian trying to summon enough adrenaline to perform. The extended manicured claws bore down on the snarling creature. It wouldn't be enough.

They slashed at exposed bits of skull, carving out an eye socket, but they couldn't puncture bone. They dug as the creature grabbed at them.

Rick raced over and shot it in the spine.

The creature's croaking groan crescendoed. Progress.

"Move!" Rick wheezed, and the nearly useless civilians backed off. Rick found the exposed bit of skull and unleashed another round. "Go back to the hell you crawled from," he muttered.

The groaning stopped and its mangled hands unclenched. It lay limp and lifeless.

He called out in Human, not quite shouting, "Use the harpoon to sever its head. Pull out whatever is in its ribcage. Lo-sats have two hearts. This probably does, too. Gunners, assist the left side."

As he finished the sentence, a pained roar echoed from behind him.

Apatay.

The monstrosity pulled Apatay to the floor in its death throes. Rick sprinted over, but his left gunners beat him. They erupted gunfire all over the creature until it lay dead, a smoldering mess of plasma dust and charred scales.

The scent threatened to spiral Rick into his dark place. His time before joining Earthquake. His time with the enemy. The suicide missions. The good people they lost. The air support that never came on that final mission. Blekk tentacles strangling him. *No, damn it.* Makawe pincers snapping his bones. *Not now.* Blood. Screams. Shouts. Alone.

No.

He forced his eyes shut.

Years of therapy weren't about to evaporate. Soft sands on bright shores. Wavegulls cawing. Another inhale. Amanda humming holiday tunes. Exhale. His graduation. Mom still alive. Inhale. His former best friend patching him after a mission.

Rick opened his eyes again to Apatay's mangled leg on display. He lacked a medbot or way to save his life. This was beyond the first aid he could do.

He approached the wailing civilian. If this were a Human, he would have crouched, but Rick was eye level just by standing. "I can't take you with us. You can stay here and wait for us to come back, maybe with medical supplies. I could also end it now for you, put you out of your misery. I know how to make it painless." He hoped his diction conveyed that the second offer was a mercy, not a threat.

Apatay whimpered. "Leave me here."

Rick nodded. "If you don't make it, I'll make sure you have a proper funeral ritual. I'll find a way to inform your family." He'd give one of his own the same courtesy.

Rick turned to the rest. Down one. But whatever else came their way, he knew how to deal with it. "Let's head down the left corridor behind the tanks. That's where the doctor doesn't want us to be."

Rick wondered why the cold-hearted bastard hadn't gotten on the PA. Maybe he got distracted by something else. Unlikely. These assholes tended to be single-minded. Odds were he assumed his night-mares would take care of them, and he could study the remnants later.

By the time they funneled into a double file line, they had passed the fourth of the sixteen tanks on this side.

Thud-slap. Thud-slap.

Shit.

"Anyone else hear that?" Rick asked.

A few tentative nods.

He recoiled on the Arkoudae. "What do you smell? Is another one coming up on us?"

Thud-slap. Thud-slap.

The prisoners sniffed the air around them. Again, showing their lack of training. An Arkouda who really knew how to sniff for something would put a paw over their nose as a partial filter, like Humans would put a hand over their eyes to block extra light and see better. These weren't trackers, just like they weren't fighters.

"Yes." Kreas sniffed. "At least two."

"From where?" he demanded.

Plerosis held up a paw. "Two behind us."

Closing off the escape. Dark memories of the moon and the archaeologist resurfaced.

Thud-slap. Thud-slap.

Kreas stared at Plerosis. "What in the Nightmare are you talking about? It's in front!"

Two hulking figures approached.

Thud-slap. Thud-slap.

Plerosis scoffed. "I wasn't talking about them. I thought we all smelled those. No, the ones behind us."

Pincer maneuver. Rick wasn't having another bloodbath today. "I need an Equalizer team in front of us and another one behind. Gunners, you know what to do."

"There's another one between the tanks," Katochos barked.

Five total.

Thud-slap.

The groans were close enough to follow and iden-tify at this point.

"Take out the one on our flank first." As he spoke, the creature to the right squeezed between two tanks.

Teeth clenched, Rick shot out the two tanks on either side of the monster, letting the viscous green gloop inside bury the mutant. Its groan deepened into a howl as the liquid coated its body, solidifying within seconds of contact. As the liquid gushed forth, the stench hit Rick's nostrils like a grenade of feet, forgotten garlic, and animal decay. The Arkoudae vomited. They couldn't slash brains out like that.

The coated creature sank to its knees, which snapped on impact. As it writhed on the ground, Wystone approached it, gun raised to shoot it in the skull. As he neared it, the monster clawed at his legs, landing one vicious slash across his calf.

Wystone crumpled, cursing all the way. He loosed a few rounds, and the damn thing quit moving. Blood gushed from the wound, but if Rick tended to him now, he'd doom the others.

The next four abominations were already here.

Still, Rick muttered, "Bridan Wystone, may you find solace in the Great Mystery."

He turned his attention forward to the Equalizer team already lining up their shot. Rick moved beside them as the harpoon *ka-chunked* out. It sailed across the corridor, smacking the monstrosity in between the eyes.

Twice this team made a direct hit on the first try. He'd need to file that away. Definitely have these three train the others once there was time to breathe and debrief. If they survived.

"Good," Rick said. "Retract the chain and hit the other one." Rick turned around to monitor the rear group's shot, and something caught his eye. Of the two monsters in front of them, one sprawled on the ground, its groaning tapering to silence. The other though, which had been walking beside it in lockstep, stopped in its shambling tracks. It crouched in front of the fallen abomination. Rick cocked an eyebrow. Was it mourning? Upset?

The Equalizer team spooled the harpoon, which made a slurping sound as it retracted. The crouching monstrosity's unholy mix of fingers and claws splayed out over the fallen one's head at the site of the injury. And boggling the stretch of science and reason even further, its hands glowed.

This thing's hands glowed like the edges of an eclipse.

What followed defied logic. It spread its hands over the injured area, and the fallen one groaned again. Then its stub of a tail twitched.

Its tail twitched.

Rick's eyes bulged. "Shoot it! They heal each other."

The gunners hesitated. Sons of bitches.

Rick charged in front and shot the healer. His strength was failing; his gun's kickback demanded more effort from him. He ignited the corridor green with plasma fire, and his gunners found the courage to join. "Don't give it a centimeter. Keep up the pressure. Where's that Equalizer?"

"Ready, sir!" his team called.

The team fired, but the creature's posture must have thrown off their aim somehow. The harpoon struck the shoulder.

"Kreas, Aspida," Rick shouted in Arkouda. "It's down. Rip its head open. Get the brain or hearts. No hesitation, no mistakes."

He wheeled around to assist the rear team. They fired their Equalizer harpoon at a shambling groaner, and it connected in the abdomen. That wasn't enough to merit its companion stopping to heal it. That confirmed for Rick these things would wait until an actual death before pulling their resurrection trick. His heart raced with the possibility that the first two monsters could be revived and chase them again.

Rick reloaded his pistol as the two standing rear gunners unloaded. Scraps of fleshy scales and scaly flesh ripped away with the searing plasma, but new patches of skin bubbled over the affected area by the time the next plasma bullet made its mark. As long as they were in pairs or more, these things were functionally unkillable.

Human stubbornness and the Lo-sat's ability to regenerate in overdrive. The science of it would have enthralled him if it weren't about to kill him. The rear shamblers approached, closing the last few meters. The one which the Equalizer team didn't target opened its jaw, showing mismatched teeth and blackened gums.

Close enough to see a blinking light under the skin on its collarbone.

Rick glanced down at the blinking light on his own gravity harness.

Their nudity had been so disorienting that he'd neglected the asteroid. These monsters were stitched together with DNA from species that never evolved to live in such little gravity. Dr. Diastrevlo must have surgically implanted grav harnesses.

Monstrous. No wonder they were in agony.

"Aim for their collarbones. They have grav harnesses inside. Fry them."

Rick unleashed a round of fire on the flashing lights. The first shot missed, searing the spot on the neck where a windpipe belonged. The groan became a whistle for a fraction of a second while the flesh stitched and squelched back together to seal the wound. He adjusted his aim and fired off two bullets in close succession.

The first shot exposed the buried device—the second scorched it.

Groan lowered to gurgle as it floated toward the ceiling.

Triumphant, Rick turned to face front, greeted with the sight of Marquez, dangling midair. An abomination had him.

Like with the fallen beast, this one splayed its fingers and claws out, glowing. This glow wasn't serene iridescence from before. This was crimson.

Angry.

Aflame.

Marquez writhed as the creature immolated his torso. Odorous charred flesh attacked Rick's nostrils while Marquez's gasping screams rattled his eardrums.

"Dontrell Marquez, may God have mercy on your soul." Rick fired one bullet through the crackshot's skull, who didn't deserve this pain and humiliation.

Rick and the surviving gunners opened fire on the beast, aiming for the blinking grav harness implanted in the neck. When Marquez's corpse turned to ash, the smoldering putrid stench made the surviving Arkoudae retch.

Aimey landed the shot on the abomination's grav harness, sending the monstrosity to the ceiling. As Rick congratulated her, he saw Wystone slump to the floor. Poor guy bled out faster than Rick had assumed.

They couldn't keep doing this. Somber, Rick approached Wystone's body and removed his grav harness. Gravity might be the only reasonable way to fight these things, and a sick twist in Rick's gut told him they weren't done.

"We'll have memorials for our fallen comrades. For now, we need to head out."

With too little support, Rick led them down the corridor, cylindrical tanks on one side, vents and cables to their right. Death behind.

THIRTY

(NED)

**On a research station in
{LOCATION CLASSIFIED}**

MUI-XE WHIMPERED IN Ned's arms. "I'm sorry, Dad." La-hok's body splayed out before them. Dr. Diastrevlo had implanted a tumor in her lungs.

Ned remembered being in the opposite position, crying in his brother's arms; a ten-year-old's tears made more bitter by the belief he was too old to cry, especially in front of another male. Ned regretted raising him with that idea.

"Don't be," Ned responded through his own sobs. "You were distracted. What you were able to do this long was a miracle."

Mui-xe, perfect boy he was, attempted to heal her once the cruel doctor tossed her corpse off the surgical gurney. The boy's hands glowed like before, yet nothing happened. Somewhere between Ned's cursing out Diastrevlo's cruelty and Mui-xe's desperate cries for his mother's safety, the doctor left in a huff.

He wanted to scream and wail for his lost love, but he needed to be a father more than a husband now. There would be time to grieve after his son was safe. Choking back a sob, he forced himself to push the pain back and focus on the boy.

Consoling his son, Ned realized this didn't compute. Diastrevlo watched them suffer and took notes. Either this was a part of a grander experiment, or something stole his attention somewhere else in the lab.

Ned released Mui-xe from the embrace to grasp his late wife's cold claws. "Did your mother ever explain to you what needs to happen if she died?"

Mui-xe shook his head and wiped away a tear. Of course she hadn't said anything. Ned hadn't said anything. Why put any morbid thoughts into their already tortured son's head?

Ned wiped away another one of his son's tears. "I'm sorry for asking. It's alright. We're going to remove her claws." He met his son's wavering eyes. "She can't feel pain anymore, son. This is what your mother's people do. We take their claws because after they die, they move on to a land of peace." Having a shaman for a mother-in-law finally paid off.

"She doesn't need her claws now?"

"No." Ned forced a smile. "Because now nobody will ever try to hurt her again. Her claws are her final gift to you." He clasped her dead hand into a fist, some dim part of him hoping that might create a pulse.

"When you're a bit older, I'll tell you how we met. But now, we need to—" It dawned on Ned that he had no idea how to remove the claws without violating layers of taboo if he did it incorrectly. If a tiny chance persisted for any of them to enjoy an afterlife, he wanted to ensure she'd arrive the right way.

Gently, he laid her on the floor and stood, pulling Mui-xe with him. "What we need to do is escape Dr. Diastrevlo." He squeezed his hand tight. "I don't like asking you to do this, but I need you to use your abilities to get us out of here."

Mui-xe looked up at him with his innocent red eyes. "What do you mean?"

"When Dr. Diastrevlo came close to killing you with the gasses—" Ned bit hard on the words. He squeezed in a breath before continuing, "Your hands. You ignited them somehow. Do you remember how you brought the heat from your hands? Is it like when you would heal me or your mom?"

Mui-xe stared at his hands, examining both sides. "I'm not sure. It just happened."

"Have you tried doing it again?" Ned asked.

The boy shook his head. Ned escorted him to the duraglass partition, but not the side used to observe Mui-xe during Diastrevlo's torture sessions. He took him to the side looking out into the rest of the observation room, where the sick doctor would watch the daily assault on their poor son.

"Place your hands on the glass. Good. I need you to think back to when that happened. Do you remember it?"

Hands pushing against the glass, Mui-xe gave a meek nod.

"Alright. Try to remember how you felt then." Ned hated himself for asking his son to relive any of his trauma, but he had no other options. "Remember what you felt."

"How?"

"Do you remember how you felt?"

"Sad...? Angry? Scared?"

"Hands steady. Why were you sad?"

"I thought if Diastrevlo got what he wanted from me, he'd throw you and Mom away."

Ned cocked an eyebrow. "Why would he throw us away?"

"He was jealous of Mom, I think. He didn't like how she was smarter than him. If he figured out how my body works, I thought he would get rid of you both."

If this were true, Mui-xe subconsciously obfuscated Diastrevlo's research. The determined noncooperation arose from the desire to protect his parents. His body might not have been healing itself as much as mutating to somehow better safeguard them.

Yet Diastrevlo had no reason to kill La-hok with an implanted tumor. Unless he'd completed his twisted experiment. The doctor had left in a hurry.

Maybe they weren't alone. Someone else arrived at the lab, perhaps—leaving Diastrevlo occupied and distracted.

After silence without progress, Ned probed again. "Remember that sad feeling that you might lose me and Mom. You said you were angry and scared, too. Why angry?"

Mui-xe stared at the floor, straining to push more against the duraglass partition. "I'm always angry when he's around. I even get mad thinking about him."

"I see. And why were you scared?"

Mui-xe inhaled deeply, fighting tears. "It just hurt so bad."

"That's something I can relate to," Ned said. "Try to capture those feelings. Dr. Diastrevlo killed—" He choked on the words, his blood pressure rising. "He killed your mother. Remember the pain."

Mui-xe strained, pushing against the glass, driving his feet that used to be smaller than Ned's, almost enough to hit it with his shoulder.

Nothing.

Reminding his son of trauma may not have been the best way to bring out his power, but it seemed like his ability to heal sprung from deep compassion. Anger bringing this fire out seemed plausible, but maybe that was Ned's surging adrenaline overtaking his reason.

Ned scanned their furniture. Maybe he could attack the duraglass, and Mui-xe could heal him. He could rip out every computer from the wall, the terrarium for La-hok's food, her solar lamp. At this point, he'd be willing to punch it until every bone in his hand shattered.

Mui-xe lowered his hands, lip quivering. "I don't know what to do."

"It's alright, son. I'm sorry I don't know what to tell you. We'll figure it out."

A troop of people entered the observation room. A Human woman, an Arkouda, and a pair of Lo-sats. This could be a trick.

Without eye contact, Ned whispered to Mui-xe. "Hide. Stay silent until I call for you. Understand?"

Mui-xe ran under Ned's cot, contorting his lanky body to fit.

THIRTY-ONE

(JOKΛ)

In a creepy lab, except holy *skata* there's some dude here pounding on a window!

JOKA APPROACHED THE duraglass partition, unable to believe they'd finally found this guy. Ned Porandi banged on the other side, screaming something. He bore the face of someone with dwindling options.

Joka peered over her shoulder at the others. "This could be another hologram trick."

Doh-riss pointed behind the captive scientist. "There's a body in there with him."

Joka's eyes widened. A Lo-sat woman crumpled on the floor. That must be the wife. *Oh Earth, did he kill her?*

"Probably a trick," Bikkolos said. "If it's not, someone in that much distress can be dangerous."

Joka was close enough now that Ned's muffled shouts were audible.

He was swearing in Arkouda, not Human. "Diastrevlo, you sonofabitch! Show yourself! You killed her." Tears streaked down this guy's face.

Joka reached out to the duraglass and looked back at the inspector. "It's not a trick. That's actual emotion right there. This Diastrevlo dude had none of that. Plus, he's locked up, remember?"

Binh snorted. "Yeah, Dick Puncher is right. Mr. Personality back there definitely did not have a contingency for his family treasures getting knocked into his spleen."

Joka kept her attention on Ned. "Can you hear me?"

Ned's expression cooled as he lowered his fist. "Who are you?"

She jabbed a calloused thumb over her shoulder toward Doh-riss. "We work for Symphora." A smile parted her lips, which faltered upon remembering their departure. "We got your message and came to rescue you. And that cop behind me has been searching for you and your wife since your kidnapping."

Ned observed them, his face a topographical nightmare to read. The mention of Symphora shifted his expression, a mix of sorrow and joy she didn't understand. He sighed and winced hard. "Is S-symphora c-coming?"

Joka looked back to Doh-riss, who shrugged. "Um, Symphora is ... laying low. That's why it's us, and not, you know ... her."

Tears streaked the man's face, but he didn't sob. "D-do you know a w-way out?"

Doh-riss nodded and moved to a control panel, puzzling over the buttons.

Wincing, Joka fixated on the Lo-sat body on the floor. "Does she need help?"

New moisture formed on his eyelids. "Diastrevlo tortured her and left before she died. I think your arrival distracted him." After a wince and a sigh, his tone hardened. "Where's Diastrevlo? We're not safe here."

"Sure we are." Joka smiled and folded her arms. "We found him and locked him up in one of his own rooms."

Ned's face fell. "You didn't kill him?"

Bikkolos sneered. "I'm a government agent. I can't kill anyone who needs to go to trial."

Ned huffed, fogging the duraglass. "You can't hold him here. He has all kinds of bots and places to sneak around. If you didn't kill him, he is not where you left him. He'll return any second." His breathing quickened, and his eyes bulged. "Can you get me out of here?"

"Yeah." Joka turned to the others. "Let's find some buttons to lift this thing up. See the hydraulics in the corner? There must be a way to lift the partition."

Doh-riss hunched over the nearest computer station, combing over buttons and commands. Binh strolled to the next nearest one, casually examining the command board as if browsing a menu.

Bikkolos tapped the glass with his paw. "Do you have any idea how we can open this from our side?"

Ned shook his head. "I haven't seen it open since La-hok and I were brought here. That was years ago."

Years of losing to Marka and Kah-renn in card games taught Joka this Ned guy was hiding something. The way his gaze strayed slightly then snapped back to attention, like he was catching himself in some subconscious lapse.

Sweat beaded on Joka's neck. Maybe this guy killed his wife. Snapped from all the pressure. Or he knew something he wouldn't share. As she left the glass and examined the monitoring station nearest her, she let out a sigh.

He also didn't have reason to trust them. He'd requested Symphora and got … them.

The inspector found the mechanism to operate the lift. The partition sank into the floor, shaking Joka to the point the vibrations rattled her spine and threatened her balance.

When the partition lowered enough for Ned's head to poke over the other side, Binh and Doh-riss jogged over to Joka.

Doh-riss hissed in her ear. "He's not alone in there."

Binh switched languages and spoke Human. "Someone scared shitless. Pheromones strong enough to penetrate this sterile chemical cloud the good doctor liked."

Bikkolos' ear perked up, and he glared at Ned. "Who're you hiding?"

Ned slumped, turned to his left, and croaked something in Lo-sat. It sounded like a name. He continued in Arkouda. "You can come out now."

Joka's eyes widened. A boy crawled out from under a naval cot. Human facial structure, but with the eyeridges and tail of a Lo-sat. Skin and flesh mixed together in ways she didn't think were possible. His red eyes bore into her soul. While his gait and demeanor suggested a child, his Lo-sat height made him taller than Joka.

When their eyes met, Joka sensed a kindred spirit in him. This poor kid was an outcast who'd never fit in anywhere, either.

This was the secret. This kid's existence explained why Diastrevlo held them hostage. Ned and his wife had created a hybrid.

"Hi." She tried to smile as warmly as possible. "My name is Joka Bunear. We came here to rescue you and your dad."

The kid sidestepped behind Ned even though they were the same height.

A part of Joka died knowing this kid may have spent his whole life only knowing his parents and that Diastrevlo creep. Maybe also the lab aide the sicko murdered. Seeing other people must be overwhelming.

"Your dad called my boss," Doh-riss said. A half smile curled around the boy's mouth, wrinkling the scales around his lipped snout. "He asked us to come save you. I'm sorry we didn't get here sooner to save your mom."

The kid glanced back to the crumpled body on the floor and gulped back tears.

"No, no, no, I'm so sorry," Doh-riss pleaded. She peered down at Ned. "Sorry."

He waved his hand. "This is still new. Mui-xe..." The kid looked over. Ned pulled the boy close. "We need to go. I'll carry your mom."

As Joka glanced around the room, a brick formed in her gut. Five adults, one child, one corpse. The battledart was damaged, and Bikkolos couldn't have much room in his police speeder. Unless this dirtbag had another ship laying around somewhere they could pinch, they weren't all escaping this rock.

"Ned," Joka asked, "did Dr. Diastrevlo ever leave the asteroid?"

Ned's eyes widened. "He would be gone for random amounts of time. Days or weeks sometimes. I have no clue where he went."

Doh-riss scooted beside Ned and extended her tail toward Mui-xe. "There's another larger asteroid connected to this one. Some kind of elevator. Do you know where it is? Mui-xe, I'll help you with your mother's claws. Did she tell you what to craft?"

The boy shook his head.

Joka cast a glance up at Binh; he was quieter than she'd come to expect. Seeing this kid must be throwing him.

Doh-riss stroked the boy's cheek with her tail; he recoiled and flinched. Ned reassured him, and the boy pinched the end of her tail. Doh-riss looked back to Ned. "Once we're safe, we'll deal with her claws. You can help him. Did she ever tell you?"

"Yes, but I don't know what she'd say now."

Bikkolos folded his arms. "We need another ship. I still need to arrest Diastrevlo."

The group trudged toward the observation room's exit, Joka and Doh-riss at the front, Bikkolos in the rear, grumbling about needing his equipment back so he could snap pictures and collect more evidence. "I can't even call for backup," he muttered.

Binh glanced over his shoulder, and Joka fully expected him to make some comment about the Arkouda's Sleeping Goddess religion, but he observed the boy instead.

When they entered the sprawling corridor, the lights had changed. Noticeably dimmer.

"Shit," Joka whispered.

Doh-riss hissed, "Stop. There's a child around."

"This ain't good," Binh said. "Sad-sack the scientist was right. Flatdick escaped."

Joka scanned the corridor. All the previously closed doors now gaped open, including the one they'd shoved Dr. Diastrevlo into. Joka motioned for everyone to follow her to the room they locked him in.

Empty.

"Shit," she whispered.

Bikkolos edged around her. "You were right, Mr. Porandi. He escaped."

Ned clutched his wife's corpse tight, breathing harder. "We're leaving. He'll have a trap for us some-where." He fumbled around for her grav harness and lowered the setting.

Doh-riss took a sharp sniff. "I can catch the trace of our scent from where we were before we got dragged in there. That should lead to the entrance."

"We'll follow you," Joka said. "Should we expect more security?"

Mui-xe croaked in his tiny voice, too scratchy to be a prepubescent Human and too soft to be a young

Lo-sat. "Diastrevlo has lots of robots. I don't know where they are."

"Something else must be going on," Joka mused.

"Or it's a trap," Binh said.

After a few more twists in Doh-riss' path, they arrived at the stairwell leading to the surface.

A *thud-thud-slap* echoed from the top of the stairs. Slow, plodding, deliberate.

Everyone stopped. Bikkolos and the Lo-sats sniffed furiously, eyes wide.

With an "oompf," Ned shuffled his dead wife's body to his shoulders. The tip of her tail nearly dragged across the floor.

"Ned, what's coming?" Joka asked.

"I have no idea."

A PA system boomed, announcing from out of sight. "Surrender Batch Thirty-two. The rest of you may leave." It was the emotionless voice of Dr. Diastrevlo.

"Thirty-two?" Joka asked.

Ned scowled and shouted back, "You're not getting him."

Thud-thud-slap. Whatever descended the stairs was close.

The PA system buzzed. "If you want Batch Thirty-two to live, surrender it."

Joka realized what lurked on the other side of this threat. A pair of feet appeared at the top of the steps. Not quite the feet of a Human or a Lo-sat but some painful mesh of the two. Unlike little Mui-xe, these feet belonged to a fully-formed adult. Eyes wide, Joka glanced back to Mui-xe. Whatever approached was the adult version of him.

She stared at Ned and mouthed, "Is he really your son?"

No response came because Ned fixated on the feet. Each step revealed more of a leg. Gray-brown skin and scales meshed together. A tail too short to be prehensile like Binh's and Doh-riss'.

Scar tissue and stretch marks littered the naked torso, like it had grown too fast.

Binh retreated a step. "What in the *nguc*?"

Bikkolos advanced, addressing the interloper. "Get your hands and tail as high as you can reach when you come down. No sudden moves."

Thud-thud-slap.

After its footsteps was the unmistakable tremolo of a groan, drawing nearer with each step.

Low enough for Joka to see its collarbone, she noticed a blinking light, reminding her of the fancier grav harnesses Arkoudae and Lo-sats would wear. Her gut twisted as its face came into view. As it continued its groan, all of its mouth lay open and exposed. Teeth more akin to rocks littered the inside. She hoped for its sake it had the monthly Lo-sat appetite.

When its red eyes came into view, Joka realized whatever this was, man or woman, Human or Lo-sat, it was brain dead. The gaze which didn't lock on anything reminded her of when Kah-renn's older sister got hit by a falling engine block on the Calamity—Symphora had to put her out of her misery.

This aberration before here was just a walking collection of agony. Her pity for the thing matched her compulsion to shit herself.

She raised quivering hands in a placating gesture and spoke in Arkouda. "W-we don't want any trouble. Just let us go, alright?"

Doh-riss repeated the message in Lo-sat.

Nothing. Brain dead.

Mui-xe let out a wail, and Ned shuddered.

Bikkolos closed the distance and stood in front, blocking off the advancing creature. "Stay where you are, by order of the Collective."

Another shambling step.

Thud-thud-slap.

This thing couldn't understand them or lacked the capacity to respond. Its eyes lacked cognition. Just agony.

Upon reaching the bottom of the stairs, something curious happened with its hands.

They glowed.

Joka wouldn't have noticed it at first, but its hands, an impossible mixture of fingers and claws, glowed in time with the blinking grav harness implanted under its skin. The crimson glow shifted to blue and then white, as if heating up.

Its groan crescendoed to a howl, and it raised its hands.

Two fiery pillars erupted from its palms. Joka banked left, diving out of the way, Doh-riss with her. The men dodged to the right.

They couldn't reason with this creature.

Doh-riss shouted over the flames. "We have to distract this so they can escape."

"Get the kid out of here!" Joka called to the men. "We can handle it!"

Over the crackling fire, she caught some protest from Bikkolos and an exasperated moan from Binh. As they circled to get around the creature shooting fire, Joka dove under the pillar of flame.

The men had clambered up the steps. They just needed to incapacitate this thing, and they'd join them.

Easy.

She yanked on the thing's tail, forcing its aim to falter. The flames petered out for a half-second, which Doh-riss used to wrap her tail around its neck.

Joka twisted the thing's tail, and it slashed down at her with its half-clawed hand.

It ripped through her flight suit and took a chunk of her arm.

"*Skata!*" Bleeding in altered gravity wasn't good.

"Focus!" Doh-riss groaned.

Joka collected herself and debated punching the thing's mess of genitalia. Instead, she stomped on the ankle and then the insole.

Nothing.

Meanwhile, Doh-riss made progress wrangling the arms.

Huffing footsteps against metal told her the men reached the stairs. Just a little longer.

Joka clenched her teeth and punched the disaster between this thing's legs.

Nothing.

The women managed to wrestle it to the floor, and its hands whitened again.

"No!" Doh-riss hissed. She bit the thing's collarbone where the blinking lights were and yanked out the embedded grav harness with her teeth. Joka expected the creature to go limp and keel over at that moment, but instead, the mesh of scales and skin squelched and gulped to realign itself, covering the fresh wound with scar tissue.

Doh-riss spat out the grav harness, and the two of them rolled away from the rising body. It floated toward the ceiling. As Joka prepared her victory dance, a thought struck her.

The ceiling wasn't high.

Its hands ignited. In a flash, flames poured toward her.

Time slowed to a crawl as Joka accepted her death.

She raised her forearms in feeble self-defense as if they could save her from the billowing inferno already searing her exposed hairs.

Despite the emotional part of her brain screaming how much she didn't want to die, the logical part of her brain accepted her death.

At least she nut-punched someone who abused a child. Not the worst heroic action out there.

Doh-riss would never know she was a truer friend than any Joka ever had or how much Joka hated herself for her cruelty.

As the first flames licked Joka's face, her last sight was Doh-riss.

Diving over her.

Time snapped back, and Joka rolled away again. She pulled the yelling Doh-riss out of the flames' path, but her long body slowed Joka's progress. The creature's groan melted into a whimper.

The creature's red eyes lightened to pink, then imploded with a wet snap. The whimper dissipated into silence, and the creature hung limp. Whatever capacity it had to regenerate wounds couldn't handle the lack of gravity and altered blood flow.

Flames on Doh-riss' back singed Joka's eyebrows. Joka hadn't acted fast enough.

Doh-riss coughed and shrieked as Joka smothered the last tongue of flame. With a huff, Joka heaved her over.

Her once-green facial scales had smoldered to a ruddy auburn, and the left side of her face had burnt off, revealing blackened muscles and exposed bone. When she blinked, scales flaked off.

"Doh-riss, I'll get you out of here, I—"

"S-s-stop. Take my claws."

"NO! You'll—"

Doh-riss raised a shaky hand to her snout, then bit hard with a wince and a crunch. She opened her snout, severed claws plinking to the floor.

"P-p-promise me something." Slivers of scales fell from her in rivulets with each movement.

"I'll get you home. I'll—"

"Don't swear around the boy."

In one breath, Joka managed to sob and laugh. "Is this a joke?"

Doh-riss displayed no mirth. This wasn't the running joke Joka had assumed it was this whole time.

"Before Symphora found me..."

"You don't have to say it," Joka said. "I know."

A tear escaped Doh-riss' good eye. "The men who would buy me would say awful things while they used me." She coughed. "When I heard foul words, it reminded me of them. The boy... I don't want him..."

"I'm so s-sorry." Joka cradled her as the last flames dissipated around them. "I'll make sure he l-lives a good life." Tears stung her eyes while memories of her unkindness attacked her heart. "What should I do w-with your claws? Do you have family?"

Doh-riss blinked hard and coughed. She tilted her head to Joka, eye glossing over. "Just you, sister."

She went limp in Joka's arms.

Brushing away tears, Joka stuffed Doh-riss' claws into a pouch on her flight suit, opposite the damaged side. She'd find a way to use them and honor her. After one last look at her friend's declawed body, she climbed the stairs.

Tears clouded her vision, but she let them flow. Her arm tingled, and she could stretch enough of her fingers to know she'd be able to pilot again.

Not that Doh-riss would.

As she ascended, she realized she'd need to give Ned her flight suit if he were to survive a ride in the battledart. But Mui-xe? Either his Lo-sat physiology would allow him to survive the trip or die because of his Human biology. Ned and Mui-xe's only hope would be to ride in Bikkolos' squad ship if it had a holding cell meant for Human criminals.

Assuming they could escape Diastrevlo. A chill crawled up her spine, realizing this creep might be watching from afar.

THIRTY-TWO

(RICK)

In the laboratory of nightmares

ELEVEN OF RICK'S recruits and five prisoners of war entered this murder pit of science. Nine and four strode beside him now. Of those nine, both Equalizer teams remained intact with three gunners. They'd taken out seven of Diastrevlo's experiments.

He knew how to kill them but had no clue how many more lurked.

They exited the tank room through reinforced double doors. Each step made him wonder when Diastrevlo would threaten them over the PA again. Rick exhaled, noticing his breath fog in front of his face.

Interesting. This near-freezing temperature might keep the abominations away since Lo-sats were cold-blooded.

This asteroid was big enough to hide a small settlement. Anywhere between one and five hundred people could be hidden away. A cruel monster like this Diastrevlo character might even have double that amount, cramming people into unsanitary conditions.

Or maybe storage tanks stored them until desired. Rick clenched his fist around his gun. He'd kill this sonofabitch if he laid eyes on him. Diastrevlo hadn't expected them to survive this far. He might be fleeing or preparing another trap. Maybe something distracted him, too.

To their left lay another double-reinforced door. The sign to its left, written in block Arkouda letters: LIVE SPECIMENS.

Rick hailed the weaker of the two Equalizer teams. Time for them to earn their keep.

"Let's bust down this door," Rick said. "See who's inside."

They fired the harpoon, puncturing the door with a satisfying metallic crunch.

They retracted the chain, adjusted their aim up, fired, and repeated until they created enough of a hole to walk through.

Rick hadn't considered the door-opening applications of the Equalizer, but it was proving useful. He ventured through the opening first, arriving in a decontamination room. Made sense.

Tubes descended from the ceiling and hissed out decontamination spray, still following their programming despite the unusual intrusion. He could barely smell the spray's ammonia odor through the laboratory's chill.

More unsettling was the lack of alarm at their entrance. They either weren't expected to get this far, or they were walking into a trap.

The second set of doors wasn't locked. When they opened it, another cavernous room greeted them, carved into the asteroid's rock. Artificial oxygen pumps ran along the ceiling. But scattered on the floor were rows upon rows of tents. In between those tents were the telltale signs of glowing cookpans along with cheap cooking oil odors.

The noise of Human voices hit him hard. These were Human-sized tents. But the scores of voices weren't speaking Human. He strained to hear, but not one stray Human word reached his ears. These people, somewhere around two hundred if he had to guess, were all speaking Arkouda.

He advanced, and an armed and armored Arkouda approached. Rick stiffened and threw out his arm to halt his recruits, then repositioned himself to conceal his missing arm.

The approaching Arkouda ignored Rick entirely and addressed Katochos and the other captives.

"We weren't expecting a new shipment today. Why do they have weapons?"

Eyeing Rick, Katochos grimaced. "These Humans are hunters. We gave them clearance to carry firearms."

The armored Arkouda eyed the Humans. "No firearms allowed in here. Why'd you come from that door?"

Rick stole a glance around the rows of tents. As far as he could tell, only about five other Arkoudae milled about this shanty town.

Rick sneered and addressed the guard. "We're here to rescue them. You can assist or get out of the way."

The Arkouda's eyes flitted between Rick and the captives.

Katochos added, "Do what he says."

"You found homes for them all?" the guard asked.

Rick cocked an eyebrow. "What do you think these people are here for?"

The guard peered over Rick's head, addressing the prisoners. "Are these Humans all there—mentally? Do they know where they are?"

Katochos stammered, "Y-you know what, why don't you tell them? They might believe it if it came from you."

This ought to be good.

With a heavy sigh, the Arkouda dropped to a knee to meet Rick's eye level, like he was a damn child. "This is a refugee camp. By the look of your weapons, I'm assuming you've been living off the grid for a few years. There's a bad group of Humans out there called Earthquake. They attack and kill Humans who don't align with their cause. All these people here lost their homes because of them. Our job is to find new homes for these people. The other guards ensure no fights erupt while waiting for their new homes."

Rick clenched his jaw. "That can't be true."

The Arkouda indicated the tents behind him. "Talk to them if you don't believe me."

Katochos stepped forward. "Do any of the other guards use that door we came through?"

"Only the camp director. It's why I'm a bit surprised to see you." He pointed to another door on the cavern's opposite side. "That's our quarters. What, need the bathroom or something?"

Rick took a deep breath. "So a few Humans will leave periodically with the camp director? And you never see them again?"

The guard laughed. "Why would we see them again? He finds them new homes."

"Where do the new refugees usually enter?" Rick asked.

From his periphery, Rick spied a group of children forming around one of the tents nearer to them.

"The camp director sends a bot down here through that door to escort the new people. They're usually brought out while comatose. The government agency who funds us is worried about Earthquake finding these people again and then attacking us here."

Rick's mind reeled—the other commanders were brutal, but attacking other Humans made him want to vomit or punch something. Earthquake fought for all Humans, not just the ones who shared their politics. But then he remembered the archaeologist. He had been ready to kill her.

The only question was whether this guard knew what else transpired in this facility.

"Have you been through that door, ever?" Rick asked.

The guard sneered. "No, I haven't."

The crowd of kids swelled, attracting some adults. A few approached Rick's crew. One kid clutched a doll the same way his sister had before she disappeared.

Katochos waved his paws in a placating gesture. "We saw some disturbing things coming in. We don't think you're aware of the whole story. You really haven't gone through that other door?"

The Arkouda guard rose from his crouch, and a paw drifted to a holstered pistol. "You … look familiar. Who are you, exactly?"

Rick advanced. "I told you. We're here to rescue them. You can assist or get out of the way."

A refugee inched close enough for Rick to see her features. She was close enough to see his too, and those of his recruits, which included his haircut and the matching ones atop his recruits' heads. Her eyes lingered on their tattoos.

She raised a finger at them. "Earthquake!"

More people came over. Many screamed.

The guard whipped out his pistol and pointed it at Rick. His gunners fanned out and drew their own weapons, and the two Equalizer teams stood at the ready. A few muttered some taunts.

Rick stood his ground but rotated his pistol to the side to demonstrate he wasn't aiming it. "You don't understand what's happening here. These people are never being reunited with their families. The camp director is experimenting on them."

Katochos bristled and bared his teeth. "He speaks the truth. We saw it ourselves. The Humans are turned into … unnatural things."

The guard gripped his pistol and clicked off the safety. "Sounds like a load of *skata*." He shifted his aim from Rick to one of his men holding an Equalizer. "Drop your weapons." With his free paw, he tapped a plate on his armor and spoke into a comm. "I need backup by the director's entrance."

The five Arkouda heads that towered over the tents swiveled toward them and lumbered over.

Shit. "I don't want a bloodbath. If you come with us, they'll show you. There are enough Citizens there for a valid testimony."

The guard sneered. "Them doing your bidding invalidates their status."

One of the other Arkouda with Rick gasped, and another joined Katochos. "They are more trustworthy than your camp director. He's a criminal."

"We get our funding from the Collective government. Last warning, Humans. Drop your weapons."

"You first," Rick hissed.

The other guards had arrived, and the whole camp broke into a cacophony of shouts. Frantic people banged on the guard's door.

Rick didn't have any other choice. "Team one, take your shot. Team two, hit his closest companion once he's in range."

Cha-thunk!

An Equalizer harpoon raced over Rick's head, nailing the guard in the sternum, forcing him to the cave floor. The *whizz-crack* was followed by the thud of armor hitting the asteroid rock.

"Retract and prepare the next shot," Rick called. He wheeled around on his four captives. "They were going to kill us and you. I'm sorry it had to be this—"

The *shoom* of a plasma rifle interrupted him. Eyes wide, Rick watched helplessly as the bullet ripped into Aimey's head. Down one more gunner.

Rick aimed and shot off a round of suppressive fire at the offender. Not that it did any good. Even the budget security guard version of Collective armor defied any plasma bullets. It did make the guard flinch at least.

But in the time it took Rick to do that, more plasma shots connected with the members of the better Equalizer team. They crumpled to the floor, their skin sizzling. The worse Equalizer team shot their harpoon, taking out another guard. Two down, four remaining.

"Hurry up and take another shot!"

Rick ducked and dove toward Aimey's corpse. He snatched the dead woman's gravity harness, then rolled toward the dropped Equalizer. Sweat poured from his forehead, stinging his eyes.

He didn't care. He let it burn.

Dropping his pistol, he slapped the grav harness onto the end of the Equalizer's barrel and thumbed the setting to make it as light as possible. The targeting computer had already lined up a shot.

He clenched the Equalizer's trigger as it rose.

He only had one chance.

The harpoon whistled toward the target, hitting the guard in the face. Rick hadn't accounted for how the altered gravity on it would affect the firing accuracy. A half-second later, and it would have missed entirely.

Metal slicing fur, muscle, bone, brain, and then the same things in reverse produced wet cracks not meant for Human ears.

Rick didn't have time to celebrate. He clutched the barrel with his armpit and adjusted the grav harness to normal gravity, then spun out of its way as it fell to the ground.

The remaining guards stopped in their tracks. They dropped their pistols.

"We surrender," the one on the left said.

"We accept," Rick said. "On two conditions. First, deactivate your armor. Second, get these civilians to calm down. They're in real danger but not from us."

All four of them stared at Rick, slack-jawed. Rick knew they were realizing for the first time that a Human could be a capable warrior, not only an uneducated trigger-happy dullard like propaganda had conditioned them to think.

Rick examined his own men. He had an Equalizer team and one gunner still standing. His Arkouda captives now outnumbered him and his recruits. Not good.

"Go on," Rick said, pointing with his pistol. "Let's get that armor deactivated. You're wearing something underneath, right?"

The guards exchanged looks. This wasn't the cushy job they'd signed up for. They weren't hardened soldiers like Rick had expected. He took no pleasure in ordering their comrade's deaths and would need to learn those three names to add them to his list.

The list of lives he'd taken had grown too large, and he couldn't just go off memory anymore. He only wanted to add one more today: Diastrevlo.

These guards were unknowing and unwilling pawns in a bigger game. But Diastrevlo getting money from the Collective and also targeting loyalist Humans didn't add up. Diastrevlo should be going for Earthquake members if the government were putting him up to it. Another rat was at work, Rick knew. He would uncover the truth before he left this rock.

The surviving guards removed and deactivated their armor, kicking them over to Rick.

His surviving gunner grabbed the grav harnesses from the dead and affixed them to the discarded armor, letting them float. At Rick's command, he took out the chain from the discarded Equalizer harpoon and strung the floating suits of armor together. The gunner protested, saying he'd rather take the cannon, but Rick trusted his captives to carry it. They didn't need to know the harpoons were more expensive than the cannons themselves. That was half the reason they went on retractable chains.

The defeated guards, along with Rick's Arkouda prisoners, managed to calm the Humans from their frenzy. They got them to dutifully line up, and Rick counted them. One hundred sixty-two.

They hadn't heard any threats from Diastrevlo still. That sonofabitch either concocted something nasty or escaped.

Rick addressed the crowd of refugees, explaining the truth of their predicament. After a few sentences, he realized he'd need to speak in Arkouda instead of Human since the kids in the crowd gave him confused looks at hearing what should have been their native language. That cut to the core.

The expressions among the crowd were clear: they didn't trust him.

The damned Arokudae had to vouch for him, only because his original prisoners were so insistent. But they understood that Rick would kill them if they didn't.

Aspida told the crowd Rick had a warhive to take them to. That seemed to reassure a few, knowing they'd be in a military craft, not whatever Earthquake used.

Yet the Human faces before him were not ones of people happily joining their saviors. These were the faces of the twice-vanquished. In their eyes, Rick was a monster. He'd killed an Arkouda in front of them, and his squad had killed two others.

Some of the Human adults may have even recognized Rick: the traitor. He had no clue what kind of lies they'd been fed about him. A disgrace and embarrassment, a cause of shame, or a bloodthirsty anarchist.

He now had many loyalist Humans who saw him as an enemy. If they mutinied, he couldn't defend himself. If the captured Arkoudae turned against him and his recruits, they wouldn't stand a chance.

Rick signaled to the crowd they'd move out. "We'll get to our warhive, and I'll take you to a place where there's room to settle, or we can start actually finding your families."

More than a few faces staring back at him suggested they'd rather stay, but the defeat in their eyes showed they knew they had no choice.

This mission shouldn't have transpired like this. The doll-clutching kid's face made the ghost of his sister surface in his mind. *What would she think of me now?*

As they retraced their steps through the airlock and the blasted doors, Rick wondered if any of the monsters' bodies had reanimated somehow. He could lead a dead sprint to the exit, likely still closed off.

Using the Equalizer to open the other reinforced door had worked, so he could do that again.

He clenched his fist, hoping they would only have the abominations' corpses to greet them. Maybe then these people would see the truth and understand Rick had come to save them. The Collective didn't really care. Or at least it enabled people like Diastrevlo.

The doctor's looming specter held Rick near panic. This scientist had every reason to silence Rick and torch this whole operation as a failed experiment. These monsters were the beginning of something horrible. Perhaps this would be the next fight he'd have in the conflict against the Collective. Hulking Human monsters to fight instead of risking Collective soldiers. Win-win for the Collective if they could pull it off. Each casualty on both sides furthered their cause of suppressing Humans.

Rick's stomach turned. He'd find whoever authorized money for Diastrevlo in the government and rip out their throat personally.

He couldn't imagine how Monsieur Tecton would take the news.

The group shuffled through the tank room where they'd been attacked. The dead bodies of Rick's troops who had their grav harnesses removed thudded against the ceiling. A visceral stain on the ceiling marked where one of the abominations had died. Blood on the floor displayed where two others did, and two empty shattered tanks marked where the one who killed Wystone died. No bodies of the monsters themselves, though.

Either the monstrosities had some special way to decompose immediately, or Diastrevlo had hidden the bodies.

The captured Arkoudae, guards and civilians alike, marched behind Rick, in front of his troops. The horde of confused and kidnapped refugees followed in the rear. They neared the middle of the tank room, and Rick could make out Apatay where he'd left him, sitting against the wall. Breathing.

One positive, at least. Proof Rick stuck to his word.

When they passed the threshold of the room's middle, some decontamination arms descended.

Weird. Something must be malfunctioning. Or they'd sprung a trap.

Rick's eyes widened as the decontamination arms hissed to life, spraying a dark mist, aimed at the Arkoudae.

Katochos growled, covering his nose.

This mist didn't affect any of the Humans.

Rick tempted fate, inhaling deeply. Nothing. He felt fine. "What is this?"

"I don't know," the guard who'd surrendered cried.

"I can't smell anything," Aspida wheezed.

"You can't either?" Kreas said.

Rick tensed. "Can you see and hear?"

Through a cough, Katochos replied, "Yes. All the other senses are fine, but I can't smell for *skata*."

A deep crease formed in Rick's brow.

Diastrevlo was messing with them. But attacking his own kind didn't make sense. However, now the doctor could throw some other horrors at them, and their Arkouda captives wouldn't be able to smell it coming.

"Let's keep moving. We'll get everyone safe." Rick motioned for the crowd to continue behind him. Apatay waved them over, weak but alive.

"I promised I'd come back," Rick said. "What happened to the monsters' bodies?"

Apatay groaned. "I went in and out of consciousness. I don't know." His voice grated a bit lower than earlier, maybe a side effect of losing a good amount of blood.

"Right." Rick offered his hand to help the Arkouda stand. "We need to move fast. Dr. Diastrevlo could be planning his next ambush."

Apatay gripped stronger than expected and nearly incapacitated Rick with its force as he stood erect. As the wounded Arkouda stood, Rick realized the reinforced door that had locked them in with the abominations had lifted. He offered an Equalizer to use as a crutch, but Apatay refused. He walked with less of a limp than Rick would have guessed.

"So you found the Humans," Apatay mused. "Are they boarding the warhive?"

Rick glared at the gaping stairwell. "Apatay, were you unconscious when this door lifted back up?"

Apatay looked over his shoulder. "I suppose so."

Rick turned to the group. "We have a modified scrapper that'll ferry you to the warhive in groups of thirty. We'll figure out who in the Collective funded this operation. However many friends and families you had in this community that you never saw again, those people you believe found a home … were murdered. With someone using government money. They will know justice."

Rick set out with Katochos and the Equalizer team; his point person, a younger woman named Dvantz, had a functioning sidearm, just in case. Rick had the impression her teammates had slowed her down.

She deserved a chance to prove herself. After he had blundered on the moon with the archaeologist in trusting the wrong person, he needed to be more careful. Possibly too careful, since he didn't trust anyone besides Amanda, and she wasn't a fighter.

Not physically, at least.

Katochos and the Equalizer team covered Rick's back as he plumbed the depths of this larger asteroid while the refugees were funneled to safety above. Maybe if he could find the elevator connecting it to the smaller synchronized asteroid, he'd find more answers.

Considering the time which had passed since Dr. Diastrevlo made any threats or even hinted at his presence, Rick assumed the scientist must have escaped after doing something to those monsters' bodies. His skin crawled at the thought. Those monsters were Human once. They'd had dreams, goals, families. Souls. No more, thanks to the twisted doctor.

Maybe Rick had written them off as abominations to be killed, not sentient beings deserving of help. The word "murderer" surfaced in Rick's mind, but he shook it off.

As they traversed the room with the tanks, Rick addressed Katochos. "Be honest. Do you have any idea who in the Collective might want to do this? Use loyalist Humans instead of Earthquake sympathizers?"

Katochos shrugged. "Whoever can benefit from the conflict and profit from both sides. You know more about the government than I do, it seems."

"That's not exactly a good sign."

His gunner, Dvantz, scanned the area, almost to the point of twitching.

Rick nudged her. "Find the middle ground. Not too tense, not too relaxed."

Down the hallway again, Rick realized how much the shanty town cavern and tank room occupied the complex. Most of whatever else was dug must be for wiring, vents, and circuitry. Not many people were living here full time by the lack of comforts. They examined a few other rooms. One greenhouse—limp vegetation and shriveled fungi were there, ready for meager consumption yet not diverse enough to provide a healthy diet. Conspicuously absent was food for the Lo-sat victims, which still couldn't be located.

There would need to be a zoo's worth of rodents and lagomorphs to keep comparable numbers of Lo-sats filled and healthy, and that was just for one month.

Yet as Rick traversed the halls, the other rooms were mostly spare scientific equipment: beakers and burners meant for Arkouda paws and Human specimens.

As he readied to call it quits, one more door caught his eye, double-reinforced like the one to the Human refugees. Yet this door stood unmarked. Rick signaled to Dvantz, and her team launched a harpoon at the door. They yanked it open after three shots.

Rick had expected another cavern full of impoverished Lo-sats, but what he got instead made him stop short. This room measured about the size of a standard kitchen. One green tube, comparable to the tanks in the first room, stood in the center, a web of wiring and hoses protruding from it.

Unlike those other tanks, this one was occupied. A Lo-sat woman floated inside.

Beside this tube lay a monitor.

In simple Arkouda, it read out the vital signs for her.

Rick's eyes widened.

She was alive.

Katochos gasped. "Those numbers don't make sense."

Leaning forward, Rick's eyes flitted between the vital signs and the woman in the tank. The readout said she'd only been alive for a few days, but whoever occupied the tank looked like an adult woman.

Katochos pointed at one line in the bottom corner Rick had missed. "This is why those numbers look wrong."

Rick read the words aloud, not believing what left his mouth. "Clone seventy-two."

A shudder rocked Rick's spine, so forceful he nearly dropped his gun. The cost to keep Humans barely alive was lower than that of cloning, and kidnapping Lo-sats en masse would draw unwanted attention.

Humans were expendable. Cheap. Rick clenched his teeth so hard they might have shattered. "That's why we haven't found a Lo-sat colony here. The Humans were forcefully spliced with clones of whoever this is."

Dvantz piped up. "But those walking freakshows…"

Rick stiffened as he exhaled. "Whatever allowed them to instantly heal must also have aged them faster. Dvantz, snap pictures of this. Then we're going to trash this room."

She complied, but Katochos shot Rick a glare.

Rick craned his neck to meet Katochos' gaze. "This is sick. Diastrevlo escaped. We're destroying as much of his research as we can. No more monsters. Are you religious, Katochos?"

The Arkouda got out of Dvantz's way and nodded gravely.

"Are these things part of the Goddess' Dream or her Nightmare?" Rick asked. The ensuing silence proved answer enough. "Nothing good will come of this guy's research. I've been around enough tortured Lo-sats to know that clone is in agony. I'm putting her out of her misery. Like it or not, I'm torching this room, and when we get back to the warhive, we're blowing this asteroid to shrapnel."

Dvantz faltered. "We can use this research. If Earthquake got ahold of this tech—"

Rick wheeled on her. "No. More. Monsters."

In a flash, Katochos snarled, ripping the computer out of its socket. The green fluid in the tank ignited—the clone's eyes whipped open.

She flailed inside the tank. Katochos threw the computer at the tank, the fluid spilled out, and the clone collapsed in a heap.

No breathing. No movement. A tense minute passed.

Rick glared at the Arkouda while the Equalizer team stared in shock.

"What was that for?" Rick demanded.

Katochos shuddered. "I don't know if clones count as real people to the Goddess, but I know She'll sort it out when She wakes. Maybe I've taken an innocent life," he straightened and glared at Dvantz, "but I'll be condemned to the Nightmare if I let Earthquake get this technology."

Rick stared at the dead clone, wondering if she'd ever been sentient enough to name herself.

They left the room, returning to the sprawling corridor, its end finally in sight. One rounded door, big enough for an Arkouda appeared against the wall as they approached.

A sign over it read "To Landing Pad."

"If this takes us to an empty hangar," Rick said, "we'll know for sure Diastrevlo escaped."

The door opened for them without difficulty, revealing an elevator. "This'll take us to the smaller asteroid," Rick said with mild confidence. "Get those breather masks on in case we're put out in the open."

Stuffing Rick, an Arkouda, and three Humans holding a harpoon cannon in an elevator was a tight squeeze, but they managed. After a chime dinged, the door opened to the surface.

After traversing a small path across the rocky topography, they came to the promised landing pad. It wasn't empty as Rick had expected, but instead held two mismatched ships.

One battledart.

One Collective military police speeder.

"Diastrevlo hasn't fled yet?" Rick spun around, desperately searching the nearby space for any telltale signs of ships. He radioed the warhive. *"Do a scan to see if any ships left after we arrived."*

A few seconds passed before the response came from the bridge.

"The scanner says nothing after us."

"These ships are what the doctor uses as a cover, I bet." Rick smirked and turned to his group. "I don't know how, but we beat Diastrevlo here. We'll make sure he gets a nasty surprise."

At his command, the five of them took position and hid behind the ships. Rick kept his eyes on the ground, scanning for feet.

After a few minutes, gentle surface vibrations caught his attention.

"Boss," Dvantz whispered, "on our left."

Rick peeked out from his cover.

A Lo-sat and an Arkouda approached. He recognized them both.

THIRTY-THREE

(INSPECTOR)

Below the surface of {REDACTED}, Asteroid field in {LOCATION CLASSIFIED}

ANOTHER PLUME OF flame erupted behind Inspector Bikkolos on the stairwell, followed by a shrieking hiss—the wail of a Lo-sat in unspeakable pain, one he knew too well, although it had been years since he heard it so close.

The shriek must have come from Doh-riss. Whether Joka had died in that fight, he didn't want to guess. Not that he could smell anything over the flames.

"We have to help them," Ned pleaded. He huffed hard. He would slow them down. Mui-xe didn't have the same issues navigating the steps and helped his father walk.

"Respectfully, you're not in charge. They bought us time, and we need to honor that. Hand your wife to me. I'll carry her." Bikkolos pitied him, having to climb steps as a Human, especially weighed down with a corpse. Even with his late wife's grav harness adjusted and his son holding the tail, he was struggling under the weight.

Tears streamed down Mui-xe's face. The sterile smell-canceling chemicals were dissipating, and Bikkolos caught the salt odor.

Bikkolos accepted the woman's corpse. The practical part of his brain hated carrying around literal dead weight during an escape, but his memory of losing comrades-in-arms was powerful enough to shut those thoughts out.

The boy offered his hand to assist Ned's climb.

"There's no telling what we'll run into on the surface," Binh said. "What's to say the good doctor didn't deploy more mutants by our ships? Fun little valet service?"

"We have no way of knowing." Bikkolos arched his neck to see above the top step.

Releasing his son's hand, Ned sprang with new energy, able to keep pace with Bikkolos and Binh. "I can protect my family."

"How so?" Binh asked. "You got some fireball boogers hiding in that beak of a nose? Will you shoot that at one of Diastrevlo's creepies?"

"No," Ned said. "When we get to the top of the steps, give me my wife back, and I'll show you."

Bikkolos eyed him. The scientist probably had an invention of some sort, but why hadn't he used it against Diastrevlo? "Let's just hope we don't run into any trouble. We'll give the ladies a few minutes before we take off."

They reached the top of the stairs, hatch door still open, suspended in the lack of gravity. Gently, Bikkolos handed La-hok's body to Ned. Ned pressed some device on his wrist, clutched Mui-xe tight, and then disappeared.

Both Inspector Bikkolos and Binh immediately sniffed around to find Ned and his family.

The sterile odor had dissipated enough that Bikkolos could make out Ned and Mui-xe's location, mostly because of La-hok's corpse—the pheromones she'd released in death were enough to signal the trauma of her final moments, and they'd linger in Bikkolos' memory for years, assuming they survived.

"Nice disappearing trick," Bikkolos said.

Ned's voice came from the void. "Thanks. If I could mask smells, I would have escaped a while ago. Diastrevlo stole this technology from me."

Binh tsked. "That's how he got the drop on all of us. I bet that's why he used that nasty cleaning chemical so we couldn't tell the difference."

"We also didn't get much chance to smell that creature coming." Bikkolos' instinct was to call it a monster, but he wanted to consider the boy's feelings. Mui-xe may have had the wherewithal to see the symmetry between himself and the thing Diastrevlo sent to stop them. Ned certainly did. The presence of the creature raised more questions than it answered, but that would have to wait. "I see our ships over there. Let's head over."

Binh sniffed and located the invisible family. "Don't get scared, kid. You're safe."

They marched toward their ships, sweet relief. Bikkolos was so focused on keeping olfactory track of Ned and Mui-xe that he ignored what loomed in front of him.

Until it was too late.

A Human voice called out from behind the ships. "That's close enough."

Bikkolos' hearts dropped. That voice sounded familiar.

Binh unleashed so many anxious pheromones that he couldn't smell Ned anymore.

The inspector's former friend stepped out. Another unarmored Arkouda flanked him, along with three Humans, working together to carry an intimidating-looking tube.

Rick Crith stared Bikkolos straight in the eye. Years of fomented hate had crusted over months of deep friendship.

"Why're you here?" Rick asked.

Binh stammered. "Hey, hey, hey, I was avoiding—"

Rick unholstered a pistol and shot at the rocks in front of Binh's feet. "Not you."

Binh cast a glance at Bikkolos. Of course the Lo-sat had no idea they had history. The fact Rick might shoot first and ask questions later dug like a jagged claw into Bikkolos' stomach.

"I work with the police now, Rick. No more active combat."

Rick advanced. "Give me a real answer."

"I came here looking for two kidnapped scientists. A Human and a Lo-sat. I didn't know you'd be here."

"How'd you find the thief?"

Binh chuckled and scratched the back of his neck frills. "You know me. I got caught up in someone else's mess. Hey, if I knew you'd be here, I would've hopped out an airlock."

Rick's gaze flitted between them. "Did you find Diastrevlo?"

Bikkolos made a show of displaying his empty paws. "Yeah. But he escaped. We don't know where he is."

"You're both full of *skata*," Rick said. "I can't trust either of you. Get on your knees and put your hands behind your heads."

The Arkouda and three Humans with him tensed.

"Don't do this, Rick," Bikkolos pleaded. Seeing the steel in the eyes of a man he once considered his brother, he did as commanded. "I'm sorry about what hap—"

"Wait!" came a voice from nowhere. Ned.

No. Bikkolos' heart thudded.

Ned and Mui-xe stepped into view, the illusion falling. Mui-xe's tail was missing, though. Somehow, Ned had altered the illusion. Mui-xe looked like a Human child, a smaller version of Ned. La-hok's body was revealed on Ned's shoulders.

"They're not lying." Ned's appearance garnered gasps from the Humans around Rick and a tsk from the Arkouda. He probably got a whiff of them but couldn't quite place what he smelled.

Ned advanced toward Rick, who squinted at La-hok's body.

"I'll tell you everything you want to know about Dr. Diastrevlo," Ned said. "I don't know or really care what your issue with these two are. I have no other way off this asteroid if you kill them. We'll go with you. Please, my son has seen enough."

Rick gazed at Mui-xe. Bikkolos' paws beaded with sweat. He knew Rick had fallen, grown disillusioned, joined terrorists. But Rick would never hurt a child.

"This device you used to conceal yourself," Rick said. "I want it."

"Done," Ned said. "Can you guarantee our safety?"

"Yours," Rick responded. "And your son's, provided you cooperate. Theirs," he indicated Bikkolos and Binh, "is another matter entirely."

Binh had finally ended his outpouring of anxious pheromones long enough for Bikkolos to get his bearings again. A familiar scent wafted over.

The Human woman, Joka. Alone. Binh must have sensed it too since he dared to rise from his kneeling position.

"Rick," Binh said, using the Human pronunciation. "I saw some nasty shit in there. I'm guessing you did, too. I see it now in a way I never could when I was preoccupied being snarky: you're right. Not Earthquake, *you*. Humans are treated like dirt. *You*, not Earthquake, deserve help. I want to work for *you*. For real this time. I'll even give you my private contact info for pings," he rattled off some numbers, a bit louder, "so if you say no here and let me live, you can contact me."

Rick appraised him with a cocked eyebrow. Bikkolos realized Binh shouted his ping address so Joka could hear. Even if Rick disappeared, as long as

Binh was with him, Joka could track them. Maybe that meant Symphora could come to the rescue.

Inspector Bikkolos tempted fate and rose from his crouch. He also spoke in Human. "Rick, you know I'll work with you. I can get pardons. News about your demands broadcasted through news networks. I can get you in contact with the right people, work out negotiations. Take the fact that I came here looking for a Human as proof you can trust me."

After one last look at the boy, Rick holstered his pistol. He must not have wanted to kill anyone in front of the child. Rick met the tall kid's gaze. "You're all coming on my ship. You'll get a meal and shower."

He shot Bikkolos and Binh a glare, using his eyes to shout, "You have one chance."

THIRTY-FOUR

(JOKΛ)

**On a stupid ass-teroid. Carrying her dead
friend's claws like a normal person.**

DOH-RISS' CLAWS IN Joka's pocket weighed her
down, almost as much as the biting wound in her
arm. Hopefully those monsters weren't venomous.
She imagined Binh making an STD joke and thought
about how she'd punch him, which helped the pain
more than it should have.

Living with Lo-sats, Joka knew she could leave
Doh-riss' body unattended guilt-free since she had
her claws, yet the sick feeling of somehow disre-
specting her friend—sister—lingered. As she climbed
steps, which were practically a series of stacked walls,
the guilt lay in how long it took before she saw Doh-
riss as a friend and how much longer before treating
her as one.

The chemical cleaner odor dissipated as she ascended. She hoped Binh and Inspector Bikkolos would trace her scent and wouldn't leave her for dead.

At the top step, sweating her ass off, she spied Bikkolos and Binh, but Ned wasn't anywhere to be found. What the hell? Maybe Ned and Mui-xe were hiding or something. She didn't see them behind any rocky outcroppings or anything after a quick scan. Maybe they had already loaded themselves into the ship and the other two were waiting for her and Doh-riss. Her heart sank with the realization she'd need to tell other people what happened to her.

She tiptoed close enough to see the now-damaged battledart she pilfered from Earthquake and a police speeder, then saw another Arkouda.

Her eyes widened, and she forgot about the pain in her arm for a second. Diastrevlo?

Inching closer, she realized the Arkouda wasn't alone. Four other Humans were there, all wearing shades of green and blue.

Another step forward.

The Human in front of the group only had one arm.

Rick Crith.

Heart sputtering, she darted behind a rocky out-cropping, praying to God and the Great Mystery and a few of Doh-riss' gods for good measure that nobody noticed her. She closed her eyes, desperate to focus and hear more, wishing Doh-riss were here.

A new voice joined the conversation.

Ned.

Shaking, Joka peeked around her cover and saw Ned, dead wife draped over his shoulders, and a vague outline she assumed must be Mui-xe.

Where did they come from?

Either way, she strained to listen. Ned sounded meek as if he were surrendering to Earthquake.

Oh, come on.

And then, Binh did too.

Of course he had to be obnoxious and extra loud.

But he didn't have a nickname for Rick. In the time she'd known him, he'd never directly addressed anyone by name. The bits of conversation in Lo-sat between him and Doh-riss reinforced this, and the thought of her friend made her wince.

Binh blurted out his ping address. She assumed it was some insult to Rick, insinuating he wanted to be best friends forever, but then it hit her.

Binh could smell her.

He knew she was close. Rick didn't.

Binh wanted *her* to have his contact information, not Rick.

She withdrew her omni-tablet and recorded his ping address. If they traded messages, she could track them. Rick could hop into warp speed on his stupid little stolen warhive, but Joka could track him as long as Binh had a way to send her pings. All she needed was two, and she could triangulate from there.

Then Bikkolos surrendered, too.

Joka's pulse quickened.

She'd gotten pings from the Calamity. One from Devy and the slew from Iasona. If she could pop that information into whatever software Bikkolos had on his police speeder, she could discover the Calamity's location and where it would be if it were still in transit. She could get reinforcements from Symphora herself. They could save them and avenge Doh-riss. All she needed to do was get into Bikkolos' speeder.

That's why the three of them were surrendering to Rick. They were giving her a chance.

Her pulse and breathing slowed.

Doh-riss and these guys believed in her competence.

She would go to Symphora and make her see reason, pariah status be damned. With Bikkolos on their side, they could get pardons. The Collective government would hear Symphora's side of the story and get the full truth. Pardons for everyone. Joka, and more importantly, Doh-riss would get the hero status she deserved.

Joka clenched her fists. This was her time to shine and be the mega badass. Then she glanced at the pouch of Doh-riss' claws. Badbutt.

She waited for her companions to leave with Rick. After some cautious glances out to where they were, she crept toward Bikkolos' police cruiser.

Even though the monster damaged her flight suit, she could navigate this safely: it wasn't designed for dogfighting in space with crazy gravimetric adjustments every second.

The speeder welcomed her since Bikkolos must have left it open or found some way to open it for her remotely. She carefully turned down the setting on her gravity harness and hop-floated into the cockpit.

The inside control panels required a minute to acclimate to, but she soon found her bearings.

She whipped out her omni-tablet and pulled up the information from the pings from the Calamity. She smirked, knowing Devy and Iasona were actually being useful for a change—a comment that Dohriss would've appreciated. Pulling out the metadata from them took some trial and error, but she found it. Long-ass string of numbers that were the coordinates. She punched them into Bikkolos' tracking computer, punching in the literal sense—the buttons were not designed for a puny Human.

As the onboard software beeped its calculations, she cast an eye above. A warhive floated nearby. No question about it: Rick had taken it.

Once the calculations finished, Joka plotted the autopilot path to the Calamity. This would let her save the little boy, his dad, and Inspector Bikkolos. Crap, maybe even Binh.

THIRTY-FIVE

(RICK)

Aboard the warhive rechristened *Noryang*, hyper-space lane toward New Lodestone

RICK'S BODY ACHED from the ice treatment. His abs burned from all the barking as much as his arm and shoulder from the shooting. He toweled off and dressed.

Sealed separately in the brig were the damn thief, the scientist and his kid who'd hand over their cloaking technology, and an Arkouda he'd once considered a friend. If everyone spoke truthfully, this was decent consolation for the number of fighters he lost today.

The nanite repair bots hadn't finished work on the warhive's comms array, so Rick initiated a call to Monsieur Tecton from one of the scrappers in the hangar.

As the connection established, Rick got a flash of his reflection in the screen. That mission had aged him. He wished it made him bald so he didn't have to sport the ridiculous Earthquake hairstyle. Those monsters, the deaths, and seeing Bikkolos all created new wrinkles in his forehead. Seeing Ten-trom increased the depth of the bags under his eyes. If it hadn't been for that kid being right there, he might have killed both of them on the spot. That wasn't the kind of person he wanted to be.

A twinge struck him. He might become that person if he wasn't careful.

The screen clicked on, and the chipper image of Monsieur Tecton replaced Rick's reflection. The twisted smile on his face made Rick want to punch something. The only consolation was the Leader hadn't accepted this call in his government offices or at his home. Finally, a sign he listened to Rick.

"Rick..." The Leader's smile soured to a scowl. "It seems you disobeyed me."

"Correct." Rick focused all of his attention on keeping his face neutral. "The information I had required action. You'll be glad I did, too, for what I found."

"Worth risking your career over?"

"A colony of Humans. Almost two hundred souls. They were bovee cattle, waiting to be experimented on without knowing it." Rick grimaced. "They thought they were in a refugee camp. They also thought we were the bad guys."

"Loyalists, then?" Tecton asked.

"They said they were victimized by us. That our operatives attacked and harassed them. Stole from them."

No surprise flickered. A fly could have landed on Tecton's face, and he wouldn't have flinched.

Rick's nostrils flared. "Did you know about this?"

Tecton waved his left hand in front of the screen. "If they're Loyalists, who cares?"

"We should." Rick's anger threatened his vital signs.

Tecton licked his lips. "You said experiments. What was happening there?"

Rick let out a long exhale. "Dr. Diastrevlo was performing some kind of horrific surgeries or cloning to build Human and Lo-sat hybrids. They were like walking corpses."

No surprise at that information, either. Politicians must be trained in keeping straight faces. "How'd they fight?"

Rick glared at his boss until he couldn't stomach the silence any longer. "I didn't say we were attacked."

Tecton shrugged. "But you were, right? You lost some fighters today. How about your polar bear prisoners that you should have executed?"

Rick fought the urge to sneer at the slur. "Yes, we were attacked by Diastrevlo's monsters, and yes, we suffered casualties. It would've been more without the Arkouda prisoners. Capturing the *Noryang* took a heavier toll than the *Salamis*." Rick lowered his voice. "I lost a lot of people today. Those prisoners also piloted the warhive."

Tecton tsked. "I'm sure. And what about Diastrevlo's lab? What'd you do to it?"

"I fired up the warhive's turrets and destroyed the whole damn asteroid. His research needed to be sent to Hell. What he made in there," Rick shuddered, "should never see the light of day. His funding came from the Collective government."

The Leader wrinkled his nose. "Or he was privately wealthy. He probably developed something marketable and bankrolled his operation there. Don't worry too much about it. You can't keep following this trail. It's a distraction. Go defend New Lodestone."

Rick straightened. "Have you been doing your part, Monsieur?"

"Hey, you don't talk to me like that—"

"Have you been trying to get the judiciaries and magistrates to listen to our demands?"

"You have no idea what I'm—"

"You're right. You're letting the other field team leaders kidnap, kill, and rob Loyalists while I'm persuading them to join us. Meanwhile, you're not using your position in the government to—"

Tecton actually muted Rick. The leader acted satisfied with himself, despite the purple shade creeping into his face. "The Collective spat you out. I took you in. You're forgetting your place. Get your skinny ass back to New Lodestone. You'll either get your next orders there, or I'll have some *armed* men escort you out. One word from me, and you'll be on the other side of those homeless shelters you love so much."

The connection cut from Tecton's end.

The bastard never gave Rick a chance to say anything about Porandi's cloaking technology. That might be for the best at this point.

Rick stomped out of the hangar toward the brig. He'd get this damn scientist to show him how to use his cloaking technology. If it could be employed wide-scale, it would tip the coming conflict between Earthquake and the Collective in his favor. As the thought surfaced, he realized he may need to contend with Earthquake itself if Tecton had had enough of Rick's renegade behavior. He passed a few recruits on his way to the brig. With each one, he wondered where their loyalties would lie if there were a schism between him and Tecton. That also raised the question of the other leaders. They were the ones more likely to take Tecton's place in the organization if he died or resigned, not Rick. They advanced because of their brutality and xenophobia. Rick was the only one making positive strides. He clenched his fist.

Earthquake was Humanity's only chance, and he would be damned if he let a bunch of racist buffoons ruin it.

He approached the brig chamber holding the scientist and his kid, pistol at the ready, just in case the scientist tried anything sneaky with his image inducer. He could be waiting at the door, ready to pounce. Why, he couldn't guess, but he'd had enough bizarre shit attack him in the last few years that he couldn't take chances.

He retraced his steps to his quarters to don his armor and considered grabbing Bikkolos to have a stronger nose by his side. But talking to a backstabbing bastard made Rick's blood boil too much. Tentrom had pledged his loyalty, for whatever that was worth. The thief sounded sincere, but Rick couldn't risk it. The two of them and Porandi had some chance to bond, and they could be planning something, even though Bikkolos was spineless and Ten-trom couldn't get trust if he stole it.

His armor, comprised of sliced and refitted Collective armor, painted the emerald and azure of Earthquake, fit well, although it came with the memory of the day's fight. After securing it, he returned to the brig, passing by Katochos' cell. He wanted to get the Arkouda he was beginning to trust, but a dead Lo-sat in the cell would complicate precise smelling.

Besides, Rick wanted another look at that corpse. He had a hunch he didn't like but needed to verify.

When Rick initiated the unlock sequence on the scientist's cell, he heard Porandi squeal an exasperated, "Quick!"

Eyebrow cocked, Rick entered.

The scientist and his son, seated in front of the Lo-sat's body, looked up at him. The boy seemed out of breath.

Rick angled his hips in a way that the other man would see his holstered gun, just in case he got any ideas.

"I'm here for the promised technology," Rick said. "Hand it over."

The boy cast a nervous glance at his father, forcing a repressed memory from Rick's childhood to the surface.

Rick retreated a step. "I'm sorry. You're trying to take care of your son and grieve." He inclined his head respectfully toward the body. "My name is Rick Crith. I represent free Humans outside the Collective."

The scientist nodded. "Thank you for rescuing us, Mr. Crith. My name is Ned Porandi, and this is my son."

Rick guessed how Amanda would react in this situation. Kids loved her. He met the tall child's eye level. "You can call me Rick. What's your name?"

The kid looked to Porandi as if for permission or guidance.

Porandi answered. "This is Mui-xe. My wife took such good care of him that I wanted him to have a Lo-sat name."

Rick's eyebrow arched, but he forced it back down. He'd seen enough orphans to know what kinds of bonds they could have with stepparents.

"So this was your mom, Mui-xe?" Rick asked.

The boy nodded, which gave Rick the second he needed to examine the body. Sweat beaded on the back of his neck. This was the woman from the tanks. Or rather, he'd seen her clone. Her DNA was twisted and manipulated, fused with unwilling Humans, to make Diastrevlo's monsters. He couldn't tell Porandi here. Not now with the boy there.

"I had to bring her body aboard. I don't know the right way to remove her claws. She died shortly before you and the ... others came."

"The detective and the Lo-sat?" Rick asked.

The scientist blinked hard. "Yes, them. Yes."

He's hiding something. "The Lo-sat we brought aboard knows how. I'll have him show you before much longer." He let a moment of respectful silence pass before making eye contact with Porandi. "I still need that device."

The boy cast another glance at his father. *He's in on it, too.*

Rick brought his face within an inch of Porandi's. "There a problem?"

The scientist checked his wrist—where he touched when the device deactivated before. The innocuous and small device wouldn't get a second glance from anybody. Casual onlookers would brush it off as jewelry or a low-tech wristpiece. "I won't give it to you on this ship," he said. "Not until my son and I are somewhere safe."

"No." Rick tried to toe the line of being firm without threatening in front of the kid. "You will be placed somewhere safe after I get it. My simpler solution is to take it."

Porandi gulped, and sweat beaded on the guy's forehead.

Rick rose to his full height, letting Porandi feel the size differential between them. "I'm not leaving without that device."

The kid shivered.

Porandi stood, pulling the boy close to him. "Can you get me new clothes for my son first? He's freezing."

"Enough stalling," Rick fumed. "Don't make me step over her body to take it from you."

Breathing heavy, the scientist pulled the boy behind him, obscuring Rick's view. "Can you promise me you'll leave us alone until we land?"

"No." Rick stepped around the corpse, and Porandi shuffled to keep the boy obscured.

"I'm begging you," Porandi said. "Just not now. I will hand it over, just, please, no—!"

Rick lunged, snatching the scientist's wrist. He dug his fingers into Porandi until the man yelped, sinking to his knees.

"And I'm begging you," Rick spat. "Pull the damn thing off your wrist. Don't make me hurt you in front of your son."

"No!"

It was the boy.

The kid pounced on Rick, wrapping himself around Rick's stomach. A mismatched plink of fingers went into the armor, as if the kid's fingers were different sizes. Rick couldn't feel anything through his protection. He kept his grip on Porandi.

"Get off my dad!" the kid shouted, clutching Rick's waist.

Rick ignored him, putting his focus into his grip on the scientist. He knew he'd start cutting off circulation soon. He dug his thumb toward the wristpiece's strap. He'd pry it off.

Porandi slapped Rick's hand, feebly trying to remove it. Too weak.

Rick did pity the guy, but he couldn't stand any more secrets on his ship. As he maneuvered his thumb under the strap, an acrid, smoky stench attacked his nostrils, and his abdomen warmed. He glanced down.

The kid's hands glowed.

The pad on Rick's armor was melting. *Shit.*

In one motion, Rick jerked his hips and thumb, snagging the device from Porandi's wrist and throwing the boy off.

As the melted and burnt fibers smoldered, Rick stared in horror as the boy rolled away on the floor, glow fading from his hands. When he came to the wall, Rick got a better view. This kid wasn't Human.

A mesh of skin and scales. Stumpy tail bobbing above the floor. Hands a jumble of fingers and claws. Protruding nose and jaw formed a rudimentary snout. Marbled red eyes.

The child version of the monsters he'd seen in Diastrevlo's lab whimpered in front of him.

Rick unholstered his pistol. "No more nightmares," he whispered. One more name for his list. He pulled the trigger.

"No!" Porandi, this time.

Shoom!

The sudden outburst made Rick miss the boy, hitting the floor centimeters away, leaving a smoldering chunk of charred metal.

"Please, no. He was protecting me. Mui-xe, let's calm down."

The gangly boy sank to his knees, and thin streaks leaked from his eyes.

Exhaling with the knowledge that he was prepared to murder a child, Rick holstered his pistol with a trembling hand. Keeping his torso to the boy, he gazed at the scientist. "This is why you hesitated."

Rick's heart beat faster than it had in years. He had pulled a gun on a damn child. The only nightmare in this room was him. Moisture beaded around his eyelids.

Porandi nursed his wrist. "Please understand—"

"The technology you used to create him..." Rick inhaled deep and blinked away the budding tears. "Do you know what Dr. Diastrevlo did with it?"

The scientist jogged over to the boy, rubbing his shoulders. "We saw."

"Did the inspector and thief know?"

"Yes," Porandi said. "They all did."

Rick fixated on the word "all" for a second longer than he should have. Porandi could very well still be hiding something. "I'll give you some time to collect yourself."

As Rick spoke, the boy caressed his father's injured wrist. After a moment, his hands glowed again, iridescent. A calmer shimmer than before. Porandi stretched his hands anew and rotated his wrist as if Rick had never touched him.

Rick blinked hard. How long before this boy turned into one of those monstrosities? Maybe this kid wouldn't turn out like the others. Or maybe the others were innocent victims like this kid. He inhaled deep. "Mui-xe… I'm sorry. I'll send in the Lo-sat to help you with her claws. Then we can take care of your mom."

Rick turned toward the door. Before he entered the combination to open it, he glanced at his feet to avoid his reflection in the screen.

Once in the brig corridor, he examined the cloaking device in his hand. If Porandi had created this, he must truly be a genius. As he turned the wristpiece over, he got a ping.

[Dvantz is dead. Someone pushed her out an airlock.]

Rick clenched his teeth. Someone was sabotaging him. Without even knowing the full circumstances, he had a list of suspects.

Ten-trom, even though he'd never killed anyone.

Spineless Bikkolos: a Collective agent on an Earthquake ship.

The technocrats who already tried selling him out.

Diastrevlo's lab guards.

A painful memory surfaced of his old second-in-command mutinying against him on that damn moon with the archaeologist. Maybe Tecton got to one of the more radical people in his employ and decided to off those most loyal to Rick.

There would be hell to pay.

THIRTY-SIX

(NED)

**In a holding cell smaller than the one
Dr. Diastrevlo gave him**

MUI-XE TREMBLED IN Ned's arms. "I'm sorry, Dad."

"I'm grateful you supported me. Really brave." Ned caressed his son's cheek with his thumb, bumping over the mesh of scaled skin.

"Is he going to be like Diastrevlo?" Mui-xe asked.

Ned winced—the boy pondered who would be the next cruel person to torture and experiment on him. A kid on his first starship should have fun and exciting thoughts, but with the cramped setting and Crith's intimidation, Ned understood why Mui-xe acted like a frightened animal backed into a corner. Even if Rick didn't want to exploit Mui-xe, others aboard would inevitably find out. He wished he could contact Maynard. Maybe he could find a way there, despite it all. They could live in the monastery or near it. The monks would keep their presence as silent as their prayers.

A shrill beep chimed from the door, indicating the door would open. Ned braced and positioned himself to obscure his son from whoever came inside. Not that it did any good against Rick.

"Hey, if it isn't the only Human smart enough to marry a Lo-sat." Binh's buttery voice came through in flawless Human. The Lo-sat thief entered, and the door closed behind him.

When they first met, Ned didn't have a chance to process Binh's grayed scales. He must have some kind of genetic condition which prevented him from shedding. Ned wondered how that would feel, and his only assumption was incredible pain. The gray pallor would make him stand out from other Lo-sats.

Binh waved his tail toward Mui-xe and took a knee in front of La-hok's body. Rigor mortis had set in, and Ned worried he'd violated a taboo with how long they waited. "Lefty sent me in here to assist." His gaze drifted toward Mui-xe, and he spoke in Lo-sat. He didn't have the same accent as La-hok and her mother, but Ned understood the gist of it. "Good tidings, young kin. The Human who-wished-he-could-re-grow-limbs sent me to help you with your egg bearer."

Mui-xe smiled.

Binh cocked an eyeridge and switched languages back to Human. "You know Human and Lo-sat, huh? You know Arkouda, too?"

Mui-xe glanced at Ned before responding. "Not all that well. Human was hard for my mom to speak, and Lo-sat is tough for my dad. We usually spoke in Arkouda."

"She could make a literal person from a petri dish, but she couldn't flatten her tongue enough to speak Human?" Binh tsked.

Mui-xe stared daggers at him. "Don't talk about her that way."

"Sorry, kid. Joking around is a defense mechanism. Your mom was really smart if she could make you. And your dad was really smart to stay away from other Humans. Isn't their hair gross?" Binh pointed a claw at Ned's stubble. "Look at that. Yuck. It gets everywhere. And you know what's even grosser about Humans? Lots of 'em drink milk. They even make other food with it."

Mui-xe's expression softened.

"You know a lot about Humans," Ned mused.

"Grew up on Earth. It's why I'm so unpleasant. Then there's the unfortunate amount of time I had to spend under Lefty's bootheel with his happy gang."

Ned cocked an eyebrow. Binh's parents must've been among the few colonists who settled Earth after the Eleva War. He would've been part of a ruling minority class, hated by the native majority by virtue of his birth.

Binh rummaged through the pouch on the diagonal chest piece he wore and withdrew a lockpick. Ned squinted at it. Impressive detail; the material looked crafted from Lo-sat claw. He handed the lockpick to Mui-xe. "This is what I made with my dad's claws. It's a ... key I use sometimes. What we make from claws is like a way to remember them. Did your mom tell you what some Lo-sats think happen when we die?"

Mui-xe returned the lockpick. "Their souls go somewhere peaceful, so they can't bring their claws."

Ned's gut twisted at his son's use of the word "they," like he didn't feel connected to La-hok's culture and that part of his identity. Ned also wondered if he'd do the same thing to describe Humanity.

"Yeah," Binh said. "But I'm not too sure if they're right. When my dad died, my sister and I couldn't agree about what to do with his claws. She and my dad didn't really like the choices I was making in life, so…" He sighed with his whole body. "So I made this as a way to make fun of them. My sister never told me what she made with the rest of his claws."

Ned broke the silence. "La-hok never told us what we should make out of her claws or how to remove them. I-I don't know if we—"

Binh waved his tail in front of Ned's lips. "When it comes to Lo-sat rituals, there's so many rules and variations you'll get something wrong no matter what you do. Probably like parenting, huh? I had a knife, but Lefty confiscated it." He focused on Mui-xe and switched languages to Lo-sat. "I'll use my claws to dig into her scales and remove hers. It'll seem gross, but once these claws are off, she's truly dead. Remember where she told you she was going if that's easier. You don't have to watch."

Ned sat on the floor beside Binh. "Anything I should do?"

Binh shrugged. "Be a dad."

Without waiting for any reaction or response from Ned, he snatched La-hok's hand and dug his claws into her thumb, making a stiff squelch. With a series of wet snaps, her thumb claw came loose, which Binh placed on the floor beside him as if removing screws from a piece of machinery. He went one by one down both hands until he had all eight claws. "Here, kid." He handed them to Mui-xe, letting them fall into his hands. "If you got a pouch or something, keep them together. We can take care of her body now. Remember, that body is not your mom anymore. She's moved on." Binh rose from his crouch then eyed Mui-xe. "Have you ever shed your skin? Or did your mom?"

Mui-xe shook his head. "I never did, but my mom told me about shedding her skin when she was a girl."

"I don't shed either." Binh pointed to his grayed scales. "Got a fun disease. 'Stare-at-the-gray-kid-itis.' But that body on the floor, just think of it as skin that shed, okay? Her belief is that she moved on."

"So what do we make?" Ned asked.

"That's what you have to figure out," Binh replied. "Before I go, I gotta send a ping." He winked at Mui-xe. "These ladies can't get enough of me."

THIRTY-SEVEN

(JOKA)

Exiting hyperspace outside the Collective frontier in Inspector Bikkolos' police speeder, temporarily named *Binhsux Mk II*

WHILE THE WHIRLWIND of crimson and vermillion streaks of hyperspace settled around her borrowed ship, Joka's omni-tablet chimed with a ping notification.

[Binh: Remember, you won't be able to ball punch your way through negotiations this time. Smartypants and the kid are fine. Locked onto our location yet?]

[Joka: I have a hunch where you're going. Send me another update in an hour.]

The Calamity loomed before her, and Joka's heart sank—she flew a police speeder toward an armed station full of criminals.

A string of curses flew from her mouth, which she censored upon remembering Doh-riss' claws in her pocket. She took a deep breath. They wouldn't shoot a police speeder. That would cause more trouble. Joka pulled up the pings on her omni-tablet and found the last one from Iasona. She hadn't responded when she got it initially but took a chance now.

[Joka: If anyone sees a police speeder inbound, it's me. I can get Symphora a pardon and all of us cleared. Let me dock.]

Thirty seconds passed. The Calamity loomed close enough for her to notice the details of the mismatched turrets. Apparent disorganization would create some difficulty for a more sophisticated system to defend against them. Maybe if the Collective fleet attacked the station, they'd stand a chance.

An Arkouda's voice dribbled over the public channel on the comm. "Joka Bunear, is that really you?" Iasona. Thank Earth.

"Yeah. Don't mind the police speeder. It's a long story. Can I dock?"

"What happened to the battledart you stole?"

Joka wished she slurped the booze in the glove compartment. "Come on, Iasona. Nobody was flying that scrap pile any time soon, and you know it. Besides, I left my flight suit schematics for Symphora. That had to be worth way more."

Iasona chuckled. "I'm messing with you. Before we let you in, can you disable the speeder's tracking software? Or did you already do that when you stole this speeder?"

"I didn't steal this, but yeah, I will. So, uh, Iasona… am I like public enemy number one?"

Iasona didn't respond immediately, but Joka caught some background noise suggesting Iasona shifted her noticeable girth in her chair. "Why hasn't Doh-riss said anything? Did you get separated? Is she with you?"

"She… um…" A thousand replies formed in her mind, and none of them did justice to the truth. "We… I have her claws." She winced away a tear.

"Oh no. I hope she finds her place in the Goddess' Dream."

She had a comment ready about how that was probably religiously insensitive, but she brushed it off. Wasn't the time for disagreements.

The blast door over the Calamity's main hangar retracted and revealed the oxygen bubble. Through the purple-hued field, rows of unflown battledarts hung out like bored chumps, the occasional routine inspection their only excitement. Symphora hadn't gone on a single mission in months. That felt so wrong.

Joka slowed the speeder and switched the auto-pilot to the docking mode. Her insides lurched as the gravity adjusted.

Inside the hangar, a smattering of mechanics and engineers were there, staring at her.

Marka and Devy sulked at the front of the group. Kah-renn crouched behind a ship, probably rolling dice with one of the younger mechanics.

The hangar's interior certainly seemed smaller than the last time. None of the girls looked like they'd seen real sunlight since before she left. No shore leave. Probably only the barest of supply runs. Meaning Joka had something they might want. The salt-and-must odor of sweat and shed fur smacked her hard.

Joka rose from the cockpit and waved with a dumb smile like she wasn't a total pariah. "Hiya, ladies." She had to open her eyes wider to accommodate for the too dim and too yellow hangar lights, which definitely made her look unhinged.

Stares.

Awkward.

"I brought some hooch," she announced.

Kah-renn chortled from the back. "Welcome home, Bunear!"

"Shut up." Marka marched toward Bikkolos' ship. "You've got a lot of explaining to do. Where's Doh-riss?"

Joka knitted her eyebrows. "Surprised you care." Joka addressed the whole group as she descended from the ship, floating down with the assistance of her grav harness. "Look, I know I left on weird circumstances."

"That's putting it mildly," Devy said.

Joka scowled, then pulled out a pouch from her pocket. "These are Doh-riss' claws."

That shut everyone up.

"I've been through some," her lips formed the word *skata*, but she remembered what she held, "some rough times, to say the least. Doh-riss and I followed a lead. It led me to a cop who can get Symphora a pardon and us cleared. That's how I got this ship. I need to get to Symphora—"

"Watch your mouth."

Every head in the room whipped around to the back where Symphora stood, arms folded, flanked by the surviving member of her strike team.

"Joka Bunear." Symphora let the name hang in the air. She waved Joka over. People parted to make a path. Kah-renn whistled a funeral march tune, which got some awkward giggles.

When Joka reached the bottom of the stairwell and stared up at Symphora, the mohawked Arkouda huffed. "My office, now."

Joka peered over her shoulder to the mechanics and engineers. More support staff had trickled into the hangar. She thought she caught Iasona from her periphery.

All eyes on her, Joka straightened. "No. Everyone needs to hear."

A menagerie of gasps, scoffs, and murmurs ran through the gathered women.

Symphora's left ear twitched. "How about I toss you out an airlock?"

"Symphora, I got a chance to see a bit of the galaxy, and you are an absolute legend. People swapped stories about you that Doh-riss and I never even heard before. You're more than someone who fills losers with bullet holes. You mean something to regular people, not just us."

Symphora adjusted herself. Looked like she'd skipped her exercise regimen the last few weeks. Skipped some meals, too.

Joka clenched her fists, pouch tight in her grasp. "We got a distress call from someone who really needed help, and you passed." Deep breath in. Probably her last one. "Because you were afraid of getting in trouble. Well, you were already in trouble. We all knew you were innocent, you knew it, and lots of people think you're innocent, too. But you were scared."

Breathing deep, she turned from Symphora to face the rest of the crowd. "Doh-riss and I went to help that person who reached out. And guess what? Earthquake got there, too. We needed backup, and we didn't have any. Doh-riss and I, two mechanics, had to get into a fight." She hoisted the pouch aloft. "I'm taking suggestions for how we should memorialize her, by the way. The person who needed our help is now with Earthquake. I know where they're going, and we can head them off. If we stop them, the Collective will have no choice but to pardon all of us."

Now it was Symphora's turn to clench her paws. "So you're trying to shame me over one single person? You want to endanger everyone on this ship over one person?"

Doh-riss would.

Joka turned back around. "Yes. And I think the real Symphora would, too. Not this scared old woman in front of me." She considered what would be the consequences of shitting herself in that moment. Pooping herself, not shitting herself. Doh-riss wouldn't want her to shit herself. "Symphora, you represent defending people who can't stand up for themselves. If you stop, Earthquake is the only option. You risked yourself for all of us over the years, and we all wanted to give that back to you by helping you here. For every kid you rescue, there's someone else getting lost." A tear welled, realizing it was a dice roll she and Doh-riss were saved as kids. "Do you want Earthquake to pick them up? And this guy who asked for help? You saved him years ago. He still saw you as a superhero. Let's get the Calamity back in gear and show the galaxy that Symphora and her gang still mean something."

Murmurs ran through the crowd. Joka couldn't parse them all out, but they ranged from "Who's this bitch think she is?" to "This bitch has a point." Everyone at least agreed on Joka's bitchiness. Except maybe Doh-riss since she was still technically present.

Symphora descended the stairs.

Joka's heart raced, and sweat beaded on her forehead.

Symphora leaned over Joka, letting her feel the height and size differential. "Scared old woman, huh? I've killed for less."

Too late to back down. "Prove me wrong."

Snarling, Symphora raised her paw. This would hurt.

The paw came down, landing on Joka's shoulder. Symphora twisted Joka around in her vicelike grip. "Maybe this bitch is right, and I'm washed up. But I'd rather die fighting than hiding." She turned her gaze to the crowd. "Who's with this old hag?"

Kah-renn piped up from the crowd. "You know I am!"

Marka laughed. "I'll smack these terrorists with my toolbox if I have to."

More cheers erupted. Fists, paws, and claws pumped in the air, and a chant rang out. "Sym-pho-ra! Sym-pho-ra!"

But the name didn't belong to her anymore. It belonged to all of them.

Once the cheers rang loud enough to shake the floor, Symphora leaned down to Joka's ear. "You know I'm going to make you clean toilets for talking to me like that, right?"

Joka sighed. "They can be dirty until we kick Earthquake's ass. Also, I'm going to need some medical attention for a wound on my arm before I can clean anything."

Symphora chuckled. "Did you make her claws into a spine for yourself?"

"I didn't have to."

"Earthquake is no joke," Symphora said. "You know where they're going?"

"Yeah, thanks to that police speeder."

"And you're positive your contact can get us pardoned?"

Of course not. "Definitely."

"Good." Symphora straightened and unleashed a roar; the force pushed the cheers into reverent silence. "Before we head out, we need to make some initial preparations. Make sure everyone's station is oiled, cleaned, and ready for some tail-kicking. Department heads, meet in my office for a strategy session."

As Joka followed Symphora up the steps, Marka followed. Joka caught a glimpse of Devy, who offered an apologetic smile.

A chill ran through Joka's spine as she considered the long-term ramifications of Rick and those Earthquake chumps getting their hands on Mui-xe and exploiting him for their own purposes. The stuff they could accomplish with Ned's technology made her shudder. Even the news of Dr. Diastrevlo making these monsters with Collective government money would bring more support for Earthquake.

Joka exhaled. That's why she needed to rescue Ned.

THIRTY-EIGHT

(RICK)

**Aboard the *Noryang*. Searching
for the damn saboteur**

RICK PULLED BACK his fist and smacked Ten-trom in the snout. The crunch echoed in the tight brig corridor.

"I had nothing to do with it!" the Lo-sat wailed.

Another hit. This one under the snout, cracking a dormant wart. "You're hiding something." The force from Rick's blow hurled the thief to the floor, and Rick used the opportunity to stomp on his tail.

"I was with the brainiac and the kid." Ten-trom feebly put his claws in front of his face.

"Say the names of your victims," Rick commanded.

"Nobody." The thief wheezed between words. "You grabbed my weapon and locked me up."

"Wrong." Rick lifted his boot.

"Wait…" He waved his claws frantically. "I have a half-sister on Earth. S-send my claws to her."

Staring into Ten-trom's marbled eyes, Rick saw the kid again. The kid he had prepared to murder. Then he saw the archaeologist he threatened. His jaw trembled. Threatening the weak and defenseless was what the Collective did to Humans.

"I'm … sorry." He pulled away when he got a ping on his omni-tablet.

Another dead body had been found.

The bloodied and battered thief stared back at Rick, heaving between coughing up blood.

Rick's gaze lowered to his hand. The Lo-sat's cyan blood sat on his skin, glistening. The skin on his knuckles had broken in a few places.

Without fanfare, Rick dragged Ten-trom by the tail to Porandi's cell. When he opened the door, the boy and his father were seated, inspecting the woman's claws. Wordless, Rick rolled the thief into their cell, then exited, locking the door behind him. If the boy could create heat like the laboratory's monsters, maybe he could heal a Lo-sat like he did for Porandi's hand.

Rick exchanged more pings with the bridge crew as he left the brig. Another person had died because he wanted to torture the thief. The logical part of his brain knew that Ten-trom was an unlikely candidate, but the primal part of him wanted to make him hurt. Rick couldn't let his trauma make his decisions for him. He'd find the killer and exact justice.

The *clank-clank* of Rick's boots echoed through the corridor like a banshee from Earth's mythology as he brought up a new ping. He contacted his manager on the Shaka station.

[Rick: Can't dock now. There's a saboteur. Forward any communication from the Leader to me before you respond. I will deal with the saboteur before we dock.]

[Shaka manager: Understood. Standing by.]

At least something was going right.

Rick entered the elevator and reached up for the engineering deck's button. He relished remodeling the interior of these ships. Everything meant for an Arkouda's reach slowed them down.

But the Arkouda aboard were the people he needed to see.

When Rick stepped foot in the engine room, the three present Arkoudae stood at attention. Katochos worked on the bridge. Allegedly. Hopefully.

Rick scanned their eyes, unable to read them. "Where's Apatay?"

Aspida shifted, round ears wiggling. "We haven't seen him since we came back aboard."

"He was acting strangely," Kreas offered.

"Nearly dying while fighting a monster will change a person," Rick said, almost more to himself, fighting a bad memory.

"That's why we didn't say anything," Plerosis said. "But it was also for such a short period of time before he disappeared."

Rick stroked his chin, reminding him of a forgotten bruise. "Was anything else off about him?"

The three Arkoudae exchanged glances and shrugged. "We couldn't get his scent because of all the Humans we picked up," Aspida said.

Kreas' eyes bulged. "Not that Humans smell bad. There were a lot of you, and—"

"I get it." Rick waved his hand. "Overload. But what about now? Would you be able to sniff out Apatay now?"

"What's wrong?" Kreas asked.

Rick envied their olfactory powers and wished he could smell through a lie. "Somebody on this ship is hiding something from me. You've all seen that I do what I say I'll do. If any of you are hiding something from me, understand I will find out and kill you. Get a read on my scent right now. Am I telling the truth?"

Jittery nods. He didn't like the sting of satisfaction their discomfort and fear gave him.

"So," Rick said, "anything you'd like to share?"

Kreas scratched behind his ears. "Apatay did ask about where you kept the armor and weapons from the soldiers you killed to take over the ship. He didn't act like he was in much pain, either."

Rick cocked an eyebrow. "He was there when it happened."

Plerosis stared at his feet. "He said it all happened so fast that he couldn't remember. And he didn't want to talk about the event or the pain."

Rick fired a ping to the bridge.

[Shut off all escape pod access. Nobody leaves this ship without my say-so. Is Katochos there?]

As he left the three captives in the engine room, the response came.

[Done. No new deaths to report. Katochos is here, too. He hasn't left.]

Rick descended the elevator and returned to the brig. His first stop was to the three cells holding the guards who'd surrendered. He examined each one through the viewscreen. Each was as unarmed and unarmored as when they surrendered, and the cell gate log showed no entry or exit since departure.

Breath held tight, he approached the cell door he'd been dreading. The conversation he didn't want to have.

He opened the door of the man he once considered his best friend, the man who was the final reason he had to defect from the Collective.

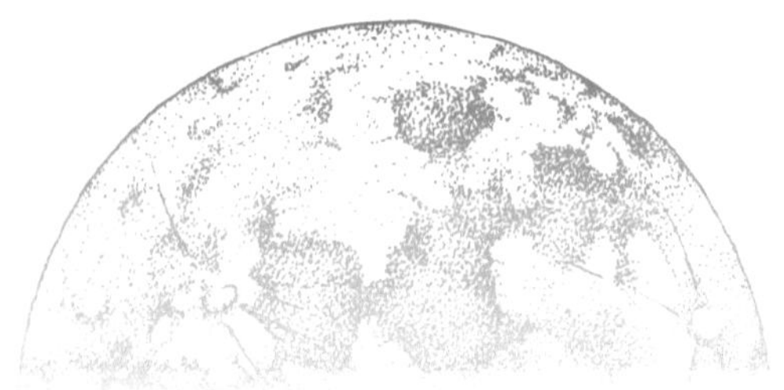

THIRTY-NINE

(INSPECTOR)

In a holding cell aboard Rick's warhive renamed something only a Human history buff would appreciate

THE HOLDING CELL door *whooshed* open, revealing the grizzled face of somebody Inspector Bikkolos used to know.

Seeing the empty space where Rick's arm used to be was a claw in his gut. The one physical injury he couldn't patch.

"I wasn't expecting you." Bikkolos puckered his cheeks for the proper Human pronunciation.

"There's a saboteur." The ice in Rick's voice could chill a star. They used to hustle rookies in angle-ball together. They'd clinked glasses in pubs. They attended therapy together. This couldn't be what the Goddess dreamed for them.

Bikkolos sighed. "Rick, check the entrance logs. I haven't—"

"I know." Rick entered the cell without closing the door behind him. "I need help."

Bikkolos flattened his ears. "You trust me?"

"No."

Bikkolos sat on the cell's bench to meet Rick's eye level. "You know I wasn't the one who denied you the prosthetic. I was the sorry cub who had to break the news to you."

"Don't bring up ancient history," Rick said. "Just be a damn detective. Use your fancy new title."

Rick emitted a pheromone. Subtle. If there had been more people in the room with them, Bikkolos might not have noticed.

With one sniff, Bikkolos smelled the truth. Bearing bad news did not cause the grudge.

An apology for never sticking up for him formed on Bikkolos' muzzle, but he swallowed the words. Rick wouldn't accept the apology; there was business to handle.

"What do you know of Dr. Diastrevlo?" Rick asked, gesturing for Bikkolos to follow him from the cell.

"Very little. What I pieced together is he abducted Ned Porandi and his wife to steal their technology."

"What else do you know about Porandi?"

Bikkolos wasn't sure how much Rick knew, so he had to measure his words. "Benedict Porandi. Goes by 'Ned.' Orphan saved by Symphora, a self-taught scientist, denied by several universities." Bikkolos considered mentioning Ned would've earned a doctorate if

Collective universities had welcomed Humans earlier, but Rick knew that.

Something about the name or backstory struck a chord in Rick based on a new pheromone he emitted, but Bikkolos couldn't put his paw on what specifically. They turned toward an elevator.

"Did Diastrevlo make Mui-xe or did the scientists?"

Bikkolos' hearts beat faster, thinking of what Earthquake might do with Mui-xe. "They did. From what I gather, Diastrevlo spent the last few years experimenting on the boy to replicate what they did. I'm guessing you saw his mistakes."

Rick's pheromone signature shifted like when they used to trade war stories in therapy sessions together.

"Don't sniff answers off me," Rick said. "You know it pisses me off."

"Sorry." He huffed an awkward chuckle. "Hard not to. Can't turn off my nose." He almost let his old nickname for Rick roll off his tongue, but he shoved it down. The elevator opened. The fact that Rick would get in a cramped elevator together suggested Rick had come to trust him again.

Or he had some new way to kill him. His former best friend who once went into a burning home to rescue a kid's Therimar Floofer was now slaughtering civilians.

"I didn't know about their kid," Bikkolos said. "I would've come with more backup."

"I'm hiding the boy," Rick said. "Earthquake can't know about him. Neither can the Collective."

Bikkolos cocked an eyebrow. He couldn't begin to imagine what ricocheted around Rick's mind, but he breathed through his mouth to avoid accidental smelling.

"What else?" Bikkolos asked.

"No," Rick said. "You tell me."

"Well, you saw Porandi's image inducer. That was an interesting bauble."

"Did he make more than one?" Rick asked.

"If he didn't, Diastrevlo made his own version."

A new pheromone erupted from Rick, too powerful to ignore. In front of the still-closed elevator door, Rick craned his neck to meet Bikkolos' gaze. "Say my mom's name."

The officer folded his arms, leaned back, and appraised the man before him. "You told me you were an orphan. That you grew up on a space station near Earth. You sent my mom a nice card on Earth's Mother's Day."

Rick slackened, and the previous pheromone dissipated. "Diastrevlo is aboard this ship. He's picking off the members of my team, one by one. He used his own image inducer to impersonate my crew."

"That's your saboteur," Bikkolos said. "We'll find him." He wished to add something about it being like the good old days. What he would give to crack a joke, crack open a can of mead, or crack an enemy's skull together.

Part of him considered telling Rick about how much *skata* was tossed his way for having a Human friend.

The names he was called, especially by his parents.

The stares.

Back then, Rick's attitude toward the stigma had been, "Let's prove them wrong." But they were kids then. Nothing Bikkolos could say would erase how he failed him when he needed a real friend to step in.

Inspector Bikkolos resigned to keep that to himself, burying that with the other feelings he couldn't understand. The mission mattered more than reviving a friendship long dead.

The elevator opened to the mess hall. In between tables in neat rows sat suits of Collective armor and weapons sized for an Arkouda. Some of them still had indigo blood stains on them. Bikkolos got a whiff of who these soldiers were and their shameful fear that their lives were taken by Humans.

Rick nudged the inspector. "Can you smell if any are missing?"

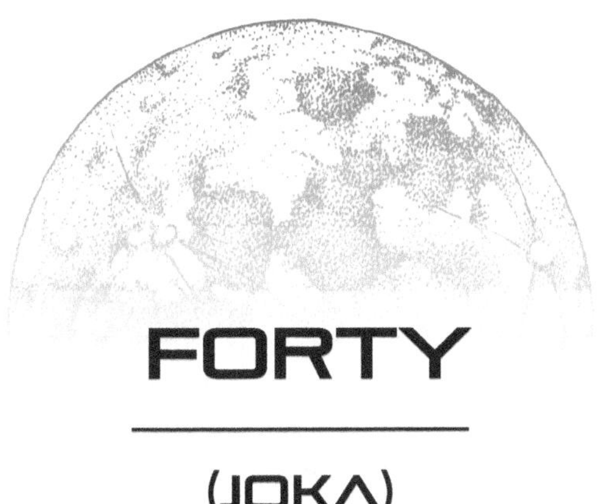

FORTY

(JOKΛ)

In Symphora's office on the Calamity, cruising through hyperspace toward New Lodestone, where she definitely wouldn't get killed by a terrorist

POTENTIALLY CAREENING INTO a bloodbath wasn't lost on anybody. Earthquake had two warhives, and it was only a matter of time before the Collective mustered a force to reclaim what Earthquake liberated.

Joka sat razor-straight in the too-big chair. She refused to slouch; nobody would condescend to her anymore. "They have weapons strong enough to puncture Collective military armor." Her painkiller kicked in, but the medgel around the wound on her arm itched. It would definitely leave a scar, but not a sexy one.

Marka bristled. "Really? What is it, the war-hive cannons?"

Symphora shot her a glare. "Let a bitch talk."

A smirk snuck onto Joka's face. "No. I saw it." The smile and any pretense of mirth faded. "They have cannons which take three of them to hold. These things shoot high-powered spears on chains. They rip through armor like paper."

Iasona chewed on the end of her paw, a decently gross nervous habit. "But the armor we have here isn't as good as what the military uses. Any ground forces we send against them will get slaughtered."

Joka raised a finger. "Only if you're slow and aren't paying attention. Their success with this weapon has been when the other side didn't know what they were up against. Collective soldiers always assumed they were invincible, so they didn't take them seriously."

Symphora leaned back in her chair, rubbing the end of her chin. "Even less so because they're Human."

"I wasn't going to say that," Joka said. "But yeah, that's definitely part of it."

Symphora huffed through her nostrils. "I was guilty of the same crime. Too many people dismiss Humans for one reason or another." Symphora stared at the other Arkoudae in the room. "That won't happen on my station anymore. I underestimated a Human, and now I have to eat *skata*. If we have to fight these Earthquake people, we have to respect our enemy."

Marka flattened her ears. "That still doesn't solve the problem of us not having our best fighters anymore."

"Maybe not," Joka said. "Their leader is this mid-life crisis guy; first Human allowed into the Collective military." The older women in the room gave half-nods as if they vaguely remembered the story. Joka pinched the bridge of her nose. "It's the guy who shows up on the news vids and everyone shouts for him to take his shirt off?"

That garnered much more recognition, and Joka thought she heard someone mutter about him being single.

"He knows how Collective soldiers fight," Joka said. "He trained his people to counter that. So the less we act like the military, the less prepared they'll be to fight us."

Symphora drummed her paws against the metal table. The chief engineer winced on each new series of taps. "Fine," Symphora said. "Everybody who can hold a gun gets one. Only rule is to save the innocent. But what's preventing the Collective military from showing up? We're still wanted. That hypothetical pardon you promised hasn't come through yet."

"We need to rescue a few people on the warhive. The police inspector who said he can get it for us is held prisoner there as well as the guy who asked for help in the first place."

Marka glared at Joka. "You aren't at the level to order us around like that."

Symphora placed a heavy paw on Marka's. "Yes she is. She understands what we're all about," Symphora's gaze turned to Joka, "better than most of us."

Symphora righted herself, then eyed everyone individually. "That's the other thing we need to discuss. I'm going to die on this mission."

Gasps and protests from the Arkoudae followed, but Joka folded her arms.

Symphora waved a paw to silence them. "Joka was right. I wimped out. I swore to protect the defenseless, and I made excuses to get out of it. I've lost my edge. I'm going to die on this mission, and I'm taking as many assholes down with me as I can."

"How can you be positive?" Marka asked.

"Did you get a vision in a dream?" Iasona asked.

Symphora shook her head. "If I survive, I'll let everyone else think I died. My story ends fighting, not fleeing."

"So you'll abandon us?" Iasona asked.

"I'll change my name and go to an old folk's den. Or wander around a jungle world somewhere."

Joka decided to tempt every religion's concept of fate. "Sounds like you're still scared."

Symphora pounded a furry fist on the table. "I let you embarrass me once today. Don't think you can—!"

"No." Joka used her new favorite word. "You're scared to adapt. There are other ways to fight for the weak besides killing sick jerks. Improve society. Start a bigger outreach program for victims. Open a soup kitchen or a women's shelter. Manage operations on the Calamity. But don't think the fight is over if we win today against Earthquake and definitely don't blame anyone but yourself."

Through cringes and winces, the other eyes in the room darted toward Symphora. Arms folded tight over her chest, she leaned forward. "Too bad Tur couldn't make her employee review now after your little trip."

"Little trip?" Joka said. "Try dangerous mission." She exhaled through clenched teeth, fighting for composure. "These Earthquake people ... have a point. Humans are mistreated. If your mission, ma'am, is protect people who can't defend themselves, that applies to the whole Human species since we've been persecuted since First Contact."

She expected the whole "we civilized you" argument or "we saved you from yourselves" or "Earth was a dying wasteland" line. She'd heard them all before.

Fighting the burgeoning memory of Earthquake's attack on the space elevator, Joka continued. "Seeing Collective soldiers slaughtered, knowing Humans were experimented on... Earthquake's motives make sense. Symphora, if you stop, they will fill that void. Do you want a terrorist group to pick up where you left off because you're worried about losing your edge?"

Symphora slackened. "Even though I paint my wins and losses on my battledart, I don't know how many people I really have saved over the years. How many scared kids I picked up and offered a place to stay or dropped off at a legitimate orphanage. I don't remember picking you specifically or even when or where I found you. But I do know I was more selective about which Humans I invited on. Tur was wrong about your potential." Symphora smiled. "I was right, though."

Joka relaxed her shoulders and sighed. "Thank you."

"Now," Symphora said, "if one of these Earthquakers offs me, take a whole-station vote on who will take over next. I'm not naming a successor since we all might bite the big one today."

Joka steeled herself for the coming fight, praying she wasn't already too late to save Ned and his son. "Ma'am, a lot of the people in Earthquake see you as a hero. I have an idea to use that to our advantage. Do we have enough helmets for everyone? I want to make a modification to them."

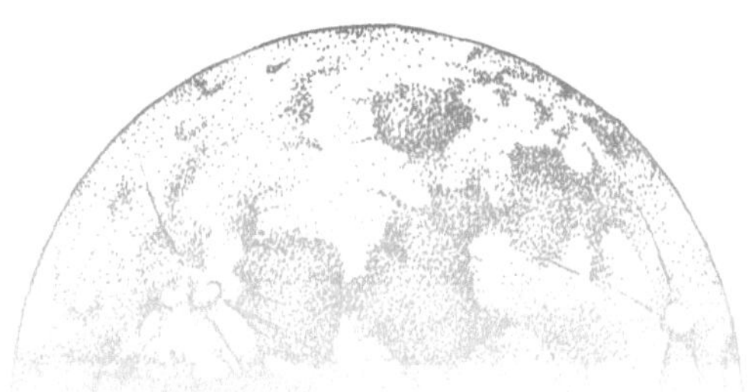

FORTY-ONE

(NED)

Trying to be a dad

ON THE FLOOR of their holding cell, Ned consoled his exhausted son. The level of trauma heaped upon this kid was cosmically unfair, and a dark part of Ned was grateful he could focus on his grieving son more than his own loss. Binh's words eased Ned's conscience.

The cell door opened with a *whoosh*.

Rick Crith entered.

His gaze was far off, and he held a pistol upright, much in the manner a scientist would wield a full syringe.

Binh sniffed. "Wait—"

A rush of air passed, knocking Binh to the floor.

Jagged scars appeared on his snout, spaced out. Clawmarks.

Ned's hairs stood on end. "Mui-xe, get behind me…"

Rick remained motionless, but another rush of air passed, and Binh lifted off the floor, through the open cell door. Once the Lo-sat was in the hallway, Rick turned to the cell door and it closed.

"Dad," Mui-xe croaked. "It's not him."

Another onrush of air hit, and a sharp pain went into Ned's neck. A needle.

Within a single heartbeat, Ned's body convulsed. Struggling to keep his eyes open, he watched Mui-xe twitch and crumple to the floor.

A neurosomatic toxin burned Ned's lungs. Dr. Diastrevlo had come for him, using the image inducer to disguise himself as Rick. The foul Arkouda paralyzed Mui-xe as well. The boy wouldn't be able to heal him.

No more experiments.

This wasn't the life Ned wanted for his son, but maybe someone else could give that to him. There had to be someone who could save Mui-xe from Dr. Diastrevlo one last time.

With his last strength, Ned averted his gaze from the heartless Arkouda disguised as a heartless man, so his last sight would be of his late wife and perfect son. His final thought was a prayer, begging for a reunion somehow in an afterlife. Hers, his, anyone's, as long as they could be together and have another chance.

Unable to breathe, he closed his eyes for the last time. His brain shut down, and all he saw was a white light.

Beckoning.

FORTY-TWO

(RICK)

Aboard the *Noryang*. Standing shoulder-to-elbow with a spineless bastard

IN THE *NORYANG'S* mess hall, Rick pointed at the Arkouda-sized handguns in front of Bikkolos. "Grab one," he barked. "Snag an Equalizer gun and leave it in the elevator, too."

Bikkolos shot him an "are you sure" glance, and Rick nodded. The pair left the mess hall.

If Dr. Diastrevlo could impersonate Rick, he could impersonate anybody.

Rick didn't trust pings now, so he radioed up to Herrod. "Any more casualties?"

"No sir," came the staticky reply as the elevator opened. Sounded like him.

"Read me their names again."

Bikkolos cocked his head. "Trying to remember their names to inform their families?"

"Partially. I also want to see if there's a connection." Rick eyed the weapons cache. He called Herrod again. "What's the status of the escape pods? Still locked?"

A pause bubbled over the clatter. "Sorry, Commander. They haven't been locked yet. The guy you told to lock them was killed."

The pair entered the elevator; he and Bikkolos ascended in silence, which was a relief. In their younger days, Bikkolos would've wanted to discuss feelings. He used to be the rare person who would ask, "How are you?" seeking an actual answer. Rick wondered what happened to him to lose that sensibility, but this wasn't the time for them to rekindle their dead friendship. They would never go back to the pubs and shoot angleballs or share cheap booze.

Arriving on the bridge, Rick barked orders. "Nobody leaves until I return. The saboteur is among us."

A few of the people on the bridge scowled at him.

He didn't have time for this bullshit. "Katochos, take a good sniff. Am I me?"

Katochos cocked his head. "Yeah..."

"I'll explain when the saboteur is dead," Rick said, meeting their gazes. "Then the first round is on me once we're safe."

Rick sprinted back to the elevator, nearly tackling Bikkolos on his run there. He pointed at the chief engineer. "Shut off the ship's artificial gravity."

"Sir?"

"That's an order. Shut it off. Strap yourselves in. Do not turn it back on until you hear back from me."

As the engineer complied, Rick's body rose. His organs twisted in anger and his grav harness chirped uselessly. "Don't allow me on the bridge unless I'm holding the bloody stump of an Arkouda head." That earned a nervous glance from Bikkolos and Katochos.

He gripped the elevator panel and pushed himself inside.

In front of him, an Equalizer gun, now weightless, floated up in front of him, which he grabbed. He thought of the first Humans in space, the pioneers who braved the stars without the aid of artificial gravity, the technology from the Arkouda that came at too high a cost.

When he reached the brig level, the guard he'd stationed there, Dion, flailed about in the absence of gravity. "What the hell, boss?"

Rick's nostrils flared. "Salvatore, what's your mother's name?"

Dion lowered his rifle and scratched the back of his head. "Uh, that's not my name..."

Rick exhaled. "Good. Don't let anyone into the brig. Ask me the same question when I come out. If I respond with anything other than 'Earth,' shoot one meter over my head."

"Sir?"

"Just do it. Ask my mother's name. Shoot a meter over my head." Rick maneuvered to the holding cells, less adroit than he would have liked. He hadn't turned off his grav harness and floated in natural gravity since the incident on the damn moon with the archaeologist, a memory he wished he could forget. But that lesson taught him he could fight weightless, and things more massive than him, like an Arkouda, wouldn't do as well.

Equalizer gun in hand, he used it like a paddle to propel himself to the brig door.

Hovering beside the door was Ten-trom, moaning in pain. "L-Lefty…"

If Rick weren't in zero gravity, he would have stopped in his tracks. Guilt smacked him in the stomach. "The boy didn't heal you?"

The thief cocked an eyeridge, and some white scales flaked off his face with the movement. "He d-did. Then you stormed in and pistol-whipped me in the snout and tossed me back out here."

"What?"

The Lo-sat nursed a clump of bruises on his snout, more scales shedding as he did. "When the door closed, I realized what happened. That piece of *nguc* Diastrevlo has Professor Tragedy's image inducer. He came in looking like you, then tossed my tail out."

"How'd you know?"

"Humans don't tend to leave clawmarks when they beat up innocent people. He didn't say 'damn' every ten seconds, either."

"Float over to the guard I posted back there. Tell him my mother is Earth and wait with him."

"Are you baiting me to see if I'll make a joke about your mother?"

A crease formed in Rick's forehead. "I regret assaulting you, Ten-trom, and I'm sorry Diastrevlo did. Let's leave it at that."

Once Ten-trom floated away, more white flecks of scales hung in the air.

Bracing himself, Rick opened the holding cell. The scientist who had taunted and evaded him on the asteroid floated inside, wearing Collective armor.

Three other bodies hovered over the floor:

La-hok Porandi. Rigor mortis resisted the elasticity a lack of gravity provided.

Mui-xe Porandi. Eyes shut, breathing in a fitful comatose state.

Ned Porandi. No visible chest movement.

With a cold stare, Dr. Diastrevlo faced Rick. "Stow your weapon. Batch Thirty-two is alive. I surrender."

They floated and glared at each other. "No, you don't. Make peace with your Goddess."

Dr. Diastrevlo pushed himself closer to the floor. "I'm worth more alive. With Batch Thirty-two, I can make an army for you." A weaker person might have begged, yet Diastrevlo's request had less emotion than a weapon—blunt and even.

"I'm not stupid. My boss told you to pick off the fighters. You were going to kill me and give yourself to Tecton. No loyalty to the Collective, huh?"

He eyed Rick with the furrowed brow of a scientist evaluating controls and variables. "My loyalty is to science. I will write my chapter in the book of life. It doesn't matter who funds my research."

Rick gripped the massive gun. Monsieur Tecton would want this madman to manufacture nightmares for him to fight the Collective. What kind of horrors would he do to the hybrid boy, beyond what he already did to the poor kid already? Not to mention the abominations in his laboratory.

"Loyal to science?" Rick barked. "Is that why you used stolen Human technology to hide?"

The scientist checked his wrist, where the modified holoprojector was. It seemed cruder than Ned's sleek design. While he was distracted, Rick shot the Equalizer gun. The harpoon removed a chunk from the monster's neck. It tunneled through, carrying blood, staining his fur purple. In a howl, he turned his head to meet Rick's eye line.

Shit. He missed the spinal cord.

No time to reload. Bubbles of indigo blood rose from the wound. Rick kicked up his leg, which brought his sidearm near his hand as he released the Equalizer.

With a roar, the scientist lunged toward him, paw raised to strike. Rick grabbed his sidearm, but the brute batted it away. Above, the harpoon's chain danced in the lack of gravity. Heaving, Rick reached for the chain, then yanked it so the harpoon would float to him. Diastrevlo swiped at Rick and removed a chunk of Rick's cheek. Searing pain made him curse as blood bubbled from the wound. That would leave a scar. In normal gravity, it would have been his jaw instead of a layer of flesh.

The Arkouda swiped again with the other paw to finish the job, but Rick kicked off his paw for momentum. Rotating in the absence of gravity, Rick spun to shove the weapon into the monster's heart.

Snarling, Diastrevlo batted it away before Rick could make the plunge.

Teeth clenched, Rick knew he only had one chance to level the field. He couldn't overcome the weight imbalance, but he had one option for changing his mass. Moving the harpoon so that he could hold the pole under his chin, Rick thumbed his grav harness.

His insides roiled as he descended, the only thing in the room to experience artificial gravity. Rick rotated the harpoon in his hand, then dug the harpoon into Diastrevlo's eye, leaving him winking in death. "No more nightmares."

The number of monsters in the room decreased from two to one.

Hateful vomit burned in his throat.

Rick holstered his sidearm and reached for Diastrevlo's corpse, grateful for the lack of gravity around the body.

Rick floated over to the limp Mui-xe, chest billowing with weak inhales. Maybe Bikkolos could figure out how to bring this kid into consciousness, but it would have to be in secret. A smile came across Rick's face as he realized he now had a second image inducer in his possession. He could sneak the kid to the infirmary and set Bikkolos to work.

A ping came from the surface and Rick's heart raced.

[Amanda: Reports are saying your new warhive is up there but silent. What's going on?]

Rick considered using this as an opportunity to tell her what she meant to him. But that was outside mission parameters.

[We had a situation on board I wanted to handle before communicating. We're fine now.]

[Amanda: No you're not. Shaka station's monitors said expect company exiting hyperspace.]

Rick set down his omni-tablet and began sawing off Diastrevlo's head with the Equalizer harpoon. The scientist's face, frozen and expressionless in death as in life, stared back at Rick as he worked. Company wasn't exactly something he wanted right now. Perhaps it was the Collective military, coming to reclaim the 'hives and New Lodestone. Or maybe it was Tecton's sycophants coming to relieve Rick from power. He couldn't imagine anyone else showing up.

When he exited the brig, a stuttering Dion eyed Rick's new cheek scar. "W-what's your m-mom's name?"

"Earth," Rick said.

Ten-trom sniffed. "That blood's gonna leave a stain, Lefty. Or should I say Cheeky?"

A minute later, when Rick entered the bridge, holding the severed head of Dr. Diastrevlo, everyone released a collective sigh except Bikkolos and Katochos. The engineer returned the ship's gravity to Human standard. When Rick floated down, he dropped Diastrevlo's head. "We need to scramble the scrappers. Whoever can fight or fly a ship—prepare asap. Ring up the *Salamis*. We need to coordinate for some guests."

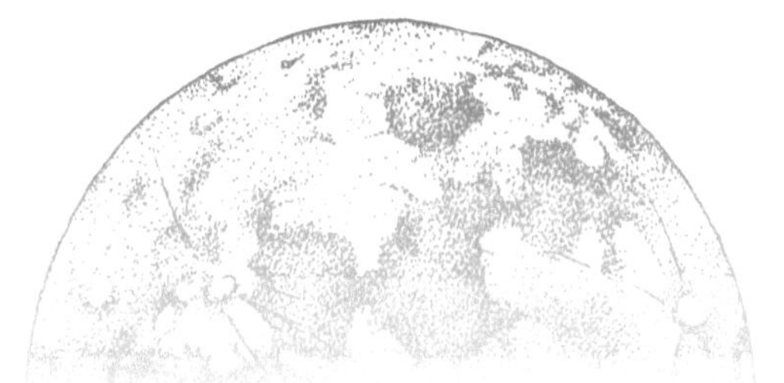

FORTY-THREE

(JOKΛ)

Wait—two warhives? FFFFUUUU—

THE CALAMITY SNAPPED out of hyperspace, just outside New Lodestone's magnetosphere. Joka and the other department heads steadied themselves on the bridge.

Symphora snarled. "Which one do we assault?"

Joka scratched her head. One warhive sat docked on the station: likely the one she and Doh-riss snuck onto.

Iasona piped up. "Ma'am, scans detect signs of other ships."

Symphora wheeled on her. "Who is it?"

Iasona averted her eyes. "Uh, Blekker pirates, ma'am."

Joka's heart froze. She didn't know they'd be there.

"That's not all," Iasona continued. "Deep range scans say someone else is about to exit hyperspace, too."

Symphora glared at her. "Who?"

"Collective military."

Pirates, military, terrorists, and their gang all coming together over this planet. Joka's mouth went dry. "Symphora, if we can extract the prisoners from the warhives, we should be able to negotiate our pardons."

Marka tutted from behind them. "And the pirates will ignore us?"

Symphora pushed Iasona away from the scanner. "Does anyone know how to sign in Blekker?"

"I heard Kah-renn dated a Blekk once," Iasona said. After some eyes bored into her, she shrank back. "That might have been a rumor."

"The Blekker can understand Arkouda at least, right?" Joka asked. "Or maybe they'll turn around once—"

The public channel buzzed; a male Lo-sat voice came over.

"Hail, Calamity station and the legendary Symphora. I'm translating for the Drowned Star. You can turn around. There's nothing for you here."

Joka cocked an eyebrow. The Blekk must have a few translators on board, and a Lo-sat's nimble tail could approximate the Blekker sign language.

Symphora barked into the comm. "How about you stay the Nightmare away from us? Earthquake is about to get trounced by the Collective. We need something Earthquake has. Get outta here before the fleet shows up."

Joka wasn't exactly a skilled or seasoned negotiator, but she understood deep in her bones Symphora just pissed on people who did not like being toilets. These pirates weren't small-time crooks she could scare. If they were protecting a backwater like New Lodestone, they must be confident they could take on the Collective fleet.

From the viewscreen, a trio of Blekk pirate warships came into view. While not as big as a warhive, each one had weapons enough to terrorize entire caravans. Their shape evoked a hateful, jagged icicle. Dots emerged from the ships' sides.

The translator came back over the comm. "Hail, Calamity and the legendary Symphora. We will flood your station. The skull of Symphora will be a fine decoration for our captain's quarters."

A new voice emerged on the public channel: Human, speaking an accented Arkouda. "Hey, we don't want to fight you, Symphora, but this planet is ours. This is your only chance to back the hell off. The Drowned Star are with us."

Joka squinted out the viewscreen. The warhive docked on the space elevator retracted its bridge. It would turn around soon to open fire.

Symphora glared at Joka. "The warhive closer to us is the one we can blow up, right? The other one will have the prisoners?"

Joka shook her head. "The small number of prisoners I've been talking about are on the farther warhive. There are still captives on the closer one."

Symphora turned to the chief engineer. "Set all turrets to fire on the Drowned Star ships." She fixed her gaze on Marka.

"Everyone who can fly a ship or hold a gun needs to get in a battledart." Finally, Symphora turned to Joka. "I made some more flight suits. You'd be surprised how many bored mechanics, engineers, and other support staff liked your designs and wanted one for themselves. All the Humans aboard are able to take part now, thanks to you."

Joka smiled, which faded upon realizing they may be marching into their death.

"You were the only one who learned how to fly a battledart, but the others can safely hide in the back of them to be an extra gun arm once the cockpits fly open in those warhives." Symphora turned on the PA system. "We're getting hit from both sides, ladies. We'll let our turrets take care of the pirates, and we'll all fly out to take on Earthquake. The Blekk want to board us so they can kill me in person. They'll get a fun surprise when they come up to an empty station."

She turned the comm back to the public channel. "You know, I never fought a Blekk pirate before. I'll be in the top offices. Translator, tell the pirates to take a sharp left if they can get in the hangar. This bitch is challenging all their raiders to single combat."

Another Human voice broke through and spoke in better-pronounced Arkouda. "Symphora…"

Joka's stomach tightened. She recognized the voice.

Rick Crith.

"…there's no reason for bloodshed. Why are you here?"

Symphora snarled. "I don't have time to flap my gums with everyone who gets their paws on a comm device. You have something I want."

"This is the ranking officer and liberator of New Lodestone. I'm the authority here of both these warhives and the space elevator. What do you want?"

"All the prisoners you have on both your warhives, on the surface, on the space elevator, I don't care. You're surrendering every individual person to me. Do what you want with your plunder."

"No." No hesitation. "We need the prisoners to bargain for our independence."

Images of Bikkolos, Ned, Mui-xe, even Binh flashed through Joka's mind along with the countless others she and Doh-riss saw the day of the massacre. All those people were just tools to be used.

"Automated turrets and defense systems are ready," Marka announced.

Symphora clutched the comms device. "You already sicced the Drowned Star pirates on us. We'll send them back to where they came from, and we're getting those prisoners. If we have to mow through you first, so be it. Come aboard the Calamity if you want. I'll be on the top floor. Find me." She turned to the rest of the group. "Let's get the Nightmare out of here," Symphora barked. "Everyone got their new helmets ready to go?"

In response, a chorus of gang members held their modified helmets aloft. Each one, Arkouda, Lo-sat, or Human, all carried a new design.

Each one had a red plastoid mohawk grafted to the top. Everyone was Symphora today.

———

Dashing to the hangar, Joka wished she could have Doh-riss help her with the battledart's weapons. Her claws clinking in Joka's pouch would have to suffice.

Nestled in the battledart's cockpit, stretching as much as possible to reach the controls, Joka puffed a slow exhale. She was ready.

The Calamity's oxygen bubble opened, and a swarm of ships poured out—sleek battledarts, heavy skirmishers chonkier than a Therimar Floofer, and one decommissioned cruiser held together by glue and friendship. Every person aboard the station left, except Marka and Devy, who Joka nominated to make manual repairs to the station as needed. Hey, somebody had to order the repair nanobots around. Might as well be two people who sucked.

To her left, a cargo ship full of armed women departed, sporting their new mohawk helmets. They knew they would lose a few good women in their assault, but they'd look rad as hell doing it and take some Earthquake scumbags with them. An empty cargo ship meant to save prisoners followed behind. They were part of the contingent assaulting the nearer warhive, the one Joka and Doh-riss originally escaped from.

Taxiing to the mauve oxygen bubble, Joka's knuckles turned white around the controls. Searing lime-colored plasma bolts whizzed in every direction outside. She turned on the autopilot and zoomed from the hangar. Within seconds, an orange, pluming explosion snapped her attention above.

Someone was gone already.

Behind, the Calamity's automated systems traded shots with the Blekk pirates, which left all the fire against Earthquake to the pilots. The 'hives were meant to deal with big scale threats, not individual battledarts and cargo ships. The warhives' turrets powered and rotated toward the Calamity. No fighters poured out of either one. It shocked Joka at first as she dodged shrapnel, but for all the battledarts Earthquake had, they couldn't pilot them. Rather, modified scrapper ships exited the 'hives and the space station.

She would've cursed were it not for Doh-riss' claws pressing against her. Joka hopped on the shared channel. "Those scrappers are modded. That's how Earthquake conquered this planet in the first place. The strong magnetosphere powers them up. Stay away from their magnetic tractor beams."

"You heard her, ladies," Symphora said over the channel. "Their armor is too thick for us to waste our time with them. Just outrun them. We'll zoom into the hangars and get the prisoners."

A series of affirmatives sounded off as fighters and cargos broke away toward the two warhives. Both 'hives wasted shots firing on Symphora's gang. For how long the main turrets took, their few shots were easy enough to dodge. The problem would arise once they came within range of the smaller autoturrets lining the hull.

Splintered groups maneuvered toward the stolen Collective warships like Earth lemmings to a cliff.

Symphora scoffed. "Don't let the symbols and paint job fool you. We're not fighting Collective military. These are terrorists who stole from them. They beat the Collective because the military underestimated them. Don't make that mistake. Remember, there are people we need to save. Let's see who can get some clawmarks painted on today!"

Joka smirked as she banked right. She flew under Symphora's wing. The flotilla zoomed like two buzzing swarms of stingflies. The only ship left inside the Calamity was Symphora's own battledart. She piloted one of the junkers. It was a smart move, Joka thought. If they knew who she was, they might recognize her ship instead of falling for the ruse and storming the empty Calamity. Joka was just as glad for that since tangling with a Blekk pirate appealed to her almost as much as dealing with Diastrevlo's laboratory monsters. She'd take a plasma bullet to the head over getting strangled by a Blekk's tentacles.

Scrappers emerged from the warhives in a slow pod, and supporting fire came from the smaller autoturrets. One plasma bolt whizzed by Joka, lighting up her cockpit emerald for a second. She shuddered, trusting the autopilot more than her own reflexes.

Her trigger finger begged to engage with the scrapper ships, blow them to heck for siding with Earthquake and Rick the Prick, but she stayed her hand and aimed instead for the nearest autoturret. She missed terribly, even with the targeting software, but then she twisted and rolled downward, going under the scrapper pod before they could fire off any magnetic beams.

The autoturrets continued their relentless assault—two friendlies exploded, sending shrapnel in every direction. While she wondered which of her sisters had just bitten the dust, she forced herself to focus on the task at hand. She couldn't recognize any of the ships anymore since Symphora and the others were all in different battledarts and cargoes than usual. Symphora's fear from the last debacle had become a more calculated caution. It wasn't hiding as much as tactical camouflage. Above her, the scrappers unleashed their magnetic beams, mauve rays reaching out for the metallic ships.

Joka grabbed her comm. "If you're caught in their magnetic beam, turn off your thrusters. Wait until they throw you or something, and then turn it on. If you return fire, aim for the magnets, not the hull."

As she passed beneath the scrapper pod, another one ignited and imploded.

Screams coming over the public channel told her it wasn't enough to stop more death.

She punched the thrust, racing toward the hangar. As she crested upward, she let off another shot at an autoturret, then banked back down as the return fire came. Wouldn't be much longer now.

Her ship penetrated the oxygen bubble. Once inside, she prepared to smash the trigger like it owed her money, but then she realized that the only ships in here were unused battledarts and cargo ships. The scrappers were their only fighting force, and those had left. A few other ships poured in behind her, and Joka initiated the touchdown. As she readied to leave the cockpit, Earthquake troops funneled into the hangar, carrying their deadly harpoon cannons.

Getting impaled by one would be a horrific death, but maybe they wouldn't shoot her. She glanced over her shoulder. Only a few ships made it inside. Blooming explosions peppered space outside like fireworks, shown through the veil of the mauve oxygen bubble.

As she hopped from the cockpit, she realized that her grav harness and flight suit's adjusters stopped. Not from malfunction. For the first time since she could remember, no gentle buzz pulsed from her collarbone as a cheap piece of technology adjusted to her to help her survive in someone else's default gravity. Rick must have set the warhive to Human standards. Even though she had technically spent her life in an artificial gravity field, she either moved too sluggish or too quickly for it to ever feel proper. All Humans' lives were spent in a weird bout of spinal and knee soreness. Ligaments and tendons needed frequent medical attention, not that they had reliable access to it. But here, the setting was something evolution prepared her to feel. Like how she imagined Earth.

One of them shouted in Human, "That's the tiny bitch Rick warned us about!"

Joka sneered, and as other cockpits opened around her, she had the confidence to respond, "Yes, the heck I am." She whispered an apology to her pouch and unholstered her pistol and fired a few shots. She didn't hit anyone, but her firing caused them to scatter, at least for a second. She adjusted her grav harness and floated down to the hangar floor, then reset it. Her stomach gave a gurgle as her body adjusted.

"What?" an Earthquake member called out. "Check the mohawk! That's Symphora!"

In the moment of distraction, Joka lined up a shot on the nearest Earthquake member. With a deep breath, she pulled the trigger. Direct shot to the hand. One less gunner to fight them. Focus shifted back to Joka.

Symphora hopped from her battledart and landed with a thud, shaking the hangar floor. She fired off her assault rifle but missed. Not good.

Eyes wide, Joka shouted in Arkouda, "Adjust your aim and grav harness! This is Human standard gravity. They're wearing Collective armor. Aim for their heads and exposed joints."

More cockpits whooshed open. Lo-sats, Arkoudae, and Humans jumped out. All sported their new mohawk helmets. They weren't Symphora's gang anymore. They were all Symphora. Joining the legend. Inheriting it.

Stuck in the middle of this skirmish, having to duck behind battledarts while plasma bolts flew, failed to meet Joka's expectation of a moment most glorious.

Shots were traded and then Equalizer harpoons were fired. In the altered gravity, not everyone heeded Joka's advice to dodge. They had a severe disadvantage from operating in Human gravity.

Two Arkoudae went down.

A howl rattled Joka's bones.

Symphora herself held up her rifle as a rally point. "Focus fire on the cannon teams! Avenge our sisters!" When she finished, she fired another round at

Earthquake, plasma fire lighting up her face green for brief flashes.

Symphora regained her status: the woman people conjured stories and legends about.

Joka fired, grazing a leg, enough for the plasma heat to scorch the thigh pad.

Scanning the hangar, Joka counted five sisters writhing on the floor to the eight Earthquake members. How many more recruits Rick had in reserve remained unknown, but the stream of ships into the hangar had stopped. Hopefully, Joka's counterparts on the other warhive realized they needed to adjust their gravity to fight on proper terms. She found the exit, blocked off by a surly Earthquake gunner. Breathing deep, back pressed against a battledart wing, she realized that when she aimed for the shoulder, she hit a hand. Aiming for the leg, she grazed the thigh.

Leaving cover and adjusting her aim, she fired her pistol at the guy guarding the door, hitting him in the kneecap where the strips of repurposed Collective armor didn't protect. He collapsed with a howl, dropping his weapon, which Joka fired at.

"Joka cleared the door," Symphora shouted. "Let's mop up and push forward behind her!"

The sisters shouted affirmatives while more plasma fire erupted. By the time Joka shimmied the door open, she turned around to find two more of the gang on the floor with the remainder of the Earthquake recruits.

On the other side of the door stood two looming figures, much taller than her.

Inspector Bikkolos and Binh, the latter holding an oblong box, supporting it with his tail.

"Special delivery for Nut Puncher." Binh seemed different. Greener, somehow. She didn't have time to analyze him.

The inspector glared at Binh before turning to Joka. "We need to get this … package down to the surface. Care to help?"

Joka's eyes widened, understanding the true nature of the crate.

FORTY-FOUR

(RICK)

**Aboard the *Noryang*. Orbit above
New Lodestone, Boudica System,
Independent Human space**

RICK GLARED AT the scanner. He had two minutes before the Collective fleet arrived. Symphora could've ravaged the hangar, but he couldn't be sure, since all the gang members sported the red mohawk—even the Humans and Lo-sats. Teeth clenched, he faced the last of his crew. He'd dismissed Bikkolos to the infirmary to take care of the kid. All his pilots were deployed. His fighters were holding off the inevitable in the hangar.

Inevitable defeat.

An update came from the *Salamis.*

[We're overrun. We didn't have enough Equalizers to take out Symphora's fighters. The real Symphora is here. There's a huge Arkouda bitch with a mohawk. A bunch of Humans were in her group. We didn't expect them to attack us.]

After a deep sigh, Rick shot a ping back.

[I'm surrendering. Save the lives of as many people on board as possible. Use the prisoners as leverage. You might not be dealing with the real Symphora.]

He might not be, either.

"We lost," Rick said to his remaining crew. "No shame in admitting defeat. Get down to the hangar, arms up. Leave your guns here."

Grimacing, Rick turned on the PA system. "Earthquake, this is Commander Crith. Stand down. They beat us. Symphora, or whoever is in charge, we surrender."

Before he would go down to face Symphora in person, he had one last call to make. With a wave, he dismissed his crew. "I'll be down after I inform the Leader."

Once the last one left, Rick fired up Porandi's image inducer to change his appearance. After a few tense seconds, the screen of his omni-tablet materialized, revealing the snarling face of Monsieur Tecton.

"Rick, this had better be—" Tecton's angular features drooped. "Who are you? Where's Crith?"

Mimicking an Earther accent, Rick responded, "Dead, sir. Symphora's gang is here. They're massacring us."

Tecton touched a finger to his lips. Calculating bastard. "There's an Arkouda scientist aboard. Dr. Diastrevlo. He needs to get out alive. Send him to me."

Rick's facial muscles tensed, and he worried for a second he'd broken the illusion. "Sir?"

"He's friendly to us. Working on something top secret." After a second, he hastily added, "Crith knew. Get the scientist on an escape pod. He's more important than anyone else aboard, got it?"

At least Rick had confirmation of his suspicion. Didn't soften the sting, though. "Understood. The Collective fleet is inbound. They'll be here in seconds. What should we do?"

Tecton gave a half-shrug. "Kill as many of Symphora's rabble as you can. Then when the Collective shows up, fight them. Simple."

"Thank you, sir. Any further orders?"

"Never surrender. Blow up the warhives if you have to take out more of them. Crith took prisoners. Execute them."

"Of course, sir," Rick said.

The transmission cut off.

He sent a ping down to Bikkolos.

[Did Diastrevlo's image inducer work? Are you in position?]

After a moment, the response came.

[Bikkolos: Yes, we got there before the rest of your crew. We're aboard one of Symphora's troop transport ships. We found the Human woman you told us about.]

[Rick: There's a monastery on New Lodestone where the boy can be kept hidden.]

[Bikkolos: I know the place. We'll make sure he gets there.]

Rick's eyebrows arched, but he remembered what his mole intercepted, that Brother Maynard had a nephew. Then Rick's blood froze. The mole. The final loose end.

He shot off a ping to Amanda.

[Tell the mole to get the hell out of the monastery.]

As Rick prepared to enter the elevator, an automated alarm blared.

The Collective fleet had arrived.

Rick had lost the battle. He'd lost the war. Worse, he'd lost the person he was supposed to be. And he was done with Earthquake.

FORTY-FIVE

(INSPECTOR)

Aboard the mobile magistrate's station, "Frontier Adjudicator." Collective space. One week later.

AFTER THE COLLECTIVE had reclaimed the hijacked warhives, it had been a grueling few days to reach this deposition. Inspector Bikkolos' stomach rumbled loudly enough to catch the attention of the people seated beside him. He thought about how the boy hadn't asked for anything since coming to, and how Rick and Joka were shocked when he requested Binh watch the boy while they had these delegations today.

Inspector Bikkolos approached the magistrate's bench. "Mr. Crith has agreed to cooperate and provide information. I would like to remind the court that the prisoners were returned unharmed." A row

400

of crusty Arkouda lawyers and an ambassador's clerk fidgeted in the chairs surrounding them, casting glares down their snouts.

Without waiting for an invitation, Rick moved beside his former friend. "Monsieur Jacques Tecton, one of the few Provincial representatives in the Collective government, funded illegal research. He was the mastermind behind the terrorist organization called Earthquake."

The magistrate, an older Arkouda woman, frowned at Rick. "An organization you were once a part of."

"Yes," Rick said. "The Collective has treated Humans horribly."

Inspector Bikkolos puffed out his chest. "You saw the evidence. Hundreds of Human abductions unreported. Then they were experimented on like cattle. If we gave Humans, Makawe, or Blekk the respect they deserved, we wouldn't have these issues."

The magistrate grunted and waved a paw. "I don't have the authority to overturn any laws. I can negotiate terms. Your comment is noted, inspector. You cannot grant a pardon to Mr. Crith over here."

"I don't need *skata*," Rick said. "Let New Lodestone be a Human sanctuary. No Collective presence needed. We will happily trade or keep to ourselves. The planet is uninhabitable to Arkoudae and Lo-sats."

Bikkolos nodded. "The magnetic field is too intense."

"What's the population?" the magistrate asked.

"There's only a few settlements," Rick said. "A one-space elevator kind of planet."

"You already returned the warhives, so pay taxes, and it'll be a sanctuary."

Rick's nostrils flared. "No taxes."

Inspector Bikkolos raised his paw. "There's a monastery on the planet, ma'am. If a non-cult status religious order ran the planet, could we leave them in peace?"

The magistrate glared at Bikkolos. "I hardly see—"

"Ma'am." Bikkolos glared back. "We let down Humans now, then expect Earthquake to grow. Their last leader wanted some semblance of secrecy and had a commander like Rick trying to minimize civilian casualties. Do you really want to keep slapping Humans in the face?"

With a heavy sigh, the magistrate rose from the bench. "The planet New Lodestone will be recognized as an independent monastic community with a refugee sanctuary. No taxation. The space elevator will be subject to weapons' checks." She cast a glance at the bench of lawyers. "Start the paperwork."

"We need to be able to defend ourselves," Rick said.

"Let me finish," the magistrate hissed. "The weapons checks will ensure nothing beyond reasonable defensive mechanisms and asteroid destruction are in place or under construction."

"You honestly think we could amass a fleet without a space factory? There won't be any need," Rick said. "Anyone still loyal to Earthquake will be removed from New Sodestone. If what Tecton allowed wasn't a reason for them to abandon the group, I don't want them on my planet."

Bikkolos winced. Those last two words would get him in trouble.

The magistrate scowled. "That's the other issue, Mr. Crith. You will not be in charge. I can authorize leaving a settlement on an unimportant world alone, but I cannot abide you walking free. You will be incarcerated for your crimes against the Collective."

Bikkolos clenched his fist. "His information is leading to arrests. He stopped—"

Rick placed his hand on Bikkolos' wrist. "I'll go." He stared up at the magistrate. "Lock me up or take me out back and shoot me. Will you respect the inspector's pardon for the other person we discussed?"

"Yes." The magistrate's expression cooled. "Then it's settled. We'll sign off and you will be admitted to prison, Mr. Crith. Your cooperation here will be noted."

As Bikkolos shook his head and prepared another argument, his eyes drifted to where Rick had touched his wrist. He noticed the image inducer. The Collective wouldn't hold Rick for long, it seemed.

The two former friends locked eyes for a moment.

"Thanks for standing up for me," Rick said. "I'll write to you. We'll catch up."

FORTY-SIX

(JOKΛ)

**Inside the Great Mystery Monastery,
New Lodestone, Boudica System.
Independent Human Zone**

THE GUY RUNNING the monastery resembled Ned way too much: ridged browlines, dark eyes, and conquered trauma. Joka knew they were brothers, but still. Practically twins—even though Brother Maynard had scars and wrinkles to prove his increased age. That or Mui-xe's abilities had removed Ned's.

The monks unnerved Joka the tiniest bit—these quiet, friendly men proved a sharp contrast to the rough and tumble women she'd spent her life around. The boy would do well here.

Sitting in the courtyard with Mui-xe, Binh, and Brother Maynard, Joka scratched her head. "I'm sorry about your parents. They wanted a better life for you. You'll be safe here."

"I guess," Mui-xe croaked. He had a hollow look in his eyes Joka hadn't seen since her own childhood. The poor kid watched both parents die and was now with a stranger wearing his dad's face.

Brother Maynard patted the boy's shoulder. "She's right." His gaze turned to Joka. "He has a grandmother, too. On his mother's side—a shaman on Vee." Removing his hand, he added. "We'll find a way to let you visit her, Mui-xe."

Binh feigned gagging. "This planet's headache field is one thing, but these holy types freak me out."

Brother Maynard cocked an eyebrow. "Not a fan of organized religions?"

Binh shrugged. "I'm more interested in disorganized religion, but I can never figure out when they meet. Nobody ever has a pamphlet or anything. It's all very—"

Joka elbowed him in the ribs. "I hope you run out of your sensory-dampening medicine before we leave. Mui-xe, don't heal him from the bruise I just gave him. Remember what I told you?"

He offered a weak nod.

Joka supplied the punchline through an awkward chuckle. "The first healing is free. The rest cost credits." She took the boy's hand in hers. "I know we're kinda all strangers, and this is a lot. We'll find a way to let your grandma know you're safe. She'll help you with your mom's claws."

"We couldn't take you to her," Binh said, massaging the spot where Joka hit him. "You're safer here where the Collective doesn't have so many eyes. Shamans can make medicine. She'll find a way to visit you on this planet without getting a migraine from the magnetism. You sure you don't feel any magnetic pull?"

Mui-xe shook his head as his eyes roamed Binh's new scales. The emerald sheen made Binh a different person entirely. But then he opened his mouth and destroyed the notion.

Joka gave the boy an awkward hug.

"Enjoy it, kid," Binh said. "Living with these guys, you probably won't be able to touch another girl."

"And you won't touch another woman living with that personality," Joka replied.

Brother Maynard shook his head. "We won't force him to take the vows if he doesn't want to join our order when he's of age." He winked at Mui-xe, rubbed his bald head, and made a squeaking noise. "But you already match us up top, so…"

They made their final goodbyes, then Joka and Binh headed toward the waiting autocab at the end of the monastery's walkway.

"How bad are the headaches?" Joka asked.

"I want to get the *nguc* off-world before my medicine runs out. I swore I'd never come back here, but I feel bad for the kid. Had to see him off." He opened the autocab door for her.

Smirking, she reached into her jacket and withdrew a small jar. She shook it in his snout when he entered after her.

"You *ke-nok* Humans have the weirdest ways to seduce a guy."

"Swear jar. You're three credits in the hole."

Eyeridges lowered, Binh studied the jar and gave a sniff. "That's what you made with her claws, huh?"

"Yeah. Every credit goes to a women's shelter."

"Heh. So what's next for you, O' mighty Nut Puncher?"

"I recall you telling me about a Human archaeologist who had a run-in with you and Crith a few years ago."

Binh's eyeridges raised. "I already hate where this is going. I did not end on good terms with her."

"You're taking me to her." Joka cast a glance skyward. "Besides the fact that you owe her an apology, I've been authorized to offer her a job."

FORTY-SEVEN

(RICK)

**Bolivar Settlement, New Lodestone,
Boudica System. Independent Human Zone.
One year later.**

AS THE SPACE elevator shuttle descended from orbit, Rick stared into the viewscreen. Maybe this damn planet was magnetic in more ways than one. For a flicker of a moment, he saw his reflection. His head and silhouette had finally corrected themselves after his misguided years with Earthquake. His hair grew naturally again and the weight of command no longer pulled down his shoulders. The damned tattoos finally began fading but hadn't vanished. Getting them removed might raise the wrong eyebrows.

He released a sigh and exited the shuttle, his whole life in the knapsack draped over his shoulder. A few other passengers filed out in front of him. A dejected mother ushered two children in front of her; they must've spent the last of their money to get here. Thinking a current member of Earthquake caused that for her family set his blood boiling. Tecton had lost his seat in the Provincial Collective government and had been arrested, and official reports claimed he took his life in prison.

Officially dead. Like Rick.

While he doubted Tecton had an image inducer like Rick, knowing his former employer connived with Dr. Diastrevlo, anything was possible. Rick theorized Tecton's fanatics busted him out, and he still led Earthquake from the shadows.

Not to mention the mole he'd planted in the monastery last year. He had no clue if or what messages the mole had gotten, but Rick couldn't be too careful.

As the neat line of refugees funneled out of the space elevator's car, some Great Mystery monks stood outside, welcoming and ushering them. Seemed like the monks had a change of heart. Maybe Ten-trom and Bunear talked some sense into them. Approaching the settlement, he saw prefabricated housing units: egg-shaped homes erected in a hurry, cheap and portable. Perfect for this kind of operation, and a much better alternative than living in a cave with armed guards patrolling.

Yet between the rows of prefab homes was something he hadn't expected.

Community. Shacks and stalls of people selling produce, tools, clothes, and crafts. A street musician on the corner strumming a Human-sized *fithar*.

Sweat beaded on the back of his neck once he caught sight of the faded tattoo on the guy's neck. Rick avoided eye contact and drew his hood over his face a little more. He didn't want to fire up the image inducer if possible. Navigating the settlement, he approached Bolivar City proper, which displayed few changes other than the conspicuous absence of Tecton's image or name on signs and plaques along with Earthquake recruitment posters.

The homeless shelter wasn't spared from the purge. After a half kilometer of traversing the settlement too small to be a proper city, he found the building where he once staged his operations, now named the Bolivar City Homeless Shelter.

With a deep breath, Rick stepped inside. There wasn't much activity in the cafeteria area. Only two or three people were actually eating a meal. The rest of the activity was on the line, where people were boxing up meals. He recognized more of the people, too. Their hair had grown out and their tattoos were faded, inked over, or removed. In the corner, a dentist hovered over someone in a lounging chair. After a blink, Rick realized it was a former recruit of his, sans tattoos and haircut.

He crept toward the line of people boxing food and tugged on the shirt sleeve of a volunteer he didn't recognize. Without making eye contact and forcing an accent, he said, "I'm searching for Amanda Martinez."

The volunteer shot him a quick glance. "She's a busy lady, pops. Have an appointment?"

The angelic voice interrupted. "He's an old friend. Come on to my office."

Rick locked eyes with the most perfect woman in the galaxy. Maybe he should have used the image inducer, but he wondered if even that would have fooled her.

He followed her through the shelter he once considered his. Seeing this much activity on the line without a greater number eating inside gave him pause. Technically, it was the end goal all along. He stole glances at a few of the packaged boxes' stamps and realized these were mostly going off-world.

"So..." Amanda closed her office door behind them. "I'm assuming you finally have money for my new refrigerators? You had to come back from the grave to deliver it, I see."

"Heh." Rick grabbed the seat across from her desk. "I don't have any money to give. Being dead makes collecting a paycheck challenging."

Amanda's eyes widened. "Oh God, is that why you're here? Are you—?"

Rick waved. "No. I'm not much into staying in one place. I'm sorry it took so long to contact you."

"I knew you weren't dead. They would have plastered your face on more news feeds and had bigger stories about it." She tucked a rogue curl behind her ear, and Rick noticed the thin scarf around her neck, obscuring the faded Earthquake tattoo. "What brings you here?"

"I'm on the hunt. Do you have any more ties here to Jacques Tecton?"

"One dead man hunting another, huh?"

Rick nodded.

"Well, I'm not sorry to say I don't. I scrubbed this place clean of his stink once you outed him. Everyone who wanted to help stayed. The people who called me a traitor were shown the door. After I pulled the mole, Brother Maynard at the monastery pledged his support for the shelter. As far as I know, Rick... nobody on this planet has had any contact with that dirtbag Tecton."

"Good."

Amanda frowned. "I'm sorry. You were probably hoping for a lead."

"Don't be. Besides, there's one other matter to discuss with you."

Her frown flipped into a bright smile. "You came for my aunt's number! Would you mind shaving?" She pantomimed stroking a beard. "She likes those older military pictures of you. I don't know how she'll do with your stubble."

A chuckle escaped. "Not quite. Have you been keeping up with the new person in the Collective government who is in charge of Frontier Affairs?"

"Yeah, actually. I guess I'd thought Symphora was a legend. Weird to see her so old."

Rick nodded. "Someone got into her head about new methods to make a difference without killing people in ways that would make a statue barf. But have you heard about her platform?"

"Something with reducing crime on the Frontier?" Her tone suggested she only had the energy and time to read headlines.

"Better," Rick said. "She's pushing for more Human representation in the Collective government. Tecton's seat has remained vacant with all the investigations going on."

Rick gazed into her eyes. She was too young for him, and he was too horrible for her. "Amanda, it should be you in that seat. I know someone who can get in touch with Symphora. You're the one who should raise Humanity in the social order. You're the best of us. You're perfect."

Amanda leaned back in her chair. "Is this your way of telling me you're never forking over the money for new appliances?"

"Among other things." He blew a slow breath through his nostrils.

"You think I'm qualified?"

"The way I see it," Rick said, "good government runs like a homeless shelter. Feed and shelter people who need it. Get the people who don't need it to help out. Seems like you eradicated homelessness here."

"It's easier when I don't have to divert funds for people experimenting with new weapons in the basement. I'll … consider it," she said. "What'll you do?"

Rick's eyes narrowed. "I'm going to find Jacques Tecton. I'll make sure he answers for his crimes. I made a 'no more monsters' promise. For that to come true, I need to take him out."

Amanda nodded. "When will the fight stop, Rick?"

"When we reach true equality."

"You think that's possible?" The whole galaxy shimmered in her eyes.

"Dunno." Rick let a smile poke through. "But I'll die trying if I have to."

She shook her head and chuckled. "You never change."

"If you get that open seat and I survive, I'll buy a new refrigerator for the shelter. How's that?"

"It's a start."

Joka and Binh found some purpose to move forward, but there's a big galaxy out there, and Rick has one more name to add to his list. It's also Amanda's turn to shine. Look for the third book in the series in Summer of 2024.

Several professional scientists offered guidance. Any scientific mistakes are the author's, not theirs. Or hey, maybe the author put them in there for the sake of the story.

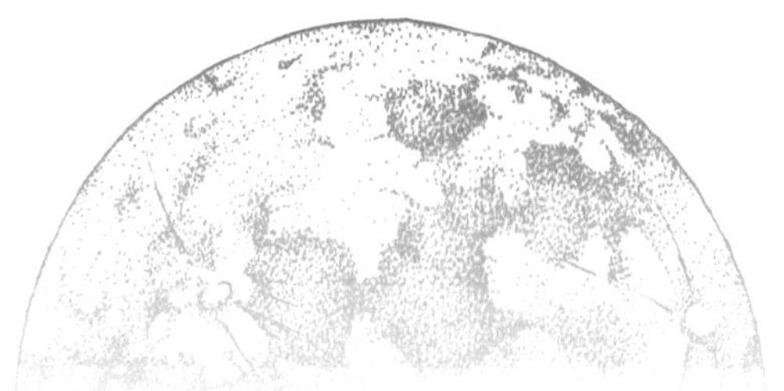

BOOK CLUB QUESTIONS:

1. There are several themes in *Severed Squadron*, such as prejudice, loss, inadequacy, and friendship. Which were you most drawn to and why?

2. Both Joka and Rick have a mentor whom they sour on. Where do you see the differences between their reactions to their changing opinions?

3. What's your theory on the clones Dr. Diastrevlo made?

4. How would the story have changed if Doh-riss' and Joka's roles were switched?

5. Why do you think Binh cleaned up his act around Mui-xe?

6. Do you think Rick is truly repentant? Explain why or why not.

7. Where do you see the symmetry and dissonance in Symphora's gang and Earthquake?

8. Would you have given the book a different title? Explain your reasoning.

9. What do you think Earthquake will do now that they have access to Dr. Diastrevlo's stolen technology?

10. Which character felt the most real to you and why?

AUTHOR BIO

PC IS A science fiction and fantasy author from the Great Lakes region of the USA. Sci fi has been a deep love for PC, growing up on Star Wars movies and reading the Animorphs series. The Star Wars novels along with classic sci fi greats like Asimov and Le Guin are constant sources of inspiration and wonder. PC loves taking his daughters to the zoo and the occasional sushi or taco date with his wife. With the help of friendly scientists and science documentaries, PC tries to blend what is just on the technological horizon with the impossible in his stories. PC is a NaNoWriMo winner and an active critiquer in the Scribophile community.

Be sure to follow PC on Twitter for updates. @nottingham_pc

Visit PC's website at authorpcnottingham.com and sign up for the newsletter.